The Thorn Tree

The Thorn Tree

Heather G. Marshall

MP PUBLISHING

The Thorn Tree

First edition published in 2014 by

MP Publishing
12 Strathallan Crescent, Douglas, Isle of Man IM2 4NR British Isles
mppublishingusa.com

Jacket designed by Alison Graihagh Crellin.

Publisher's Cataloging-in-Publication data

Marshall, Heather G.
　　The thorn tree / Heather G. Marshall.
　　p. cm.
　　ISBN 978-1-84982-307-4

1. Mother-daughter relationship --Fiction. 2. Scotland --Fiction. 3. Family --Fiction.
4. Domestic fiction. I. Title.

PR6063.A6744 Th 2014
823/.914 --dc23

ISBN 978-1-84982-307-4
10 9 8 7 6 5 4 3 2 1
Also available in eBook

In memory of my grannies and great-aunts—in particular,
Jessie, Meg, and Mina.

ONE
Agatha

As the last of the summer night lifted, giving in to an early dawn, Agatha Stuart sunk her slim fingers into the tub, cradling the hard kernels of the snowdrop bulbs through the water one at a time, mapping the haggard filaments of thin roots softened by soaking in preparation for planting. Outside, headlights shining down the skinny coast road in front of her cottage declared the approach of the man who would collect the girl, her great-niece, from the Glasgow airport. Agatha could have driven herself, having learned how during the war, when she lived in Glasgow and was not much more than a girl herself. The war had taught many lessons; but not all were worth carrying into peace, and Agatha preferred her old bicycle, which she'd found in the shed and repaired when she moved to the island. She didn't care that it was a man's bicycle, nor that people had, for nearly ten years now, been saying she should stop altogether lest she fall and break a hip. She liked the feeling of riding up and down the coast road with the wind pulling strands of her hair out and tossing them around, sometimes helping with the work of the pedaling, sometimes testing her lungs and legs and will.

Agatha bent to put on her boots, ignoring the inevitable creak in her old bones. She rose, dried her hands on her apron before she picked up the photograph. A teenaged girl in dark clothing, wild-haired, with eyes that glared into the camera. Not just defiant—something else haunted her drawn face.

Faint hints of sunlight began to emerge as Agatha crossed her garden, handed the man the picture, waved him off, and then stood with her hands braced on the closed gate, watching the car make its way toward The String Road that led up and over the middle of the island. When it disappeared, Agatha turned toward the cottage, but then stopped. She turned again, the morning breeze a tickle, and passed through the gate, rubbing her hand over the sign she'd had carved to rename the cottage when she'd taken it over: *An Garbh-choire*, after The Black Cuillins with their looming peaks, in whose shadow she'd spent her girlhood. Their names included *Am Bastier*—The Executioner—*Sgurr a Ghreadaidh*—The Peak of Torment— and, of course, *An Garbh-choire*—The Wild Cauldron. "Rough corrie" was the literal translation, but here was one of the few instances in which Agatha felt the more fanciful version fitting.

Agatha lifted her hand from the gate, stepped from the smooth of the pavement to the pebbly beach, and then picked her way over seaweed-tangled stones, surefooted but not foolhardy on the slick shore. When she reached her sitting rocks, she lowered herself and took in a breath deep enough to be seen from the road, had there been anyone to see. The pungent aroma of seaweed filled her. A rogue wave leapt up at her, ahead of the tide.

She recalled the first girl, Fiona, brought to her cottage early in the summer of 1978—slouching there at the gate, with her long hair below her backside, split ends swirling in the wind, hiding the girl from view. Fiona, eldest of Agatha's great-nieces: first of that generation, first to grow her whole life with a television and a telephone and the ability to see around the world, first to be unable to see her way to herself. First to come to Agatha in the cottage on the western edge of Arran, off the west coast of Scotland. At the end of the summer, Agatha packed Fiona back to Canada, hair just as long but pinned back enough to see in or out.

When Fiona left, Agatha had felt a tightness creeping in just below her navel, a feeling someone else might have called panic.

After a lifetime spent with too many people in too-small spaces, Agatha was going to be alone. In this solitude, would she grow into herself, full and wide like the sea, or would she, instead, do as her mother had and close inward, becoming tighter and smaller until there was nothing left but a shriveled cage of a body? She hadn't been alone long enough to find out.

Agatha took a deep breath, let go of the memories of Fiona and of her own mother, and, instead of facing north as she typically did, turned her body west, the direction from which the girl was coming. Hope—who surely hadn't been told that her life nearly began in the cottage, with her father out of the picture for months, then turning up at the last minute. She would get her first impressions of the land all to herself, without Agatha to distract her. By the time she reached The Cauldron, she'd already have begun to know this land. Perhaps the land would allow Agatha to help the girl reconnect with herself; perhaps it would be learning about her family; perhaps something else altogether. As she had done with the others, Agatha would offer pieces of herself and see what spoke back.

She rose, wiping hands damp from the spray against her apron. Time for a cup of tea and a bit of toast and her Sudoku.

Inside, Agatha sat at her dark, polished table. The leaves, which could extend the table for a setting for six, had never been used; she'd never needed space for more than two. Agatha lifted her rose-patterned teacup and took a small sip, thinking of the girl who'd given it to her, one of Fiona's cousins whom Agatha had invited to the cottage, having heard she was tired of siblings or parents or both.

Each time, she thought her new girl would be the last. Then another far-flung family member would return. A niece from Australia scraped a tremendous suitcase through the garden gate at the end of her marriage. Fiona, again, on the run from a future that was slow taking shape. In 1991, there had been one lad, for one week; Agatha thought he might do her in, but he'd gone as quickly as he arrived, deciding university might be okay after all. There had been Margaret, her youngest sister's only daughter, in 1996. And then Agatha's youngest sister herself—Ellsie, who was mother of Margaret, grandmother of Hope; Ellsie, who was dying of cancer.

When she finished the tea, toast, and puzzle, Agatha turned the cup over in the saucer and waited a moment. Lifting the cup, she stared at the pattern of the tea leaves. Only a couple of distinct beads of tea, so not many tears indicated. And just the one clump, a small one at that, meaning only a little trouble, and not of her doing. Agatha rarely read the leaves anymore, but it seemed right on such an important morning. She wondered whether the girl would be the kind who would sneer at such superstition. Perhaps she would be one of those not sure what to make of it, or one who would be afraid to make a wrong move, taking the reading too literally. Perhaps the girl would be like her—one who would seek a whisper of truth in whatever form it might take.

She washed the cup, saucer, and plate. She rinsed the teapot. She checked the cottage again, found it to her liking, though it wouldn't be to the girl's, not at first. Other than the snowdrops, there was only her wash left, hanging on an indoor line on a pulley system she'd made in the kitchen. She checked that too, and, finding her garments still damp, pulled on her black gardening shoes and fetched the bulbs.

Snowdrops again—*Galanthus nivalis*, like the ones she planted for Ellsie, being too old by then to carry a memorial sapling to her favorite grove, like the willow and elm and hawthorn she'd planted for her mother and Aunt Wina, and for Donagh.

Agatha turned and turned the soil, breaking apart large, dark clumps that might threaten the new growth. When she had created a fine texture, she knelt and dug what she hoped would be the perfect spots from which the bulbs would sprout and grow. As she hollowed out the wells in the soil, Agatha wondered how Hope would take to this place—a reluctant transplant, fatherless again, and this time all too aware of it, as Agatha had once been, at just about the same age.

TWO
Hope

Hope Carver hunched in the passenger seat of the little car, her skateboard wedged across her lap, every muscle stiff as if she were wrapped in a straitjacket. The driver, Davey, leaned over the wheel and pointed out Glasgow's city center as they pulled out of the airport parking lot: bleak buildings rising toward a cloudy sky almost the same shade of grey.

"Yer auntie will maybe take you," he said as he turned the car in the opposite direction. Hope didn't answer. The buildings lowered and spread apart as they drove away from civilization.

Hope had expected Scotland to be all grey rock and sharp cliffs, something that would suit her mood, but all she could see were miles of rolling hills, fields dotted with dingy-looking sheep and cows bedded down in the damp grass. Davey rolled down the window a couple of inches, enough to let in the cold, the odd spit of rain and the smell of the countryside through which they now drove—the odors of the grass, the wet road, the persistent whiff of animal waste. Hope pressed the button to roll up the window, found the child lock on and felt the color rise in her neck. Out of the corner of her eye, she caught Davey looking. She leaned away.

"Your auntie wanted you to experience the Scottish countryside. Sights, sounds, smells. She loves it all does our Agatha."

"Smells like shit."

"It is shit." Davey turned back to the road. "The Scottish word for it is dung."

Hope leaned her head back and closed her eyes. It worked like a charm, shutting Davey up and shutting out the sights her aunt apparently wanted her to see. She let her back sink into the seat and wrapped her arms around her board, letting herself bounce and sway to the bumps and curves in the road. At length, she opened one eye, met a rock wall on her side of the road and rolling fields beyond it. More sheep, more cows, more shit.

She hadn't fought her mother as they drove to the airport, had focused all her attention on the texts hitting her cell phone from her best friend Katie. Was there a way she could avoid this banishment to the cottage of Great-aunt Agatha, the ancient crone she knew only as the voice on the other end of the phone once a year on her birthday? In the Glasgow Airport lobby she'd considered it again, just for a second, darting out the door to the transit stop and seeing how far she could get with the hundred dollars in cash she'd snuck out of her mother's purse. If she changed the money, dollars to pounds, how far would that take her? Enough to show them—what, she wasn't sure. But before she could take a step, there had been a strong hand on her elbow, and she was caught in the vise grip of the hairy knuckles belonging to the paunchy little man her mother had said might meet her on the other side. Great-aunt Agatha's prisoner transport. Hope wondered if he got a lot of runners.

The car slowed, and she cracked her eyes open far enough to see a ticketing gate and a low metal ramp leading onto a ferry, a line of cars and brake lights up ahead of them. She didn't try to understand Davey's thick accent when he stopped and chatted with the ticketing agent. The car stopped, then started again, moving slowly up the ramp. The engine reverberated inside the ferry.

A hand on her arm again. Reluctantly, she lifted her gaze. He was supposed to be her mother's age, this greying man whose face was too close to hers.

"We're no allowed to stay in the car."

Hope turned away. She looked out and found herself in the belly of the ferry, tall metal walls rising around them like a floating jail. The cars were parked so close to each other Hope had to get out sideways, skateboard pressed so tightly against her it might have been another limb.

"I'm away for a coffee. You look as though you could do with one."

Hope shook her head.

"Fair enough. I'll be in the canteen if you need me."

Hope didn't spare a backward glance as she climbed the stairs to the top deck.

Outside, she sat alone under a clearing sky, holding her skateboard to her chest as she watched the houses in the villages along the shore get smaller, studying the trees that grew only on one side, limbs pointing inland, bare trunks left to face whatever weather the sea brought. She held herself there, still, staring at the trees that had bent to the will of the wind. Wasn't that what she'd done—bent to the will of her mother? Margaret had tried to get her father to bend to her will as well, and he had, bent and bent until something snapped.

As the trees shrank and disappeared from view, Hope moved to the edge of the boat. At least the sea had blown away the smells of animal shit. An occasional cold spit of sea landed on her hand or cheek, a shock at first. The wind swirled, blowing long strands of hair into her face. She had to work to hold her ground, such a different feeling from home, where she felt rooted in place by the still, humid air. She stood against the rail for an hour, until the announcement over the loudspeaker to return to the car. Back in the passenger seat, she closed her eyes and remained silent, feeling the car descend the metal ramp again, the curve of road, the rise and fall, the inevitable slowing and stopping.

"That's you, then."

Davey hopped out of the car, had Hope's bags on the ground beside her and the passenger door open in the time it took her to unbuckle her seatbelt.

The cottage was smaller than she'd expected, whitewashed and weathered, with a large front garden penned in by an ancient-looking rock wall. In the garden knelt a lady who looked as old as the rocky shore, tucking one of her hands into a hollow in the dirt like a miniature grave. Her long, slender fingers looked like the kind that would always be digging into something. Hope watched from outside the gate, one hand on a carved wooden sign that held the cottage's name. Great-aunt Agatha peered over her horn-rimmed glasses with glacial blue-grey eyes.

"Don't just stand there, lassie." Her Scottish voice carried clearly though her head drooped toward the earth, long white hair meeting black soil. "It isn't as though you're a stranger come looking for lodgings." She patted soil over the bulb, sealing it into the moist darkness. The muck had tattooed her hands, sticking under every one of her nails and curling across her fingertips, around her cuticles and over the backs of her hands, the same hands that would be making Hope's meals.

The gate creaked when Hope pushed it open and stepped into the garden. Mounds of turned earth surrounded her like landmines. A tidy row of lettuce led toward the squat white cottage.

Great-aunt Agatha stood, flicked at her apron. Bits of muck swayed wildly on a frayed strand of wool hanging from her elbow. She stepped in Hope's direction.

"Hope," she said. "Welcome to Arran."

Hope took the welcome in the way she would have taken it from a competitor at a skate park—not so much "Come in, make yourself at home" as something along the lines of "Thanks for coming so I can show you up." Agatha scrutinized her from her long, loose red hair to her skull-adorned Chuck Taylor sneakers, and in her head Hope nicknamed her Auntie Aaaag, the same way she nicknamed competitors new to the skate park. The same way she herself had earned the nickname The Carver.

"Bring in your bag, then," Auntie Aaaag said. "You look fair fit for it."

Of course she was fair fit for it. Hope was fit enough for just about anything; she'd gotten that way by skateboarding during nearly all her free time. Fitness was a benefit she hadn't expected and a perk, perhaps redeeming, that her mother failed to notice.

"Mmmuh." Auntie Aaag made the loud, old-lady kissing noise as she nuzzled her pale ridges of skin against Hope's cheek. She held Hope at arm's length, then glanced at the suitcase and the skateboard. "I'll just get the kettle on for you. You'll need a cup of tea after your journey."

The whistle of the kettle filled the tiny kitchen. Suspended—not nearly high enough to avoid Hope's head—Agatha's slip, long underwear, padded bra, and granny panties sagged from a string that ran the length of the ceiling. Agatha moved back and forth so briskly she made the underwear sway as she warmed the pot, put the kettle back on to heat again, sprinkled in the tea leaves. Hope gripped her board more tightly. This woman in the kitchen was lean and brisk, just like her mother. Would she find Agatha to be like her mother in other ways—to have, for instance, lost whatever hint of sweetness she might once have possessed?

Agatha tugged a knitted cozy over the teapot. The cozy looked as though it had been made from cast-off wool not good enough for any other project. Had Hope been the tea, she'd have preferred to go cold. The pot went on a bronze tray that looked older than Agatha, followed by two saucers, teacups, and a miniature pitcher of milk covered by a tiny linen cloth. Little beads dripped around the edges. Each saucer cradled an unpolished silver spoon. Agatha lifted the tray, glanced at Hope, then turned toward the door that led further into her life.

"You can leave your things there until we've taken our tea," she called as she passed through the door, the tray balanced on one hand.

Hope didn't move. The door closed. The cups clinked on the tray as Agatha set it down on something in what Hope already thought of as the inner Agdom.

"Or you can stand there while I take tea for the both of us," Agatha's voice cut through the door.

Hope hesitated a moment longer before finally setting down her case and board. She pressed through the door, not sure what to expect, surprised nonetheless by the weight of the drapes in dark floral patterns that hung like sentinels at the edges of the windows, by the deep red upholstery that seemed to dare anyone to sit on the couch or chairs. The heavy furniture soaked up the scant light from the lacy doilies perched on the arms and backs of the couch and chairs and the weak sunlight slipping through the curtains.

"You must have had quite a journey." Agatha poured milk into the bottom of both cups. "Davey got you okay at the airport, obviously." The tea went in next, brown like liquid dirt. The tray didn't offer any sugar. Agatha lifted the cup and saucer and put it in front of the place on the couch where she wanted Hope to sit. Hope took the next seat over from the teacup and stretched her legs out in front of her.

Agatha sip-sip-sipped her tea on the other side of the tiny living room. She didn't remind Hope at all of her youngest sister, Hope's grandmother. Hope had called this plump, round woman Granny Mac, and had loved just about everything about her. Granny Mac had smiled at everything, kept a separate compartment in her suitcase for the candy she always brought with her from Scotland. "Wee Hope's secret sweetie place," she'd called it. Hope had never known her grandfather.

Granny Mac had looked fine when she'd last visited. Soon after, though, she wrote saying she was moving in with her big sister, Agatha, and that Hope could write to her there at the cottage. Despite starting several letters in the middle of math class, Hope managed to finish only one and had not quite gotten around to putting it in the envelope that would have transported the letter from one side of the Atlantic to the other before Agatha was on the other end of the phone, out of season for a birthday call, saying Granny Mac was dead.

Hope's mother had come to Scotland for the funeral. She'd decided it wasn't appropriate for Hope to come—too expensive and too much time away from school. Then, Hope thought she would never see the place where her grandmother had died. She wasn't sure how she felt about being wrong.

Sitting on the couch in the front room of the cottage, Hope began to think that anyone beyond a certain age—say, twenty—might have time to die while Agatha sipped her cup of tea. When she finished at last, Agatha put the cup down on the tray, slapped her hands on her legs, and stood.

"Right then," she said. "Since you've finished your tea, you can get your case and I'll show you to your room."

Hope hadn't touched her tea. She rose nonetheless, retrieved her baggage, and followed Agatha out of the front room, into the dark hall and up the skinny stairs.

Agatha did not switch on any of the lights as they went, leaving Hope to follow her dark outline. At the top of the stairs, Agatha turned toward the front of the house and held open the door to the room that faced the sea. Two twin beds huddled in the scant light, against pale walls of watery yellow. Dark curtains cut a frame for the faint outline of rocky coast and the rumpled grey waters outside, just visible through the lace panels.

"There you are." One edge of Agatha's lips curled, a smile. "Home sweet home, for a while anyway. You can unpack your things into the drawers there, and that wardrobe." She pointed to a tall wooden thing that looked old enough to have been hers when she was Hope's age. "You'll want forty winks to help you over the jet lag. Don't take too long, though, or you'll not sleep tonight." Agatha stepped out of the room and started to pull the door closed. "I'll be in the front garden if you need me." She shut the door tightly.

Hope listened to her creak down the stairs, then set down her case. She pulled the heavy drapes closed and sat down on the bed nearest the window, farthest away from the wall that met up with the next room, which she guessed to be Agatha's. Every inch of space she could claim for herself felt important.

Hope opened her case. She'd packed her clothes, some bike and skateboard magazines, extra griptape and wheels. Tucked down below those layers lay the last note her father had written her, a photo of the two of them, her father's favorite hoodie and, rolled inside the sweatshirt, a Lortab bottle, worth bringing because it was a last connection between Hope and her father, the final thread in his disappearance and her exile.

Hope did not take the photo out of the case; she merely wanted to confirm it was with her. She pulled the sweatshirt over her head. She fingered the Lortab bottle tucked inside the front pocket.

The bed was made so tightly Hope had to maneuver into it as though she were getting into a sleeping bag. *Even the beds here are like little prisons.* Hope wiggled some space for herself under the sheets and blankets and then closed her eyes to shut out the itchy tiredness, along with any thoughts about whatever might come next in this place.

THREE
Margaret

Well before dawn, Margaret gave up on sleep. She swung her legs out from under the covers, seeking an escape from a night of staring at the ceiling, imagining Hope's journey over the Atlantic. It was still far too early to call Agatha when she rose, so she ran instead, twice her usual route. At the final bend, she imagined Hope making her way off the plane, staring out at a grey city she'd never known.

Back home, Margaret peeled herself out of her running skirt and socks, hauled her matching tank top and jog bra over her head and into the washing machine in one move. Naked on the bare black and white tiles of the laundry room, she closed the lid on the washing machine and just stood there, staring at the chrome under her hand. *Did I do the right thing? Should I have gone too?* Her stomach pulled in on itself. Her mind fluttered, searching for other options or answers and landing on more questions. Margaret gripped the edges of the washing machine. Would this doubt ever let her go? She stood tall. She glanced at the clock. She could make the early morning yoga class.

The instructor told her to set an intention, to find something she'd like to bring in more of or something she'd like to release. Margaret did both: bring in peace, release anger. By the time Hope came home, she might be all peace, no anger—flexible, ready to take on whatever pose was required in being the single mother of a teenager.

In the car, after yoga, the clock blinked 7:03. Noon in Scotland, on Arran. Hope should be with Agatha, in the cottage that had fallen to Agatha after the rest of the family left, like so many other Scots, spreading west to Canada and the United States, south to England, east to Australia, all for better wages and what they thought would be easier lives. How would her own life, and Hope's, have differed had Margaret stayed fifteen years before? How many times had she chased that long-dead possibility in the months since she'd discovered Brad was using again?

She pushed away the playback of things she could have done differently, things that might have made her a better wife and mother. She put the car in gear. She breathed in deeply— Ujjayi breath filled with peace and the scent of worn leather.

Until recently, Margaret had considered nothing other than step-by-step forward motion. It was why she liked running. It was why, after all these years, she still took joy in the onward propulsion of each step, ignoring the fact that, no matter how much she varied the pace or the route, she ended where she'd begun.

Was that what she'd set up for Hope?

At home, the electric kettle lit as she dialed Aunt Agatha's number.

"Aunt Agatha. Did Hope arrive okay?"

"She did indeed."

"And?"

"And?"

"And how does she look?"

"Like a girl who has been sent three thousand miles to stay with a woman who looks three thousand years old."

"Aunt Agatha."

"She looks a sturdy girl, Margaret. What is it you'd like to hear? I've sent her upstairs to rest and gather herself." Agatha paused. "Shall I get her?"

"Yes." Margaret shifted on the cool tile. "No. Don't disturb her rest."

"Shall I have her ring you when she comes down?"

"Yes." Margaret hesitated. "No." Her feet seemed to suck up the chill of the tile. She should buy a nice little throw rug to put below the kitchen desk. "If she asks to."

Silence then, and their breath.

"Margaret. You're sure you'll not come yourself?"

"I have to work." Margaret shifted the phone to the other ear.

"Aye." Another pause. "We'll ring if need be, then. Or you will."

"Yes."

"Right, then. I'm away to my garden."

Margaret held the phone a moment after Agatha hung up, then hurried upstairs to shower. Under the hottest water the nozzle offered, the questions, and the slow-motion replay that sometimes accompanied them, began again.

Had it been almost a year and a half already since that morning when Margaret had lounged (could she even remember how to lounge?) on the patio, the second cup of post-run coffee, strong and creamy and sweet, steaming up at her? There had been no soccer game to take Hope to, no egg to scramble or protein smoothie to blend for Brad before an early morning personal training client. Margaret had been alone for the first Saturday in who knew how long.

She put off any showings until noon, not difficult since she didn't have many clients then. She'd only recently returned to work. Before Hope, she'd been an accountant, but she hadn't quite been able to stand the thought of the rows of numbers and pudgy clients wanting tax breaks for which they weren't remotely qualified. One of the women on the PTA suggested she try real estate. First year out, she'd made Gold Ring, the top sellers' circle. She'd earned a break—the time to sit on the porch on a bright February morning that held the promise of spring.

When she heard the back door open, her stomach lurched. The rhythm of Hope's voice wafted out to her. Margaret expected her husband and daughter to come bubbling back prattling tales of dirt and rock-hopping, campfire grits and gear, but not for another day. Margaret hopped out of her chaise, coffee sloshing over the rim of the mug.

Before she made it all the way into the kitchen, the smell of stale beer and Lysol struck her. Only after she got closer did she catch the more predictable odors: tent and sweat, dirt and fire.

"Don't be mad, Mom." Hope's eyes, wide and clear, seemed to take up the room.

Brad hung between bike-racing teammate Bert and some guy she didn't recognize; her husband was sweating in the cool air, leg in a cast, envelope with what appeared to be X-rays in his hand, the bitter beer and antiseptic smells rolling off him. Hope stood to one side.

Margaret stepped up, slid her arm around Hope's shoulder. At almost thirteen, Hope stood eye to eye with her. "Mad?" She turned to Brad. "What happened?"

"Nothing spectacular."

"Looks pretty dramatic."

"He's heavier than he looks," Bert said. "Let's get this boy lying down and then he can tell you." They settled Brad on the sofa.

He'd crashed his bike the evening before—no faceplant or bike-and-body-turning endo, just a weak landing after a bunny hop over a log he could just about have ridden across, then a slide into a nearby oak.

"I thought I was good," Brad said. He'd popped a few ibuprofen when they got back to the tent, washed them down with beer. They sat around the campfire, drinking. None of them had realized the extent of the damage until the morning. Brad woke with an ankle twice its normal size; he hadn't been able to stand. Still, he'd ridden most of the way back to the car, one-legged, and then passed out in the back seat on the way to the hospital.

"He didn't want me to call and worry you," Bert said. "Broken ankle. Fractured fibula and tibia."

Brad squinted. Margaret couldn't tell if it was pain or an attempt at a weak smile.

They left him sinking into the cushions on the couch. In the driveway, Bert offered a cheerful honk of the horn as if he'd just dropped off Brad after any normal Tuesday night ride.

In the doorway to the den, Margaret surveyed Brad, with his bare toes peeking up over the cushions. Her Brad—who made his living training other people to top-place finishes, who raced himself, leading his team to win after win, who had been fluid and graceful and in motion from the moment she first saw him—slumped on the sofa. She flopped onto the loveseat next to Hope, pulled out the X-rays, and held them to the light. Hope leaned into her. Brad, shot up with pain meds, closed his eyes.

"You okay?" Margaret asked Hope.

"*I* didn't crash."

"You weren't scared, being out there with Dad not able to walk? And in the ER?"

"It's just the woods, Mom. And the hospital, you know, where they heal people?" Hope leaned her head on Margaret's shoulder. "Dad was great."

Margaret nodded. She wrapped her arm around Hope, pulled her in, drawing close to her the scents of dirt and tent and sweat, earthy and still somehow sweet. "Why did you think I'd be mad?"

Hope shrugged. "You said I was too young to go with all those guys out in the woods and someone could get hurt, and someone did, only I don't think it's the someone you thought."

Margaret squeezed her. "I'm not mad, Hope. Go get clean. I'll start the wash."

"What about Dad?"

"Look at him."

Brad's mouth hung open. His hand hung off the edge of the sofa.

"I'll be right there in the laundry room if he needs something." Margaret tucked the X-rays back into the folder. She glanced back at Brad. She lifted the bottle beside them. Lortab. *Take one, as needed, for pain.*

Was there something she could have done differently that morning that would have set them on a different course? Something that would have meant that seventeen months later, she would not be standing in an overheated lather in the shower, preparing to step out of it into an empty house, husband who knew where and daughter three thousand miles away?

Margaret dried quickly and slipped into the clothes she'd laid out the night before. In fluid movement, she hurried down the stairs, out the back door, into her car, and down the driveway, past her neatly cropped lawn and the crape myrtles at the end of the drive. Somehow their blossoms offended her, so pendulous, so boldly seductive. And didn't these plants shed it all in the autumn, going beyond the normal release of blossoms, the dropping of leaves? She'd looked up their proper name when they first bought the house. *Lagerstroemia fauriei.* Imported in the 1950s as part of a breeding program, the myrtles weren't content to be merely bare-armed like other trees—they stripped off even their bark in the winter, showing it all in public parks, mall lots, medians, trailer parks. She should dig them up, replace them with something sturdier, evergreen.

She accelerated down Live Oak Lane, pulling out after rush-hour traffic instead of well in advance of it as she usually did. She pushed in the CD she'd bought at the studio, meant to bring back the feeling of the yoga, to remind her of her intentions. Margaret breathed in. Her ribs expanded. Her shoulders rose almost to her cheeks. She exhaled, too quickly. She tried again. And again, nearly hyperventilating. If she was breathing any feeling, it was confusion, followed closely by irritation. She pressed the SAAB beyond the speed limit, began her mental checklist—checking in with staff, checking email, new prospects, a showing at eleven, followed by a drive through the Bent Creek and Shutter's Plantation subdivisions. She accelerated around the curve onto Bent Creek Avenue, met the scurrying hump of an opossum, its bare tail obscene, erect, pointing behind it. She swerved, clipped the curb, righted the car, swore at the rodent, drove on, restarted the list.

Halfway through the list and just beyond the turn out of the subdivision onto Bridwell Road, she heard the thwack start, then the rumble that indicated she'd clipped the curb with enough force to flatten her tire. She pulled to the edge of the road and pushed on her hazard lights. She glanced in the rearview. A small bonus of being late: the road was clear.

She lifted the emergency triangle out of the trunk, paced back the requisite fifteen feet, placed the triangle in the middle of the lane. Should she call Triple A? She scanned the area. Bent Creek was still in view. The house she'd pulled over in front of wasn't like the new ones in the neighborhood—white clapboard, a relic from the farm days. Triple A would likely take ages. She smoothed her skirt, slid the lug wrench and jack from their compartment.

Margaret crouched by the tire in the humid morning air. She tugged. The lug nut wouldn't budge. She tried another. And a third. She stood. She breathed in. She placed one foot, in its shiny, pointy shoe, on the wrench. She pressed with as much force as her hundred-and-twenty-five-pound body could muster. Nothing. She bounced a little. The nut creaked a small bit. Margaret bounced again. A sigh of release. Margaret moved to the next one.

"You look like you could use a little help." A voice came from behind her, scratchy and deep, as she bounced on the last lug.

Margaret let out a small squawk. She removed the lug wrench, turned. Her light eyes met dark, liquid ones, deeply set in what looked to be a permanently tanned, crosshatched face, too old to be a threat, especially when the face was connected to a body that leaned heavily on a carved cane.

"Excuse me?" Since childhood, Margaret had taken pride in not needing help.

"Thought you might want a little help on account of…" The man hesitated, taking in the whole of Margaret as though measuring why she might need help. "…that teen-tiny little skirt not being the usual costume for tire changing. And on account of…" He paused again. "Well, you look like you need help."

Margaret leaned back slightly on her slim heels. She pressed her lips together. Purchased from the new summer line at Ann Taylor, her skirt was the perfect length for any occasion. As Margaret straightened to her stiletto-aided five eight, the man lifted his weight off his cane, pulled up beyond her.

"Thank you. I've got it." She bent, reattached the wrench, met little resistance.

"Folks don't know their neighbors nowadays." The man stayed behind her.

Margaret loosened the lug nuts fully. She added *trip to the car dealer* to her list.

"Used to be folk knew everyone for miles. Stopped in to visit."

Margaret clopped to the trunk. She had begun to perspire. With the spare balanced on the ground with one hand and the wrench in the other, Margaret stooped to roll the tire forward. A brown, crinkled hand landed next to hers.

"Honey, I'm hunkered down here anyhow." The man's face was too close to hers, his skin freshly shaven and smelling of Old Spice. Margaret pressed forward again.

When she eased the tire onto the wheel and turned for the lug nuts, she found the man's hand again, pale silver cones shining in his outstretched palm. Margaret met his eyes. She lifted a nut, turned back to the tire.

"Now folks don't even slow down to see who's there—don't hardly wave."

She took a second nut, slowly this time, a bird pulling a worm from the ground.

They went like this for the rest of the tire change, Margaret pecking a lug from the open palm, the man offering a sentence between each.

"Been here all along. Me, I mean. Ain't no 'we' no more." He turned to face his house. Margaret turned with him, the last nut in her hand. "Unless you count the land. Five acres and me, all that's left of ninety-nine acres, eleven brothers and sisters, two daughters, two hunting hounds, a prize heifer, and a wife."

Margaret twisted toward the little white house with its neat lawn in front and fields behind. How many times had she passed it? Huge sunflowers lined the front fence. Tall corn rose in the back field. Tomato and cucumber vines wound around trellises. Pepper plants climbed neatly placed dowel rods. It hadn't struck Margaret until she crouched below this old man, nearly changed tire in front of her, that the little house might have been the homestead for a full-blown working farm, once upon a time.

Margaret lowered the jack. She set to tightening the lug nuts.

"You ought to let me finish that."

Margaret hesitated.

"You're not telling me those pretty hands can tighten a lug nut good as these." He held out his hands, the veins like the foothills, long fingers like rivers.

He was right. She didn't want the tire coming off. And he'd probably be faster.

She stood and gestured to the tire. The man nearly creaked to a squat. Ropes of muscle in his forearm stood out as he pulled each nut tight.

He lifted the flat on his way back to standing, headed for the trunk without asking, slid everything back in, closed it. He wiped his hand on the leg of his pants, extended it.

"Clyde Bridwell."

Margaret looked at her own hand, in need of a wipe, but not on an Ann Taylor skirt.

"You'll want to wash up. Miss…?"

"Carver. Margaret Carver. And I wouldn't want to inconvenience you."

"I wouldn't let you, hon." Clyde's eyes showed a slight narrowing. "Wherever you're headed in that getup, you don't need to look like you come from being a shade-tree mechanic."

Margaret lathered with a lined bar of soap, watched the water swirl in the sink. She dried her hands on a worn blue towel embossed with a faded duck.

Clyde stood at the end of the hall when she came out. "You in too much hurry for a cup of coffee?"

She glanced, she thought surreptitiously, at her watch. "I…"

"You youngsters. Too busy to stop." Clyde's lip curled at one side. "I might have something to say you'd be interested in."

"Could I have a rain check?" The question surprised Margaret even as she asked it.

The other side of Clyde's lip curled. He nodded slightly. "Sure, hon, a rain check."

Margaret pulled carefully onto Bridwell Road, tried to restart her list but found herself backtracking through her morning instead, reliving the rising early, the 4:30 run, her manicured hand against the bark of the myrtle, yoga, her call to Aunt Agatha, complete with all the details and all the doubt.

"Good God, Margaret." She looked at herself in the rearview. "It's done." She pressed hard on the accelerator, her mother's voice in her head. *The only poor decision is indecision. Pick the thing and move forward.*

FOUR
Hope and Margaret

Before she arrived at Great-aunt Agatha's cottage, Hope's plans for her summer had consisted of finding ways to avoid her mother and to make some sort of connection with her missing father. Just three days before she tucked herself into the tight little bed on Arran, Hope had lain on her back, bum on the edge of her own bed in her house in Terra Pines, muscular legs dangling over the side. A white pill rested on her tongue. Her bare feet poked out from her favorite pajama bottoms, the black ones with the white skulls. Hope tucked her left hand up into the right sleeve of what had been her father's favorite hoodie. She did the same on the other side, making a kind of straitjacket. The medicine bottle, one tablet left, nestled in her fist. Hope swallowed. She waited for the little capsule to dissolve and work its magic, disconnecting her from herself, the way she imagined it must have done for her father.

In the six months since her dad had disappeared, her mother had taken to extremes: silences, scrutiny, obsessively rearranging their house. Hope lay under one of her mother's most recent makeovers, a gauzy canopy of mosquito netting that matched new window sheers and the coordinated dust ruffle. The yip of the neighbors' Shih Tzu slid through the screen of her open window. Her mother hated the little dog. Hope had never cared much one way or the other; however, she'd recently started to find a tiny amount of glee in emphasizing the *shit* in the dog's name. "Oh. Is that the *shit*-zoo barking again?" she liked to ask.

"*Sheet*," her mother said. "It's *sheet*-zoo."

Hope had looked it up after the last exchange. It was neither. The correct pronunciation was *sureds*, Mandarin for lion. Hope decided she might actually like the little dog then, finding kindred in a creature known for being intense, intelligent, and loyal. She ignored what might have been some other similarities—like the fact that, when it's not clear who's in charge, these dogs become anxious, untrustworthy, and obstinate. They develop "behavioral issues," like snapping, biting, and obsessive barking, the kind of barking that wafted across the yard and through Hope's window as she lay on her bed waiting for the pill to do its work.

Hope pulled inward, away from the barking and the canopy. She rode her memory and the dissolving pill back to before her father left—before he took the first pill, before he even felt the pain, all the way to the night of the accident.

They'd ridden through the woods, branches snapping beneath them, headlamps flashing, Hope in the middle of the line of cyclists on the single-track trail in the thick of Issaqueena forest, breathless behind her father, keeping up and feeling as though her smile had taken over her whole body.

The replay flashed across the dark screen of Hope's closed eyelids. Fragments of remembered images—the trail as her light hit raw red clay or brown roots or dark, dry pine needles. As the pill worked harder, her memory clamped down on the image of her father ahead of her, disappearing for a moment until her headlamp found him, his body slamming into the pine tree. Hope's hand around the pill bottle slackened; she reached for the gauze of the canopy, pulled it around her, wrapped herself up, and drifted with the memory of her father.

When she awoke hours later, the late-afternoon sun hammered through the window. Hope found herself enveloped in the mosquito netting and a light sweat. Her stomach growled; her hands felt larger than normal, and as she pulled them out of the sweatshirt sleeves, the Lortab bottle fell onto the bed, brown and innocent-looking. The white label that bore her father's name faced the comforter, leaving the warning labels to stare at Hope. She didn't need to read them, had already studied the bottle enough times to know exactly what they said.

Warning: May cause drowsiness. Alcohol intensifies effect.
Use care using machinery.
Warning: Taking more than the recommended dose may
cause breathing problems.

At least a couple of warnings were missing. Hope wasn't going to think of that, though. She cut herself off the way she used to cut off any line of thought concerning the ways in which she might crash trying a hard trick on her skateboard. You go where your eyes go, where your head turns, where you think. You think of crashing, you wind up bleeding on the ground. You think of crashing, you think of your father, of his crash, the one on the bike, the one that leads to a kind of crash that takes place on the sofa in the living room, the kind that leads to you lying on your bed one sunny June day taking your father's leftover meds. Another smile, then a tight little laugh, which made her head hurt. Had her brain shrunk?

She tried to roll out of the netting and instead pulled it tighter. She rolled in the opposite direction, but the thing just got tighter and made her sweat, which made her head hurt more. She heard a tearing sound, kept rolling. The sound again, a definite rip. *Fuck it.* She slithered to the end of the bed, slid down, and wriggled out.

Hope tucked the bottle in her stash box in the far corner under the bed, alongside her journal, camera, and the last note from her father. A quick stocktaking proved she and her mosquito-netting cocoon were both the worse for this little escapade. It was worth it, though.

In the kitchen, her mother's pink running shoes rested by the door, her pink visor perched on the table, and black (slimming) spandex skorts flowed over the laundry hamper.

Mom must have had some last-minute call: some ritzy client with an urgent need to see one mini-castle or another—the kind of extreme rush that required Mom to leave some evidence of herself, instead of erasing all proof that she even lived there before taking off. Hope shrugged, pulled down the Raisin Bran Crunch, poured the milk, and pulled herself onto the counter, imagining her mother saying, "Hope, honey, why would you put your bottom where I'm going to fix our food?" Hope wiggled a little, dipped in her spoon and shoveled as much cereal as would fit into her mouth. The crunch made her head hurt more. Still, it was the closest she'd come, out of all the things she'd tried so far, to connecting with her dad since he'd pulled out of the driveway a cold, clear night in January.

Margaret pushed through the back door, keys in her mouth, her expanding file with client notes cradled in one arm and her pink canvas grocery bags dangling from the other. She found Hope perched on the counter, a bowl of cereal in her left hand while the other held a spoon, full, aloft and not directly over the bowl. Milk dripped onto the counter. Margaret's lips tightened. How many times did a person have to ask that you not put your backside—in pajamas, even, at five p.m.—on a food preparation surface? She'd thought about showing Hope slides of bacteria, but what she imagined she would find disgusted her, and she had more than enough on her plate these days.

Couldn't her daughter at least do her the courtesy of pretending to care that she'd been caught, and jump down instead of making Margaret say the thing she always said?

She set down her papers, hung the keys on the hook, put the bags side by side on the alcove counter in the wall of cupboards by the back door. When she turned toward the drawer that held the dishrags, Hope turned too, slowly, mouth filled with Raisin Bran, spoon now submerged. Hope's spine rounded, sleepy eyes half-hooded.

"Oh. You're here," Hope slurred.

Not *Hi, Mom.* Not *How are you?* Just *You're here.* Weren't they always here? It had been a joke in the car, years ago. *Are we there yet? No, darling, we're never there, always here.*

Margaret lifted out the extra-firm tofu and a salmon fillet, heard Hope slide from the counter, the clink of the spoon in the sink, the clack of the bowl. *Dishwasher*, she thought. *Rinse the bowl and then put it in the dishwasher.* Margaret turned, met what was available of Hope's eyes, took two steps closer with the tofu still in one hand and the salmon in the other. Hope gazed at her, pupils too narrow for the light. Margaret's stomach rolled. Hadn't Brad's eyes looked precisely like that when he was using?

"Hope?"

"'s me."

Margaret continued toward the fridge, mind racing. Ask directly? What kid would say *Sure, Mom, I've been taking some recreational drugs while you were at work*? She slid open the meat drawer, lined the salmon up next to the Cajun turkey Hope liked. She placed the tofu into one of the vegetable crispers, next to the bok choy and the leeks. Did tofu even belong there? Margaret shook her head. She closed the fridge and turned; she found Hope in front of her. She had to look up slightly, another recent development, to meet Hope's eyes. Margaret took in a quick breath, tried to sound pleasant, casual, unsuspecting.

"So, what did you get into today?"

Hope shrugged and stepped back, making space between them.

"Did you stay at home all day? Katie come over?" Margaret asked.

Hope pressed between Margaret and the fridge. "No and no," Hope said.

"So where did you get to?"

"Why does it matter?"

"I'm just interested."

Hope raised an eyebrow, which emphasized her droopy eyelids.

"Did you go skate?"

"Sure."

"At the park? Or where?"

Margaret moved toward the grocery bags, pulled out lemon ginger tea, crunchy almond butter, a bag of Granny Smiths, firm and tart.

"Sure."

"At the park?"

"Sure."

Margaret opened the cabinet closest to Hope.

"Anyone interesting there?"

"Mom." Hope stood up straight, unhooding her eyes. "I skated. I came back here, I lay on my bed. I had a little nap. And then a little bowl of cereal. And then my mother came in and started to interrogate me. Anything else you'd like to know?"

Margaret turned away, faced the sink, swallowed the rising lump in her throat.

"Yes, there is." She turned back to face Hope. She smiled. "I'd like to know if you could please put your bowl in the dishwasher."

Slouching, Hope slid her feet across the floor to the sink, eyes lowered again. She lifted the bowl, held it high, then the spoon, raised both eyebrows.

Margaret went back to the bags, lifted out the remaining groceries and opened another cabinet door, which shielded her from all but the sounds of Hope putting the bowl and spoon away, shutting the dishwasher too aggressively, opening and closing the fridge door on the way past, opening and closing the door to the den as she passed through. Margaret held onto the top of the cabinet door, head hanging, nauseous, listening to Hope's faint footsteps up the stairs and down the hall to her room. A bead of sweat ran down Margaret's spine. She shivered.

Hope stood at the foot of her bed, gathered a clump of thick, wavy hair and piled it on top of her head. What to do with the torn netting? She stretched, arched her back, released her hair.

She tied the netting into a knot that dangled over the bed. She nodded, then flopped down under it. Later, her mother poked her head around the door.

"Cute netting," her mother said. "Glad you're taking an interest in making things pretty."

"Whatever," Hope said.

Just after midnight, Hope slid from her room to move the Lortab to a more secure hiding place: the bottom of her skateboard toolbox in the tool room off the garage, between her griptape and extra wheels. Her mother never ventured in there. She texted her BFF, Katie. *Rescue me.*

After her morning run, Margaret sat at the kitchen table, plain Greek yogurt and steaming green tea in front of her. She dipped the tip of the spoon into the yogurt, lifted it, held it in midair. She listened. Could those be Hope's footsteps on the stairs, so early? She eased the tip of the spoon into her mouth, sucked in a little of the creamy white. Protein, probiotics, good for bone density and digestion. She swallowed, heard footsteps again. Margaret set down the spoon, turned, met Hope coming through the door, fully clothed, skateboard tucked under her arm.

"Hope." Margaret cleared her throat.

"Mom." Hope moved past her.

"You're up early."

Hope shoved her head into the fridge, pulled out a half gallon of orange juice, shook it. Outside, a car horn honked.

"Don't mind if I take this, do you?"

"Take it where?" Margaret scraped back her chair.

"Katie's taking me to breakfast. She needs some driving practice before her mom takes the car to work. And then we're going to the skate park. Free Friday, all day, for regulars. Bye." The door shut.

Margaret scurried after Hope, napkin dropping from her lap. She arrived in the driveway in time to watch them pull away. Even though they weren't looking, Margaret waved. She had a sudden impulse to call Katie's mother, ask for the courtesy of advanced warning if she was going to pull into Margaret's driveway and take Hope for the day. Allie likely thought she was doing Margaret a favor; Katie and Hope had been best friends since they walked into kindergarten. Margaret turned for the kitchen, glancing at her watch. She had over an hour before she had to leave for the office, grab the files she needed, meet clients at the estate on the edge of Tubs Mountain, just north of town.

She abandoned her yogurt and went to the mosquito netting first. She knelt on Hope's bed and untied the knot. The gauze spilled around her, filtering the light except through the hole where the netting was torn. What had possessed Hope to make such an angry rip? Margaret pressed her lips together and climbed down from the bed. Again, she knelt, this time reaching under the dust ruffle, blindly pulling out a skateboard shoe that had been pronounced lost long ago, scrunched algebra notes, a torn copy of *The Giver*, Snickers wrappers (Margaret had never even seen Hope eat a Snickers). She had almost reached the back corner when her phone alarm when off. Time to go. *Shit.* She shoved everything back under the bed and sat up.

No. She would clear her schedule, give herself time to see if Hope really was hiding something from her. She would not be so naively hopeful, the way she had been with Brad.

Margaret rooted through the closet, past old skateboard wheels, faded swimsuits, and forgotten hairclips. She was reminded of her own mother, long ago, standing over a swept pile of junk from Margaret's closet floor, her bun beginning to unravel, broom firmly planted, proclaiming Margaret a slut. Margaret had been devastated, had run from the house, three miles to her best friend Trig's.

"Your mum?" Trig had asked. "Your uptight Scottish mother said the word *slut*? Does it mean the same thing over there?"

They looked it up in Trig's den, both of them relieved, giggling, when they found that the first definition was not, as Margaret had thought, related to sex, but to being slovenly or untidy. Her closet hadn't been anywhere close to as bad as Hope's was.

Margaret sat back on her haunches. Surely Hope hadn't hidden anything in there. Not with any thought of finding it again, anyway.

Under the bed again, Margaret unearthed a little metal box with a diary and some other odds and ends. She knelt in the middle of the floor, pushed her hair back from her face. Had she imagined the look in Hope's eyes, so much like Brad's when he'd been strung out on Lortab? Had she made a false connection between Hope's anger and the rolling boil in Brad, months later, after he started with the cocaine again?

Margaret opened the diary to a random page. Tuesday, February ninth—sixteen months ago. *Dad is showing me how to change the derailleur. He has already shown me how to do tire changes, even on the back, when you have to get the wheel away from all the gear sprockets.* She flipped to a page a few days later. I love being in his tool room. *Mom calls it the Cave. Now it's the bike cave and the skate cave 'cause Dad is letting me keep my stuff there.*

Under the bare bulb in the Cave, Margaret pulled open the drawers on Brad's red toolbox. A nut fell to the floor, followed by a screw or two a few drawers down. Margaret left them where they lay. Drawer to drawer, top to bottom. At her side, Brad's bikes dangled from the ceiling. Where was he that he didn't need his beloved bikes? In the corner, neatly propped, a smaller toolbox rested beside a blank skateboard, a neat row of wheels, sheets of griptape. Margaret's skin prickled as she lifted the lid on the box.

Onto the floor went Allen wrenches, an inner tube, more skate and bike tools Margaret didn't know the names of, until Margaret unearthed not a plastic baggie but a brown bottle. She stopped, stood, stepped out into the sunlight. She shook the bottle. One pill left. Hadn't she thrown all Brad's meds out not a month ago? Hadn't she wiped her hand across his shelf in the bathroom cabinet—his former shelf—sweeping the lot into a thirty-gallon trash bag? Her face burned. This was definitely Brad's prescription. And there had definitely been more than one pill in the bottle when Margaret had last seen it.

Cycling.

Skateboarding.

Bike repair.

Lortab.

Christ. Were there other ways in which Hope might follow in her father's footsteps? Margaret pressed her hand to her forehead.

"Oh."

She turned, leaned against the doorframe, thought she might weep.

The ring of phone stopped her. She tucked the Lortab bottle into the waist of her pants, sniffed, wiped her nose with the back of her hand—how many decades since she'd done that?— pulled the phone from its sheath. Unknown. A new client? Hope, using some Goth boy's phone at the skate park? Margaret cleared her throat.

"Margaret Carver."

"Hallo, Maggie. How are you?"

Of course: Auntie Agatha, on her monthly—sometimes more often—call. Sometimes Agatha's name flashed on her screen; sometimes things got jumbled on the way across the Atlantic and Margaret's phone said Agatha was Unknown.

"Well, thank you. And you?" Margaret replied.

"I'm very well, pet."

Margaret turned her eyes to the ceiling. *Dear God, if she launches into that damned dream of hers with the witch and the portent of doom again, or if she starts digging for information I don't want to give, please let it be okay that I hang up on her.* Margaret needed to focus on rescuing Hope.

"Just taking a break from my garden and thinking of you having to share the bathroom with those orchids I was growing all those years ago," Agatha continued.

Fifteen years ago, Margaret had lifted the plants out of the bathtub every evening before she ran her bath, there being no showerhead then in Aunt Agatha's little bathroom. Each morning, Aunt Agatha had checked on the orchids; her long fingers cradled the blossoms as though she could divine precisely what the plant needed just by touch. And hadn't she?

"Are you," Margaret cleared her throat again. "Are you growing orchids now?"

"Ocht, no, pet. It's the wrong season. I've just brought in some cuttings and I was away into the loo to arrange a few of them and somehow it made me think of you. I was thinking how lovely it would be if you and Hope came for a holiday—get the pair of you away from that rotten South Carolina heat and into some lovely Scottish air."

Agatha prattled on while Margaret fingered the Lortab bottle, stomach clenching. She tried to take silent, calming breaths, gave herself the hiccups while Agatha outlined places and people and things she and Hope would like.

"Is that you hiccupping? Away and get some water. Quite sure you're all right?"

"Yes, Auntie Agatha. Bye."

Margaret hung up, lunged inside, grabbed at the edges of the sink, gasped air. What to do? She'd done what she thought was right with Brad and now she was minus a husband, Hope was minus a father, and no matter how hard she tried, the pair of them—Hope and Margaret—were rapidly losing each other. Even her past life as an accountant couldn't help her balance these scales.

Margaret pulled herself upright. She wiped her face on a dishtowel. She blew her nose. She turned for the computer. There were places that could help with this, weren't there? Summer camps with a little extra? She printed out page after page, shocked at the number of camps and the variety, not to mention the cost. When she heard the mail truck drive past, she pushed back the chair. How long had she sat? She looked at her watch. There was still time.

Margaret corralled the printouts into a stack on the kitchen table, set the Lortab bottle on top. Quickly, she erased evidence of her rummaging in the Cave and in Hope's room. She would go to the grocery store, come home, prepare a nice meal. She would wait for Hope. They would discuss this calmly.

Hope climbed the chain-link fence behind the tallest half-pipe, ignoring the chorus of *what the ef*s behind her. Below, on the ledge at the top of the half-pipe, her board waited, freshly griptaped, new bearings in the wheels. Today, a new trick: jumping from the top of the fence, leaping into a moment in the air that would hold a microcosm of possibilities—she could land perfectly, roll into the bowl with the pace gained from the extra pressure exerted on the skateboard, launch up the other side, wheelie grab, maybe with enough air there to flip (the flip itself holding another little moment of air and its own Fibonacci spiral of chance); or else that first moment would offer a slightly missed landing, feet still on the board, extra momentum but without the elegant balance, the chance for the grab and flip; or else there would be a near-total miss, a tumble into the bowl, the bleeding. Every time she tried a higher launch, she increased the risk of falling, bleeding, insides oozing out onto the smooth wood, bright red and beautiful in the sunlight, metallic on the tongue, delicious.

Hope reached the top of the fence, bent over, hands and feet clinging. She bent her knees, let go with one hand and then let the other rise slowly. Behind her, a straight drop to concrete, how many feet, she wasn't sure. She grinned. She held her arms wide, eyes on the fence opposite her, on the other side of the half-pipe.

She leapt, no twist or flip this time, just straight down. Her feet thumped onto the board—perfect. She felt the clunk as she crossed the lip, entered the downflow of the half-pipe. She crouched, gained momentum, flowed up the other side. Hope grabbed, fingers on the smooth underside of the board and thumb on gritty griptape, body turning in the air, an inch to spare before she reconnected with the board, the air whooshing along with the rush of blood in her ears, back down to the belly and then the easy roll up the other side and back onto the ledge. At the top, she saw Katie's mother standing at the gate into the park. No time to go again. Next time, she would go higher.

The garage door was lowered, as usual, when Hope arrived home from the skate park. Finding her mother's car inside, Hope clenched her teeth, robbed of the usual peace she got before Mom got home from work. Out of the corner of her eye, Hope noticed the door to the tool room slightly open. Her chest tightened. Could her dad have come home? She peeked into the darkness. Everything seemed in order. Her father's touring bike, mountain bike, and racing bike hung where he'd left them; the table saws stood in place.

Hope stepped fully in, felt around for her skateboard toolbox, found and unlatched it. She lifted the box to her face, squinted, made out nuts and bolts, a roll of griptape, everything except the Lortab bottle. She stood in the doorway with the toolbox in her hands, too late to catch Katie. Should she go into the house or turn and head for refuge on foot—Katie's house, or even back to the skate park? Before she could decide, the back door opened. Her mother still wore the yoga pants from this morning.

"Come on in, sweetheart. You're earlier than I expected. I'm making spicy sausage jambalaya, your favorite. Thought I'd have it all done by the time you got here."

Inside, her mom grabbed a pile of papers from the table.

"What's that?"

"Just something I was working on." She turned away from Hope. "Wash your hands. It's just about ready."

Hope sat, skateboard on her lap. Her mom set the pile of papers, face down, on the counter. Hope noted the bottle-sized bulge in her mother's yoga pants. What game was this? She went for the papers.

"Let those be, please."

"What are they?"

"Just set them down, please. Let's have a nice meal."

Hope turned them over. On the first page, bright-faced girls played hockey in pleated skirts. The page underneath held rosy-cheeked teens in Patagonia gear, attached to ropes along a cliff face. Of course. Mom had already taken Hope's bike, after Hope had gone to one of her father's old night-riding spots trying to find him. She'd shut down Hope's Facebook and Twitter and even her Tumblr photoblog. Now was she researching ways to get rid of Hope too.

"Spicy sausage jambalaya?" Hope asked.

"Yes. Doesn't it smell good?"

"And then what?" Hope held up the paper. "Mom."

Hope's mother left the spoon in the pot. She sighed. She turned, hands gripping the counter at the edges of the stove.

"Can't we just have a nice meal, Hope?"

"Can't you just tell me what this is?" Hope waved the papers.

Glancing from the girls on the page to Hope's fraying jeans and Chopper t-shirt, Margaret breathed deeply. "I just wish you could..."

"You wish I could, what? You wish I could be like one of these happy little preppies?" The girls in the photo might look like standard-issue private school harpies, but Hope suspected these were no standard-issue summer camps. She knew of a few kids who'd been sent off like this. Their parents got the first whiff of pot or booze, panicked, and shipped them away. A posse of girls just one grade up had done their time at rehab "camps"—Outward Bound for three weeks, some place in Montana for twenty-eight days, a couple of them even gone for forty-two days. Was that supposed to sound like less or more than six weeks?

"I wish you could choose to see the beauty in yourself instead of choosing to take drugs," Mom said. "I wish you would wear nice, bright, flattering clothes and let your face show instead of shrouding yourself. You could..."

"This is about yesterday, isn't it?"

"...smile. You have a lovely smile. You..."

"The one time you came home early and noticed."

"…could play a team sport. Get a varsity letter. You're fit and athletic. You…"

"I took one little Lortab, Mom." Hope stood.

"What?"

"*One* pill, Mom."

Hope's mother pulled the bottle out of her pocket. "One?" She rolled it in her hand, studied Hope. "That's all it takes."

"This is ridiculous. I'm going to Katie's." Hope went for the door.

"I think you need some time away from here," Mom said.

Hope stopped. She held her breath.

"You can choose. Or I can choose." Mom set down the bottle, gently, squared her shoulders and curled the edges of her lips into a smile as deliberately as if she was drawing it on with lipstick. Mom the clown. "You can choose one of these places or," Mom hesitated, "or you could go to Scotland.

"Yes. You could stay with Auntie Agatha. She bakes the most wonderful scones and bannock and praties," Mom said, using her *let's have a nice meal* tone, as if she was talking about sending Hope on the trip as some kind of treat, as if Hope had never heard of her grandmother's spinster sister and her solitary cottage on some island off the west coast of Scotland.

"Great," Hope said. "I'll be tortured and fat." She folded her arms. "Only from the scones. Bannocks and praties sound like rodents." Hope made the list in her head. *Mouse, rat, opossum, nutria, pratie, squirrel, bat, bannock.*

She turned away. The light over the kitchen table suddenly seemed harsh, bouncing off her mother's new sunshine-yellow paint job. Hope waved in the direction of the wall.

"That's what you want," she said. "A sunshine girl, all hap-hap-happy. A little you-clone—Mini-Margaret—for your Christmas cards."

No wonder her father had left. No wonder he hadn't made it to rehab. Or come home.

Hope moved within inches of her mother, spoke quietly. "Well, I'm not you, and I'm not yellow. I'm…" Hope stammered.

"I'm, I'm..." Her eyes darted to a bag of groceries on the counter. "I'm eggplant!" she said. "I'm dark and ripe and full of seeds to sprout and grow, and you can't stop me from growing any way I want."

She turned, passed through the door to the den, chose not to slam it.

"Go on and send me to Great-auntie Agatha. It's grey and rocky there—maybe I'll fit in."

In the dark, hours later, Margaret's manicured fingers wrapped around Hope's doorknob. She turned it and inched the door open. Under the mosquito netting, Hope lay curled into herself, the blankets pulled up to her chin, thick waves of auburn hair covering her face. Margaret's shoulders rounded. She opened the door a little more, stepped in, hesitated there in the dark, in the middle of her daughter's bedroom. How was this the same girl Margaret had read to, sometimes lying under the covers, more often sitting on the edge of the bed, some heavy text Hope had chosen on her lap while her daughter curled her body around Margaret, her small freckled hand propping up her chin? There had been the big cat book Hope had put on her Christmas list when she was six, a follow-on to the previous year's request for birds of prey picture books. They had exhausted the selection in the children's section at Barnes & Noble by September. Hope searched online by herself, developed a short list for Santa. Margaret had warned her that she might not like the books, meant for adults. The first night she read from one, Margaret felt her daughter's body shift against her, her legs stretching out, so recently shed of their baby pudge. Hope rolled onto her back. Margaret kept reading, checking Hope in her peripheral vision, anticipating a request to stop and select one of the older, easier books.

Mom? She could still remember Hope so clearly—little hands tucked under her as she lay back, her hair fanning out across the pillow. *Don't you love the scientific names?*

Sure, honey.

They skipped back to the beginning with the dictionary beside them, read all the names again, Margaret's slim white finger—bare-nailed then, cuticles in need of a trim, a fleck of grime still clinging from pushing Hope on the playground swing—running below the words alongside Hope's finger, the pitch of her voice high against Hope's already slightly husky one. *Neofelis nebulosa*, clouded leopard; *Oreailurus jacobita*, Andean mountain cat; *Acinonyx jubatus*, cheetah.

Margaret had smiled, reminded of her own childhood—not of cats or scientific names, but just the pleasure of learning things. How many nights had she shunned a storybook and brought her father something from the encyclopedia instead? Sometimes they just chose a volume number, opened, read: Julius Caesar one night, American Revolution the next; Communism, Hadrian's Wall, it didn't matter.

In the middle of Hope's dark room, nearly a decade after the big cat books, Margaret wrapped her arms around herself. The only scientific names she'd run her fingers under recently had been related to Brad and his addiction. How many mornings had she risen before him, trying to know, hoping it would help her understand, sitting in her office whispering the names for the roots of the drugs he took—*Papaver somniferum*, the poppy, and *Papaver bracteatum*, from which might come 3-methylmorphine, codeine, or thebaine, converted to hyrocodone, combined with paracetamol to become Lortab. She'd done the same research after she found out about the cocaine— all this on top of researching new houses for clients and new clients for herself, as if there was an amount of money she could make that Brad wouldn't spend.

Could it help them if Margaret might once more be allowed to sit on Hope's bed, running her finger over these names, explaining the danger, the way they could take a person from him or herself?

Margaret carefully pulled the door closed, stood in the hall, rolled the Lortab bottle in her hand. She tiptoed downstairs, not turning on any lights, across the bare heart pine floor and into the screened porch. She sat in the hanging chair Brad and Hope had talked her into just two years ago. *Tacky*, she'd said. *Fun*, Brad countered, winking at Hope. Her shoulders had tensed then. Why was she always the outsider?

Holding the memory as well as the Lortab bottle, Margaret spun in the chair; she pulled her knees up to her chin, wrapped her arms around her legs, rested her forehead on her knees and breathed into herself. Crickets and cicadas vied for the rhythm of the night. The neighborhood owl added a couple of hoots—telling them off or joining in, who knew?

Margaret's shoulders began to shake slightly, then her head.

"No," she whispered into her legs. "No no no no."

Her mother's voice, in her head. *That's enough*. What she'd said after she rested her meaty, age-spotted hands on Margaret's shoulders when Margaret had begun to weep in the receiving line at her father's funeral, the piper tooting "Flowers of the Forest" in the background, Mummy holding Margaret in her hard, slate eyes. *It will be all right*. A quick, hard squeeze of the shoulders, and then her mother stepped back into her spot, kissed the next person's cheek, accepted condolences, asked about the woman's child or cat, Margaret couldn't quite make out.

In the chair on the screened porch, Margaret straightened her legs; she gave each cheek a firm brush to banish the tears. It would only be all right if she made it so. And she obviously hadn't been making it so, or she wouldn't be cradling herself and a nearly empty bottle of pain medicine in an abandoned chair in the middle of the night.

In the kitchen, lit by her laptop, Margaret flipped through the printouts. Each one looked as bad as the next. She fanned them in her hand. The sun-and-moon-framed clock over the windows ticking: 2:23. 2:24. 7:24 in Scotland. *It will be all right*. Just saying it might be enough for dealing with the dead.

She hoped Agatha would pick up right away; she hoped Agatha would be out in the garden already, or across the street on the rocks by the sea, or else on some plant-gathering mission. Then she would have another few minutes, an hour, perhaps even a whole day to pretend that it would be all right, that she would be all right enough to give Hope what she needed.

Agatha picked up on the third ring, saying the number as people used to, seeming neither surprised at the sound of Margaret's voice, nor as though she'd been sitting there waiting for it.

"Hiccups are gone, I hear," Aunt Agatha said.

Margaret had forgotten them, thought for a moment Aunt Agatha meant something else.

"I," Margaret said. "Hope." She paused.

"Yes, pet, what about you and Hope?"

"She. I found." Margaret stopped. What right did she have to bother an old woman with her failings as a mother? Agatha probably hadn't even finished her first cup of tea. Agatha wasn't a mom.

"Fourteen can be a hard age," Agatha said, "without complications."

"It's not that. Yes, it is. Oh. I just don't know what to do with her anymore."

"All right, pet. Calm yourself a minute and just start with what has upset you so much you want to hear my quavery old voice twice in less than twenty-four hours."

Margaret blurted out about the Lortab, Hope's general darkening, hanging out with the Goth boys on the edges of the crowd at school, the impenetrable wall Hope was building against her. As she spoke, Agatha was quiet, saying only "aye," "oh aye?" or "aye, of course," as though it was all perfectly natural.

"I went online and looked at summer camps, you know, ones that specialize in these sorts of things. I thought we could talk about it, sort of rationally, and then." Margaret paused.

Silence on the other end of the line.

"And then we had a fight and I said she could come and stay with you. I don't know why I said it, especially without asking. It's not exactly the same as coming for vacation and..."

"I can't believe you even thought of sending her to strangers, Margaret. Of course you'll send her here. Just put her on a plane."

When she hung up, Margaret washed and dried her face. She fed the stack of printouts through the shredder. She would sleep, for a few hours anyway. In the morning she would make the reservations before she ran.

Hope woke just after five a.m., the moon a sliver outside her window, the crickets still rubbing their racket, the sky beginning to pale. She listened to the house. Likely her mother was up meditating or getting ready for a run. Perhaps she was researching more summer camps. Hope imagined herself in a cabin full of potheads, pillheads, drunks. Not that different from school. She rolled over, tried to sleep, failed, rolled the other direction, tried again until she heard the back door shut. 5:33. Mom going for her run. Hope flung back the covers. She had time to raid the fridge and tuck herself back in.

On the kitchen table, under the empty Lortab bottle, she found a stack of papers. She lifted the bottle. The paper beneath held not a summer camp printout, but airline reservations.

Hope McNairn Carver, unaccompanied minor. Terra Pines to Atlanta to Glasgow. Below the tight font, Margaret's curly script detailed how Hope would get from there to Great-aunt Agatha's cottage. *Shit.*

Hope pocketed the bottle. She lay her head down on top of the reservation. Was this what her father felt when her mother had tried to force him into rehab? A connection to Dad, at last, only this wouldn't bring him home either.

When she heard her mother's footsteps in the garage, Hope straightened. She wiped her eyes. Before the door had fully closed behind her mother, Hope held up the printout, rolled her eyes, slapped the paper back down on the table and runway-walked to her room. Twenty-one or twenty-eight days, or even six weeks away from this shit couldn't be all bad.

On the way to the airport, Margaret faced the road, eyes hidden under dark Dolce & Gabbanas. She scanned Hope in her peripheral vision. Had her daughter's spine been that straight since Brad left? Hope sat, hands in pockets, eyes forward, hidden under her own sunglasses—unearthed at Goodwill, vintage 1981, by the looks of them.

"Would you like to listen to some music?" Margaret asked.

"Sure."

Margaret reached for the radio. Hope dug in her pocket, pressed her bluebottle-colored earbuds into her ears. Of course. How could Margaret have thought they might share a few moments of music? Was Hope even listening to music in there? Rings of sweat began to form under Margaret's arms, even though she had the air conditioning in the SAAB set to sixty-eight, white air blasting from the vents.

In the tiny airport, Margaret paid the fee to walk Hope to the gate and wait. She offered a soft drink, a candy bar. Hope selected water, shunned the snack. She dug the money out of her own pocket while Margaret rooted in her oversized bag for her wallet. On the faux leather seats, Hope pushed in her headphones again; Margaret laid a hand on Hope's knee, felt the muscle underneath, toned and strong. She squeezed.

"Hope."

Hope removed one earbud, jutted her chin forward.

"You have the instructions? You'll come through customs…"

"Mom. I got it. I'm sure I can make it to Auntie Agatha's Home for Wayward Girls just fine."

"It's not." Margaret shifted closer. She wrapped an arm around her daughter, felt the slim shoulder, muscular there as well. Did her daughter know her own power? Did she know even a little of her own beauty? The slight curve starting at her waist, lean arms and legs—not one of those scrawny girls who looked as though they pecked at scraps instead of eating whole meals, but a fit, healthy girl, five eight already. Margaret swept Hope's hair behind her shoulders, rubbed her hand across Hope's back. Hope shifted her head, hiding beneath the shroud of her hair.

"I love you, Hope."

Hope shifted forward in her seat. "I do want a snack."

When Hope returned, the flight attendant called for early boarders. Hope allowed Margaret to hug her, pressing her smaller frame against Hope's. Had she reciprocated, Margaret would just about have disappeared into Hope's long arms, broad shoulders. Hope held her arms away from Margaret's body.

"Bye." Hope began to turn within Margaret's embrace.

Margaret held her hand to her chest, palm flat, resisting an urge to clutch at her silk blouse as Hope made her way to the plane. Margaret pressed her palm against the window as the plane taxied, just in case Hope was watching. She lifted her hand as the plane lifted, dropped it to her side when the plane flew beyond her view.

On her run the next morning, Margaret imagined Hope awakening over the Atlantic, almost in Scotland. As she made her way to yoga, she pictured the flight attendant seeing Hope through customs and immigration, safely to Agatha. After the call to Agatha and the flat tire and the offer of a rain check, Margaret clutched her steering wheel, breathed in.

Her mother might have been able to simply make decisions and move forward. Once upon a time, Margaret had been capable of the same thing. Not anymore. On her out breath, Margaret whispered, "Hope is okay. You've done the right thing." In her gut, though, questions roiled: *Is she? Have you?*

FIVE
Agatha and Hope

Agatha closed the door to her guest room—Hope's room for the foreseeable future—and made for her gardening boots and the rest of her snowdrops. Outside the cottage, a goat waited for her. Stubborn, hollow-horned, and bearded, the creature had broken away from her herd.

"What a silly girl," Agatha had said, out loud, the first time the goat ambled around the corner of the cottage a couple weeks before.

Agatha had shaken her head then, thinking of the bravado so many people inferred after seeing the herds of wild goats rambling across the Scottish landscape. All false. In fact, goats were far less hardy than sheep or cattle. They needed, among other things, to be sheltered all year round. And here was this one, with her hollow toggle of skin hanging from her neck; likely she was seeking her own fortune—greener pastures, so to speak. A typical member of the genus *Capra*, she looked for what she needed in the same place day after day, when she might have been able to find something better just around the corner, if only she could let go of a little single-minded stubbornness.

As she knelt in her new flowerbed, Agatha shook her head at the goat.

"Ocht, you again?" she said.

For over an hour, she and her trowel worked steadily in the dark soil below the wall. At last Agatha stood, held her hands gently on her lower back. She looked the goat right in the eye.

"Have you nowhere better to go?"

The goat butted her horns against the wall.

Agatha laughed. "Fair enough. We'll see if it's you or the lassie upstairs who's more stubborn, won't we?"

Hope blinked her eyes open. She sat up and drew back the dark drapes and then the sheers. Her eyes landed on a hairy, curvy-horned black and white creature, hanging its head over the stone wall below. Had she dreamed the laugh that had awakened her? Down on the ground, the goat chewed. Agatha dug in the garden. Hope dropped the curtains, lay back down. Agatha's voice started up again. Was she talking to the goat? Scotland's version of Dr. Doolittle?

The clock said 12:21. 7:21, really. Had she been in her own bed, Hope would have been debating whether it was worth facing her mother to get a ride to the skate park, or better, to the old library, or to wait until Mom left and then just strap her board onto the outside of her pack. Sometimes she took some music to listen to. Sometimes Katie got to come, a bonus. The clock ticked while Hope imagined herself skating over to the stairset at the old library. Skating there was best. Street skating in general was preferable, always holding some surprise: rails to grind, stairsets and gaps to jump, ledges to drop in from, not the same old ramps week after week after week like skating vert at the skate park. And there were never any adults hovering—only other skaters watching to see Hope nail the ollie, show off a new trick, watching to see her bleed or break when she missed. Adults at the skate park stood off at the edges, like they were waiting to pluck out some tiny flaw that said Hope was all trouble. Hope's mother looked at Hope like that now, all the time, the same way Mom looked at her own face, searching for blemishes at her dresser, in front of the magnifying mirror with tweezers and blackhead squeezers and cleansers and firmers and all kinds of little bottles she thought would make her flawless.

Mom had plucked Hope out, hadn't she? Got rid of the one big blemish everyone could see a mile off and dropped her into this trash can called Arran, just like she dropped the little extra eyebrow hairs that grew at the bridge of her nose.

Would Agatha be picky like that, too? Hope listened again. Agatha's voice had been replaced by the sound of something metal disrupting dirt, *chuck-chuck, chuck-chuck*, double time against the rhythm of the ocean trying to reach her over the pebbles and rocks across the skinny street. Hope lay still and listened to the grey-green waters roll up on the shore again and again, half wishing they would roll up over her, wrap her in one big, cool wave and carry her away. She'd done her share of wishing this year, swung the same wish toward the first star she saw every night in February. At Easter, she mouthed it while she lit a candle at Katie's church.

"I made my wish," she told Katie when they got into the hard wooden pew.

"It's called a prayer if you do it here, over the candle," Katie whispered, rolling her eyes.

Hope shrugged. Whatever you called it, it didn't work.

She quit it altogether when no amount of wishing or looking or anything else she tried made her father show up by the end of school. "I resolve to be wish-free." She wrote it on the front of all her notebooks. *Wishes are for fairies. I wash my hands of wishy-washy wishes.* She set fire to her notebooks. Standing over the flames, she vowed to find other, better ways to connect with Dad.

She thought she'd left little-girl wishing behind, and then those waves washed one back up on her. Hope sucked her wish down, burrowed under the covers, and closed her eyes again.

When she woke, she thought the clock must be wrong—4:26. She pulled back the covers just enough to fling her legs free and scooted the rest of her body out. The air in the room was cool. She stood, facing away from the window, and took a deep breath. She sat back down. She slid her legs back under the covers. Could she just curl into the little bed-prison, accept her sentence, wait for parole? She rolled toward the window, closed her eyes. Her mind went immediately to the skate park. Hope felt the breeze on her face again, as she had standing on the bar on top of the chain-link fence at the skate park; she felt, again, the air, the dance in her gut, equally excited at the prospects of success and of bleeding. She pulled back the sheets, got up.

"Right," she said, the way her Granny McPherson used to say it when she was ready to take on some unpleasant task, like scrubbing the skirting boards in their kitchen. Shoulders back, head high, the way she stood at the top of the half-pipe, ready to drop in, Hope started down the stairs.

When she opened the door to the front room, Hope expected to see Agatha sip-sipping at another cup of tea. Or else she expected to see Agatha pick-picking at some bit of knitting or sewing. She definitely did not expect to see butter dribbling down Great-auntie Agatha's fingers and slithering across the back of her hand, making her scrubbed fingertips glow, pink and shiny in the scant light from a tiny fire. Agatha turned slightly, took a bite of the buttery bread in her hand. She seemed to have scrubbed so hard getting rid of all that muck from the garden that she'd rubbed her hands back to babyhood, red and drool-covered. The similarity to her youth ended at her bony knuckles. Auntie Agatha was still there, sharp and silent and ancient.

"Close the door, please. You're making a draft. *Díth céille.*"

Hope tried to ignore the Gaelic that Agatha hung off the end of her sentence. Granny Mac had had the same habit, adding Gaelic words here and there, but when she did it, her voice was kind, joking, and she explained what she meant. When Agatha did it, the words sounded sharp and tight, like secrets.

Hope had to push the door hard, over the carpet, to close it. At home, Hope barely nudged the doors and they slammed. Here, the doors fit so tightly into their frames that there wasn't room for a breath around the edges.

"That was quite a sleep." Agatha began to lick her fingers. "That's me finished in the garden, for a few days anyway."

Agatha nibbled the buttery bread, the light from the fire flickering against skin so thin Hope imagined she could

almost see her bones. Still groggy from sleep and jet lag, she
watched Agatha wrap her thin lips around each buttery, bony
finger, silently sucking out every last bit of flavor. Hope's
stomach growled.

"Bannock?" Agatha held up the plate. "I love warm bannock
by the fire when I've been outside all day; even when it's not
really cold enough, I like a small fire—always have, since I was
a wee thing, younger than you. *Gearchaile.*"

Here it was already. Bannock. Hope hadn't eaten since the
last pack of pretzels on the plane. She wouldn't have cared if it
really *was* a rodent. Hope reached for the bread, lifted, bit.

Bannock didn't taste like rodent at all. It was a little sweet and
soothing, with salty butter melting in her mouth.

"Tomorrow I'll give you a tour of the island," Agatha said.
"Part of it, at least. We'll take out the bicycles."

Hope swallowed the bite of bannock whole and started
coughing. She pictured Agatha on a bike almost as old as she,
pedaling like that woman in *The Wizard of Oz.*

"You'll need to know how to get about," Agatha said.

Hope took another bite while she digested the idea of Agatha's
spindly legs propelling a bicycle. She didn't need whatever bike
Agatha had in mind for her; she had her skateboard. Hope could
almost hear the steady thrum of her own little wheels, good
enough to get her anywhere she wanted to go.

In the morning, outside, Hope stood away from the wooden
shed that crouched in the side garden, grey as the stone of
the cottage and the granite hilltops behind. Hands in pockets,
skateboard on the ground in front of her, Hope peered around
her great-auntie, trying not to wonder what was inside. Did
Agatha own one of those original bikes with the huge front tire
and tiny back one?

Agatha pulled the door hard, angling her body toward Hope
as it opened. Hope turned her back, faced the water and the
wind coming off it, finding herself almost eye to eye with the
same hairy goat to which Agatha had been talking the day

before. This time, it had its hooves up on the low rock wall, as if it was standing at a bar, waiting to be served a drink or a sandwich.

"Right," Agatha said.

Hope faced her. The door to the shed banged against its frame. "What?"

"Right, I said. That's me nearly ready, then." Agatha lifted a meticulously wrapped brown package and put it in the basket on the front of the bike. "Just the tires to pump up. There's yours." She flicked her head in the direction of the shed. Against it lay a bike of the same grey as the rocky beach, with fat, smooth, flat tires and a saddle nearly big enough to be a recliner. Cobwebs dangled from the frame.

Hope lifted her board.

Auntie Agatha screwed the end of the hand pump to the valve on the tire and started inflating. While Agatha pumped, Hope twirled the wheels on her board, eyeing the steps that led from the house into the garden. Not much, but something, at least, she could grind or jump over.

"There," Agatha said. "So, just a few kilometers up to Catacol, then on to Lochranza." She looked at Hope's board. "You'll not go fast on those wee wheels," she said. Her lips curled, puffing her hollow cheeks outward. "Not as fast as I'll go on these big ones."

Was Aunt Agatha measuring Hope like a skater?

"Sure you'll not take the bike?" Aunt Agatha asked.

"Very."

"Suit yourself." The wind whipped wisps of Agatha's hair out in front of her, pointing the way as she wheeled the bike through the front gate. "House that gets less sunshine than any other house in Great Britain is in Lochranza," she said.

Hope remained still, the wind coming at her profile. One gust came so hard she thought even her eyebrows must be pointing windward. She refused to start plucking them— thick, dark eyebrows like her dad's—no matter how much her mother nagged. Agatha obviously hadn't been doing much plucking either.

Agatha put one foot on the pedal. Instead of swinging the other leg over the bike, she used it to push along the pavement, sort of the way Hope pushed on the board, but not the way Hope had ever seen anyone start a bike. When Agatha finally started to swing her leg over the saddle, the wind died completely. The bike lost what little speed it had gained. It wobbled. The goat bleated. Hope dropped her board, started toward Agatha, nearly reaching her just as the wind came back. Agatha's foot connected with the pedal. Both the goat and Hope stopped. It stared at her, creeping her out with its rectangular pupils and yellow eyes that never seemed to blink.

"Coming?" Agatha turned.

Hope flushed. If there was anything worse than being stuck on this island, it was having to take care of an old lady. She pushed off with a vengeance.

By the time Hope rounded the corner into Lochranza Bay and felt the wind die again, Auntie Agatha was off her bicycle and lifting her package from the basket. Any one of the houses in front of her could have been the one that got so little sun.

"How would you like to see the castle?" Agatha called to her. She pointed at what was left of a castle perched on the edge of the tide. Small fishing boats bobbed nearby. The castle had so many holes it looked as if it was struggling to remain afloat on dry land. "You'll get the key in the post office. I'll give you a tour when I come out. Only be two ticks."

Agatha and her parcel tucked into the shop—sweaters and cardigans she'd wrapped carefully in brown paper and tied with the exact right amount of string. Another woman—Hope's mother, for instance—would have plopped her knitting into some brightly patterned, designer canvas bag. Hope picked up her board. Did Agatha wish Hope to be a more neatly wrapped package? Had she pointed her in the direction of the castle so Hope wouldn't be an embarrassment, the way Margaret doled out money for the arcade in the mall when she ran into a client?

Hope considered herself: wild-haired, jeans frayed at the edges, faded black sweater with too-long sleeves unearthed from the $1 shelf at the back of the Goodwill. She scanned the village, looking for a coffee shop or skate shop or any other sign of civilization. *Probably still sharpen their pencils with knives.*

She sized up the chance of ollying right up to the front door of the shop, maybe even through it if someone opened it in time. She decided to go for it. The wheels ground against loose stones on the path as Hope pushed off. The bottom of her shoe hung perfectly on the griptape; the wheels hung on the path a little too tightly. One of the lace curtains peeled back, barely.

Pushing the board forward again, then again, Hope gathered speed. The door began to open. Both feet on the board, Hope bent her body toward it, got ready to lift off. She jumped as the door opened wider, felt the board leave her feet and begin to spin. Perfect air. Perfect timing. She lifted her eyes from her feet and they landed, not on Agatha or on the door, but on the shaggy-haired boy who was just coming out.

Her legs splayed. The board landed in front of her, carried on alone, careened into the steps. Hope landed like a yard flamingo lobbed toward the trash. Half of her clung to the path, half gathered grass stains. Her face turned as red as her hair. With each passing nanosecond, she must have looked more and more like some overripe fruit—not the dark, seedy eggplant that she'd brandished at her mother, but a bumpy beefsteak tomato fallen from the vine at the worst possible minute. Lying spattered in the shop's front garden for all of Lochranza to see, she heard, above the hot embarrassment swirling in her ears, the boy laughing at her.

Hope stood, flicked her hair from her face, didn't bother to dust her pants, went for her board.

"Sorry," the boy said, nearly choking on his ridiculously thick Scottish r's. "I know I shouldn't laugh. It's just you looked quite funny, and it's not as though you're hurt." He paused, shaking his dark hair away from his face and revealing clear blue eyes. "You're not hurt, are you? I've never seen anybody do that before."

She pushed past him into the shop.

"Met Kenny, did you?" Agatha wound her string into a tiny ball. The brown paper, sweaters removed, lay folded in the basket.

"Kenny?" Hope half turned, her hand on the open door. There he still was, at the bottom of the steps. He shrugged. "Sort of."

"I sent him out to say hello," said the woman behind the counter.

"He lives just behind us," Agatha said, as if Hope had been living there forever, as if they were roommates in college or something.

Inside the shop, shelf after shelf cradled the rounded folds of sweaters in all colors and sizes. Agatha's bony body looked like one of the ridges on the Arran-knit cabled sweaters. Her friend behind the counter, probably Kenny's great-auntie, looked like a set of rounded humps formed by ball upon ball of wool, stacked up and stuffed into a too-small bag. Kenny stepped back inside and stood there still smiling. The castle, holes and all, might have been Hope's better refuge.

"Kenny, dear, did you not introduce yourself?" Kenny's whatever-she-was asked.

Kenny stuck his hand out, pasty white and rigid in contrast to his reddening face.

Hope forced her hand to meet his, which felt rough, more like a man's hand than a boy's—a little like griptape. She pulled back quickly.

"You'll be seeing a lot of Kenny," the woman said.

Hope turned toward the counter. The old lady plopped her hands on her wide hips and leaned her body, which mostly meant her breasts, over the counter at Hope.

"Unless you find Agatha's company too riveting to want a friend your own age." She chuckled at herself, making her apron and everything she'd corralled under it flow like an ocean that didn't know which way to send its waves. Hope resisted the urge to roll her eyes only because she didn't want to share it with Kenny. "Or maybe you'd rather pal up with your great-auntie Agatha's *glaistig*." Her body rolled with a new tide of laughter.

"Don't be silly," Agatha said.

"That's no ordinary goat, as you well know, Agatha Stuart. It's a *glaistig*." The woman nodded at Hope. "A kind of a fairy woman that turns herself into a goat to look after children…" She turned to Agatha. "Or the elderly who are getting a bit frail and need a bit of help."

Agatha cleared her throat, turned to Kenny. "Might you show Hope the castle?"

"I can't just now, Miss Stuart. I've to get the shopping back to my mum." Kenny eyed a box of groceries in the corner, then turned to Hope. "Maybe another afternoon?"

Hope pulled her board closer, not caring when she felt the griptape stick to her sweater, likely making the little picks which so irritated her mother. Would Agatha notice or care? She shrugged.

"That would be lovely." Agatha turned to her friend. "Thanks, Moira."

Kenny grabbed his box and opened the door, forcing Hope to stick her skateboard out ahead of her and squeeze past him sideways.

"Nice to meet you, Hope," he said.

"You too," she said, so he wouldn't be the only liar in the room.

The skin on Hope's face stung with the wind and salty spray from the sea. Nearly back at the cottage, her body vibrated from skating for miles on rough road—one rung up from gravel. Her mind rang with questions. What had she been thinking, not fighting her mother? Why hadn't she asked how long, even? And then, suddenly as the wind had died when they rounded the corner and rode into the shelter of Lochranza Bay, her mind leapt to the night her father left.

He'd healed. He'd gone back to bike racing, finishing better and better every time he was gone. Didn't that prove he was fine? And yet her parents' fighting got worse and worse. Mom wanted him to get help; Dad said he didn't need it. Then one night her mom had called her downstairs.

Hope had known about Dad still taking the Lortab. She'd suspected there was something else, too, but she hadn't expected to sit across from them on the couch, listening to the kind of half-truths you'd expect from a guilty teenager instead of your mother, your father nodding as though he agreed. He needed therapy, related to a little part of him still not healed from the accident.

Mom sat on the loveseat. Dad scrunched in the chair in the corner, saying nothing, unfurling himself at the end, hugging Hope too hard. He didn't look back, or meet her eye once as he got into the car. He backed out of the driveway, turned down the street, and drove away.

What if she had climbed in too, felt the chilly leather against the backs of her legs? What if she'd sat there, inside the closed car, smelling the sweaty gym bag full of used cycling clothes that he never took in to wash until the day he needed them? What if she'd called bullshit on him as she would have anyone at the skate park? If she'd done any of that, or if she'd just said *I'm going with you*, where would she be?

She pictured him watching her grind some new rail in some new city, the sun poking through the clouds, him giving her that look, where his hair fell in his face and his eyebrows rose, saying *surprise me*. And didn't she? That look made her feel safe enough to try the next hardest trick, no matter what it was. They could have gone to some small town in Iowa, some city as big as New York; they could have come to Arran, even. Her father could have ridden his Kona over the hills, the way he did before the crash. Hope could almost feel the heat of his cheek against hers. Then Agatha whizzed past, wheezing.

SIX
Margaret

Eighteen years. Eighteen years since Margaret had tiptoed, sock-footed, sneakers in hand, onto the stoop of the ratty little apartment she shared with Trig on the top floor of what had once been a grand old antebellum, the kind with wide stairs and a huge front porch and columns. Sometimes it seemed to Margaret that no time had passed at all—that it must have been some other girl who had tried to keep so quiet while Trig and whomever she'd brought home the night before nestled in Trig's room, the guy's thwarted copilot piled on the sofa, the lot of them sleeping off the results of another Friday night in Five Points.

Margaret would start running as soon as her feet hit the driveway. The small amount of debris in her head from the night before was gone after the first mile. Always, she wanted more.

The start of her senior year. She'd already been approached by Elliot Bingham, Hughes Aughtry, and Windsor Cole, three of the best accounting firms. In not so many months, she'd be on her way—off the stoop and moving toward a house of her own, one with a vegetable garden in the back and neat rows of hosta in the front.

Margaret leaned forward, encouraging gravity's pull down Marion Avenue, tanned legs turning over easily. This was what she was made for—linear movement, rhythmic breathing, steady and fast, her lean body speaking of economy, a spareness that suggested she had precisely what she needed.

An empty Coors can rolled along the curb, welcoming her to Saturday morning in Five Points. Behind it, rounding the corner at the other end of the block, ran a blond, bare-chested and glistening, his shirt flapping from the side of his shorts.

Margaret had never met anyone this early in Five Points—not upright, at any rate. She held her course, mesmerized by long legs the color of honey. As she passed him, she pressed harder. Breathless and overheated, Margaret slowed where she'd seen him turn onto the street. She risked a turn of the head, found him doing the same. The image of him followed her home and up the steps, into the shower and out, disrupted her studying. Trig noticed, dragged the specifics out of her, sent her out at precisely the same time the following Saturday. Trig even piled herself and a large coffee onto a bench in Five Points, in case the guy turned out to be a creep or Margaret turned back.

There he was, Brad Carver, stretching already when she got there, majoring in Parks, Recreation and Tourism Management. How many miles did they cover on the subsequent Saturday mornings, soon adding in the weekdays as well, spilling their secrets to the rhythm of their feet on the pavement? He'd started running, he said, in high school, with his mother, when she lifted herself from the sofa, poured out the last bottle of vodka and swore never to drink again. The running kept Brad going even when his mother returned to the sofa and the bottle.

By the time the first hard frost rolled around that year, Brad sat beside Margaret on the stoop, tying his shoes and heading out with her on Saturday mornings. He made her laugh. She kept the pace steady. A year later, Trig was her maid of honor.

How did that Brad, fluid and flawless, connect to the man he became just a few years later, the addict who healed himself and came to Scotland to prove himself to her? How did he connect to the man on the sofa fourteen years after that? What should Margaret have noticed, done differently to help him after the accident? Should she have tried harder to console him? Made a bigger fuss over the healing? Paid no attention to it at all?

Weeks after Margaret had jumped out of her chair on the porch to find Brad home early with his leg in a cast, she sat beside him on the sofa. It was mid-March; Brad should have been racing the spring series, gauging how to train for the season ahead. Instead he was slouched on the couch, leg propped on the coffee table. Brad glared at a new set of X-rays, an accusation.

Margaret put her hand on his leg, squeezed.

"Surgery," he said.

"Oh, honey. I'm sorry." She patted his leg, smooth and lithe as ever, as though he was still training.

His quad tensed against her. He pressed up.

"What do you need? I'll get it."

"I'll get it. And what I don't need is for you to feel sorry for me." He hopped to the kitchen, came back with a bottle of Sweetwater 420, popped off the cap, swigged down a Lortab with the cool pale ale.

"Should you be doing those together?"

Brad turned to her, eyes wide and steady. "It's a beer, Margaret."

It was the beginning of a new afternoon ritual, this beer, replacing his run or ride.

The first surgery didn't take. Margaret tried to encourage, to empathize. Brad tensed, tucked into himself and his beer and Lortab. At home after the second failed surgery, he raised his pint glass to her, sneered. "Only a few more weeks." As if it was her fault.

A few more weeks of Brad replacing work and exercise with feeling sorry for himself and imprinting his softening body on the sofa. He'd gone from a weekly routine of six runs, three hard bike rides, and workouts with clients to twelve-ounce curls on the couch. Repeats that used to take place up seven-percent-grade hills had been replaced with returns to the bathroom down the hall. Margaret brought him books from the library, which he used as beer coasters. She offered to take him along when she went on scouting rides for properties; he declined. The only time Brad was animated was when Hope was home, telling him about ollying and other nuances of her newfound love, skateboarding. What possessed Brad to give Hope the board the previous Christmas, Margaret didn't know. She'd been to the skate park, noted that the kids weren't the clean-cut ones from the soccer team, but the darker kind who seemed to show a wanton disregard for damn near everything, including their own safety. If Hope wasn't careful, she was going to end up on the sofa beside her father.

Margaret rounded up more clients. Real estate had a plushness that had been missing from the black and white of accounting. She hadn't realized work could be fun.

In the mornings, she passed in front of Brad on the sofa. His gaze on her made her gut roll. She could no longer bring herself to meet it, couldn't think what to do or say that wouldn't sound like pity to him. She worked harder, longer. They needed the money. Brad drove Hope to school and to the skate park and nowhere else.

Should she have refused clients? Sat on the sofa and cried for him? Should she have had a beer with him? Gone with them to the skate park?

Perhaps if she had done any of those things, she might have found herself somewhere (anywhere) other than struggling to maintain some semblance of decent posture in the curvy red plastic chair in the Sears car repair waiting room. Brad gone. Hope gone. Tire flat. The dealer too busy to fit her in.

The grime-flecked floor and ergonomically incorrect seating seemed to be forcing her up and out, into the adjoining mall. Anything was better than sitting, rigid, hoping the questions wouldn't start.

She strode past a pair of geriatric mall walkers on the way out of Sears. They were about the same age as Clyde Bridwell, a man and a woman, only they were all white tennis shoes and pale, age-spotted forearms, in contrast to Clyde's dark lace-ups and permatan. She passed them and then stopped, caught by the sweet smell of American Eagle perfume wafting out of the store. Brightly colored pants dangled like party streamers from the high racks. Patterned blouses with skinny belts nestled beside them.

"He-ey. Welcome to American Eagle. Can I help you?" The clerk's cheeks puffed out. Perfectly straight teeth beamed at Margaret, framed by glossy lips.

"Yes," Margaret said. "Yes, you can." She glanced upward at the choices, then back at the girl. "I need to get a little something for my daughter."

"Cool. Birthday? Early back-to-school?" The girl leaned in like a co-conspirator. "Or just a little sercy?"

Margaret hadn't heard the word—*sercy*, short for surprise— since her dad died. "No, actually, it's. She's." Margaret hesitated. "She's overseas."

"Ooh. Foreign exchange. How fun."

The girl guided her toward pants, blouses, sweaters (normally an irritation, arriving early for fall when it was triple digits outside). Margaret stepped back out of the store twenty minutes later, flush with visions of Hope as a brightly clad, confident teenager—cheered by the notion that even a little thing like this might help Hope care for herself instead of focusing on a man who had abandoned them, and who was coming back who knew when, if ever.

On the way back to Sears, Margaret stopped at Starbucks for a rooibos chai: decadent, deserved, a celebration of taking charge. Another elderly couple in line ahead of her, pink-cheeked and glowy, reminded her again of Clyde and of the rain check. She wanted that off her list.

On Clyde's porch, Margaret balanced her chai and a black coffee, cream and sugar perched on top, along with a bag containing a blueberry muffin, a cinnamon scone, and a pecan bar. She knocked. Waited. Knocked again, harder. Maybe he wasn't home. Would leaving the treats on the mat count?

"No need to pound a hole in the door." Leaning on rail at the corner of the porch, Clyde gave the sense that he'd been there all along, watching.

"Mr. Bridwell. Thought I'd make good on that rain check."

"Thought you was getting a rain check from me, not the other way round."

"The least I could do after your kindness this morning."

Clyde moved toward her, slowly, face craning forward like a cat sniffing something unknown, trying to decide whether to play with it or eat it. He stopped short, smoothed back his Brylcreemed white hair.

"All right, then. Make yourself at home." Clyde nodded toward the porch swing and a pair of metal chairs that crouched in front of the rail.

Margaret moved toward them. Behind her, the screen door *thwacked* shut. Margaret set the coffee and tea and sweets on a little end table between the chairs and then took a seat. The metal of the chair felt cool through her skirt. She crossed her legs. Her skirt rose and she pulled it closer to her knees, remembering Clyde's reference to its teen-tinyness. She uncrossed her legs. She stood.

"Thought we might require a plate or two."

Margaret spun at the sound of Clyde's voice behind her. She cleared her throat. "You scared me."

"You scare easy."

Clyde set down two mugs as well.

"Mildred never could abide the sight of a person taking their drink from anything except a real cup or glass." Clyde lifted the lid from his coffee. "Nobody et or drank much outside their own homes when we was youngsters. Reckon it was round the time we married—nineteen and fifty-one—when folks first started with the drive-up and all. Mildred said we'd eat at home or else with folks we knew. Wouldn't put a thing to her lips if she didn't know who made it. She wasn't just particular about who cooked it, neither. Back then, we knew who grew it or raised it and who harvested or slaughtered it. Even knew who ground it up for grits." Clyde sipped. He raised his mug. "This was the first stuff Mildred let in her house not knowing where it came from. Before that we had chicory. Then the kids brought RC cola. Mildred made them pour it in a glass. Wasn't no arguing with her, neither. I reckon after forty-seven years, some of her stuck."

Clyde poured what would fit into his mug, one eye on Margaret as she lifted the lid from her tea, pulled the other mug over, poured. She nudged the bag toward him. "A little something sweet."

"That's right nice of you." Clyde pulled out the muffin, then the pecan bar, then the scone, and set them on a plate. "Ladies first."

"Oh, not for me. I got them for you."

"You wouldn't expect me to eat all that by myself."

"You could save some for…"

"Or to eat alone, right here in front of you."

"I don't mind at all."

"Mildred would never forgive me."

Margaret lifted her tea.

"You think when they're dead and gone you can do as you please, but they're still there, like they're watching and you can't even argue with them." He pushed the plate closer to Margaret. "Go ahead."

"Really, you could save them."

"Or you could." Clyde sat back.

They sipped a minute. Cars swished by. Crows lifted and landed in nearby trees.

Margaret clenched her jaw. She lifted the pecan bar. She could nibble the nuts off the top—protein, at least. Clyde took the muffin, bit in, examined what remained. "Right big, aren't they?" Clyde chewed slowly. He swallowed. "I recall Mildred's muffins. Roll the berries right off the bush, making it look like they were hurrying into her palms, like they *wanted* to be part of a Mildred Bridwell muffin." Clyde studied the muffin again.

"If you don't like it…"

"Oh, I like it." He bit. He started the methodical chewing. "You're making me feel bad, me chewing away here and you not touching your little pecan tart."

Margaret nibbled a nut.

"Now, you wouldn't eat the nuts off the top and leave a fine crust, would you? Mildred could bake a fine, buttery crust. Believe I still have a recipe. I'll get it." He leaned forward, preparing to rise. "I might have something else, too."

"Don't trouble yourself."

He stepped toward the door.

Margaret considered tossing the pecan bar over the porch. She didn't keep her body in shape eating like that. She and Brad had both taken care of themselves, until the accident. It had seemed to come naturally to Brad; for her, it required discipline, a constant vigil so she wouldn't become one of those dimple-thighed women on the PTA, women like her own mother had been, bodies spreading like softening butter. "Really, thank you, but there's no need to trouble yourself." The pecan bar still sat on the plate on her lap. Clyde turned.

"I'll look later."

She should just stand, say *Thanks, but I have to be going. Thanks, but I have to make supper.*

He'd see the lie. She bit.

Clyde kept on with tales of Mildred, expert at beheading chickens, superior at biscuit baking.

"A fine mother, too." Clyde looked off toward the drive. "Shouldn't have had to shoulder the blame for Ruth Ann."

"Ruth Ann?"

"Nothing." Clyde turned his gaze back toward Margaret. "You're missing." He searched her eyes. "You're missing out. That's not but one good mouthful you got left there."

"I'm full, really."

"You can't waste it."

"I could save it."

Clyde leaned in. "You won't. Just take the bite. Do you good."

On the street, the traffic had disappeared. The heat of the day finally hinted at surrender.

Margaret sniffed, cleared her throat and bit. "I really should be going." She stood. "And you really have to keep the scone."

Clyde reached for his cane, pressed to full height. "If you'll come back by, I could give you..." Clyde hesitated. He glanced from Margaret to the shed at the side of the driveway and back to Margaret again. "I could give you Mildred's recipe."

"I don't bake anymore."

Clyde nodded. "Come get the recipe anyhow. There might be some other things I could dig up to help you, too."

In the dusk Margaret stepped off the porch, stomach swirling with the sweet pecan bar in it, a slight headache starting. At least Clyde was keeping the scone. And her debt was paid.

At home, Margaret climbed the stairs with her tea steaming in one hand and a real estate map and her bags from the mall in the other. She set the bags beside her desk and spread the aerial map on it, prospecting. From this view, her neighborhood looked like a maze, full of false starts, little dead-end cul-de-sacs, the lines of houses like so many hedges, obscuring the way out. Margaret put her finger on the lone expanse. Five acres, right there on the corner of Bent Creek Avenue and Bridwell Road.

She rubbed her forehead. The headache pounded. She lifted the tea, sweet lemon and ginger steam wrapping around her, somehow making it worse. She set it down.

She pulled off her clothes beside the bed and didn't bother picking them up and putting them in the hamper, a thing she had never done, except for those few times in college after she, tipsy, and Trig, drunk, had climbed the stairs leaning into each other, nearly two decades ago.

Margaret slid into the sheets, smooth and crisp and cool, Egyptian cotton. She'd bought them in Atlanta, on a spree with Trig, how long ago? They'd stood in front of rows of sheets, different thread counts, colors, prices.

"You got to be sure it's the real thing," Trig warned her. "The right kind of cotton."

Gossypium barbadense, Trig meant, from which sheets like these were traditionally made. Nowadays, they were just as likely woven with both *barbadense* and the common *Gossypium hirsutum*. Trig claimed it was still possible to get the real deal. Margaret had lifted one of the packages, plastic so shiny she saw a reflection of herself.

Through all that glossy packaging, how would you know? Did anyone know what was real anymore? And did it matter, if it felt right? Margaret lay back, closed her eyes, and slept instantly.

When she woke before the alarm, having hardly wrinkled the sheets, she sat up and pushed back her smooth lilac wrapping, noting the clothes strewn on the floor, the map unfurled over her desk, the half-drunk cup of tea, all looking like that old apartment might have had she not been vigilant with Trig. Margaret swung her legs out from under the covers, planted her feet on the hardwood. Her gaze landed on the American Eagle bags, slumped against each other in the corner.

The Hope who had developed over the past year wouldn't be caught dead in any of what Margaret had bought. She lifted her blouse, tights, shoes. Was it possible that, on Arran, Hope would try on a little light? Margaret stuffed her skirt into the dry cleaning sack. Hope had to wear something. This was what Margaret was willing to buy. She was not going to contribute one thread further to the darkening of her daughter.

Margaret put her room to rights. She folded the map. She sat. She pulled out a sheet of her personalized stationery.

Hi, Hope. She crumpled the sheet. She had to set the good example. This was a letter from mother to daughter, not a note to be passed in class.

Dear Hope. By the time Hope got the letter she would have been there for at least a week. *You'll be settled by now.* What if she wasn't settled at all? What if she was holed up in the room, staring out the window at the grey sea, unsettled as ever, throwing Agatha off balance? Margaret crumpled the page.

Dear Hope,

I hope you're all settled in on Arran and have discovered… what? The bannock again? Margaret recalled Hope's sneer when she'd said it during their argument. She hoped her daughter was discovering a life not driven by trying to find a man who was lost, discovering a life with sea air and something more wholesome than skateboards and punk boys. How could she phrase it?

Margaret looked at the clock. 5:10. Hope and Agatha would be long since up. She could phone. And say what? Even the call to Agatha had been stilted.

Trig would know what to say, but asking for help would mean having to explain everything to her. She'd hardly even spoken to Trig since Brad left. Trig would be asleep for another two hours anyway. Margaret pushed back her chair. She would write after her run. She always had a clearer head after some time in the fresh air and the simple, repeated motion of putting one foot in front of the other.

SEVEN
Hope

Hope dragged herself down the stairs and into the front room the next morning, hunched against what she expected to be an onslaught of questions from Agatha, the same kind her mother always had at the ready. There were the daily staples: How did you sleep? What would you like for breakfast? What's your agenda for the day? These would be followed by ones related to recent events. If Margaret was on Arran, they would be something like: Wasn't Lochranza lovely? Did you think Kenny was cute?

"Toast, as you can see," Agatha said. She nodded at the silver rack on the table in front of her. She put down her paper and pen, exposing a completed Sudoku. "Porridge is still warm, on the stove. Bowls are in the cabinet just to the left." Agatha poured salt into her hand and then sprinkled it on her porridge.

Hope braced herself for the hanging panties, flags of this new land. Porridge with salt? A glass of juice would suit her better. The fridge offered milk in a pint-sized container. Literally. Like they sold at gas stations in the U.S. A lone tomato sat on the top shelf, beside a package of meat, which Hope lifted and dropped with instant regret: tongue. She closed the fridge quietly and lifted the lid on the porridge. Lumpy and pale. Oatmeal was for camping trips, chilly mornings when you crawl out of the tent and your dad has the fire and the camp stove lit up and smoking. Dad, who found berries in season and carried brown sugar for the offseason. Hope replaced the lid, returned to the front room.

"I'll take a shower."

"I'll show you how to work the heater." Agatha set down her tea.

"I'll figure it out."

"Suit yourself."

Frigid shower water rolled over Hope's shoulders with the power and temperature she imagined would come from of one of the streams outside. Goosebumps rose with every drop. She washed quickly and dressed even faster, as she had on winter camping weekends.

Back downstairs, she found the toast, tea, tablecloth, and Agatha cleared away. In their place sat two plump backpacks.

Agatha's face appeared around the kitchen door. "Green one's for you."

Hope raised an eyebrow.

Great-aunt Agatha mirrored her and came for her pack. "We'll have a nice walk—a hike, I think you call them. Maybe a lesson about good Scottish geology." Agatha extended her arm toward the door, indicating that Hope should go out ahead of her.

Hope stood, feet planted shoulder-width apart, arms at her sides. She might have been securing her balance in preparation for the first attack in a martial arts class. She glanced at the backpack, then at Agatha. The crevices of Agatha's face hid whatever she was thinking. *Two can play at that game.* Hope shrugged. She lifted her pack. She might as well see what Agatha had in store. And at least on a hike there was less risk of running into the likes of Kenny and his gran.

Outside, Agatha set the pace around the road, over a stile, across a heather-dotted field edged in gorse, and into a glen, neither of them speaking until Agatha abruptly stopped.

"Seethe." Auntie Agatha said it as if she'd discovered some new toy there in the grassy valley.

Hope stepped up, even with Agatha, then turned and looked at her. The sun jabbed at Hope's eyes. Was it possible that Agatha understood that Hope was pissed? Hope squinted. "Excuse me?"

"Shee." This time it sounded different, and Agatha pointed to a little hump of land, a mini hill not even big enough to be a skate ramp. "Shee. S-I-D-H-E. Fairy mound," she said. "Beside the tree." She pointed again. "A thorn tree—hawthorn its proper name. A fairy tree."

"I thought we were on a geology walk."

"Yes, indeed." Agatha paused, breathing deeply and loudly through her nose while she built a smile on her craggy face. "We can fill up the day with rocks upon rocks upon rocks, dear. Porphyrite." She began to move away from the hump. "Peridotite. Gneiss. Scree. Granite. Rocks from all the ages." Her smile grew. "All Scotland's ages.

"Many of the rocks in Scotland, my dear, many of the rocks here on Arran are from some of the oldest volcanic formations in the world. We can start there, walking this valley and building your knowledge with all the care the earth takes making and shaping and changing a rock. It's a long walk, tiring at times." She looked as if she was riding the edge of jolly the way Hope used to grind high rails, loving it all the more because of the knowledge that she could fall off at any minute. Hope stared at Agatha, standing there in the middle of the valley, explaining an eternal walk through rocks older than she was. *Whatever.* "I thought we'd rest here. Eat a sandwich." She said it *sang-weedge.* "Have a story to go with it. To break up our journey."

"I'm fourteen."

"Correct again." Agatha set down her backpack and lifted out a tartan blanket. "Help me with the traveling rug, then." She flicked it in Hope's direction.

Agatha spread her end of the blanket, leaving Hope's rumpled on the ground. The old woman lowered her body onto it slowly, like a time-lapse sequence of some mountain eroding.

"Real fairy tales are not for children," she said.

Agatha lifted a piece of lumpy oat bread from the basket, then a slice of smooth cheese.

"Sidhe is an Irish Gaelic word. An Irish fairy name. I suppose if I was being correct I'd keep the good Scots separate entirely from the Irish, but I'd an Irish…" She hesitated. "… an Irish uncle. By marriage. Your great-granny's youngest sister's husband. He was lovely. A lovely storyteller." She centered the cheese on the coarse bread, then bit in. "Donagh. Donagh Padraig Joseph O'Leary his full name." Agatha bit again, took her time chewing the pale, homemade bread. "Basket's just there if you fancy anything."

Hope almost wished she was one of those cheerleadery meal-skippers.

"Donagh came over looking for work, first in England, like so many Irish have at one time or another. He came north, to Glasgow, as they did, for the shipyards, just about at the same time as our Auntie Edwina—Wina, we called her—came south to be part of something she thought would be larger and brighter than where she was from. She got it in the form of a tenement flat in Cathcart and Donagh O'Leary from County Cork. She used to tell us how she walked down Sauchiehall Street one day in 1927—this the happy time between the wars, mind you. Somehow she'd got herself off track—not a big surprise if you knew Wina. She hadn't noticed that she'd wandered off Sauchiehall Street until she came round the corner, found herself by the river, and ran straight into him." Agatha bit and chewed again. "Donagh with the wild dark eyes and the wilder curly hair, aye looking as though he was up to something, those eyes calling for you to go along with him. It was magic from the start, Auntie Wina said."

Agatha seemed to be telling the story as much to herself as she was to Hope. Sitting there on the hump of grass, chewing her cheese and telling her tales, she might have been planted by the Scottish Tourist Board.

Hope grabbed a thick wedge of bread.

"Before any of us on Skye even knew it, wild Donagh had Wina away over the water to meet his relations. When they came back, they settled in Glasgow, though Donagh later claimed he never really felt settled there." Agatha's tongue darted out to catch a stray bit of crust that had settled on the side of her mouth. "So he, they, ended here, on the shore of Arran. In the house you're staying in now." Agatha pulled out a flask and started to unscrew the cap. Steam from the tea rose up to coil in wisps of her hair. "Wina had just the one story. Donagh was her only tale. But Donagh, you'd have thought he knew all the fairy world himself—the Seelie and the Unseelie and all the ancient warriors from this world and the other." She sipped, held the flask in the direction of Hope.

Hope shook her head.

"Us five girls—me and Ellsie, your gran, and Aileen and Anna and Mairi—we all huddled round him. By the fire in the cottage on Skye when he came for us after Da died, and then in the flat in Glasgow and again by the fire in the cottage here, more interested really in being closest to the glimmer in Donagh's eye than near the flame of the fire."

Agatha swallowed the last of the tea in one gulp; she shook her head as she screwed the cup back on to the flask lid.

"I suppose the younger ones wished he was their da." She looked right at Hope. "We all missed our da. I did anyway, and Aileen, I think because we were the eldest, the ones who remembered him best. Donagh and his stories made it that wee bit easier. 'Round the fire, we forgot we missed him."

What sort of person forgets she misses her dad?

Agatha wrapped the bread back in its tea towel and laid it in the basket.

"So what about the fairies?" Hope asked.

Agatha paused, looked up. The sun shone into the crevices on her face and neck, making her skin even whiter and casting shadows between the ridges. She folded down the lid of the basket, stood up straight. Agatha wasn't one of those stooped women Hope had seen in the food court in the mall or at the nursing home where Katie's grandmother lived.

"You are, of course, correct," Agatha said. "Fourteen is the wrong age for fairy stories." She brushed some crumbs off her skirt.

Hope looked at her watch: 1:03 p.m. Minus five equals 8:03 a.m. If Hope had been at home, Margaret would have been calling her from work, telling her to get up and start the day,

as though it was a school day, as though she would be heading
for the awning at the front of the building where she and Katie
stood, before and after school, to the left of the crowd. The
smoker boys stood there too, not right with them, but not too
far away either. Some of them skated. They never hung out with
Hope and Katie, but sometimes at the park they swapped new
tricks. That was why they didn't mind Hope and Katie standing
near them.

Dad never cared where they stood when he dropped them
off or picked them up either. Dad was just happy to see them.

Mom minded. When she pulled up, she rolled her eyes up
toward her frosted fringe, unless she was wearing her Dolce
& Gabbana sunglasses. In the mornings, she told them to
go straight in, but she never stayed to see if they did. In the
afternoons, she always had something to say.

"You girls," she'd squeak. "You girls can do soooo much better
than those boys." She'd drop her voice down low for *those*. "You
ought to be front and center."

She'd turn and throw a smile to where the preppy posse
stood. More than once Mom's smile met one of theirs. On those
days, Hope's mother raised her hand, pumped up her smile,
and waved her girliest wave. Someone always matched it, all
glimmering white teeth and cutesy wave.

"See," Mom once said. She swung around in her seat to look
at Hope and Katie. "You two girls are at least as cute as that."
She nodded, as if she had to reassure herself that it was true.
She flicked her hand in the direction of Hope's red Spitfire shirt.
"You just need to dress up a little now and then."

Hope didn't need to look at Katie to know she was thinking
the same: that no one in the preppy posse was their friend or
Margaret's, no matter how many sparkly little waves they shared.

At least on Arran, Hope didn't have to put up with Margaret's
attempts at camaraderie with prep central. Maybe the first good
thing about being three thousand miles away.

When Hope turned back toward Agatha, she found only the
impression of her aunt, pressed into the grass where her bony

body had rested. Hope looked in the direction from which they'd come, found another goat, or the same one, chewing and staring. She turned again, into the sun, and found Agatha's dark form trudging along.

The goat ambled past her. If it really was a woman, as Kenny's gran said, what kind of woman was she? One like Hope's mother or Auntie Agatha, or one Hope might like? Was there such a woman?

Hunch-shouldered, Hope walked with the goat, moving along at her own pace, land sloping up on either side of her, straight-spined Aunt Agatha ahead. Aunt Agatha, who forgot she missed her father. When had she realized he wasn't coming home? Who had told her? Had Aunt Agatha's mother been like Hope's, withholding what she knew until it was too late to do anything?

Margaret had stood at the edge of the Cave, not even putting her feet on the threshold, the night before Dad was due home. Hope had been putting new griptape on her board.

"Come in and have supper," Mom said.

"I need to finish this."

"Leave it, please."

"It won't take long."

"Hope." Mom exhaled heavily through her nostrils. "Please. There's something I need to say."

Hope held her board at her chest, the griptape untrimmed around the edges.

"I want to have this ready for Dad coming home."

"I know. That's what I need to talk about." Her mother turned for the house.

"So talk here."

"We should sit."

Hope lifted the X-acto knife and began to slice at the ragged edge.

"Your father isn't where he's supposed to be."

"I know where he is."

"You do?" Margaret took one step closer to the Cave.

"Do you think I'm totally dumb?"

"Of course not, Hope."

"Really?" The X-acto knife dangled from Hope's hand. "I know what 'extra therapy' means. I know Dad went to rehab."

"He didn't."

"Mom. Oh my God. Can you just be honest?"

"I'm trying. You're right. We said 'extra therapy' when we meant rehab. Your father had some problems…"

"Finally. I know, Mom. I know Dad had some 'problems' with pills. I have eyes." Hope shook her head and turned back to her board.

"Honey, he didn't get there. That's what I'm trying to tell you."

"What?" Hope's body remained bent to the board; her hands stilled in place.

"The place called. Then he called."

"Where is he?"

"I don't know. He wouldn't tell me." Her mother reached for her. "Come in. Let's sit. Eat. Talk it through."

"Wait. My father, who was supposed to go to rehab, never got there? When did he call?"

"A couple of weeks ago."

"What? Why didn't you tell me?"

"I thought he'd call again. Or just come home." Margaret closed her eyes for a long moment. "Now, I'm not so sure he's going to do either."

"He has to," Hope said. Her eyes darted from her mother to her board to Dad's stuff. "His bikes are here."

In the light from the bare bulb, Hope and her mother stared at each other, silent for a few minutes. Hope set down the knife.

"If you'd let him heal the way he wanted to, he wouldn't have gone at all." Hope pushed past her mother. "He was doing better." She tossed the board onto the driveway, pushed off, and made for Katie's.

Of course her mother called before she got there. Of course she didn't tell the whole story—a mother-daughter spat, she said to Katie's mother. They hid in Katie's room until Allie made Hope go home, citing the no-sleepovers-on-school-nights rule. Katie texted her after she got home. *Maybe he'll come home tomorrow anyway.*

Hope spent the next evening in the Cave, finishing her griptape, oiling the bikes. Three times, she heard the back door open—her mother checking on her without actually showing her face—then close again a few minutes later. At eleven, Mom circled back to the edge of the Cave.

"Come in," she said. "He has to come home sometime." She hovered in the door. "I'll find him. Please come in."

Hope kept oiling the chain, turning the pedal around and around.

"I have ice cream," Mom said. "Chunky Monkey."

At least Agatha had had something more solid than ice cream to help her stop missing her father.

Hope walked on, behind Agatha, for miles in Glen Rosa. They took no breaks, didn't stop until the land began to rise more sharply toward what Agatha called the saddle, a kind of natural wall of land between two valleys. A great rise of rock called Cir Mhor stuck up on the left of it, and on the right, craggy Goat Fell climbed toward the sky.

"From the indicator up there, you can see Ireland," Agatha said, pointing to the top of Goat Fell. "Takes the whole day for me to get myself there. Tourists get dropped off at Brodick Castle on the eastern side and walk it in an hour or so. The way we've come is much better." She sighed. "I can only do it at the peak of the year, when the sun hangs on until nearly midnight. There's still light enough for me for a while yet, though we are, of course, already past the solstice."

Goat Fell looked like a massive pile of grey rocks of all sizes and shapes, sort of like the self-portrait Hope did in Mr. Ramos's class in the spring. Picasso-style, they sketched their odd-looking selves with eyes staring in the wrong direction, faces all twisted. When they got to the painting part, most people slashed bright colors back and forth across their canvasses as though they were painting a booth at the state fair. Hope painted herself in shades of grey. She got bonus points for picking up on the grey period. A girl from the preppy posse—Hope and Katie nicknamed them Preppy Possums after that—accused her of being a suck-up. Only Katie knew Hope well enough to know that she would never do that.

Standing there on the saddle only a few months after the Picasso painting, Hope grimaced an Aunt Agatha excuse for a smile. Arran should be perfect for her—grey sky, grey water, great big grey rocks, and matching great-auntie.

EIGHT
Agatha

As Agatha had lifted the basket and moved away from Hope down the gently sloping hill, she'd thought of her father over seventy years ago, on Skye.

The eldest of five, and, like her father, not in need of much rest, Agatha had stepped into the dark of many a morning with him. The scent of seaweed and black muck and dung filled their noses and lungs, waking them fully as they lifted peat from the stack outside to rebuild the fire Da smothered before bed every night. Inside, her sisters tucked into each other, filling the space she left when she slipped out. Across the cottage, under layers of woven wool, Mammy curled in too, alone in the bed she shared with Da.

Mostly, Mammy woke when the fire roared, sliding out from under her covers to lift the oats that had been soaking the night through. She got them rolling to set Da on his way. Some mornings, though, he set out with a bit of day-old bannock in his pocket before any of the rest of them woke.

"Get the porridge on for your mam," he'd say to Agatha, and away he'd go, flipping his cap onto his head and swinging his arms as though keeping time to a jig only he heard. On days that began in that way, Agatha's mother jangled all about the place as though she'd a load of pulsing energy within her that couldn't find its way to the thing it was meant to power. The minute he ducked his head and came in the door, her energy focused. He grounded her.

In those days, in their cottage and many of the older ones on Skye, you saw a man's head first. The thatched roofs hung low, forcing the doors to be built even lower, so anyone of much height was forced to hunch and, before his body hurried in after him, present his face. This was what Agatha's father did after his day of work, and men like Angus Donald, who flipped off his grey cap and let his black hair unfurl into their cottage before he pulled in his body and took his seat by their fire. There they told tales about those they claimed had built cottages like theirs on the west of Skye, the little people, fairies, in the days when it had been safe for them to be seen on the land, before they'd been forced to live within the hills. The low-slung shelters just made sense to Agatha—the thatch not too high to patch and the ceilings low enough to hold down around them the heat from the fire and from their own selves and the breath of whoever was the storyteller of the night. From September to nearly June, they were especially grateful for those low ceilings as they hunched close and tried to content themselves being wrapped in stories and in the scents of peat and wool and hard-worked bodies.

Before it was theirs, the cottage belonged to Agatha's mother's family. It had been built by her grandparents when they brought their family to an easier life, sailing away from where generations of them had lived, twelve miles further out to sea on the Shiant Isles. They brought with them the clothes on their backs and their resilience and their tales, gathered from the myths of the great Celtic warriors, men like Ossian and Cuchulainn and women like Sgathaich, the warrior queen, and from their own families. As they had on the Shiants, they clung closely together, cattle under the same roof, adding to the warmth.

Although Agatha heard some stories of her parents' child-hoods on those tiny islands in the middle of the wide waters, the one she remembered best was of her mother and father's first encounter on Skye. When her father told it, he referred to himself by his whole name, as though he was telling it about another person entirely.

"Calum Stuibhart could not recall a day without Ellsie McLeod," he'd begin. "Until, that is, the moment his father made him and the rest of the Stuibharts huddle into their boat and roll over the waters to Skye. The McLeods did the same in their own vessel. Each family found their own place and set to the hard work of resettling on Skye." Although in later tellings, Calum spoke in English, he preferred the rhythm of the Gaelic as he told of the waters that looked like the great Cuillins, the mountains near which they would settle, dark grey and jagged under caps of freezing white. "A strapping lad of thirteen," he went on, "with nearly black hair and flinty eyes but tall already and broad, young Calum pined for the lovely Ellsie." He claimed that, all the time on the waters and then building a cottage and cutting and drying and stacking the peat and all the other loads of things he'd to do to help his father make the new life they wanted on Skye, Calum imagined Ellsie's thick, auburn hair, her waist, already taking the shape of a young woman, her freckled hands. Though he'd known her from their youngest years, he realized in those months of cutting and stacking and thatching that he missed her in a different way than he missed the others. He thought of all the new lads on Skye who she might be meeting. "Young Calum worked harder," he said, "looking for the day his own father would be satisfied that they'd made a good start and allow Calum to roam free for a bit." He tried not to think about the fact that there were likely thousands of boys his age on Skye, rather than the few in the ten or so families with whom he'd shared the Shiants.

"Three months, Calum had, to think about Ellsie and whether she'd forgotten him and what he might do make sure she remembered him over whatever others might come to meet her. By the time his father turned to him, a turve of peat in his hand and said, 'Well done, lad. Away you go and have some fun,' Calum knew precisely what he'd do.

"He ran up over the hill and down to the shore, pinched a rowing boat not nearly sturdy enough for Skye's southwestern waters, whose moods change faster than a toddler. Calum was equal parts luck and determination, though, and made the most of both to reel in three salmon so big they looked as though they'd been about those waters long enough to think themselves completely safe from man and bird. With these fish in hand, Calum Stuibhart replaced what could then safely be called a borrowed vessel and marched himself from the rocks across the field to Ellsie's cottage. Upon encountering the low-slung door, Calum first thrust through the fish and then his face, ducking as though he was already a man."

Agatha's father told how he found Agatha's mother and her older brother and younger sister hunched by the fire. Her father mended a net at the table and her mother sat, spinning yarn.

"*Is mise Calum Stuibhart. Ciamar a tha sibh?*" I'm Calum Stuart. How are you?

"*Tha mi gu math.*" Ellsie giggled, saying she was well.

"*De an t'ainm a tha oirbh?*" he asked, as though he hadn't known her name from its very beginning.

"*Is mise Ellsie,*" she threw her hair back over her shoulder and stood.

I am happy to know you, he said, still using the formal Gaelic.

Agatha's grandfather might have thought him a little soft in the head and sent him packing had he not had those fish. Agatha's grandmother knew the look on him as he took Ellsie's hand. Young Calum had caught more than salmon that day.

It would be years—until they married—before he brought more fish like that to Agatha's mother, but when he did, he did it as he had that first time, presenting the fish, ducking his head, and removing his cap as though he was a stranger come courting. Each time, he introduced himself as though still in hopes of winning the lassie's heart. "*Is mise Calum Stuibhart.*" Always, he ended the exchange as he had the first time: *I am happy to know you.*

This began a tradition that continued whenever her father came through the door with an especially good catch. This is what Agatha imagined as she lay in bed, side by side with her sisters, and heard him whisper to Angus Donald, who'd stayed too late the night before to make his way back to the village.

"How's about a bit of fresh?"

"Is it not too cold?"

"Ah, come on, just the pair of us, gaining on the waters and the wind and bringing a wee surprise, eh? A lovely belly warmer?"

Agatha's tongue tingled, the memory of a bit of freshness rekindled just at the time when she'd feared she might have lost altogether the feel of tender fish against her tongue. They were, by then, more than a month past the solstice and the night had begun to part earlier and allow the day in longer. Still, it was a long way to spring. The full moon and the nearly clear skies drew the pair of them to the challenge. Agatha slid out and over to the fire with them and felt her Da's hand, calluses catching in her hair.

"You'll be wanting to help, then, *doithín*," he said. By then he spoke a mix of Gaelic and stilted English. "You'll keep our secret a wee while—let her suss for herself where we've gone." He nodded over at her mother. "If I'm lucky, I'll have a great big catch before she's it sorted out."

Agatha pulled on her sheepskin mittens, struggled against a sudden gust of wind to wrap extra woolens around herself. She tramped down to the shore with them, guided as much by memory as by their lanterns or the moon. She gave them a last push with all her might and watched them row away into a perfect light breeze to see what they could make of the day and the waters. How often had her father come in with a fistful of fish when others came back with nothing but a salty burn on their faces and an empty net?

Just after midday, Agatha finished spinning the last of the yarn that had been cleaned and carded after the last shearing. Her mother stood at the table, making bannock but flinging flour when she should have been letting it settle, thinking her father had gone away into Carbost with Angus. The two sisters closest in age to Agatha had already run off to play, over the hill somewhere. The baby, another Ellsie, and the next eldest,

Mairi, stood on stools, side by side with their mother, imitating her every flail of the arm. Agatha escaped down to the rocks in search of good skipping stones and maybe a glimpse of her da and Angus, making their way back in the distance. She found a good perch, a few lovely flat stones, and Rory MacKimmon.

Rory and Agatha had been born on the same day, he in the cottage by the shore and she in hers. His mother took ill and so Agatha's mother nursed the pair for months. When the time came for him to go and sleep in his own house, the two were said to have keened louder than a *caoineag*, a witch who visits in dreams and visions, crying a portent. Rory and Agatha kept their racket going and refused food until they were brought back to each other.

As they stood together on the shore, looking for a glimpse of Calum, Agatha had no memory of a day without Rory. They threw stone after stone, not needing to say anything. They could have gone on like that for hours, only something caught Agatha's eye, a dark patch on the sea. She watched it spread, whitecaps rise, and she pointed. Rory lifted his cap and they both sat, staring at the black clouds reaching long wisps like witches' fingers down to the waters, seeming to call the sea skyward. Something shifted in her gullet, low, and she thought she should maybe spoil the surprise, tell her mother that her father hadn't gone into the village, back to Angus's house as she thought.

"*Is mise Calum Stuibhart*," Agatha whispered. She told Rory she had spinning yet to finish and turned back toward the cottage, not yet in need of going in face first.

As though she didn't believe Agatha, her mother set out across the threshold in the direction of the shore. Agatha went behind and saw her mother smile when she found the boat missing. Mammy looked out to sea after him, the squall already gone. "*Is mise Calum.*"

She took to an extra sweeping out of the cottage and another milking of the cow, to take up the hours until Calum came. By the time the night began to creep in, Agatha's mammy had the cottage spotless, and so went down the shore with her light and waited, as she had so often, to guide him in.

When the dark settled fully, Agatha went as well. She found her mother silent and still, holding the lantern high, her face set straight out toward the sea. Mammy did not shift even her eyes to acknowledge Agatha there. The wind lifted their hair, swept in under Agatha's shawl, rising as it often did with the moon at that time of year. As she picked her way over the rocks toward Rory's, Agatha felt little need to hurry, her movements fluid and unpanicked. The wind swept up her sleeves and skirt and down her neck, gathering chill from the waters beside her, blowing steadily, which made her comfortable in it.

Rory's father opened the cottage door. "Young Agatha."

Rory turned from banking the fire, rose. Agatha should have been scraping the scales off some big, bulgy-eyed fish by then. "Is he not back?"

In the time it took her to shake her head and turn outward again, Rory and his father had their heavy sweaters and boots and caps on. In the time it took her to get back to the cottage and send word to Angus's family in Carbost, Rory and his father had their own lanterns lit and were pushing away from the shore. Agatha's stomach clenched at the sight of them, even though they'd hug the crannies of the coastline and leave the farther-out places to a bigger vessel and more men from the village, if necessary. The smell of the seaweed cut into her, no longer seeming fresh and full of possibility, but overwhelmingly pungent and salty, like aged winter meats; it wrapped around her, a clinging, slimy scent that would not release.

The next morning, Agatha picked back and forth between her mother and the cluster of larger rocks at the edge of the bay. When she could no longer stand neither being able to do nor see, she climbed the hill on the south edge of the bay, scrambling along the path the sheep made, slipping more than once and finding her hands in dark muck or sheep dung and not caring as long as she was moving to a better vantage point. From the top she could see west and south easily, and a little north up the minch between Skye and Lewis. The trawler from the village passed inward, men scurrying on board. Below her, Rory's mother came out and wrapped a blanket around her mother. Through the lot of it, Mammy stood, lantern in hand, not moving even as the tide came in around the rocks, bringing closer and closer the idea that Da was dead.

Rory climbed toward Agatha, his head angled toward his feet as though it was his first time on land. When he reached the top, he stood, his jacketed shoulder catching her dark shawl. He handed her a pebble, smooth and flat, opened his palm to show he had one as well. Together, they cast them out, watched them fall to the wide waters, too far below to hear when they sank. Rory plunged his hands in his pockets, lifted his shoulders toward his ears. "My ma says to tell you to tend your sisters."

When Agatha got there she found there was no need; someone, or they themselves, had tucked them into the big bed and smothered the fire. Agatha lifted the peat and built it back, as though it was morning again, as though she'd hear his whisper, as though they could start the day fresh. She sat the night there, where she'd last felt her father's hand and voice on her. She dozed a little and wakened fully at the whisper of the wind rising with the sun.

Agatha looked over at the beds, counted four in the big one and none in the other. She didn't bother starting the porridge, went instead to the rocks. Her mother stood, keening for the one soul who knew her beyond the marrow, straight through to the rock and the roaring air that made her who she was. Her mother stood through the day's search and until darkness fell again, weeping, whispering, "*Is mise Calum*" again and again until she fell into the arms of a man from the village whose name Agatha did not know, come to offer condolences. He carried her up the hill and tucked her in beside her other girls.

In the morning, while Ellsie slept, Agatha lined the sisters up in front of the fire and told them their father had been claimed by the sea, that he wasn't bringing fish or himself across their threshold again.

"D'you mean he's been caught?" This from Mairi, then five.

"Caught?"

"Aye. Instead of him catching the fishes, they've caught him."

"You might say. Not the fishes, though, but the waters themselves have taken him."

Mairi nodded as though she understood and then her face turned to tears. She gasped. "Will they scrape him and split open his tummy and cook him?"

"Ah, no, *doithín*." Agatha pulled her close, sitting on the floor in front of the fire. "It's not like that at all. He's only gone into the waters, become part of the lovely waters now, instead of being part of us."

Mairi fell silent then. Little Ellsie joined her on Agatha's knee and Anna tucked in on her other side. Aileen, only two years younger than Agatha, climbed back into bed with their mother.

Mairi brightened a bit and said, "Maybe our da will become a selkie and come back to us." Calum had told them many a selkie story there by the fire, conjured tales of the magical creatures who came onto land and captured the hearts of men or women and lured them out to sea.

Rory's mother saved Agatha from having to dash Mairi's hopes. She came along with Rory behind, carrying food for them as though they hadn't already put away their store for winter. Agatha's mother slept through Rory and his mother and several others, only sitting up at dusk and sliding out from under the blankets and taking her lantern down to wait by the rocks until the dark settled completely. When she came back in, she stood and stared at the five girls by the fire as though she wasn't sure how they had arrived there.

"You'll want your tea." She set the lantern on the table; all that electric energy she'd had was gone, pouring out in tears and trying to will their father back from the sea.

Three days later, while Ellsie waited with a lantern, the sea delivered to an inlet just southwest one splintered oar, not near any known hideaway for fish of any sort. The waters would not return the bodies of Calum or Angus or any other piece of their boat.

Ellsie moved through those days as though she was no more in her body than Calum must have been by then, coming back to herself as the night began to settle and marching to the rocks to keen and light the way for a man who could no longer see. It fell to Agatha to become something between mother and father, while her own mother stood still, her tears washing amongst the tide flowing in around the rocks. It fell to Agatha to slide from bed before light and wrest from the stack the peat that had been cut and dried and stacked by her father's hands. She lifted that peat that had last been touched by him, imagining that touching the peat with her hand was as good as touching his own hand. She stepped into his footprints—back to the cottage, over to the fire, handling the tools that had been his to make the fire roar, ready for her mother to awaken and lift the pot of oats that had been soaking overnight. Except her mother slept, so after Agatha put her hands and feet where her father had put his, she did the same for her mother, making the porridge hot in the morning and helping move them through the days until it was time to tuck in her sisters at night and then to smother the fire. These things and more fell to Agatha and so, on the third day, she decided that it also fell to her to dig from her mother's treasure box under her bed the address of Aunt Wina and Uncle Donagh, and to write to them, in Glasgow, to say that her father was dead.

In the seven decades that followed, Agatha had wasted not a moment pondering what other choice she might have made.

NINE
Margaret

Light had barely begun to seep into the sky, but the air was heavy with moisture already, a month premature for this kind of humidity. Margaret began to sweat before she reached the first streetlight. She passed another jogger, lumbering like one of the divorcees on a fitness kick at the gym. His awkward gait reminded her of Brad just after he received the all-clear to walk. Was it only last September? The month had brought an early cold snap along with the doctor's approval, at last. After the first trip to the gym, the same day as the doctor's visit, he shoved himself through the back door red-faced and angry, all sore leg and bruised ego, and made straight for the fridge. He flopped down on the sofa, lifted his beer, slugged some down and then slammed the bottle on the coffee table. He stood. He hobbled back outside. Margaret went after him, started to say—what, she couldn't remember. He didn't let her get past his name, turned around, put one hand on each of her shoulders, squeezed hard, then pushed her away and limped out past the crape myrtles.

"Please be patient with yourself." Margaret's voice sounded like her younger self, pleading with her mother for a new toy. She was as successful with her plea to Brad, then, as she had been with her mother years before. Defiant stubbornness seemed to serve Brad better than patience: within a couple weeks, he was on the stationary bike, saying he'd found a new trainer. He took to recovery like a sprinter coming from the back of the pack at the end of a race, passing everyone, stride smooth. The South

Carolina season was winding down, but Brad was in shape, looking for races in Florida to test himself.

Margaret came down the stairs one morning and found him pacing the kitchen, looking as though he'd returned to the Brad she'd always known, lithe and strong and sipping coffee instead of beer, a printout from USA Track and Field in his other hand. He waved the sheet.

"Lauderdale," he said. "A 10k in Lauderdale in three weeks."

"So go."

Hope wanted to go with him. Uncharacteristically, he declined. The new trainer was going instead, he said. He came back, bright-eyed and waving a third-place age category medal. He gathered more steam as the weeks passed.

The second Sunday in October, Margaret woke, rolled over, and reached for him. They had the house to themselves; Hope was spending the night at Katie's. Margaret's hand landed on cool sheets. She found him tying his shoes on the back steps.

"Brad?"

"Hill repeats." He didn't look up.

"This early? On a Sunday? Come back to bed."

"Gotta keep building." He leapt off the step and started down the drive, turning at the end, grinning. In the dark, Margaret caught the edge of the look in his eyes, so intense, so familiar. It struck the hard part in the center of her chest.

She dug in the storage boxes under their bed, in the medicine cabinet, under the kitchen sink, in the tool room. She stood in the open doorway, staring down the drive. Was she wrong, or just looking in the wrong places? She tried the door on Brad's car, found it unlocked. The baggie peeked out from under his seat—not even well hidden, as though he wanted her to know.

She cleaned the kitchen counters until he came back an hour and a half later, plonked himself on the sofa, shed shoes, socks, shirt. They lay flaccid on the floor beside him. Margaret came around the corner, drying her shaking hands with a towel, the pit in her stomach stretching wide. "Brad? You been taking some stuff again?"

"It's no big deal." His voice was tight, belligerent. His slim chest was back to its lean, pre-crash weight; his torso glistened.

She wanted to sit down next to him, to feel the smooth of his leg, freshly shaven for the next bike race, against the smooth of hers. She wanted to take his hand, lean her head against his shoulder, close her eyes, believe.

She held up the bag. The smallest of Ziplocs, snack size, white clinging in the corners. "What if Hope had found this?"

"Hope wouldn't."

She dropped the bag on the table. That wasn't what she wanted to say. This wasn't about Hope. Some part of her thought he'd respond better to Hope than to her.

"You're going to stop this, right?" She tried to keep her voice light, heard it rise, heard the snap of the t. "You know where it goes."

"I know where it's gone so far, Margaret. It's got me up off the sofa, back into business, back into shape, running, coaching, working."

"And you know where else it will take you if you don't stop."

He stepped closer to her, bent to pick up the bag, held it in front of her face. "I know it's got my body back in good enough shape for you to look at again."

"That's not true."

"Your sudden interest in me is pure coincidence?"

"You were hurt. You spent all day on the couch. You weren't healing. You pushed me away. I was concentrating on making ends meet."

"You mean turbocharging your career."

"For us. So we could keep living. Keep our house."

"And you're not still doing that?"

"What do you mean? You know I am."

"But you suddenly have time to look at me again."

"You hardly let me near you."

"You hardly tried."

"Brad, this isn't about any of that. It's about the drugs."

"Is it? Or is it about you wanting to be on top—to be the

big dog in the house? Maybe you liked it when I wasn't so fast. Maybe you just can't stand the competition."

"Brad."

He lifted his shoes, took the baggy, and stalked out of the house.

Margaret sat down, the smell of Brad's sweat fresh on the couch, layered over the lingering scent of stale beer. She suspected that, in addition to the cocaine, he was using the Lortab beyond its prescribed time, sliding one in every night before bed, earlier in the day on weekends. She should have known it was too good to be true, how fast he'd transitioned from lying on the sofa, his bones refusing to knit, to racing. She pulled a cushion to her. She hoped he'd come home; she hoped he wouldn't. She thought of cleaning the bathrooms, of going for a run, of calling and saying Hope had to come home from Katie's. She lifted the phone, thought of calling Trig. She set it back down, lifted the remote, set it back down. She lay down on the couch. She breathed in Brad. She closed her eyes. The months since the accident folded in on her. All she wanted was sleep.

Brad's lips on her shoulder seemed like a dream, gently repeating up her neck. She held her eyes closed, lingering between sleep and waking, wanting the dream of it to go on, not wanting to open her eyes and see the real man and respond. He moved to her face, ear, cheek, eyes, kept going.

"I'm sorry, Margaret." He slid an arm around her.

She kept her eyes closed.

"I'm okay, Margaret." He lifted her into his arms, carried her as he had when they were first married and again when they bought this house.

She kept her eyes closed, breathing in the dream.

"It's not like before."

Up the stairs and into their room.

"I love you, Margaret."

Margaret wrapped herself around him, felt the press of his

skin against hers, the metal sweat as she breathed him in, eyes still closed.

She woke the next morning consumed by the notion that she should show Brad she loved him enough to give up something herself. She stopped drinking coffee. She dumped sugar, held the practice like a talisman, convinced it would help.

Margaret watched his legs with that fluid rotation, smooth and fast until the curve in the road that morning and every morning after. She took to glancing through the car windows, pulling ajar the door of the tool room. She held herself back from opening the car, pulling wide the tool room door, digging in drawers. She should trust him. She did trust him. Didn't she? He had done this on his own all those years ago, after all. Surely he could do it again, this time with her support.

Thanksgiving morning dawned clear and bright, Brad by her side when she rolled out of bed to start the turkey. He stepped into the kitchen just as she opened the oven door to slide it in.

"She'll be ready in perfect time. We'll eat at two," Margaret said.

"Two?"

"We always eat at two."

"You could've asked."

"I thought…" Margaret closed the oven door.

"What? You thought you'd do it your way? I have a long run scheduled."

"Go long tomorrow." She stood.

"I'm meeting my trainer."

"On Thanksgiving?"

Margaret turned to face Brad and found his back, heading through the door to the den. Stunned, she stayed in the kitchen, following his movements through the thump of his feet up the stairs, down the hall. Could she make out the pulling open of his drawer? Silence, meaning he must be lacing his shoes. Training for an Ironman was one thing, but did the long run really have to be on Thanksgiving Day? She resisted the impulse to check his eyes when he came back down.

"I'll be back at three," he said. "Is an hour that big a deal?"

She kissed his cheek. "Three," she said.

The bird was half done by the time Hope came down, asking where Dad was, when dinner was, could she go to the skate park after.

"On Thanksgiving?" Christ, was that all she could say?

The Brad she loved seemed to come back through the door after his long run. He showered, took his seat at the table, carved the turkey, served her, kissing her cheek as he set the plate down.

"Thanks for letting me run," he said, his voice smooth and sweet.

Margaret's stomach clenched. Wasn't this part of the rhythm, too?

She thought they were on the same page. When he asked what she wanted for Christmas, she said, "You, clean."

He lay on the bed after a long ride. He nodded. He would go where he'd gone when Margaret was pregnant with Hope. She would stay in Terra Pines, wait for him. It had been his idea to tell Hope it was just a little extra therapy, a lingering issue related to his crash. Could Margaret hang on until the New Year, so they could give Hope a normal Christmas? Of course.

After he left, Margaret told no one. She couldn't even face Trig. She planned to tuck into herself for the twenty-six days he would be gone. She had plenty to do, between work and Hope.

Trig called the first morning after Brad left, her voice on the message as big and brassy as her hair. "Hey, girl, saw you in the car line. Brad forget how to drive for you? Call me."

Margaret spied her heading into Whole Foods the next morning. She dialed Trig's home number, said she'd be in touch, said her schedule was busy, busy, busy for the next few weeks. She started scurrying through the car line, arriving early so she wouldn't have to answer Trig's questions about why Brad suddenly wasn't in his usual places.

Aunt Agatha called (didn't she always?), claiming her uncanny sense of timing, going on about her *caoineag* dream, as she had fifteen years before. Agatha called so often she was bound to land on or near every little upset. Margaret held the phone away from her ear, unpacked the groceries, waited for Agatha to take a breath, and told her they were just fine, thank you, Brad was healing nicely, just away getting therapy to take care of one last little detail. She hung up.

She believed herself until the rehab center called, asking for Brad and refusing to tell her anything, citing the medical privacy act. She called his cell phone. It went directly to voicemail; the mailbox was full. She thought of calling Agatha. She thought of calling Trig. But if she did, if she said out loud that Brad hadn't gone (she'd first have to explain where he was supposed to have gone), that she had no idea where he was, it would somehow make it real. She stood in the middle of the kitchen, paralyzed for a few minutes. When she moved, it was to her spice cabinet. She alphabetized the dried herbs and spices. Later, she picked up Hope from school. She delayed calling his friends to ask if they'd seen him. And then Brad called, collect, in the middle of the afternoon, a couple of days later, the number displaying as Unavailable on the phone in her office.

"Where are you? Are you at the clinic? Brad?"

"I have to do this my way, Margaret."

"What way, Brad? Where are you?"

"I'm getting myself together."

"Brad. Brad, give me a number."

He hung up.

Margaret called his list of friends and running and cycling buddies, crying, saying again and again, to Bert and Mike and other guys she'd barely met, "Have you seen Brad? Will you call me if you do?" She hated the pity in their voices, but not enough to stop her from calling the next person. *Sorry. Sorry, Margaret. Sorry, sorry, sorry.*

She searched the house, the tool room, pulling everywhere wide open and then putting it back together before Hope returned from school. She said nothing to her daughter. They ate dinner, spent the evening as though everything was normal.

Margaret laid herself down that night. Head on the pillow, she felt the questions crowding in.

Should she have driven him? Insisted he go sooner? Her mind jumped to years past, landed on arguments, small moments in time, did the same thing the next night and the next. What if she'd done something differently? Could she have been enough for him? What if he was still in town? She visited his favorite riding and running spots; she hid in the woods to see if he would turn up. She sat across the table from Hope every night, imagining the words she would say, feeling her throat tighten, the bile build in her stomach—finally forcing the words out the night before Brad was supposed to come home. Then there were the questions from Hope, not to mention the accusations. Margaret started making lists, moment to moment forward movements. She had to keep going, one step at a time.

She recited her list out loud as she turned onto Bridwell Road not long after dawn the day after the opossum mishap. She'd run, showered, dressed, wrapped the package for Hope and put it on her back seat, ready to mail. The streetlight on the corner illuminated an old oak, then wandered across the road to the fence that created the boundary between Bent Creek subdivision and the rest of the world. As she made the turn out of the subdivision, another light pierced the corner of Margaret's eye: a small one, on Clyde Bridwell's porch. Her head turned. Clyde's hand rose.

Margaret raised her hand in reply. She gunned the gas, continued the list, jumped when the phone rang through her speakers. She let it roll to voicemail when she saw it was Trig, tried to keep the list going while Trig yelled through her stereo. "Margaret MacPherson Carver, answer your damn phone. I know Brad's gone. And Hope. Quit playing ostrich. You can come to me, or I'll come to you."

Margaret picked up.

—

Just before noon, Margaret stepped down Trig's path, past the neatly trimmed azaleas. Trig stood on her front porch, arms outstretched, reminding Margaret a little of an azalea herself: evergreen, just like subgenera *tsutsuji*, genus *Rhododendron*. The showy shrub lined up outside homes across the southeast with no regard to socioeconomic status or ethnicity or anything else. Come April, trailer parks, suburban cul-de-sacs, and the front doors of downtown condos burst into brilliant color.

Even in middle school, Trig had been like that. They'd left school in June as plain little seventh graders. When Trig returned in late August, she was all lipstick and big hair and boobs, while Margaret was still bare-barked, like a crape myrtle in winter, waiting to bloom.

Trig still had plenty of bloom left, though Margaret couldn't say she was disappointed to note a little wilting: the slight sag in Trig's check, little lines from the corners of Trig's eyes, reaching outward like threads stretching toward her hair.

"Margaret, honey, you look great." She circled her arms around Margaret's waist.

The scent of vanilla pulled at Margaret as soon as she stepped into the foyer. White lilies rose from cut glass vases on matching display tables. Mirrors reflected each other, making the long, lean blossoms appear to be infinite.

"Your house looks great," Margaret said, following Trig to the kitchen.

"Coffee?" The smell of amaretto vaulted from the pot, mixing with the vanilla from the candles on the counter.

"I started doing tea when..." Margaret hesitated, couldn't finish her thought. "I've already had my fair share this morning."

"Well, aren't you good?" Trig's full lips tightened. She eyed Margaret, poured her coffee, followed by amaretto-flavored cream, followed by sugar. She closed her eyes and took in the first sip.

Margaret shifted on her bar stool, backless and in need of a little tightening of the screws.

"Ooh, that's good." Trig opened her eyes. "Sure you won't have some?"

"Positive." Margaret smoothed her waistband.

"So how are you?"

"Fine. Well. Thanks. You?"

"You been hiding from me."

"I've just been busy."

"Mmm-hmm."

"I have. I've pulled in three new clients and…"

"All right, then." Trig cut her off. She came around the counter. She lifted a folder from the end of the bar. "I know how you hate talking, how you love to do, do, do. I got to thinking, how long it's been since I did your logo. Since you got started. You're past due a change. So. I put together a few things, a new image. Clean, uncluttered, clear of…" She stopped. "We'll get you on the right path."

Outside the window, the sun, a thin yellow, hung low in a pale blue sky, cloudless, clear.

"You need a new you, Margaret. Not even Margaret. You need something to snap you out of." Trig patted her hair. "You need something snappy in this tight little market." She pulled a sheet from the folder. "A logo, lean and bold, a new name, even."

"MacPherson. You think I should go back to MacPherson?"

"Why not?"

"Brad."

"Brad? Honey. When's the last time you took a good look at Brad? You really want to waste yourself waiting for him?"

Margaret tried to breathe into the tight space just below her breastbone. Breathe in peace. But something else slithered in. She turned to Trig, eyebrow raised.

"When's the last time *you* saw Brad?"

"I don't remember exactly."

"Trig."

"What does it matter?"

"It matters. Is he here?" Margaret stood. She and Trig had lived this once before, when Margaret was first pregnant. Margaret had expected Trig to be shocked at the news she'd discovered Brad using cocaine to edge up his running, and more than a little pot to bring him back down. "Why are you the holder of Brad's secrets? Is there something between the two of you I should know about? That Mike should know about?" Margaret placed the folder on the counter.

Trig dropped her hands on Margaret's shoulders. "Take a breath."

Margaret picked off Trig's hand as though it was an errant spider.

"Margaret. Sit down. There's no secret. He turned up on my back patio. Three something in the morning. Mike nearly shot him."

"When, Trig? Why didn't you call me?"

"He was gone before I could."

"You could have called me right away."

"Really, Margaret? I could have put one hand on his scrawny shoulder and said, 'Hold there a sec, sugar, while I call your wife'?"

Margaret's eyes darted back and forth, from the wall to Trig's face to the ground.

"You're better off remembering him however he looked when he pulled out of your driveway. And I did call you, Margaret. Several times. You didn't call back. So I decided that I had something more productive for you to hear than a recap of Brad's raggedy ass. I was going to show up at your office if you hadn't answered me this morning."

Margaret sat. The amaretto and vanilla smelled almost good—rich and sweet and just the right shade of dark. "Could I have a glass of water?"

"Aw, sugar." Trig gathered Margaret in her arms, pressed against her soft, too sweet flesh.

"Tell me anyway."

She needed truth, not pity. Was this what Brad had felt when Margaret tried to console him?

"I'll tell. But we're going to set somewhere more comfortable. And you're having something decent to help wash it down."

—

Margaret gathered a coral-colored cushion to her chest. Steam rose from the mug of chai with cream that rested on the end table beside her. Margaret tried to just breathe in and out—screw peace and anger—as Trig explained how she'd been up working late in her office. She'd looked up and straight into a face so gaunt she thought she'd imagined it. Then his hand tapped on the window and Trig screamed and Mike came rumbling down the hall, .22 in hand. Brad tapped again and Trig screamed again and Mike cocked the gun and Brad called out, "It's me," in that same voice she'd heard all those years ago when it was Margaret who went to Scotland.

"It wasn't hardly Brad," Trig said. "It was more like something you'd see in a funhouse mirror."

"And then?" Margaret sucked her cheeks in, clutched the cushion to her chest.

"And then." Trig looked at her watch again. "Five o'clock somewhere. I want some Kahlua with my coffee before we go on."

Margaret hunched into the cushion, almost submerging herself by the time Trig got back. It was five o'clock in Scotland.

Trig took a hefty gulp from her own mug, then held it in midair as she told Margaret he'd asked nothing about her or the house or Hope. "Money. That was all he wanted. Claimed he needed it to get himself right." Trig slugged again. She tilted the mug as though it might make more. Margaret forced herself to sit straighter, rising out of the cushion like a turtle.

"I told him to take his sorry ass on. 'Brad, honey, it doesn't take money to get right,' that's what I said. 'You just stop the shit.' I told him he was welcome when he'd done that. I called you not five hours after I first saw his face. And then I called you again. I've stewed over showing up at your place for a week."

"A week?"

"A week. At first I thought it was just as well you didn't call me back—you were better off not knowing he was skulking around.

And then Paige said she heard Hope got sent off to Outward Bound. She's not, is she?"

"No. She's with Aunt Agatha."

"I figured. The point is, I figured if Hope was gone, it was past time I made you get yourself together."

Margaret placed the cushion exactly as she'd found it, patting it gently.

"I can't do a damned thing about Brad." Trig reached for Margaret's mug. "And neither can you. But I can do something about you, like giving you and your company a little makeover—new logo, new tagline, new name, new everything. And then I can help you with pulling a good goddamn drunk, which is something you desperately need."

"Trig?"

"Mm-hm."

"You expect me to believe that Brad showed up at three a.m., said, 'I need cash,' and you said, 'Get outta here,' and that's it? When have you ever let anyone out of your den without getting all their juice? What else did he tell you? Where has he been?"

Trig shifted in her seat, then set down her mug. "Why do you want to do this to yourself?"

"Let me worry about what I'm doing to myself."

"He didn't tell me anything that matters."

"Not to you, maybe."

Trig shook her head. "Hell, Margaret."

Brad said that he'd driven to Atlanta all those months ago, intended to go to the rehab place. Somewhere along I-85 he convinced himself he was just fine, that it was Margaret who was wrong. So what if he did a little stuff to help him stay on top? He was winning races, getting back on top of his game. How could that be so wrong? He drove to the apartment of some elite runner he knew, talked his way into trading training for the spare room.

Margaret rooted herself to the couch, fought an impulse to close her eyes and put her hands over her ears. When Hope was little, she used to cover her ears with her feet when she didn't want to hear. Margaret breathed in and listened all the same.

"He sat on that sofa and told me he'd been doing well. That he was racing and winning and getting some regular clients. He told me he was on the way to establishing himself there, that he thought he'd maybe send for Hope; he said it all would have been fine if he hadn't done a circuit race on the bike, won the damn thing and got tested. Banned from everything." Trig paused. "Sure you want more?"

Margaret nodded, held her pose, breathed as Trig made note again that, even then, what Brad thought went wrong was not that he took cocaine and Lortab and whatever else to maintain the edge he'd found again, but that he got caught.

"'Everyone does something.' That's what he said. 'If you don't, how can you expect to compete?'"

How could he have been so close and not come to Margaret? Did he sit exactly where she was sitting now, when he could have been sitting with her on their couch, where he belonged? How many times had she imagined him walking through their door, clean and filled with penance? She'd imagined moving toward him, smelling the Dove clean of him, yearning for the smooth of his cheek against hers as she had so many times. Why couldn't he have turned to her for healing? Why wasn't she enough? He hadn't even let her say goodbye.

"Reading between the lines, I'd say he spiraled down pretty fast after that," Trig said. "He was too tainted for any of the good athletes—even the amateurs—to be associated with. Seems like he was couch surfing, until the last guy's girlfriend came home and chucked him and all his stuff out. Another woman who didn't understand." Trig looked down. "He didn't exactly say this, but I'm pretty sure he's living out of his car. He said he needed money to get a place down there, then he was going to quit, prove himself.

"'Don't tell Hope'—that's what he said," Trig finished. "Told me he wanted to be on his feet before he saw her again. Thing is, Margaret, he doesn't know how far down he is."

Margaret sat in silence for a few moments, unflinching, avoiding Trig's face. She shifted on the couch, looked directly into Trig's eyes. "Do you have any idea where he is now?"

"No. I don't. And I don't think it bears wasting even a minute trying to figure out."

Margaret tried to sit straighter, but her spine already felt like an extension rod pulled to its fullest. She rummaged in her head for a sentence, a phrase, a word. She flicked through her brain the way she flicked over folders of clients. She kept landing on questions. Why couldn't he have come to her window instead of Trig's? She could have wrapped her arms around him. But would she? Would she even have been able to draw out what Trig had? Didn't Trig know this wasn't some random, hopeless addict she was suggesting that Margaret give up on? This was Margaret's whole life—everything she had built for the three of them. If she gave up on Brad, the whole thing would crumble. She and Hope would be left wandering in the rubble.

She'd sent Hope to Agatha to keep her safe while she shored things up here. She'd heard herself speak the words to Hope that Brad was gone, that she should move on, but she hadn't felt them in her gut. Part of her still thought Brad would be back, even with what Trig had just told her. Part of her wanted him to show up at the back door. Partly so she could turn him away. Partly so she could memorize the last of him, knowing that's what it was. Even now, her logic said he'd turn up eventually, in person or in the mailbox or on the phone. It made her want to put a For Sale sign in the yard. It made her want to stay forever. She'd been so intent on avoiding the shame of it that she hadn't allowed herself to think that Trig might understand enough to help her without asking questions. She lifted the folder with Trig's work in it.

"I'm ready for the makeover. I'll pass on the drunk part—I need to use this time to move forward, get myself in order before Hope comes home. Anyway, I never did get the hang of the soul-cleansing drunk like you."

—

In the late evening, Margaret sat on her own couch, the folder with Trig's makeover on the coffee table in front of her, the scent of stale beer and well-worn cast rising around her. Perhaps there was a bit of it still clinging to the plush, dark red cushions. Probably not, though, given the number of times Margaret had cleaned them. The scent that hung in Margaret's nose was a memory of the smell she'd come to associate with Brad since he'd dragged in hanging on Bert's arms. Why couldn't she shake it?

There wasn't a thing she could do to bring back the Brad who smelled of sweat and bike grease, Dove soap and shaving cream. Was there?

She shoved the coffee table aside, flung the pillows, one at a time, into the center of the den floor. She pulled the couch across the hardwood, not caring whether the foot protectors came off and allowed the sofa to gouge a track along the floor. She might like running a great big sander over the whole floor to smooth it down.

The sofa got stuck in the doorway to the kitchen. Margaret kicked the couch back into the den, then hauled it up, turned it sideways, shoved it through. She pulled it backward down the driveway, parked it beside the myrtles, its deep red voluptuousness clashing with the bold pink blossoms. She hunched over it, panting in the dusk, gulping in the thick, still summer air.

TEN
Hope

The rest of Hope's week was nothing but Agatha.

Agatha dragging the two of them across grassy fields and rocky places, talking about natural history.

Agatha leading her through the pages of a Shakespeare text that looked as though it might have come out while the author was still alive.

Agatha always there.

Agatha never flagging.

Agatha, Aag, Ag, ack.

And then Hope awoke on Saturday morning to find, on the floor outside her bedroom door, an envelope, white and flowery and adorned with perfect script, beaming up from Agatha's dark carpet. Hope bent to lift it. After three thousand miles and who knew how many hands and machines on it, the letter still smelled like her mother's smoky sweet perfume. She stuffed it in her back pocket.

Downstairs, a package, with the same perfect script as the letter, leaned against the table leg. A note balanced on the toast rack, plain and white, bearing Agatha's black scrawl. Hope lifted it. No perfume at all—just paper and ink and the faintest scent of the soap Agatha used to do the dishes, clean and crisp, with nothing extra sweet or frou-frou or fake. Agatha was outside. Hope's bum had barely made contact with the seat before she heard a rap at the back door.

We never use the back door. We, as though she'd been there long enough to belong. The knocking came again.

"Just come to deliver the eggs." Kenny held the eggs high as if to prove it.

"She's out front, I guess."

"I'll just go through, then."

Hope headed back to breakfast.

"What's in your pocket?" he asked.

"Nothing." Hope pulled it out and away from him. A trail of scent marked the envelope's path.

"Smells like something."

"It's from my mom, if you have to know."

"Sorry," he said. "I was just trying to make conversation. How come you haven't opened it? Don't you want to hear from your mum?"

"No," she said, a little too harshly.

"Oh. 'Kay," he said. "Don't you miss her?"

She sat back down at the breakfast table.

"I suppose I'd have to be away quite a while before I'd really miss my mum. All that 'Tuck in your shirt, Kenny,' 'Stand up straight, Kenny,' 'Mind your manners, Kenny.' That's probably what she'd write, if she was to write me a letter. That would stop me missing her straight away. Maybe that's what your mum has written. You should read it. Maybe it'll stop you missing her."

"I don't miss her."

He blushed. "I'll just take the eggs through." He turned when he got to the kitchen door. "You should still read it, so."

Hope set the letter on the table. Somewhere outside, Kenny's muffled voice called for Agatha. She should open the package, at least. She peeled open the lid of the box, held between her thumb and index finger a pair of pink trousers with green pinstripe. She dug a little. The deeper layers held similar fabrics. Did her mother think Agatha was schooling her in the landscape of the preppy instead of the geology of Arran? Was there even the slightest chance that the letter would explain?

Dear Hope,

I hope you're all settled in on Arran, and have discovered what a beautiful island it is. I decided to write instead of calling because you and I don't seem to be very good at talking these days. I'm writing this, sitting at the kitchen table after a run, thinking how quiet the house is without you. By the time you get this, Great-aunt Agatha will already have shown you some of the great places to explore. I'm sure she's teaching you tons as well. I hope you're enjoying her good food and hospitality.

I hope the weather isn't too cold. I know it's a shock to come from our humid, hot summer to Scotland's cool, windy one. Maybe you find it refreshing. I'm sure you've already discovered that Great-aunt Agatha makes beautiful sweaters. She's got plenty and I'm sure she'll be happy to share whatever you need. She'll also be happy to share a kind ear—maybe help you shed all the stuff I know you've been carrying around about your dad. I hope you can do that.

I hope, too, that you're learning a lot and having a great time living in another culture, especially since it's where your family came from. I'll write again soon. You can call anytime.

Love,
Mom

P.S. I'm mailing you a package—hope it gets there at the same time as this—so you have something nice to wear. ☺

Hope set down the paper and put her hands flat on the table. A sudden heat crawled up her neck. Her stomach tightened, squeezing away her hunger. In place of breakfast, she craved open space. On the other side of Agatha's hanging skivvies, her board waited by the door. She grabbed it, and then strode past Kenny in the garden, still holding the eggs. Agatha was making her way over the rocks, back toward the cottage, when Hope marched through the front gate, past the goat (still chewing), and into the wind.

Shed Dad? Have a great time in another culture? Did her mother think she'd sent Hope to some spa, an emotional fat farm where Hope could drop her dad like cellulite-ridden flab, pick up something new in the form of Agatha's (sugar-free?) Scottish culture, and clothe herself in preppy pants? Was this what her mother thought would happen after she took Hope's bike, shut down her Facebook and Twitter, claiming Hope might encounter someone unsavory? Like who? Dad?

Hope pushed the board hard and fast. Her stomach churned; her brain boiled; her quads and hamstrings and calves throbbed. All the anger she should have hurled back at her mother the morning she'd found the itinerary for Arran suddenly erupted. Mom had written the thing they'd been skirting all year. Whatever other stuff her mother had done that pissed Hope off, which was a lot and often, the line she hadn't crossed until the letter was coming out and saying she thought they were better off without Dad.

Mom had probably sat in the kitchen with her floral stationery and her green tea, steam rising, contented smile growing. How easy it had been to get rid of Dad and then, when Hope hadn't taken to the color scheme of her mother's new life, to send her to Arran to wend her way to a new, cultured, Dad-free self. Might her mother even know where her father was?

Hope pressed her board harder, past whitewashed cottages and whitewooled sheep, past grassy fields on one side and grey sea and shore on the other, past a chewing, staring goat that looked just like the chewing, staring goat to which Agatha talked. The rain started, a welcome cover for wet, red cheeks. Could she push herself out ahead of the lightning inside? She thrust the board forward until her legs ached because she'd used up her muscles, until her eyes burned because she'd cried them dry, until she thought she'd cleared enough to let the tailwind push her back to the cottage and walk back in the door in control of herself.

"Why am I here?" she said.

Agatha looked up. "For your lunch?" She gestured at the plate across from her, the table set again, the package gone. Good riddance.

"Not why did I come in from skating up and down the island and sit down in front of you. I *mean*, why am I really here, in this house, on this island, instead of skating at the old Terra Pines Main Library and getting ready to start Terra Pines High like I should be?"

Agatha put down her sandwich. A pale cluster of crumbs clung to the left edge of her lip. Her tongue reached out and grabbed them before she brought the napkin up to dab her lips. She set the napkin back in her lap and smoothed it out. "You're here to live and learn."

"I was living and learning at home."

"You weren't learning what your mother thought you ought to be learning."

"She thought I should be living in the rain, learning how to identify the rocks of all ages and wearing ugly pants?"

Agatha put both her hands flat on the table. "Perhaps the better way to phrase it is to say that your mother thought you'd taken to learning things you were better off not knowing."

"Like what?"

Great-auntie Agatha leaned in and looked right at Hope, clear eyes steady and open. "Do you really not know?"

Hope stared right back into Agatha's sea-like eyes. Was there a glimmer of a chance that Agatha Stuart would believe her?

"Do you really not know why you're here, Hope?"

"For some so-so grades." Why not start with what had seemed the least offensive thing to Mom, and see what Aunt Agatha did with it?

"Aye, that's a bit of it. A small bit. What about being truant from school?"

"I missed the bus." Hope shrugged. "I wasn't used to taking it."

"And lying to your mum about being at Katie's house when you weren't?"

"I went to ride my bike." Not entirely a lie.

"To ride your bike?"

"Yes. To ride my bike."

"You lied to your mum to ride your bike?"

"Mom. I lied to my *mom* so I could see if I could find my dad, which is more than she was doing."

Agatha and Hope sat silent for several seconds, and then Agatha's face seemed to shift. She sat slightly straighter, making more distance between them. "And what about the drugs, Hope?"

What about the drugs? As though Hope were a dealer or something. For all the things Mom could have made a meal of to Aunt Agatha—her grades, for instance, which really had dropped and about which she really couldn't make herself care anymore; the fact that her father, the most important person in her life, her fucking father, had dumped her and dropped off the edge of the world. Why didn't either of them mention that, other than saying Hope should "shed all the stuff she'd been carrying around about Dad," as though missing Dad was a pair of jeans she chose to pull on every day or an expensive hobby she'd picked up, or, hell, a drug she'd gotten hooked on? Why did they have to make out that it was Hope who was fucked up?

"What about the drugs?" Hope said. "I think you mean, Auntie Agatha, 'What about the drug?' What about the one little Lortab my mother caught me taking. Is that what you're asking?"

"Hope." She reached a hand across the table.

"It was one little place I managed to connect with Dad that Mom couldn't control. And no, it wasn't the first time, which means yes, I liked it, if that's what you want to know. And yes, I did have another *one*. Which I would have taken at some point. And that would have been it, Auntie Agatha. Not that you're likely to believe me. I wasn't going to talk a buddy into extending my prescription. I didn't like it so much I was going to fall in love with it. I didn't like it so much I was going to turn into Dad."

Hope pulled herself up. Her words hung in the air. She wanted to suck the last of them back in or blow them away, fast. She concentrated on calming her voice.

"I wasn't out getting plastered at the cool-kid parties that Mom thought I should go to. I just wanted to find my dad. Why can't you get that?" She pushed her chair away from the table. "People in this family make no sense. Mom tells you whatever to justify sending me halfway around the world. And you buy it, hook, line, and sinker."

Hope walked past Agatha, into the kitchen, then turned around and walked back to the table. She grabbed a sandwich and went to sit on the bottom step outside the kitchen door, her face burning in the wind while she chewed a wad of oat bread and thick smoked ham and tried to ignore the goat that seemed to be chewing in rhythm with her.

She had blurted out a truth worse than any fact she might have told Agatha about where she'd been when she lied to Mom and missed the bus. She'd betrayed her dad and she couldn't even find him to say sorry. Whatever slim chance she'd had of finding him in Terra Pines was gone. She hadn't fought her mother once the tickets were booked, somehow thinking her mother was sending her for only a few weeks. *To live and learn* sounded as though it could take the rest of one of their lives, and Agatha hadn't even told her what she was supposed to learn. If it was to walk and talk and dress like her mother, it would take both their lifetimes.

Tears again. She swallowed them.

She felt as though she'd dropped in on the tallest half-pipe she'd ever seen when she'd arrived at Aunt Agatha's cottage. The half-pipe was getting steeper and steeper as she rode down toward the bowl, never getting any closer to the safe curve of its belly, never able to reach the place where she could launch herself up the other side and over the lip at the top. She put her head in her hands. The last bit of sandwich stuck in her throat. Hope forced it and the tears down. Damned if she would let the old lady see her cry. She needed to know the exact size of this half-pipe of exile.

Inside, she slid into the seat across from Agatha.

"What exactly am I supposed to live and learn?"

Agatha pushed back her chair, left the teapot and the rest of the sandwiches and even her crumby plate and then she left the room. Hope listened to her steps on the creaky stairs.

Agatha came back laden with a pile of dusty photo albums. "A bit of family history for you." She sat on the couch. "Try not to roll your eyes too much, dear." She blew dust off a slim white box on top of them, lifted the lid, her eyes on Hope. Pulling out an old photo album, Agatha set everything else on the floor and waited for Hope to join her. The book crinkled when she opened it, as reluctant as Hope to be exposed to living and learning.

Hope folded her arms over her chest, felt the raised lettering on the Spitfire logo against her bare skin.

"Yes," Agatha said. "This is a good beginning." She set her bony pointer finger down on the black page below a photo of a solemn little boy on a bleak day, his pale knees poking out between dark shorts and socks that looked as though they had lost the energy to stay up on his calves. "Calum Dalgleish Stuibhart. Your great-grandfather. My da," she said. "Here he'd be only five or six, but already sent to work the land every day with his da. He'd have been thankful at that age that it was only a wee spot they had there on the Shiants.

"Born in 1900—first baby born the Shiants in the New Year. First baby of the century."

Auntie Agatha turned the creaky pages in her photo album, showing a straight-lipped teenager in baggy trousers and a jacket standing in a field that might as well have been on Arran. Here was where Agatha got her serious-looking face. Was it a trait of the Stuart family that stayed the same from place to place, or had it more to do with the life they led? Was that why her mother had so little sweetness left in her? Would Hope become like that without Dad there to show her how to enjoy herself, or did she have enough of him built into her?

Agatha stroked her way through the albums, one photo after another, telling the stories that went with each, stories that carried the family from one world war to another and from the island Agatha was born on to the "big city of Glasgow;"

stories that seemed to offer everything except the answer to the question Hope asked. When Agatha snapped the fourth album shut, she said, "I think everyone should know where they come from, and who in the world they can call family." She paused. "Some people learn because they live in the place they belong, amid their family—their big, extended family with cousins and aunts and uncles."

What cousins? Granny Mac was the only one of Hope's family to live in the U.S., and she'd come back to Scotland after Hope's grandfather died, before Hope was born.

"Others have to learn in other ways." Agatha patted the albums. "Does that answer your question?"

"I'm supposed to live and learn about family?"

"That's some of it." She set her bony hand on Hope's leg.

Hope moved out from under her. "Is there a family tree I can memorize?"

Agatha patted her own knees. "Tomorrow we'll take our rest—try just living for one day of the week."

ELEVEN
Margaret

After she caught her breath, hunched over the sofa at the curb, Margaret dusted off her hands and headed down the driveway. Instead of going straight inside to sweep away any dust bunnies exposed by the sofa removal, she paused at the door to the tool room. How many times had she stood at the edge of the Cave since Brad left? More, certainly, than when he'd been around. She remembered standing there that day in May, coming home as dusk settled, humidity up even though spring wasn't nearly over, finding the door ajar. She'd called Hope a few hours before, told her to order pizza, explained that she needed to take a client to dinner to cinch a deal.

I don't need dinner, Hope had said, spluttering something about Katie's mom inviting her over. So who had been in the tool room? Had Brad been there? If he had, was it before or after Hope left? With one finger, Margaret pulled the door fully open. Brad's bikes hung where he'd left them. Wouldn't he have taken those? Her eyes landed, then, on the gap where Hope's bike should have been. Katie's mother always picked up Hope when they went places. When she went on her own, Hope was all skateboard. The mountain bike had been something reserved for her dad. Could Hope just have gone for a ride around Bent Creek? Or was Hope doing what Margaret herself had done not three months before?

Margaret's stomach lurched as she recalled the night she had parked at the grocery store, away from the trailhead and parking lot. She'd hiked in, crouched in the woods, waited for Mike and Bert and all the others, felt the sick shame rising as she hoped for a glimpse of Brad, hoped he wasn't there at all. The next time, she'd parked in full view, waited at the trailhead, asked each man in turn. She couldn't let Hope feel what she had, again and again.

She checked the house nonetheless; she called Katie's mother. No Hope in either place.

Margaret parked in the unpaved lower lot, around the curve from the trailhead. The sky seemed to be darkening with every footstep toward the trail. Margaret didn't risk a headlamp or flashlight lest Hope see her first, and slip deeper into the woods. Thank God for the full moon. If Hope was here, had she acted on impulse or would she have calculated the phases of the moon to allow her the greatest night vision?

As she slunk around the edge of the trail, the hairs on the back of Margaret's neck stood on end. Could Hope be behind her, in the woods nearby, seeing Margaret, holding her breath as though Margaret were some sort of predator instead of her mother, trying to make a path for them both out of this tangled nightmare in which Brad had abandoned them?

When the gap in the tall pines and oak and mountain laurel and ferns that stood for the trailhead came into view, Margaret stopped. Her feet stilled; her breath halted. There stood her daughter, wild hair tumbling out from her helmet, bike propped against the trunk of a hickory, herself propped beside it. She wasn't even hiding, just waiting right out in the open.

Oh, Hope. Margaret's throat tightened. Her eyes welled. Her hand covered her mouth, as though a scream could have made its way out. *Breathe.*

Margaret stepped forward slowly, breathing in with one footfall, breathing out with the next. She didn't need to look at her watch to know that the Wednesday night mountain bike group would come careening around the last corner, bunny hop the fallen oak from last winter's freak ice storm, jam on the brakes before coasting through the parking lot. Margaret hadn't known any of this when Brad had been at home.

Mountain biking was something Brad kept for himself until Hope showed interest.

Since Brad had called, saying he was healing in his own way, Margaret had crouched, hidden, enough times to memorize the routine. If just imagining him in the line of men whizzing past could have made him manifest, he would have been home months ago.

Margaret edged closer; she touched Hope's shoulder.

Hope screamed.

"He isn't here," Margaret said.

Hope straightened.

"How do you know?"

"Hope."

"We could ask his friends."

"I have."

She'd stood where Hope was, asked each of the men as they came in, seen the embarrassment in the eyes of the few who didn't avert their gaze. She'd heard their apologies, felt the shame. Margaret didn't want Hope standing there, heart rising at the sight of every headlamp rounding the corner, falling as she realized it wasn't him again and again and again.

"Come on, honey." Margaret took hold of Hope's bike.

"That's mine." Hope pulled at the handlebars. "Dad gave it to me."

Margaret yanked the bike firmly away. "Yes, it's your bike. It's coming home. With us."

"What if he's here?"

Margaret measured her daughter. She sighed. "We can sit in the car and wait."

In the car, Margaret kept her eyes straight ahead, unable to bear the sight of her daughter's hope rising and falling twenty or more times as the men rolled in, single file. She reached for her knee when the last man rolled past. Hope flinched and pulled away, leaning her head against the door.

Margaret's mind reeled, searching for something to say. Finding nothing appropriate, she pulled away, the crunch of the tires against the dirt and rock loud in the gap between them.

At home, Hope stormed through the door.

"Just because he wasn't there tonight doesn't mean he won't be there next time," she said.

"You can't just go skulking around the woods at night." Margaret left the bike in the trunk, followed Hope into the house. "Hope, sit with me."

Hope took the stairs two at a time, closed her door. Margaret stood outside it, hand on the knob. If she went in, what would she say that might make it better? Could she even find anything to say that wouldn't make it worse?

"I love you, Hope," Margaret spoke through the door.

"Goodnight."

In her own room, Margaret sat, hands on her knees, head hanging. She wasn't going to wait for the questions to start. She hung her skirt in the walk-in closet, her back to Brad's side. She turned to face his scant dress clothes, hanging there, perfectly pressed and waiting. Damn him for holding them in this limbo. She would clear him out. She would find the right moment to sit down and talk it through with Hope; Margaret envisioned them sipping tea on the sofa, shoulder to shoulder as they had been the day Brad came home from the crash.

In the morning, she told Hope to ride the bus. When Hope was gone, she left Brad's stuff for the trash. On a hunch, she took the computer to her office, and got her tech guy to hack Hope's history. She saw Hope's messages on Facebook, her Tweets, her posts on bike forums. *Has anyone seen Brad Carver? Brad Carver, missing adult, last seen pulling out of the driveway in January.* Margaret scrolled through searches Hope had made at midnight, at two a.m., at four p.m. of race results, for personal trainers. Did she do anything other than skate and look for Brad?

Margaret decided to come home early from work; she had half a notion of baking something for them, as she had so often before she went back to work. She ran upstairs to change, came down, pushed through the kitchen door trying to recall the recipe for chocolate chunk cookies. She found Hope crouched by the window.

"Hope? What are you doing here?"

"Mom!" Hope stood. "What are you doing here?"

"You're supposed to be at school."

"You're supposed to be at work."

"Hope. I can come home from work if I need to. I was going to make cookies." Why did she feel the need to explain?

"You got me to ride the bus so you could make cookies."

"Never mind why I asked you to ride the bus. Why didn't you?"

"I missed it."

"What?"

"I missed the bus."

"Hope. You missed the bus? Why didn't you call me for a ride?"

"You said you needed me to take the bus, so I figured you had something that was keeping you busy."

"Oh, Hope." Margaret took in a deep breath. "Can you not just talk to me instead of sneaking around?"

"I might ask you the same." Hope stepped closer, her eyes full of challenge.

"Hope." Margaret's mind swirled. None of this made sense to her—not this conversation or anything that had led to it, from the crash to Brad's inability to heal to the addiction to the leaving.

Margaret was the one who got up every morning, held a job, cooked dinner, stayed the course. Still, she felt crazy trying to make sense of it all. *Dear God, please let Hope not be drowning in the same kind of doubt I wade through every day. Please let her at least have something definite to grieve.*

"Hope," Margaret said. "Your father is gone." Margaret heard her own mother's harsh tone in her voice. She winced. She tried to soften. "I'm so very sorry. I wish I was saying something different. He's gone, honey." She reached out, laid a hand on Hope's arm. "You have to move forward."

Hope jerked her arm away. "I bet you're sorry," she said, belligerent like Brad.

In the weeks that followed, Margaret started taking Hope to the library, taking a minute to watch her skate. Margaret took Hope to the skate park, tried to ignore the dark clothes, the shaggy-haired boys, the scent of cigarettes outside the door.

She took her to a therapist. Hope came out looking more sullen than when she went in.

"Isn't that where Dad went?" Hope asked in the car. "No wonder he didn't come home."

Should she have taken her again? Looked harder for Brad herself?

In the first week of summer, they seemed to settle into a rhythm, mostly silent but free of the obsessive searching. *One step at a time.* And then Margaret noticed Hope's eyes, the torn netting, felt the same stab in her gut.

How was it that Margaret had done what she thought to be all the right things and still wound up with an addict for a husband and a daughter who looked to be on her way? How was it that she wasn't enough for either of them?

Margaret slapped the door to the tool room. She had told Hope to move on, yet here she was, summer already at full boil, gawping at Brad's remains; her greatest accomplishment seemed to be that she'd managed to take the sofa to the curb. She hadn't even fed herself properly since Hope left, and there she'd sat telling Trig she wouldn't drink with her, too focused on getting herself together. She would change clothes, go to the grocery store, replenish her supply of herbal teas, buy fresh fruits and vegetables.

In the morning, she would show her staff the new name and logo. She had doubts about the variation on her first name. She had doubts about going back to her maiden name—but she had to admit, Trig was right, Mags MacPherson had a ring to it. And the double M's on the logo looked sharp. She'd show the staff in the morning, tour her clients at ten and noon. If the response to the name was positive, she'd order a new sign, and then go and get herself a new sofa. Out with the old, in with the new. She closed the door to the tool room and headed to the grocery.

At last she was making progress. Wasn't she?

TWELVE
Hope

A long, white sheet of paper rested on the tray with the tea after breakfast on Monday. Agatha handed it to Hope.

An object that is not being subjected to a force will continue to move at a constant speed in a straight line. If more than one force acts on an object along a straight line, then the forces will reinforce or cancel one another depending on their direction or magnitude. Unbalanced forces will cause changes in the speed or direction of an object's motion.

"What is this?" Hope handed it back.

"I think it maybe answers your question about why your mother wanted you here."

"Mom wants me to live and learn about force?"

"Think of you, rolling along in your life in a straight line—a line that was pointing in quite a nice direction until your dad had his accident." Agatha pressed her pointer finger down on the page below the sentence about the constant speed and straight line. "Now think of Mum and Dad as the forces acting on you and each other—the unbalancing forces that caused a change in your direction.

"Think of you, then, after all of that. Think of yourself rolling along on your skateboard, if it helps, in a straight line pointing in a new direction—consider that the line was, perhaps, pointing in a less than desirable direction." Agatha pointed at the second sentence. "Think of me as the new, unbalanced force that's meant to cause a change in the speed or direction of your motion."

"You're an unbalanced force?"

"I'm steady enough on my feet, but I think you'll agree that I'm a wee bit different than your mum or your dad and that Arran is a teeny bit different than Terra Pines and that…"

Hope held up her hand. "I get it."

"You did ask why you're here." Agatha said. "It makes the right connection. You're just here to rebalance yourself." Agatha handed Hope another sheet with a map. "Away and see what you can learn about force."

"It's summer vacation," Hope said. Her hip jutted out.

"Or else you can stay here and help me in the garden, see if I've learned enough about keeping the soil pH balanced to grow my dinner. Lunch is at noon. Tea's at six."

Hope grabbed her board and pushed out, down the coast road against the wind. She didn't get the nickname the Carver for nothing. She jumped the board up to try to grind the sea wall and found it too irregular and too low. Her foot met the pavement again and again as she gained pace, seeking something to climb and jump from, longing to replicate the microcosm of chance she'd discovered hauling herself to the tops of increasingly high ledges in Terra Pines or scaling the fence at the skate park. On Arran, even the waves that rolled in didn't swell like the ones on the Carolina coast.

The low wall ended. The land flattened. Hope stopped and looked back. Behind Aunt Agatha's house the land rose and grew edgier. Even with her eyes closed, Hope had felt Davey's car climbing away from the ferry. She'd felt the car peak and then descend. The String Road, Davey had called it.

Hope pressed around the bends of The String, away from sea level and the cottage. As the road curved away from the coast, it rose quickly, making her work harder and harder. When the last little white farmhouse ducked out of sight and even the sea seemed small and far away, Hope stopped again.

Far off, on the left, Cir Mhor and Goat Fell dug into the clouds. On the right, green fields edged with hedges and trees rolled away. Hope hopped a barbed-wire fence and trudged in the direction of the highest peaks. Surely there were outcroppings along the way. She might not be able to drop in onto the board, but she could leap, flip maybe, test how she'd land. If she had to, she could walk all the way to the top of Goat Fell.

A rise of rocks jutted upward not far from the fence. Hope set the board at its base, stepped back and shielded her eyes, not from sunlight, as she would have in Terra Pines, but from the drizzle that had begun. The outcropping rose maybe fifteen feet, not as high as she'd like, but perhaps with enough lift to show her where to go next. At the top, she inched from one edge to the other before settling on the farthest jutting rock. Wasn't this just like having the board below her? She bent. Why had she ever allowed fear to prevent this? She leapt high and away, tucked her body into itself, eyes wide as she passed layers of grey, one sharp edge coming within inches of her face before she unfurled, stretched to her full length and landed, knees sinking into the grass and muck. *Barely*. She sat for a few minutes, breathless, before she began to climb again.

From the same ledge, Hope measured the space between herself and the ground, an ecology of risk. She would add a twist. As she lifted her head, she found the same square fields rolling toward the sea—and Kenny, scurrying across the tufted grass toward her. Was it possible he hadn't seen her? She crouched, waiting.

"Escaped, have you?" Kenny made his hands look like Agatha's bony graspers. He smiled as he bent to put his hands on his knees and catch his breath.

Hope couldn't help it. She smiled back.

"I've been trying to catch you up since I saw you start up The String. Where you gaun?"

"Just going."

"When d'you have to be back?"

Hope shrugged.

"Want to go into Brodick with me? Better than slogging up this hill."

"I like the hill."

"Oh. I suppose it's a nice one, as hills go." Kenny glanced around. "Brodick's nice as well. We could take the bus and get out of the rain. Unless you like the rain, too."

She eyed him. Had Agatha sent him? Did it matter? "I don't have any money."

"No bother. My treat."

Wind and Kenny's words whistled passed them, waiting on the side of the road at the weather-beaten pole that stood for a bus stop. Kenny rambled on about bands he liked while Hope tried to remember a time she'd ever been on a bus, other than the big tour buses they got for field trips. She'd spent part of every day of her life—before Arran, of course—in a car with someone else steering. How had she felt she was living her own life, making her own choices when all along she'd only gone where she was supposed to? Agatha was right, although maybe not in the exact way she intended. Hope had been pushed around by other forces.

"Ever feel like you have no choices at all?" Hope blurted.

"About bands?" Kenny leaned closer to her, his forehead wrinkling under his wind-whipped hair.

"Not bands. Well, sometimes even bands, but mostly bigger stuff, like choices about where to go and when and why."

"D'you mean you'd rather go somewhere other than Brodick?"

"How would I know?"

"Just asking." Kenny stared, waiting for a response.

"Brodick is fine."

"There are other places. They're smaller, though. The bus goes right round the island. We could get off anywhere."

"I was really talking about bigger choices."

"Like?"

"Just. Bigger."

"Like where you live and stuff?"

"Yes. And what clothes I have. And friends."

"I know what you mean. My gran's very strict. So's my mum. They get worse the older I get." Kenny's Scottish accent made the words sound as though they took up too much space in his mouth.

"My mom got worse after Dad left."

Kenny's forehead wrinkled more. Before Hope could say the next thing, he pointed behind her. "Bus."

She climbed on after him, setting her skateboard at her feet and thinking how one of the choices that landed her on Arran was missing the bus the one day Mom wanted her to take it.

She'd missed it on purpose, having heard her mother dragging stuff down the hall late the night before. She'd peeked through her door and seen Mom lugging two black thirty-gallon trash bags over her shoulders and carrying out the awkward things Dad had left behind that couldn't be stuffed in plastic bags. In the morning, she'd told Hope to take the bus, claiming she had an appointment. She hid until Margaret left.

Hope had barely begun rummaging through the big green bin at the end of the driveway when she saw the trash truck coming. She hauled both black bags out of the bin and into the woods that led to the stream between Bent Creek and the rest of the world.

All she found worth keeping were the sweatshirt and the Lortab bottle. She wasn't sure, at that moment, why she took the bottle, with the pills still inside.

The day had been warm, sun filtering through the clouds and trees and she laid her head down, using one of the trash bags as a pillow and cuddling the other like a stuffed animal. The sound of the stream kept her company. She and Katie had crossed it once, walked right through and climbed the red clay rise on the other bank. They had taken the few steps to the edge of the trees on the other side, stood side by side and stared at the broad field that opened in front of them, bigger than all the yards on their blocks combined, a small house in the distance, not much bigger than some of the garages in Bent Creek. Hope thought of it, a vague memory, as she lay in the woods with the trash bags full of her father's stuff. She closed her eyes, clutched the Lortab. There was plenty of time before she had to figure out where to stash the trash bags so she could meet the kids coming off the bus and pretend she'd been on it. She dozed, and when she opened her eyes the sun seemed much brighter. She squinted, sat up, took a minute to remember where she was and why.

"Y'alright, hon?" A voice, hard worn, came from across the creek.

Hope stared, frozen, at the man with his wrinkled skin and smooth, slicked-back hair.

"I come down here walking. Don't mean you no harm. It's just a girl in the woods in the middle of the day with nothing but trash bags…"

"I'm fine." Hope jumped up. "I'm fine."

"Oughtn't you be fine in a school?" He looked from her to the bags and back. "You not thinking about running away, are you?" He moved away from the tree he'd been leaning against.

"No. I. I'm fine." Hope dropped the bags, fumbled to stuff the Lortab in her pocket, ran. She heard a splash behind her. She pressed as hard as she could through the trees and the yards and across the street, not looking back until she was past the crape myrtles and down the driveway and into the house, door locked. She commando-crawled over the kitchen floor to the window.

He came into sight at the edge of the neighbor's yard, dark Wrangler jeans and collared shirt, brown pointy boots out of place beside the manicured lawn. He nodded, as though marking something to himself, then turned and cut back the way he'd come. Hope relaxed. And then it registered that, after the trees and the driveway, she'd sped past her mother's car in the garage.

Hope snuck back into the woods a few days later, but the trash bags were gone. She thought she saw the old man again a few days after that, in the grocery store, but either it wasn't him or he didn't recognize her or didn't want to speak. She'd been relieved.

Who could have known that not taking the bus would turn out to be one of the things that landed her on Arran, which led to her meeting Kenny, which led to her sitting on a bus, rattling toward the north corner of the island, pushed along by the same tailwind that had pushed her and Agatha to Lochranza, while Kenny rattled off information about the landscape as they passed?

"I think we should go right the way 'round." Kenny nodded as if he'd conferred with himself on this subject and found his alter ego to be in agreement. "I'll point things out as we go and then you'll know the options and you can choose. Fair enough?"

"Sure."

They rattled on, through Lochranza and out the other side, with Kenny pointing out the house that got the least amount of sun, just as Agatha had, and then other clusters of houses, sheep, hills, rocks, bigger rocks, more sheep, all seeming to brace themselves against whatever weather was on its way.

"Coming into civilization soon," he said, as they passed the foot of Goat Fell.

"Mom would like that," Hope said. "She liked us when we looked like the standard-issue middle-class family, all civilized, which she seemed to think we did as long as Dad was there," she blurted, then clamped her mouth shut.

"There's plenty of wild places still on Arran," Kenny said.

They stopped and started, stopped and started in Brodick. Kenny pointed out the castle and a brewery and a chippie. When they left those behind, he pointed out the window again, saying, "Clauchland Hills," and then started into a story about roaming over the hills during the summer. While he talked, they passed farmhouses that dotted the southern part of the island, seeming lonely. Green fields with borders of pointy-edged shrubs left the houses exposed to the elements, reminding Hope of how she'd felt exposed to her mom's pickiness.

"What are those shrubs?" she interrupted Kenny's story.

"Gorse."

"Looks prickly."

"So it is," he said, "but beautiful, don't you think?"

"Just like my mom." Her mouth took over again. "Prickly and beautiful."

Kenny's eyes widened.

"Sorry. TMI."

"Hills," he said. "Hills I don't know the names of."

Hope chose to get off the bus just beyond the hills, in what seemed like a remote valley. They walked across the fields until they came to a circle of standing stones that looked out over the southwest side of the island. There, in the middle of them, was a goat she could have sworn was the same stupid goat that was friends with Agatha.

"Did that goat follow me?"

"Oh, aye, they're just like good dogs, follow their masters anywhere—or mistresses."

Hope frowned.

"Hallo? This is Scotland. There are goats."

She moved away, toward one of the larger stones, a grey guard perched there on the moor, impossibly tall for its width, looking as if the first good wind coming in from the sea would topple it, and yet, according to Kenny, the stones had been standing for hundreds of years.

"Do you think the people on this end of the island had to drag these rocks from the northern part to make the circles?"

"I cannae imagine it," Kenny said. "This is about as far from Goat Fell as you can get on Arran."

"It didn't seem so far on the bus."

Kenny moved over to the stone Hope was standing beside. "It's far enough. And it's a different kind of place. It always seems farther back in time to me. The people who live here would probably be insulted, but that's how I feel. I think of this piece of land being associated with the time of people running about with paint on their bodies and fairies on their shoulders an' a' that."

"Don't start with the fairies. Agatha has already threatened me with fairy tales."

Kenny waved his hands over her head as if he was a witch casting a spell. "By the oak. By the ash. By the thorn."

She pulled back. "What is that about?"

"Miss Stuart hasn't told you that old fairy bit about the sacred trees? The fairies live in them, grant wishes by them, bring luck—good and bad—by them. I've heard them all, I think, between Miss Stuart and my gran."

Hope raised an eyebrow.

"Och, don't be so stubbornly modern. Miss Stuart and my gran and their old stories are quite funny without really meaning to be."

"I'll pass."

"Fair enough."

They stood there with one hand each on the huge stone. Kenny's hands looked much older than the rest of him, broad and callused.

"What next?"

Hope shrugged. "I don't even know what the options are."

Kenny paused, looking almost as if he was out of words. "Why don't we start by getting off this moor?"

She should say sorry, she didn't mean to be harsh. Sorry, it wasn't him. Just sorry. She walked along beside Kenny, past more stones and down the same path they'd come up, trying to make that one little word come out.

Kenny hopped a ditch by the side of the road, turned and held out his hand.

"I got it," she said.

He pulled his hand back as if she'd slapped it.

Sorry.

Kenny stuffed his hands in his pockets after that and walked the rest of the way to the bus stop in silence. They took seats at the back of the bus. Hope held her board at her chest. By then, it was nearly dinnertime. Too late, for Kenny at least, to do anything but go home, but not too late for Hope to stay on until the top of The String.

She didn't even have to push to get going. She gave a couple of shoves around the first curve for some extra pace and squatted down, cruising down the middle of the road. The wind, fresh and open and so unlike the heavy air of Terra Pines, pushed back her hair as she picked up speed again and found a rhythm to carry her around every curve. The letter from her mother, her dad's accident and addiction and absence, even the image of Agatha saying she was an unbalanced force, the wind blew them all away. Down the last of the curves on the ride back to the cottage there was, for the first time in ages, only herself.

In the cottage, Hope found Agatha in her chair in the front room, working a pair of knitting needles fast. A ball of thick, dark brown yarn sat on the floor by her feet, an obedient pet waiting for the next command.

Hope's stomach growled. She hoped Agatha's old ears weren't good enough to hear it. She'd never been a meal-skipper. She'd taken her lunch to school—made it every morning—and eaten the whole thing. Sandwich or wrap at lunch and apple or banana or pear on the way home. Standing in front of Agatha, it felt more important to extend the time she had within herself than to eat.

"Aileen McGinty says you look quite impressive on that board of yours." Head bent to her knitting, Agatha raised her eyes toward Hope. "She passed you climbing The String some time ago, stopped in for a minute. Did you learn anything?"

Hope shrugged.

"I thought you maybe were learning something, since it kept you out past your lunch and your tea." Agatha began to count the stitches on her needle.

Hope set the backpack on the table. The dark wood gleamed, as though it had been not only cleared but also freshly polished.

"Where you away into Brodick, then?"

"No." Hope stood behind the couch.

Agatha finished her row of knitting, which led her to the end of her ball of wool. She attached a new ball, got her rhythm going again. "Where was it, then?"

"Just some rocks."

"Some rocks?"

"Some rocks."

Agatha put down her knitting. "Sussed out all Arran's high points, did you?"

"I liked them."

"Oh, aye?"

Aye.

"What was there to like?"

"Nothing. We just walked and talked."

"We?"

"I ran into Kenny."

"And what had he to say for himself?"

"Nothing. Just some chant."

"What chant?"

"By something, something thorns."

Agatha set down her knitting mid-row. "By oak, by ash, by thorn? Not just a chant. A blessing." Agatha crackled her way to standing. She went to Hope, put her hands on her shoulders, pushed her toward the fire. "Sit down here and don't be stubborn." She disappeared upstairs.

Hope thought to stand, to propel herself upstairs and into bed. Instead, her body settled further into the softness of the sofa. Before she could will herself up and out, Agatha was back and sitting beside her, holding an intricately carved box.

"This was made for me, so it was; carved by hand." Agatha stroked the box. "Those three trees—oak, ash, and thorn—are trees of the fairies. Hawthorns can live for four hundred years, you know. It's very bad luck to cut one down. I was told the one this box came from fell on its own." Agatha opened the box and handed Hope the comb that rested inside. "I've since come to wonder if it was the truth."

Hope turned the little comb over in her hand.

"There's no need to pretend it's more interesting than it is. Come and help me. I can't see you starve even if you did miss your tea of your own choice. You can repay me by sitting politely by the fire whilst we eat, and by pretending to listen intently whilst I tell you a story about a comb and a girl on the moor, like you were today."

Hope turned the comb over again, looked from it to the fire to Agatha to the door. She followed Agatha to the kitchen.

They brought warm bannock with melted cheese back to the fire. As Hope ate, Agatha began. The light from the flames emphasized the hills and hollows on her face as she spoke.

"This story is set in Lochranza. It's the story of a lassie just a bit older than you, sent out to drive her family's cattle into their holding pens." Agatha leaned into Hope, her face even more serious than usual. "You'll think this is a story from long ago, but it isn't. This happened during my lifetime." She sat back. "And not when I was a young thing, either.

"The lassie was hopeless. The cattle were this way and that, pell-mell all over the hill." Agatha waved her hands in the air, casting shadows that looked like some medieval festival on the walls. "Not only was the girl a hopeless drover, she'd no sense of sticking to a thing, so in less than an hour, she'd given up and decided to go away home, leaving the cows as they were and not a care about her. Just as she came around the head of the loch, which I'll show you next time we go, she saw a lad sitting next to an old piece of fence. He was a lad a bit older than Kenny and a lot better looking."

Hope blushed. Agatha went on. It wasn't so hard to listen.

"'Hallo,' he called out to her. He'd a voice even more lovely than his face. She couldn't resist it and so went over to him. She'd only just reached him when he pulled out of his pocket a beautifully carved comb. 'Have you lost a comb?' he asked. 'Not me,' she said. He asked again, though, as boys tend to.

"On the third time he asked, something in his voice changed, making it sound as if he was chanting a spell. 'I haven't lost a comb,' she said. The boy stared at her, hard, and thrust the comb into her hand, saying, 'It's yours now.'

"The girl thought how lovely and light the comb was, and how nice it would look on her drab dressing table at home, but something told her she mustn't accept it.

"Something was right, Hope, for this girl was as surely in a battle of wits for her spirit as we are in this cottage now. 'No, thank you,' the girl said, and handed back the comb. The lad let go of staring at her and looked very sad that she'd rejected his gift. 'Will you do one thing for me? Will you comb my hair?' he asked."

Agatha took a breath and patted Hope on the shoulder.

"I'm sure a girl like you would think it a strange request and have the good sense to remove yourself from such a person, but you've a lot more sense than this girl. She didn't see any harm in it, and took up the comb and began to glide it through his hair, content until she noticed sand and small seashells and starfish were falling from the lad's hair.

"She dropped the comb and turned to run away home, but found she could no more run than could one of those stones you saw this afternoon. That lassie put all her will into the idea of running, and in a minute found herself sprinting across the moor and into her house, where she blurted out the story to her parents, no doubt leaving out the bit about not having got the cows in their pens.

"Her father strode out to challenge the lad, but all he found were some shells and starfish and a small pile of white sand forming a triskell—a fairy sign—on the ground. The father went back to the cottage and hugged the daughter, glad she was safe.

"It was when the mother was in the town three days later that an old woman who lived alone by the loch hobbled over on her long, crooked limbs and told the mother that her daughter had had a lucky escape. She explained that the strange boy was the sea god Manannan Mac Lir, come to take away a mortal woman to his realm. He'd tried and failed seven years before and would no doubt try again seven years hence. She was a lucky girl to have kept hold of herself."

Agatha patted her box.

"As I have not been carried off to another realm under the sea, you may gather that it was no sea god who gave me my comb, just a very mortal young man." She put her teacup back on the tray and reached for Hope's. "I'll wash. You'll dry."

Again, Hope followed Agatha to the kitchen, stood beside her and waited for the dishes and cups to be passed. Twice, Hope turned to Agatha, mouth opening as though she might say or ask something. Agatha hesitated, cup in hand, water dripping down her forearm, raising an eyebrow as if to say, "Yes?" Hope closed her mouth, accepted the cup, dried. Neither of them said a word as they put away the dishes and then, as Agatha hung the tea towel to dry, she turned to Hope.

"Something occurred to me while you were out—something I think your mum maybe didn't tell you." Agatha stepped toward her. Hope's hand remained wrapped around the cupboard handle. "I told you you're here because your mum…"

"Mom."

"I said your mother thinks you've been getting a bit off track. I'm maybe crossing a line I shouldn't here." Agatha took a breath. "Your mother needs a bit of time to get herself pointing in the right direction as well. It's hard being a single parent."

"It's easy being a single kid?"

Agatha reached for Hope's hand. Hope dropped it to her side, leaving Agatha's to land on the bare handle.

"Is that it?" Hope asked.

"No. It isn't it. What I suspect your mother failed to be clear about is not just why you're here, but how long you're to stay. Am I right?" Agatha smoothed the tea towel, fingers moving with a nervous quickness.

Hope must have one-upped her somehow. Why couldn't she take any joy in it?

"I figured a few weeks," Hope said.

"Hope, you'll be here until you're rebalanced."

Could that mean Hope might miss starting at Terra Pines High School? Could she miss Katie turning fifteen? Could she miss not getting asked to go to homecoming, not caring, picking out something not new from her closet to wear to the skate park instead; could she miss arguing with her mother about why she was going to the skate park instead of the stupid dance? The color rose in her cheeks. Tears began to well. Her body, however, stood rigid below the laundry. Her feet planted themselves on the floor, feeling as though they were setting down roots she didn't want them to have. She wanted to stare Agatha down, but her eyes kept darting from the stove to the cupboards to the laundry as though they might somehow land on someone new in the room, someone who could help, who could cool the heat on her face, open the fist around her heart.

"I'm sorry, pet." Agatha came closer. "I just want to be honest with you."

"If you're so sorry, you wouldn't have let her send me here in the first place." Hope pulled her legs up from the roots and stepped forward. "If you're so sorry, you could send me back any time. Tomorrow, even. If you don't know how, just ask my mom. She's great at sending people long distances on short notice."

"I'm sorry only that your mother was not clear with you, Hope." Agatha made a grab in Hope's direction. "I'm not the least bit sorry you're here. And I've no intention of moving you anywhere before you're ready."

"I'm ready now."

THIRTEEN
Agatha

Agatha hadn't considered anything about readiness or balance when she'd been just about Hope's age, facing the loss of her father. She had considered no other course of action than writing to her Aunt Wina.

Stories of Agatha's Aunt Wina said she came to life in the shadow of the black hills, as locals called the Black Cuillins, which rose from the belly of *An t-Eilean Sgitheanach*, the Isle of Skye. To the non-native eye, these remains of a Paleogene volcanic center looked to be great, dark mountains, formed around a million years ago, during a time the earth's tectonic plates grew restless. America pulled westward; Scotland drew herself east. Along the split, volcanoes that would become the Cuillins sprouted, brewing and then spitting their molten insides as though to sear shut the ragged edges of the riven earth. Were they healing damage or sealing off the possibility of reconciliation? Does it matter when the urge to move is overpowering, as it was for Wina from the moment she set foot on the island? Agatha's mother and father had said that Wina seemed to overflow with energy, her long legs gliding her back and forth from the feet of the hills to the southeastern edge of the island to gaze at the shore and rising hills of Glenelg on the mainland, as though something as powerful as the earth itself pulled at her. Having had a taste of expansion in the move to Skye from the Shiant Isles, miles out to sea, Wina had grown restless, in need of still more growth.

As a young girl, Agatha knew Wina, only twelve years older; she recalled Wina's bold departure for Glasgow and her subsequent returns to Skye, bringing Donagh with her, after the births of Agatha's youngest two sisters, Mairi and Ellsie.

Two days after the services for her father, Agatha stood on the shore, wee Ellsie on her hip, watching for Wina and Donagh. The boat—commonly called the poor-man's ferry— chugged across Kylerhea Narrows, barely having to push off from Glenelg into the swift current before the men were putting down the planks that served as the gangway, first for the odd car that managed over, and then for the pedestrians. The oil from the ship's exhaust choked Agatha's nose. She raised her hand to the woman she thought was Wina. When no hand replied, it occurred to Agatha to look for the tall, curly-haired Donagh, a head above any crowd.

Already waving from the other side of the boat, Donagh came off first, stopping at the end of the gangway to guide Wina down. A sliver of sun pierced the clouds, falling on them for a moment and making clear a few little lines at the edges of Wina's eyes, crinkling upward as she landed her hand in Donagh's. This, even as they came on the heels of a funeral.

"Agatha, girl." Donagh reached for her as soon as Wina had both feet on Skye. He wrapped his big arms around her and Ellsie and pressed the pair of them into him. The rough of his jacket scraped her face, the same texture as her father's jacket, though she couldn't remember ever being pressed so hard against him.

"You'll suffocate them," Wina's voice came in under his arm as she tugged Ellsie away.

Donagh held another moment.

"Look, you've left a mark." Wina pressed her long, gloved fingers against Agatha's cheek, cool on the hot, rough place Donagh had left. "Your ma," Wina started, shifting Ellsie to her other hip and taking Agatha's arm.

"We'll see her in minutes." Donagh took the other arm. "What about the girl who sent for us?" He turned to Agatha. "How are you? Can you be as well as you look?"

Agatha felt her own heat come into her cheeks. "I'm well just now."

He hesitated. "Fair enough. And so, your ma?"

Agatha shook her head.

Wina gave her arm a squeeze. "We'll get her sorted."

Wina and Donagh held her, one on each side, until the path narrowed to sheep track, and then Wina and Agatha kept single file along it, avoiding the squelch of the taller grass where Donagh strode. Wina's pace had calmed by then. Donagh was the one who moved briskly, his long legs allowing him to veer off to the water's edge ahead of them, looking out to sea, letting them pass and then catching them up. The familiar sheep dung and seaweed scents flushed away the oil and exhaust.

Agatha stood behind when Donagh ducked his head to get through the door. The heat rose into her face as she watched him survey the cottage, the fire burning beautifully, the floors cleanly swept, the nutty smell of the oaten bread wrapped in cloth, still warm, rising to greet him. Mairi and Anna sat on their bed, playing with their clothespin dollies. Except for her mother being in bed in the middle of the afternoon, the place was perfect.

Donagh took up Calum's stool by the fire, gathered the younger three into himself. "How would you lovelies like a tale of three girls much like yourselves?" Donagh began his first story of the Seelie world. His voice danced to a faster, lighter melody than had Agatha's father's, sang a different part of the scale altogether, but in notes that could have made a harmony with Calum's deep, craggy tones.

While Donagh leaned in and whispered of the fairy world as he'd known it in Kinsale, on the mouth of the River Bandon, Wina whispered the elder Ellsie from bed to chair. She pressed her lips to Ellsie's ear again when dusk fell and together they made their way to the rocks. Wina's words gave the elder Ellsie strength enough that night to sit by the fire. In the morning, Donagh and Agatha together rekindled it. Ellsie and Wina put on the porridge. Handing the spirtle to Ellsie, Wina turned from the pot and sat on stool next to Agatha.

"You'll come with us to Glasgow," Wina said.

"Me?" Agatha leaned away slightly.

"All of you. You'll come with family and not stay here and fall to the care of strangers. Or worse."

Of course. Agatha said nothing as she made for the door. She felt Wina's eyes at her back, imagined a glance between her and Donagh.

No one followed her. She might have liked to shed some energy on pressing one or the other of them back, on being adamant about going alone to the pushout.

Agatha dug her heels into the pebbly ground, as though she could root in the impression of herself. The next tide, or a rain before it, would clear her mark. She stared down the line her father had sailed, imagining him going again, out across the gently rippling grey waters, one last time. Agatha breathed in the salt and the seaweed. Wet grass and sheep dung. She held her hands still at her sides, her head high and her breath inside her for a moment. When she exhaled, she whispered, "*Is mise Agatha*," offering her name out to the sea to follow her father's.

Along the shore, she concentrated on the feel of her foot, heel to toe over black and grey and white and purple-flecked pebbles. She tried to memorize the strain in her calf or thigh when she stepped high onto a rocky outcropping. The chance of finding Rory out on the rocks was small but she went anyway, hesitating there. She knelt, fingering a jagged black rock. Another girl might have taken the rock with her. Agatha closed her eyes, stilled her focus to just the rock in her palm, feeling its edges poke the fleshy bump below her thumb. Before she turned toward Rory's cottage, Agatha hurled the rock to the sea, watched it submerge and gave it time to find ground.

The swish of cloth on wood called Agatha to the side of the MacKimmon's cottage, where Rory and his father hunched over the bow of their small boat. Agatha watched them for several minutes before they noticed her. Almost in unison, the pair straightened.

Agatha swallowed. She didn't like to ask Mr. MacKimmon to free Rory from his work. Neither did she want to have to say, out loud, to both of them, that she was to be taken away. The three of them stood, silent, father and son with their cloths dangling limply in their hands, and Agatha with words like rocks in her closed mouth.

Mr. MacKimmon pushed back his cap and wiped his brow, sweaty even in the cold air. "What brings you round of a morning?"

I've come for a quick word with Rory. Can I just have a wee word with Rory? Could Rory have a minute?

She opened her mouth. "I've come to say we're away. To tell you that Aunt Wina and Uncle Donagh will take us." She swallowed again, lined up her spine and her shoulders and her lips and brow so as to keep herself properly balanced. "They will take us with them to Glasgow."

Mr. MacKimmon pulled his cap back into place and bent to his boat. "You're due a break, lad." He angled his head slightly toward Rory as his hand connected with the wood. "Take your time."

On the shore, the wind picked at their hair, pulled Rory's steely scent over Agatha. At length, he turned to face her, stepping close but not touching. Agatha tried to take him in, deeper than words, willing the green of his eyes and rust of his freckles and blue of his veins into her. Rory seemed to do the same, finally taking both her winter-worn hands in his rough ones as though to seal in their knowledge of each other.

They had next to nothing to pack. Everything that was worth carrying fit into three cases. Donagh sold what he could: cow, chickens, goat. The rest they gave away. Two weeks to the day since Agatha had pushed Calum out for something fresh for their family, on a wild-aired morning, they followed Donagh and Wina to Talisker Bay rather than to the Narrows. Even that was too costly for their number. Donagh had made arrangements for them all to get a lift on the boat of a local man, heading for the lower western isles.

All along the walk Agatha's mother kept turning her head back toward the cottage, barely managing to keep pace. When it was her turn to step into the dinghy that would take them to the boat, she stopped.

"What if he comes back?" She turned in the direction of the cottage. Donagh leapt around the younger girls, sloshing across the shallows to catch and guide her.

The wind whipped harder once they were on the big boat, and Ellsie said again, "What if he comes back?" Agatha read this on her lips more than heard it over the sound of the air.

As the boat grunted, Ellsie stood on the deck, unwilling to go in or below, staring alternately back at Skye and out to sea, where, unseen but well remembered, lay the Shiants. Agatha stood beside her, one hand securely wrapped around her mother's waist. She caught sight of a figure sprinting along the edge of the high hills that sheltered the bay, then standing as they pulled away. Agatha held up her hand and saw Rory hold up his, not high, but open-palmed in front of their hearts. Agatha held like that until she could no longer see the dot of him.

An observer might have remarked what a comfort Agatha was to her mother, staying out in the sharp air and wrapping her so tightly in her arms. Agatha saw the rawness of her mother, her weakness from weeping and from walking the shore, waiting, just in case. She felt Ellsie's ribs through her clothes, more prominent than ever. One gust might have carried Ellsie away. Agatha hung onto the parent she had left. Even if she was scant and had hollowed in the past fortnight, the flesh of a mother was better than none at all.

Wina came up and asked them to come down.

Only Ellsie's hair moved. Wina tried her whispering again. Not even a blink.

"Will *you* not come down, then?" Wina widened her eyes at Agatha.

"And leave her?"

Donagh came and wrapped his long fingers around Agatha's and pulled them away. He wrapped his arm where Agatha's had been and lifted her mother easily. "You'll come down, woman," he said. "Before you hurt yourself."

She bit him.

He set her back down.

"Will you, so?" He held out his hand. Agatha wrapped her arm around her mother again.

Donagh leaned the side of his body against Agatha's, warm for a minute. He shook his head, dark curls wiggling at the sides of his cap. He left the pair of them, coming back to check and shaking his head a few times until it was time to step back onto the mainland and then to the train that carried them in from the coast, along the River Clyde, to Glasgow.

The year Agatha and her family arrived, Glasgow hosted more visitors than there had been permanent residents on Skye, perhaps in the full span of its existence. The Glasgow Exhibition drew over twelve million visitors, this in addition to the hundreds of thousands of residents. There had been fewer than ten thousand on Skye.

In the dark, that first night, they made their way to one of the sandstone tenements that had begun to characterize the city, the stone so light in contrast to the dark of the Cuillins they had left. After they had settled, Agatha would learn that, when the tenements first were built during the Victorian era, whole buildings belonged to individual families on the west side of the city. Only later, as they spread south and east, did they become divided into flats. The same buildings that housed one wealthy family on the west side were adequate for eight or ten lower-class families on the east and south sides of the city.

It was to one of these flats that Agatha, age thirteen, made her way. Her mother held onto one arm and baby Ellsie perched on her hip. Donagh held Mairi, asleep on his shoulder, and one of their suitcases. Wina had one hand in Aileen's and the other in Anna's; each of them carried a suitcase in her free hand. They passed street after street of red sandstone tenements, each one indistinguishable from any other. The sky, already dark when they got off the boat, blackened as they walked.

"No stars." Agatha didn't expect a reply.

"No, pet. No stars. Streetlamps instead" came Wina's voice in the dark.

Even the streetlamps were difficult to see, so dense was the black, as though the Cuillins had liquefied and drawn down, threatening to suffocate them. Agatha would soon realize that what shipyards and factories and coal fires in homes around Glasgow released into the sky seemed to fall back to earth each night, covering the city. That first night, only Agatha noticed the difference as they trudged along, hunch-shouldered, grateful to arrive at a ground-floor flat and not to have to drag their tired bodies and scant belongings up even one flight of stairs. They didn't know, nor would they have cared, that ground-floor flats were the smallest, since the broad entryway to the building and the path to the toilet and the yard took up space that became part of the flats on the upper floors.

Agatha and her mother and sisters and aunt stood in the dimly lit entryway. Gas lamps hissed, offering as much noise as light. Donagh worked the key in the door. Agatha looked up. She'd lived all her life in a cottage barely tall enough for a person to stand. Now the weight of three other families would lie on top of them.

Not even Donagh had to duck and enter face first. He went straight to start the fire, coal, with an ignition process altogether different to peat. Wina arranged the girls in their bed, a mattress on the floor where the sofa had been. Ellsie would claim her space in what had been the dining room. During the day, they would heave the mattresses against the wall and put the flat back together, almost as it had been.

When the Glasgow Exhibition was over and the city cleared, the war seemed to hang in the distance, at first like a squall out at sea, not worth the attention of a girl learning a new city and a new school and taking in new kinds of work to feed herself and her mother and her sisters. The Military Training Act, conscripting boys aged twenty and twenty-one, didn't pull it any closer. Then the city painted her buildings in oil or water mixed with black soot. As though it wasn't enough to hide her buildings, Glasgow set to squirreling away her children, issuing an evacuation order on August 31, 1939. Agatha packed her youngest sisters—gas masks, change of underclothes, toothbrushes and the other few belongings they were allowed—then she pinned on their labels, their surname the Anglicized *Stuart* by then. Although Agatha still fell within the age range of the children being evacuated, the order was voluntary and Wina thought it best for Agatha to stay with the elder Ellsie. The chance that any of the girls would be sent to families who would take in more than one of them was nearly none, so she wouldn't be able to help her sisters anyway. In Glasgow, her work would help the family, and her presence would mean Ellsie didn't have to watch all her girls go.

As it was, Ellsie didn't watch any of them go. Wina and Agatha took the girls to Queen Street station while Ellsie wiped the breakfast dishes again, crippling waves of tears spilling into the soapy water before the girls reached the front door. New rules insisted that the streetlamps be extinguished, the trams stilled, and indoor lights turned off. Alone in bed for the first time, Agatha imagined this dark to be the way it might feel to curl up inside one of the Cuillins, safe.

By March of the following year, the girls were home, along with most of Glasgow's youngsters, the threat deemed false as the Luftwaffe concentrated on London until all at once, without warning, despite the darkened streets and buildings, the Luftwaffe took aim at Glasgow's shipyards. Just across the Clyde from where Agatha slept, a whole section of the city— the homes and shops of Clydebank—was demolished in two nights. The adjacent shipyards were left unscathed.

A week later, Agatha came in, carrying sewing Wina had collected for her—buttons, hems, other embellishments from the west side. Donagh and Wina sat, alone for once, faces close and tight.

Agatha turned. She could start her work on the back steps, in the remaining light.

"Agatha. *Doithín.* Come in," Donagh called to her.

She stopped in the front hall, fixing her eyes on the tiles that divided the paint from burgundy bottom to cream at the top. She hesitated.

"Donagh, leave her."

"She should hear it now, Wina."

Agatha looked at Donagh first, finding his normally dark eyes nearly black under his wrinkled forehead. Wina's light eyes darted about the room. Agatha did as Donagh asked.

"You're finished your school in a couple of months. I've spoken to Willie Naismith at John Brown. The shipyard, you know. The best. A place at the best yard for you. A fitter's job. You'll have better pay than your auntie." He reached his hand out and cupped Agatha's chin. "Will you have it?"

"Of course I will." Agatha would have taken whatever work was offered. And this was good work. The women of Glasgow had flocked out of their homes and out of domestic service to take up men's jobs in factories and shipyards.

The three sat a minute. Wina fingered a loose thread on the hem of her skirt. Agatha stilled her hands on top of her mending.

"I'll be away, so, after you start," Donagh said. "With the other men. It's only proper."

On the longest day of the year, Agatha watched Wina and Donagh make their way arm in arm down Langside Avenue, as though they were on the way to a picnic instead sending him off to a war. "Right," Agatha said as the pair turned the corner.

Inside, her mother sat hunched in the chair by the front window, a blouse with missing buttons idling on her knees. The sewing box closed on the table beside her. Agatha set to work, rearranging the flat to reflect that there was one fewer body to accommodate. Wina and Ellsie would share Wina's bed. Agatha hauled what she could back into place, feeling the heat rise in her body from the physical effort and from the satisfaction of having done it herself. She set out her clothes for the next day's work. Donagh had passed the mantle to her. She was determined to deserve it.

Her mother didn't acknowledge her efforts. Her sisters didn't seem to notice. This gave her all the more satisfaction.

Agatha and Wina stepped briskly, each bearing a small bag of groceries, a Friday in March, 1943, two years after Donagh left. The war by then seemed almost normal. Wina struggled more than the rest, having not had a word from Donagh in more than two months. Opposite to Agatha's mother, Wina moved as she had in her younger years, nearly running out the door to work in the mornings and constantly scrubbing at the skirting boards or the counters or the floors in the evenings. Agatha had learned to keep pace with her.

As they neared the flat, Agatha noticed the back of a man, lanky and slightly stooped, leaning heavily on a cane outside the doorway. Wina squeaked. She dropped her bag. She lurched at him, nearly making the pair of them fall into the street along with the broken eggs and rump roast that Agatha stooped to rescue.

When she stood again, fingertips yellow from the yolks, Agatha noticed the slight tightening of Donagh's lips as Wina kissed his neck.

"I thought I'd lost you," Wina said.

Agatha pulled her stare from Donagh's lips, let them meet his dark eyes. They seemed even blacker than they had the night he'd told them he was enlisting. Wina wrapped her arms round Donagh's waist, pressed herself against his side, the same side on which he held the cane, as though she didn't notice it at all. Agatha's hands became sticky with drying egg yolk. The handle of the bag dug into her palm.

"Auntie Wina." Agatha touched Wina's arm. She cocked her head toward the cane.

Wina reached for it. "He can lean on me, can't you, pet?"

Donagh unwound his arm from around Wina. He lifted the cane over her head and planted it with a clack against the stone step. He pulled himself forward, wordlessly, his too-slim torso still strong enough to force Wina to either hang on and be dragged or let go altogether, which she did.

When he folded himself onto the sofa in the sitting room, Donagh looked as much like a large insect as he did his former self. There were only the four of them when Agatha brought the tea, if she counted the shadow that Ellsie had become. Steam clouded Agatha's vision as she poured for them. Mairi dribbled in, bored with the day; she shrieked at the sight of Donagh and flung her arms around his neck.

"Sit down, Mairi." Agatha's voice was higher than usual and there was more emphasis than necessary on the t. She handed Donagh the plate with the remains of the biscuits she'd secreted away from her canteen lunch at John Brown during the week. Donagh shook his head, turned toward Wina, took one of her hands in his. With the other, he reached into his pocket.

"I should maybe have come here first." Donagh pulled from his pocket a photo. He turned it face down on his leg. "But I wanted things settled."

"First?" Wina's chin wavered. "Where have you been?"

Donagh handed her the photo, which she held in her free hand, studying it for a moment and then placing it on the table. The rest of the women leaned toward the photo. Hills rose behind a white cottage. In the corner of the frame, the sea rolled.

"It's ours."

Wina looked at Agatha before turning back to Donagh. "Ours? To do what with?"

"To live in, Wina."

Agatha stood. She took Mairi's hand and nodded in the direction of the door.

"Stay." Donagh's voice froze them, Agatha and Mairi standing, Ellsie with her tea halfway to her lips, biscuit crumbs at the edges of her mouth. "Sit down, girls."

They did as they were told. They listened as Donagh told of wading through the waters toward French soil, of the bullet catching him in the knee, of the sand, wet against his face when he fell, cold in contrast to the warmth of the blood against his leg, of the words of the rosary, a whisper on his lips, of his eyes closing and the face of Wina filling his vision—then of Agatha, of the lot of them. He imagined the sounds around him as a kind of pipe band, playing his last tune: the guns like the grace notes on a fast jig all around him and the growl of the ship engines, the drones and the splash of the men coming in droves behind him like snare drums. The soft thump of other men's bodies meeting land, limp before they fully made France, the bass drum under it all.

"I expected the Mother of God when I opened my eyes," Donagh said. "Instead I got a pocky red nose with dangling grey hairs and cheeks with red spidery veins. Doctor Ahern. I knew I wasn't in Heaven then. I didn't know whether to be glad."

No one could tell him exactly how much time he'd lost, having hit his head on one of the very few rocks on the beach when he landed and having wandered in and out of consciousness.

"You'd think I'd want nothing to do with the sea after that," he said. "But it was all I could think of when I woke. The waters, and you." He turned to Wina. "I thought they would have sent you a note."

Wina shook her head.

"Ah, Wina. I'm sorry for that."

Wina's head hung.

"I had to have this done before I came back." He reached for her hand. "Mind I took you to the waters the summer I courted you? Mind the picnic in the cove, on the far side, away from everyone."

Wina lifted her head slightly. "I mind you nearly got us stuck, the tide coming in on us."

"And so, do you mind, as well, the cottage there, where we stopped and asked the fastest way back to the ferry home?"

"Aye." Wina lifted the photo. "How?"

"Soldiers get paid."

"But how will we live there?"

He fingered the handle on the cane. There'd be no going back to the docks. "Better than we'd live here."

Before the month was out they were gone. Agatha took Wina's place in the bed with Ellsie. She had learned to survive in this huge, new place, to navigate the city streets without a father. With Wina and Donagh gone and Ellsie a shell of her former self, Agatha would be mother and father to them all.

There had been neither time nor space nor energy to ask in what ways their lives might have been different had their mother been able to rebalance herself. Later, when she thought of it, Agatha told herself that it was mainly her life that had had to change. She had sheltered the others from the worst of it. She still did.

FOURTEEN
Hope and Agatha

Hope woke to a strange *click-click, poke-a poke-a poke-a* sound rising from the front room. She lay, half asleep in the semidark that passed for a summer night. If she could figure out what made the sound, she could settle back to sleep. The bedside clock ticked along in rhythm: 11:24. 11:25. The *click-a poke-a* sound prodded again and again, not quite loud enough to hear properly, but too insistent to ignore. When the clock showed midnight, Hope gathered her body from under the sheets.

In the front room, Agatha sat at an ancient foot pedal–operated contraption that looked as much bicycle as sewing machine. As usual, a small fire smoldered in the fireplace. The only other light came from behind Agatha's shoulder in the form of a weak work light, clipped to the back of her chair and shining on her bony hands as they fed fabric through the machine. The *click-click* matched Agatha's strokes on the foot pedal and the *poke-a poke-a* went along with the needle.

In the darkest corner of night that hung beside the door, Hope was caught for a few moments between waking and sleep, transfixed by the sight of the old lady bent over her work.

"You'll get cold in that corner." Agatha did not look up or break her rhythm when she spoke.

Hope held still.

"Since you're here, you may as well have a look." Agatha pulled the fabric from the machine and held up a pair of pants. "You'll mebbe still hate them, but I had to give it a go."

Hope moved forward, squinting. She took the pants from Agatha, looking from them to her to a tidy stack of folded fabrics on the table beside the sewing machine.

Agatha had cut up some of the clothes Hope's mother sent. She had combined pieces of the least obnoxious fabrics with some that must have been her own and made them into a pair of crazy patchwork pants—crazy cool patchwork pants.

"Not ideal, I know." Agatha stood, accompanied by popping and cracking in her knees. "But maybe good enough for an island where there's nobody watching you'd want to impress." She stretched. "Your mother put in a gift receipt. I suppose she thought there was a shop like this in Glasgow." She looked at Hope. "There maybe is but I can't see that a shop that sells all this," she lifted the pink pants, still intact, "would sell anything you'd like." Agatha stepped around the sewing machine. She lowered herself to the stool in front of the fire. "If they work, we can be pleased that we've exchanged the trousers for something that fits you better." Agatha held out her hands toward the fire, leaving Hope in the work light.

Hope held the trousers in her hand, felt their softness before she took them upstairs and pulled them on, half wishing that the fit was too big or too small, half wishing she wasn't thrilled when she buttoned the button and zipped the zipper on pants that had clearly been made for her.

"They fit," she called to Agatha. *Thank you.* She should go downstairs and say those words to Aunt Agatha, or at least shout them in that direction. Somehow, she couldn't make herself be grateful out loud. "Goodnight," she said.

She tucked back into bed. The noise that had awakened her was gone, so she should have been able to sleep. Instead, she lay there, turned to the window, listening to the waves outside, thinking about Agatha making pants just for her.

She must have slept, because when she woke, the clock said 3:17. Her stomach grumbled, ready for breakfast far too soon. She listened for an Agatha sound in the other room—a snore or an old lady gurgle or something. Nothing. For a few minutes there was only Hope, the half-dark sky, and the waves. She swung her feet to the floor, pulled on the Agatha-made pants over her pajamas.

By the time she made it to the kitchen, she was fully awake and pleased to have this little slice of night for herself. She slid a piece of Agatha's oat bread into the toaster and went to the larder to see what else there might be to silence her stomach. As she opened the door, a sliver of cool air called her attention to the fact that the front door wasn't quite shut. Agatha left it like that during the day when she was in the garden or just across the street. Hope peered through the gap. A slice of rocks and sky and sea stared back. No Agatha. Not even the goat. The moon, full over the sea, seemed to be waiting.

The toast popped. She slathered on some butter, slipped her feet into her shoes and stepped out into the night. For once, the wind was barely even a breeze. Even in the dusk that passed for night, the sky held more stars than she'd ever seen. Were those the same constellations that had once held so much interest for her?

Years ago, Dad had taken her to the observatory and planetarium on winter Friday nights. They'd sat through the simulation of what they would have been able to see in the sky if not for light pollution, leaning their heads back and watching as the narrator pointed his or her laser at first one then another star, drawing out Orion, the Big Dipper, the Little Dipper, the Seven Sisters, the star signs. What were their names? Which stars made them? She walked across the street, looking up at them, all so clear.

Still in sight of the cottage, Hope plonked herself down on a boulder, butter dripping down her fingers while she chewed the warm bread. She didn't so much hear as sense something coming down the beach. She turned in its direction.

Just before the place where the land rose and curved toward Lochranza, Agatha stood, tall and slim, with her long hair blowing around her. She looked like something from the sea, with her flowing hair and clothes, taking one step and then pausing in time to the roll of the waves. The toast turned cold in Hope's hand while she sat there, stuck to her rock and staring. Agatha seemed not to see her. Hope was not completely convinced it *was* Agatha until she sat on a smaller rock next to Hope.

"When I was a lassie, any woman caught wandering the rocks by the shore in the middle of the night like this would have been accused of being selkie. Any beautiful young woman, at least," Agatha said.

Hope waited.

"Sea spirits that are beautiful on land but can't stay there, and have to take on the shape of seals to go to their homes under the sea. Only their eyes stay the same. Their lovely eyes." Agatha lifted a pebble and tossed it into the water. "Some say they're fallen angels, too bad for Heaven and too good for Hell.

"As I'm no beautiful young woman and you're no fallen angel, I suppose we can ask the same question of one another this night."

Did Agatha really want to know why she was out?

"If you want to tell me, I'll listen," she said. "If you want to listen, I'll tell." She took a deep breath. "Or if you like the silence, we can sit in it."

Hope crunched her cold toast. She licked her fingers. Agatha's shoulder barely touched hers.

"You first," Hope said.

The breeze lifted Agatha's hair away from her face, then dropped it suddenly. "The obvious answer is that I couldn't sleep, but then there's plenty to do inside, isn't there? The truth is, I come out here quite often." Agatha kept her face toward the sea, lifting a flat pebble and tossing it out. "I stopped when you were first here, just to be sure you could sleep in this new place." She glanced at what was left of Hope's bread. "Throw that to the gulls," she said. "If you're still hungry, we'll get you a fresh bit inside."

Hope glanced down at the cold remains. She tossed the toast.

"I've walked this shore once a week, at least, all the years I've lived here. It's an old lady's eccentric habit now. What I think of while I walk probably isn't of any interest to you—sad wee thoughts of a crone whose father was claimed by the sea, whose sisters are gone and whose first love floated away before even your mother was a thought."

Agatha stared out a minute, tossed another rock, making it skip several times.

"I've told you my da died out there. Got himself swept away. I was just about your age when it happened. The sea might as well have taken my ma as well."

Hope shifted on the rock, faced Agatha, met her eyes.

"I lost Rory to the sea, in a way." Agatha held Hope's gaze for another moment, then looked away. When she spoke again it was mostly to the sea. "Not to death. The sea carried him away, first to France and then all the way over to Canada."

Hope picked up a rock and threw. It landed in about the same spot as Agatha's.

"Not bad." Agatha picked up another and threw it hard, making it disappear into the night and then splash down in the distance. "Shouldn't be too hard for you to beat an old lady like me."

Hope clutched another rock in her hand. "Who was Rory?"

Agatha tossed another rock, skipping it across the water, one, two, three, four, five times.

"I'm sure it will sound silly to you, coming as you do from such a big country and modern world." Agatha sighed, almost the way Katie had sighed over Adam Evans in social studies the year before. "Rory and I grew up on Skye together. It was he who made the box and the comb. We were heartbroken when my family moved to Glasgow. He stood on the shore with me the day we left and promised to come and see me. In those days, that was like promising to come and see somebody on the other side of the world."

She threw another rock, made it skip again.

"Not a day went by I didn't think of him. I don't suppose I'd have said I loved him at that time, only that I missed my friend."

She looked at Hope. "He came, all right. Right to the front door of the flat in Glasgow. Told me he was off to the war. Told me he intended to come back and make me his wife." Agatha reached out and touched Hope's shoulder. "I'll spare you the details of the visit, except to say that he brought me the box and comb." She shook her head. "He came home from the war. Told me he'd decided to set out for a new life in Canada, said he wanted me with him." She paused. "I hope he managed it, building the life he dreamed of."

"Why didn't you go?"

"I was the man's share of the income in my house at that time. Had I left, Ma would have had five mouths to feed. She'd have had one-sixth less needed at the table with four-sixths less to put there." She put her arm around Hope. "There's a lesson in fractions for you."

Hope tensed. Agatha squeezed, then dropped her arm.

"So I come out here to the rocks and walk. The waves sweep everything clear—all my wrongs, regrets, they wear them down. Those waves sweep a sleepless night past faster than sitting in that cottage in the dark, straining these old eyes to see something." Agatha bent and lifted a pebble, casting it out to the sea—far, by the sound it made when it entered the water. Hope thought of it sinking, straight to the bottom, and then lying there, stuck until some incredibly strong storm came to churn up the sea and move it somewhere else. She felt a bit like the pebble: picked up and tossed off and sinking to the bed of this island. When she'd first stood at Agatha's gate, Hope thought she would be the storm that would churn things up.

"Your turn," Agatha said.

Hope lifted another rock, rolled it in her hand. If she told the right story to Agatha, would it earn her release? If it did, would she wear her new pants home? Would Mom magically approve since they were made by Agatha? The stone's jagged edge jabbed at the flesh beside Hope's thumb. What if she told her own story? Would Agatha think she had to patch Hope together like the trousers, or would she tell Mom the first chance she got? Hope stole a glance at Agatha out of the corner of her eye. She reminded herself of that first day at the gate, noting the similarities between this bony woman and her skinny mother. Hope flung the rock.

"I'll pass."

They sat, then, in the dark on the rocks, Agatha thinking of what she hadn't told Hope, of the tales told by the fire on Skye, of her favorites—those concerning selkies. She'd never thought they were real; even so, she had been, still was, captivated by the notion of something that could move amongst the butterfish, the lemon sole, the lesser spotted dogfish, the translucent blue slugs (*Polycera faeroensis*) with their yellow-tipped spikes. Even the conger eel, lurking in submarine caves, would have to concede the beauty of the selkies, the light they shed in the dark, churning waters.

When they were girls, it had been Mairi who said out loud that she loved them, who clung to the idea that their father had been a selkie long after they left Skye. Privately, though, even after they settled in Glasgow, Agatha thought of her father as a lovely creature moving gracefully through the sea.

She had been recalling one of those tales as she sat, head bent over the sewing machine, an afternoon in the summer Donagh was missing during the war. Mairi and young Ellsie's voices had interrupted her reverie, shooting in from the front hall, calling, "Ag, Ag, Aggie, Agathaaaa."

No doubt Mairi had found some rare dead spider or broken toy or shiny shard of a thing over which she wanted Agatha to cluck. Or else the younger Ellsie was desperate for Agatha to come and put the lid back on the overflowing midden, as though it wasn't futile. She didn't have the inclination for it. She worked all week, putting together ships, and all weekend holding together her mother and her auntie and all the rest of them. As she went out to the hall, she concentrated on softening herself, unfurrowing her brow and lowering her shoulders and relaxing her throat so she could look at whatever it was and then shoo them gently back out rather than shouting at them to be quiet and let her work.

Agatha opened the door and found herself, instead, looking at a uniformed chest. She drew her eyes up.

"Rory." She ran her palms down her blouse and skirt.

"Agatha." He leaned in, politely kissing her cheek.

She caught Mairi and young Ellsie's wide eyes, staring as the heat rose into her neck and face. She should introduce him to the wee ones, take him in to see Wina and her mother, let him give his news of Skye. She took a small step back. She hesitated.

"Let's go for a walk," she said.

Rory bent his arm, jutting out his elbow for her.

Agatha delighted in the feel of her arm in his as they walked down Langside Avenue. She led them around the first corner, out of view. Rory stopped them as soon as they'd made the turn, grasping Agatha by the shoulders.

"Let's have a proper look at you then, woman."

She stood and let him take her in, long-legged and slim-waisted, her auburn hair by then cut to her shoulders, the waves just tipping her jacket. She scanned herself as he did, wondering if he'd notice the slight puffiness below her eyes from not sleeping enough, or feel the rough of her hands from near-constant work, or the pale of her cheek, all of which normally gave her a slight tinge of pride.

"You'll have some Glasgow lads going mad for you."

"I've no such thing." She'd had a few boys prowling about, but none for whom she had the time. Standing in front of Rory, she was glad of it. "And you? You'll have left some lassie in tears by the Narrows."

"I've not, and that's why I'm here."

"To make a lassie cry?"

"I hope not." He took her arm. They strolled on, stopping again at the next corner. "Agatha, listen. I've no intention of going back. I'm glad to be shed of the scraping and the dying."

"There's a war on, Rory. I think you're making your way *into* some scraping and dying."

"The war will end, Agatha. And if I survive the scraping and dying, and I will, I can do something else. Skye feels like a battle to me, every day."

Of course. Didn't young men die there, too?

"We should go back. I didn't tell Mam I was away out. And you should say hello to her. Bring her what news you have."

"One thing first." Rory dug in his pocket, pulled out a small wooden box. "A wee minding. Just a thing I did in a few spare minutes."

Agatha rubbed her thumb over intricate swirls in the wood.

"Have a look inside."

A wooden comb nestled within, the handle matching the carvings on the outside of the box.

"Rory."

"Agatha." He grinned. "I made it from the hawthorn tree, do you remember it?"

Of course.

"Struck by lightning. Nobody noticed until she shed her leaves in the middle of summer."

"They're gorgeous."

Rory wrapped his arms around her. She tucked her head in under his and nestled there. In those few minutes, Agatha felt more rested than she had since the night before she pushed her father's boat away from the shore for the last time.

They had two weeks before she saw him off to the war in France, waved as the train pulled away, braced for what would be.

Not much more than a year later, Agatha knelt in the dark soil of the garden plot she'd rented, hands wrapped around carrot tops. A light breeze lifted and dropped her hair. She pulled a cluster of green tops, deep orange rising out of the dark dirt, and tossed them to the small pile already started. Agatha lifted her face, closed her eyes and drew in the scant warmth of the sun and of the soil at the same time, loving the feel of earth and sky. The war was over. It was a hard thing to believe, given the remaining rubble and rations. Donagh had come home and gone again, taking Wina with him. Agatha didn't dare think too much on Rory, afraid she might tempt some ridiculous harm on him as he made his way back to her. Instead, she concentrated on what was in front of her that she loved—the ground itself and the food she harvested, always amazed at what she could get from a seed or a bulb, some nicely turned earth and her hands.

Feeling a shadow block the sun, Agatha opened her eyes and found Rory to be the cause of it. He lowered himself to her, then knelt, in his uniform, face to face with her, then kissing her, arms around her.

The Rory who came back to Agatha, after those first still moments in the garden, was more restless than the one who had left. He shifted, foot to foot, when he waited for her to go out. He walked the street in fits and starts, rarely willing to stop. Even when they were still, on the train or tram, holding hands, his pinky rubbed relentlessly on her wrist. She waited for him to settle back to himself.

When he came to her, a different Saturday, putting his hand on her leg to stop her pumping the sewing machine and said, "C'mon. We're away to Arran for the day," Agatha imagined a picnic on the rocks in front of Donagh and Wina's cottage.

Instead Rory quick-stepped from the ferry to a grassy spot on the south end of the island; he spread their blanket a slight distance from the others who had come, as they apparently had, to watch the trials of the liner the Queen Elizabeth.

"Isn't she gorgeous?" Rory opened their flask. "Look at her— newly released from the war. Look at her fresh paint."

"Aye." Agatha took the smallest of sips.

Rory said nothing else as they made their way through luxurious egg salad sandwiches made from extra eggs Rory had wangled from a farmer friend in Ayrshire. Agatha watched his face as he studied the liner. She found his broad jaw and strawberry hair and freckled hands as they had always been. His body sat still, legs stretched out in front of him, calm as he had been before the war. Agatha softened. She breathed in the seaweedy scent, watching as Rory licked stray egg salad from his fingers. He rose and reached for Agatha's hands to pull her up.

Rory stood behind her, close. "She's going to sail right the way across the Atlantic, Agatha."

"Is that so?" Agatha reached for his hand, pulling him gently against her.

"Listen, Agatha." Rory wrapped both arms around her. "Come away with me. Come away from these black buildings and nights so dark we can't see even ourselves. Come away to Canada." He pulled one hand away from her, rustling in his pocket.

"Canada?" Agatha wrapped her arms around herself. "I thought. I thought." What had she thought? That they'd get married and stay in Glasgow, with or near her sisters and what was left of her mother?

Rory held the ring over Agatha's shoulder. "Will you come away to Canada and be Mrs. MacKimmon?"

Agatha had not shed a tear on the shore saying goodbye to her father, nor had she shed one on the boat, holding her mother and watching Rory disappear the first time. She thought there might be some when Donagh and Wina announced their move. And again when she parted from Rory a second time, and to war at that. Even those she restrained. Agatha could do nothing to stop those that came on the shore of Arran, watching the huge liner, named after and steered by the queen.

He straightened, turning her in to his arms. She looked into his broad, freckled face, his brow furrowed.

"How can I?" The words squeaked out.

"Never mind that. Do you want to?" He had her by the arms, his hands so tight they hurt.

In the end it hadn't mattered what Agatha wanted. She would not leave her mother and her sisters. Rory could not resist the call he felt to take to the waters. He took his time. He asked Agatha again, three times: as he booked his passage and as he packed his few belongings, and after, once more, on the shore at Greenock. Each time she said the same thing, that she couldn't, that her mother and sisters needed her.

"You're a stubborn woman," Rory said, there on the shore.

Then it was Rory who watched as Agatha stood on the shore and became smaller and smaller until she disappeared.

He'd been gone a month when Agatha slid out of bed and took the train and the ferry, alone, for the first time. A Saturday in 1945, she wakened in what counted for the dark of an early June morning, swung her feet out of the covers. Her mother, by then the smallest person in the flat, lay still, her hair on the pillow the most lively part of her; the rest of her slim body mingled with the humps in the comforter. Agatha tucked the sheets and blankets snugly around her. She slid into yesterday's clothes and held her shoes in her hand as she made her way out the front door.

Down Langside Avenue she walked, alone. There was not so much as a birdcall or a cat skulking about as she walked toward the train, stepping briskly along the street and back through the progression of memories that had led her here. Agatha stepped onto the first train of the day, feeling the pain again of Rory's hands on her arms, so present she had to rub them to be sure it was a memory. This first train would get her to Ardrossan in plenty of time to board the ferry before the weekenders and daytrippers poured themselves aboard *The Waverly* or one of the other steamers, great dollops of humanity piled onto the boats like lumps of clotted cream and strawberry jam on a fat man's scone, jiggling with joy at the prospect of going *doon the water* for the afternoon or for a day or more.

Agatha sat straight, holding still against the *ca-chuck ca-chucka* of the train. Glasgow pulled back from her, was replaced by Ayrshire moor, then rolling hills curving up from the coast, dotted with a few brave trees whose branches grew in the direction on which the wind insisted, a kind of natural Bonsai.

When she stepped off the train, she turned to face Arran before she boarded the ferry. Goat Fell, with its jagged top like a black ragged nail, rose, accusatory, from the softer, green land below. And then the whole island becoming gentler as it rolled south. Wina and Donagh would be stirring as Agatha boarded the ferry. On the other side of Arran, hidden from view, they would make the sounds of their first wiggle toward each other—the clearing of Donagh's throat, the whispers. "Mornin', *doithín*," even though Wina was too old for the word to truly fit.

On the ferry, Agatha sat with her back to Arran, watching Scotland go. How far out would you have to go in order for Scotland, and all her inhabitants, to become invisible to you?

Long before anyone with a picnic and a tartan traveling rug thought of arriving, Agatha stood on the rocks, staring out at Holy Isle, and beyond it the blue hone granite plug of an extinct volcano now called Ailsa Craig, sticking up right in the middle of the Firth of Clyde. Beyond Ailsa, unseen, rose Ireland and then the great, wide Atlantic, and on its other side, Canada. Agatha became aware of her clothes, worn already, chosen because they were handy. She stood tall, shoulders back, felt the presence and absence of Rory, wished she'd put on a bit of color to her lips or cheeks as though he hadn't said goodbye at all, stepped down the gangplank, and sailed away; as though he might come round the corner or off *The Waverly* or just appear, as he had in the front hall of the tenement, as though people dashed back and forth from Canada to say they were wrong, that they loved her enough to stay.

Her sisters at first refused to believe that there was no lad, present and in the flesh, to whom Agatha snuck out, once a month, in the dark, telling herself that it wasn't too much to take for herself: one morning and the price of a train ticket and a cup of tea on the way home, steam rising as Glasgow reeled her back in.

Who knew how long Agatha might have gone on like that had her mother's voice not slithered out to her another morning, a Saturday in March.

"Take me." Ellsie's voice was so quiet Agatha at first thought she imagined it.

She hesitated on the edge of the bed, then turned. Ellsie's long fingers wrapped around the top of the blankets, pulled up to her chest. Her white hair tentacled out from her on the pillow.

"Mammy."

"Take me to the waters with you."

The muscles closest to Agatha's spine tightened. A fluid line of cold ran down it like the run of water from her hair in a hard January rain. She'd told no one exactly where she went these mornings, and had let the sisters have their fill of taunting her with their imaginings of what she got up to.

"It's too cold, Ma."

"As though I've never felt a breeze."

Agatha stood, drew her hair back from her face, let it go.

"Once more to the waters."

"There's plenty time to go to the waters when it's fair again."

"I want to go today. With you."

They stood, the pair of them, on the rocks, not at the normal place where Agatha stood, but down a bit from Wina and Donagh's cottage. Ellsie's white hair flew out behind her, her shoulders rounded into the wind in a way they hadn't when she'd waited for Calum on Skye. They'd barely planted their feet firmly when Agatha turned, ready to go up and knock on Wina and Donagh's door, to take tea with them.

Agatha took one step and felt the scrape of her mother's fingers at her sleeve. She hesitated, wanting to move forward to the warmth of the cottage and the chatter. Ellsie's fingers hung on her cuff. Agatha turned to her mother, wrapped an arm around her, rounded herself against her mother's body, not looking out. She let herself curl into her mother for a few moments, then pulled herself up.

Agatha brushed away whatever stray flecks of sand the wind had brushed over her. She straightened her skirt. She had young sisters not twenty miles inland who needed her yet, who deserved more than what they'd get if she allowed herself to be consumed by hope or grief. She turned away from the waters, at last accepting that, like a selkie, Rory had been unable to resist a call and claim on him, so much greater than whatever claim she might have had.

It would be decades—until she moved to Arran herself—before Agatha would go to the rocks alone again. When she did, she sat, more often at night than during the day, leaning only a little into herself, not giving a hint that, like igneous rock, she'd let the loss of father and lover remain at her core while the rest of her life built up like sedimentary rock, knitted so tightly that the core could only be discerned if someone were to be, in the first place, inordinately curious, and in the second, equally determined to discover what lay at her heart.

FIFTEEN
Margaret

Layers of scent—fabric protector, new leather, some sort of cinnamon-sweet air freshener likely meant to cover up the chemical fabric protector smell—gathered around Margaret and Trig as they entered the furniture store, the third one in as many weeks.

"This one." Trig grabbed Margaret's elbow and pulled her down into a plush leather two-seater, deep and dark.

"I can hardly find myself to get out of this thing."

"Oh, fine." Trig pushed Margaret up.

The two of them gazed out over miniature den after miniature den, the possibilities stretching back toward the horizon at the end of the store, post modern to Victorian.

"You take that side and I'll take this," Trig said.

Margaret meandered through more dark leather, a couple of Bauhaus numbers. She shooed away a toupeed salesman in the middle of the art deco section.

Just past a cluster of Victorians, she turned to see how far she'd come, irritated with herself for not having found anything yet. There was no Brad at home to consider. Hope hated everything she chose right now. It should have been easy. Far from her, the light streamed through the front windows. Margaret sighed, shrugged, steeled herself to finish her side. She spun around, determined, and bumped into the broad back of a man, his bald head shining under the lights.

"Sorry," she said.

He turned. "No need to be sorry." His voice, big as his stature, was filled with rounded, slightly southern syllables. Margaret colored.

"A little overkill, isn't it?" he asked.

Margaret nodded.

"You buying a whole living room set?"

"Just a sofa."

He cocked his head.

"The old one wasn't working anymore."

"I hear you. My whole den isn't working."

Margaret laughed, a little high-pitched. She hadn't been this close to a man since Brad. She stepped back, into a Victorian, all delicate legs and curls no one could settle into. "This isn't going to work either." She sat anyway.

"I don't really know what's going to be working for me. Just thought I'd get an idea of what's out here. I don't even have a house yet to put it in," he said.

Margaret stood. "Are you looking?"

He was. Freshly transferred from Austin, Texas, Tim Arthur was in the market for just about a new everything, having leased his house in Texas, fully furnished, while he tried living in Terra Pines. Margaret handed over one of her new cards.

"Mags MacPherson? Nice to meet you."

She extended her hand, shook. "My pleasure."

He found her again before he left. She walked him to the front door, watched him climb into his red Solara, waved him off. She'd see him again in the morning. Nine a.m., her office.

She might have fought harder against Tim's idea of driving, of having her ride with him, had the sky been anything other than a perfect, clear, vivid blue, the air just a bit less humid, holding the promise of an early release from summer. She liked her car and she liked being the driver. Still, the idea of having the top down, of letting him steer, somehow appealed, at least for the few moments it took for her to get from the front door of her office to the front seat of Tim's car. She slid into the passenger seat, put one arm on the door rest, one on her lap. She shifted both hands to her lap. She lifted her list of listings, held it in both hands like a girl holding a Bible at her first Sunday school reading.

"First stop, Arco's Mill," she said.

"A mill? Like a converted one?"

"A subdivision. Where there used to be a mill. Near your new office. All new. You could pick your colors. Maybe even your living room set."

Arco's Mill, Falling Leaf Plantation, Sugar Valley, Standing Springs, Hammet Mill. Through all of these, Tim kept a poker face despite the fact that each home had all the items Tim had listed on his priorities.

"Where do you live?" He turned to her as they pulled out of the last driveway.

"Bent Creek."

"Let's look there."

"It's not close to where you work."

"Let me have a look anyway."

"I don't have the listings. I don't even know if there are any suitable ones."

"So we'll drive through today and I can get a feel, and if I like it you can look for something next time."

Almost at the corner of Live Oak and Bridwell, on the way out of the neighborhood, he asked if they'd passed her house.

"It's not for sale."

"If you pointed it out, I could pick you up tomorrow, if the weather holds."

"If my daughter were here, she'd say you were stalking me."

"Stalking? A daughter?"

"Yes, to both."

"How old?"

"Fourteen."

"You don't look old enough for that."

"Surely you can come up with better flattery than that if you're going to stalk me. Left here."

"Would it be evidence against me if I asked to buy you a coffee before I take you back to the office?" Tim's head shone in the sun. His teeth, flawlessly white and straight, beamed out of the corny grin he shot her. Tanned hands on the steering wheel. Coffee.

"Could it be tea?"

"Whatever you like. Unless you need to get home to your daughter."

"She's." Margaret paused. She folded her listings. "She's staying with my aunt tonight."

Tim leaned over his coffee, broad hands flat on the table.

"What do you like to do when you're not wandering around in other people's houses or searching for the perfect sofa?"

"I…" What did she do? "I run."

"For fun, I mean."

"Running is fun."

"So it's Friday. It's five o'clock. The office is wiped out, you've found the perfect sofa and the perfect houses for your clients, your daughter is with your aunt—or maybe even out with her friends having fun. You're going to run the night away?"

Margaret straightened. "Actually, I run in the mornings." She dunked her teabag in the cup of steaming water. "To start the day with fun." She sized up Tim. "How would you recommend I spend the Friday night in question?" Margaret leaned back, pulled her tea to her lips, only half-listening as he rattled off his suggestions.

What did she do for fun? What *had* she done for fun, even before the accident? She'd clung to a fourteen-year-old resolution to be out no more than once a week so they could have family dinners. Her social life consisted mostly of PTA meetings and real estate certification classes.

She hardly noticed that Tim had finished talking, dug into his pocket, paid the bill. He came around the table, took her cup and set it down, then pulled her upright.

"Come on."

"I haven't finished my tea."

"I'll get you another later, if it's what you still want."

Outside, she let Tim lead her to the car. They drove down a zigzag of streets and parked near the flat, grassy banks of the Pipsissewa River, which ran through the center of town. She let him take her hand and pull her out of the car. In stilettos and a skirt, Margaret watched as Tim removed his shoes and socks, rolled his trousers, and stepped up to the rocks at the edge of the water. He turned.

"Do I have to come and get you?"

"I'm not dressed for this."

"That's part of the fun."

He took two large steps toward her.

"Okay. Okay." She bent, pulled off her shoes, surprised to hear her own laugh.

They waded to the middle of the river, cool water around their ankles and calves, almost balancing out the humid summer air. Tim moved closer, his chest millimeters from her.

At home, he walked her to the door. On the front porch, he drew her to him. "You could invite me in," he said.

"Maybe next time, when I have a sofa."

He bent, lips just grazing hers at first. Margaret closed her eyes, the heat of the night and of Tim's body enveloping her.

"We don't need a sofa," he said.

"I need a sofa."

Tim nodded and let her go.

Alone inside, she leaned against the door, heart pounding. She wrapped her hands around her own waist, realized she was smiling—cheeks puffed out, eyes crinkling—and that she'd left her shoes in his car. She didn't bother with pajamas, throwing back the cool cotton and falling onto her bed under the stir of the ceiling fan. How long since she'd had such simple fun?

SIXTEEN
Agatha

Agatha first encountered treacle toffee when Donagh pulled it from his pocket and offered it round the flat not a month before the rationing started. That night, they all gained a taste for what would soon be unattainable. It would be years before they'd have it again. The feel of it in Agatha's mouth always connected to that first year in Glasgow, and so to Donagh. Sweet and slightly bitter, the treacle was a comforting distraction in those first months in the tenement.

Later, when Donagh was at war, Agatha had looked it up. Could she make it, or an approximation of it, for herself? Hold in her mouth the bittersweet that Donagh had introduced? Feel the sweet balm slide within? Not likely. It came from the syrups that remain after sugar has been refined from sugar cane—genus *Saccharum*, family *poaceae*, tribe *andropogoneae*. She could hardly get her hands on sugar, much less cane.

Over twenty years after that first taste, on her way to see Donagh on Arran, Agatha thought of it as she passed the sweet shop near the railway station. She stopped in and paid for a handful of round, individually wrapped treacle toffees.

On the train, Agatha tucked her hand into the paper bag, causing crinkles and stares from the old lady across the aisle, a further pursing of the lips when Agatha unraveled the wrapper. Who could know if it was from the sounds of the waxy paper peeling away from the hard, black sweet, or from the fact that she declined to offer the bag round? Agatha slid one oversized toffee into her mouth whole, even though she was thirty-five years old, far beyond an age at which filling one's entire mouth with anything was remotely appropriate, especially in public. Agatha's lips tried to curl into a smile as the edges of the sweet, bitter round began to melt. The toffee took up too much space to permit a smile, but the attempt caused a little of the black juice to slip out at the edges of Agatha's mouth. She didn't bother retrieving a hankie from her bag, just dabbing her lips with a bare finger. The old lady across the way tightened her gloved hands on her handbag, cleared her throat.

Agatha's eyes began to water from the delight of the toffee, and, somehow, though it wasn't like her at all, at the old lady's prim irritation. She imagined sitting by the willow and the elm, telling her own little story to Donagh, a funny one at that, something to give, in addition to the toffee, a new addition to this Saturday ritual that had developed between the pair of them since the last of her sisters left.

Agatha sucked her treacle and listed to herself the times and reasons she'd taken this train: with Rory, for the final picnic; with her mother to visit Wina and Donagh; with the younger Ellsie, along with an American, James, whom Ellsie had discovered at the Festival of Flowers and wanted to show off.

At the ferry dock, at the end of that day with Ellsie, Donagh had leaned into her. "Soon be just the pair of us." He'd angled his head in the direction of Ellsie and James.

Not even a pair. Donagh would be there on Arran, alone, and Agatha in Glasgow, alone. She'd come back the next month, struggling to abide the weeks on her own. And the month after, and then, when Ellsie married James, twice in the same month. By the time Agatha sat dabbing at leaky treacle toffee juice on the train, it had become a weekly ritual, beginning with the walk to the station, the train and the ferry and the lovely stroll over The String to the cottage. From there, she'd step out with Donagh, sometimes starting by the waters, sometimes by the road, sometimes over the stile and straight to the glen, always fitting in a trip to the willow and the elm they'd planted in memory of Wina and Agatha's mother, the elder Ellsie.

Normally Agatha and Donagh stood side by side, silent. On the day that Agatha handed Donagh his bit of toffee and he unwrapped it and slid it into his mouth, he curled his hand around hers, as if this, too, was what they had always done.

"D'you miss the flat, bursting as it was?" Donagh asked.

Agatha absorbed the feel of Donagh's fingers more than his question. "It isn't a thing I care to think about."

"You're not lonely, so?"

Agatha turned to him. "I keep up with them all, their worries and excitements."

"I remember coming to you on Skye and asking were you okay, you, a young slip then and taking on the lot of them. Do you recall the three of us, walking from the ferry?"

Agatha nodded.

"On a day not unlike today, with its swirling wind, as though the sky herself can't manage to settle. And you, saying you were fine when you couldn't possibly have been."

"If I recall correctly, I said I was fine 'now.' Now you and Wina were there."

"And so, are ye fine, with them all away?"

She thought of them all—the elder Ellsie and Wina, taken early, the pair of them, by a fast-moving cancer. Aileen, gone away to Canada on the arm of a man, flowers in her hand but no ring on her finger. Anna in Australia, already with child. Mairi, having trained to be a chartered accountant and marrying and then leaving the man on his own in Belfast while she went away to work for weeks on end in places as far-flung as India. The younger Ellsie in America with her American. All of them, like so many others, leaving the country for what they thought would be better lives.

"I'm fine just now," she said.

Agatha turned for the cottage. Donagh followed, the pair of them stretching long legs across the rough terrain, stepping easily over the Rosa Burn, the stream that marked the entry to the glen. The swirl of the winds and the call of an osprey and the squelch of damp grass underfoot stood for conversation until they climbed back over the stile out of the glen, crossed the fields of the farm next door and stepped through the back door of the cottage.

In the kitchen not long after, steam rose in Agatha's face. Donagh, beside her, arranged cups and saucers on the tray. A stray wisp of hair, still wavy and wild but now starting to show white amongst the auburn, curled out and hung at Agatha's cheek. Donagh's big fingers reached for it, pulled it out of the steam, tucked it behind her ear.

"Would you think me awful if I said you look gorgeous there?" Donagh asked.

The kettle began the moan at the start of its long whistle. Agatha held her hand on it, the heat building to the point of burning.

"Maybe."

The kettle's high scream rose. Donagh's hand landed on Agatha's as she lifted the kettle.

"Maybe you could say it anyway," she said.

Donagh poured the boiling water into the pot, closed the lid, gently, causing the china to clink, bone on bone. He turned, slid his hand into hers. Agatha felt his palm against hers, his fingers against the back of her hand—broader than Calum's, more callused than Rory's, his touch gentler than both, just there against her, neither grasping nor threatening to leave.

"You look gorgeous, Agatha."

She felt the color tiptoeing up her neck and into her cheeks; the strand of hair popped out again from behind her ear. She reached to put it back, met Donagh's hand again, stilled, dropping hers to her side while Donagh brushed back her hair.

He held his palm against her cheek, barely touching. "Absolutely gorgeous."

She thought she should say thank you. Or maybe he expected her to say something flip or to return the compliment, to say he was not at all bad himself, which was true. Donagh was fifteen years older than she but looked no more than five, still the muscled man he'd been when first he arrived on Skye over twenty years before. She glanced at the teapot, nestled in its cozy; thought of the china underneath, of the heating of the bones until they crumbled into powder, of the mixing with kaolin to become elastic so as to take new form, of the tea brewing within.

"The tea will be bitter if we leave it too long."

"Aye." Donagh turned toward it.

Agatha's fingers curled around his hand.

He turned back to her. "If need be, we can pour out the bitter and make more, sweet as you like." Donagh slid his hand, slowly, out of hers and around her waist, pressing gently, his hand in the small of her back, asking her to come closer.

He lifted Agatha's hand, lightly kissed the tip of each finger, holding her gaze all the while. Agatha slid her other hand around his waist, fingers shaking as she pulled herself against him.

We can pour out the bitter.

In the front room, decades after that first kiss, Agatha folded her morning paper in half like a piece of clothing she might have to wear somewhere special. She tucked it under her arm, retreated to the kitchen, and returned with a bowl of porridge and a shoebox.

"Eat up, Hope," she said, her voice bright. "I've a lovely lesson for us today." Agatha dug rocks from the box, setting them gently on the hard placemat at the edge of the table.

Hope slugged back the ration of orange juice that Agatha served in teensy little glasses. Agatha lifted a rock.

"Permineralization," Agatha said. "The most famous of the ways to make a fossil." She raised a rock, dark grey and embossed with what looked like the delicate legs of some lanky insect. "Petrification—that's what most people call it. They think it's the only way the earth captures things and preserves them, keeps them here for us even after their whole species is extinct." Agatha set the rock on the table, holding her hand on top of it for a moment before reaching into the box again. "There are actually four other ways in which fossils are made."

"Really? Fossil fondling?"

"I do, indeed, have some examples for you to hold." Agatha turned the rock in her hand. "And I've some lovely pictures I printed out from the Internet on Jenny Telfer's computer."

"Who is Jenny Telfer?"

"Kenny's mum, dear. Unaltered preservation, for one. This would be, for instance, when an insect becomes trapped in tree sap. In due course, the sap turns into a piece of lovely amber." Agatha stroked the fossil in her hand. *Unaltered preservation could also take place when a kiss, for instance, becomes encased in a soul and turns into its own kind of perfect amber.*

SEVENTEEN
Hope

Hope turned away from Agatha and her fossils when she heard the squeak of the letterbox flap and the flump of the mail on the floor.

"Away you go and see what we've got, then," Agatha said.

Hope returned, waving a hand-addressed letter for herself.

Agatha sat back in her chair, thumb rubbing across one of the rocks. "On you go, then—the fossils will likely keep a wee bit longer."

On the bed she didn't sleep in, Hope peeled back the stuck-down part of the envelope as slowly as Agatha sipped her tea. She lifted the flap, pulled out the lone sheet of paper, unfolded it, and read.

Hey grrrl –

Waz ↑ I wish you were here to go with me + Josh + Mike + his girlfriend Stella to Pizzarilla's – it is sooo fun out there these last weeks of summer + my Mom +Dad let me stay out later because they like Josh and they think it's much safer than, "2 young girls at the skate park." How dumb but anyway I'm glad they do. I got totally bored when you were gone at first, but now I go with Josh to the climbing gym some. I am so much better at climbing than I am at skating. 'course I'm comparing myself to you, the pro who no-one can touch. You should see if there's someplace to climb on Arran—a gym or something.

> *Guess what else? Josh already asked me to go to TP Hi*
> *homecoming. Can you believe it? I haven't even officially*
> *started hi school and I already have a date for homecoming.*
> *I shouldn't've told Mom—she already wants us to go*
> *shopping for an outfit. It's gonna be so cool anyway.*
>
> *I got ur letters but you didn't say when you were coming*
> *back. I thought u'd already be here, so I got Josh to ride*
> *me by ur house so I could ask ur Mom. I wound up not*
> *stopping cause she was getting in a convertible with some*
> *big baldy guy. Well, gotta go.*
>
> *K.T.*
>
> *(get it? K.T. –*
> *Katie but looks cooler.*
> *Josh thought it up. ☺)*

> *P.S. I saw it there again—the red car—the other morning*
> *when we drove past.*
> *P.P.S. Write soon and tell me when you're coming home.*

The letter shook in Hope's hand. *Baldy guy?* She set it on the
bed, clamped her hand on top of it, breathed, lifted her hand,
reread. She thumped downstairs, past the fossils and into the
kitchen.

"Can I call my mother?"

"I'll show you after I finish the dishes."

Show me? "Can I just call her now?"

"Aye."

Hope picked up the heavy black receiver on the phone. She
dialed the number. A smooth English-accented voice welcomed
her to Vodaphone, then told her she'd dialed a wrong number.
Hope dialed again, got the message again, hung up.

She poked her head into the kitchen. "Phone isn't working."

Agatha wiped the last dish, drained the water out of the
tub. She carefully placed the dish in the cabinet and folded the
dishtowel before she pushed through the door and walked to
the phone.

"Did you use the country code?" Agatha dialed the number, handed Hope the phone, and pointed to a sheet of paper on the desk that listed the codes. She walked away. The door to the garden shut at the same time as Margaret's voice came across the line.

"MacPherson Realty. Mags MacPherson."

Hope's chin jutted forward slightly.

"Hello?" Her mother's voice again.

"Mags? MacPherson? What the ef? You've changed your name? You've gotten rid of our name?"

"Hope." she paused. "Hi, honey. It's lovely to hear your voice."

"Lovely to hear my voice. Mom! I call up. I call up to talk to my mom, Margaret Carver, you know her? I want to talk to her—the person who sent me three thousand miles away. Where is *she*?"

"Oh." Margaret breathed in audibly. "Hope, it's okay. It's me. I'm still your mom. I'm still the same person. I'm right here."

Hope held the phone out and away. On the other end of the line this Mags (what kind of name was that?) MacPherson twittered on. MacPherson was reserved for Granny. Hope was a Carver. Margaret had been a Carver when Hope left. Was there anyone she could count on anymore? Was there any reason to hold anything back? Hope closed her eyes, visualized being at the edge of the half-pipe she'd imagined on her first day at Agatha's gate. She pressed the phone back to her face, pushed off. The words rushed out.

"You haven't been my mom since before Dad even left. You haven't told me anything about what you know about Dad or where he is or anything. You've exiled me to the far side of the planet and as soon as I'm gone, you change your name and take up with some bald convertible driver? And you think you can act like it's another beautiful day in the neighborhood?"

"Hope, calm down. Oh, Hope. Oh dear. Where is Auntie Agatha?"

Hope held the phone out again. She'd finally said just a few of the things she'd been wanting to say, and all her mother had to say was *calm down* and *where's Auntie Agatha?*

"Auntie Agatha is in the garden," Hope said, voice steady. "I'll go and tell her there's a call for her." She set down the phone, pressed through the door to the kitchen, and opened the one to the outside. She closed the door just sharply enough to make Agatha turn from her digging and squint, her eyes not able to take even the weak Scottish sun that slanted through a gap between clouds.

"What is it, pet?"

"Someone called Mags MacPherson is on the phone for you."

"Can you not write down a message?" She held up a pair of mucky hands.

"She asked specifically for you."

"Fair enough." Agatha pressed herself to standing. She tilted her head, puppy-like. "Mags MacPherson? Your mother?"

"So she says."

"*Uabhasach.*" Agatha wiped her hands on her apron, made her way inside.

Hope bent to the dirt and picked up Agatha's trowel. She stabbed the dark, fertilized earth again and again. After a few minutes, her arm aching but still wanting more, Hope lifted the spade that rested on the fence. She stepped to the left, began gouging and turning, gouging and turning, moving to the thick, wet grass rooted in peaty gley beside the plant bed. She didn't care that the peat might have been cut into neat rectangles, dried, ignited to warm the cottage. That had she left it alone, it might, after a few generations, have formed the highest rank of coal, anthracite, boasting the most carbon, the most metamorphosed. Instead of leaving the little patch of partially decayed vegetable matter to take the earth's own time with transformation, Hope and her spade took charge of things. She turned it to the sky, chopped it into smaller and smaller pieces, bent to separate clods, churned the soil to make it into finer and finer grain.

She was still digging when Agatha came back out a short while later.

"What a mess," Agatha said, standing behind Hope, hands on hips.

Hope looked down at herself, spattered in dark dirt.

"Och, not you, pet. This Mags MacPherson bit. Your mother says somebody thought it was catchy—some friend of hers who does advertising and things of that nature told her she should be something a bit more interesting than Margaret, and that using her maiden name would catch people's attention and stay in their minds. The two M's."

"Somebody was right." Hope tried to shake the dirt off her hands. The black muck hung on. Would it stain her clothes the way Terra Pines clay left its mark on whatever it touched? "What about the baldy?"

"Just a client," Agatha said. "Not to worry." Agatha rested her hand gently on Hope's shoulder. "Looks as though you've started a lovely new bed in which to plant something."

They finished turning the soil, working under a rare, bright sky and the gaze of the goat at the wall. What they might plant was irrelevant. The gritty feel of the shovel connecting with the dirt felt right. Hope bent to grab the soil, breaking up a stubborn clod; the cool muck climbed over her skin, the closest to perfect she'd felt in a long time.

EIGHTEEN
Margaret

Margaret had been hurrying to her car when the phone rang: an unidentified caller. *A new client*, she thought. Perhaps even Tim, whose number she hadn't yet programmed. She needed gas before she met him across town for a second look at a house. Margaret waved to Clarie, her office administrator, and walked briskly out the front door.

"Mags MacPherson," she'd said, the name strange on her tongue.

Hope's voice had been a surprise. In the summer sun in her treeless parking lot, her back to the door, Margaret listened to Hope say she hadn't been a mother since Brad left, heard herself ask for Agatha as though she was the child in need of help.

She's tried to explain about the rebranding. How could any of that hold meaning for Agatha? She'd stammered through an explanation of Tim.

"A client," she'd said. "He picked me up."

"Picked you up?"

"Not like that." Margaret touched her hand to her brow. "He drove us to a house showing."

"Aye."

"And even if there was something with me and Tim, isn't it okay for me to have a cup of tea with a man? Or a drink? Or some fun, Auntie Agatha. Can't I have a little fun?"

"Aye, of course you can."

"Can you say anything other than *aye*?"

"Aye, of course."

"Shit."

"Pardon?"

"Nothing."

"On you go, Margaret. I'll get Hope sorted. She'll be fine. You know what teenage girls are like."

Margaret hesitated, a line of sweat snaking down her spine. If she'd learned anything from living with Hope, it was that she knew nearly nothing about teenage girls.

"Auntie Agatha?" She was too late. The double beep sounded: call over.

Would Agatha really get Hope sorted? Was she, Margaret, entitled to some fun? Was her staff staring at her back through the windows? Could they guess that her face was scarlet, eyes brimming? She didn't turn and look. She strode to her car. Inside, she stifled the need to check herself in the mirrors, reversed, checked her watch. Just enough time to meet Tim if the lights were with her. She turned the air conditioning on high, rolled down the windows.

Tim pulled up behind Margaret as she cut the engine in the driveway of the three-bedroom Cape Cod with wooded lot and brook in the back, everything he said he wanted: built-in gas grill, rock patio, outdoor fireplace, vine-covered pergola adding to the shade. Margaret headed there first, perched on the built-in bench. "So cozy—perfect for entertaining."

He sat next to her. For a moment, all she could hear was the flow of the creek. "Nice and private," he said. His thigh, firm against hers, nudged lightly. He pressed closer, ratcheting up the heat, even in the shade.

"Let's look inside again," she said.

In the foyer, light from the second-story window poured down on them.

"This could be perfect for you," she said.

"I agree." He moved closer, his face leaning to hers.

She felt the heat rising again, warring with the cool of the climate control. Her chest tightened; her toes curled in her stilettos. Tim got close enough for her to breathe in the subtle, musky cologne of him. His lips against hers, thinner than Brad's. Margaret opened her eyes. She pulled back, pushed her hand against his chest, removed it quickly.

"I can't do this."

"Why not?"

"I can't go around kissing clients in people's foyers."

He reached for her waist, pulled her back to him, gently. "Come on. I thought I was getting to be more than a client. I thought I felt something from you."

"You did. But I. My daughter." She hung her head. "I'm married. I'm sorry. I'll get you another broker."

"Not necessary." He dropped his hand, stepped back.

She stood under the shower of sunshine in the foyer while he sauntered out the front door, pausing to look at the house again before getting in this car. When she heard the door close, she stepped out and locked the keybox.

In the car again, still in the driveway, Margaret waited until she thought he must be far enough away. Then she laid on the horn. *Brad*, she thrust the heel of her hand against the horn. *Hope*, another blast. *Shit.*

She turned for home, heavy on the gas on the highway, tires almost squealing around the corner of the off-ramp, not caring who or what might be on Hot Springs Road, just wanting to be home, even if her den was still a partially furnished cavern. Here she was, thinking she was going to get this one little thing she wanted…

The car slowed. She crushed the gas pedal to the floor. The engine died. She coasted to the grassy verge, sat, hands on the wheel, looking at the controls, wondering what the hell could be wrong and feeling it slowly settle that she had, for the very first time in her life, run out of gas. She was a mile from home. Two miles from the nearest gas station.

At least an hour, Triple A said. She'd walk. Surely there was a gas can at home. She could change her shoes and clothes. She could jog back. She stepped onto the grassy verge, heels sinking in. She took three steps, stopped, turned back to the car, climbed back into the driver's seat, pulled off her shoes and stockings, started off again, shoes in hand, pencil skirt with side ruffle preventing her from taking full strides. An hour to send help. What the hell did she pay Triple A for? And then herself—letting Hope get her so flustered that she forgot to get gas, and then letting Tim refluster her so she forgot again. *Shit.* She picked up the pace, stepping short and fast. She hiked up her skirt to free her legs.

A carload of teenagers whooped as they passed. Margaret clenched her teeth. A county roadworks crew honked. The inevitable pickup truck, faded orange, 1970s vintage, pulled off on the grass just ahead of her, four men in the front seat. Margaret stepped out onto the road, a bumpy section that the road crew had apparently not reached.

"Want a ride, sweetheart?" The driver, tanned and lined and sporting two days' worth of five o'clock shadow, poked his head out the window.

"No, thanks."

"These boys'll be happy to hop in back and make room for you, darlin'."

"No, thanks." Margaret passed the truck, asphalt heating her feet almost to the burning point.

"Lady like you ought not be walking the side of the road. Sure you don't want a ride, sugar?"

Margaret stopped. She turned. "I am so fucking sure. Thank you." She marched on. Having, for the first time, directed the F-word, out loud, at another person, she found she liked it.

"Fucking rednecks," she muttered.

"Fucking gas."

"Fucking Triple A and their fucking hour wait."

The list went on: Tim, Hope and her histrionics, Trig and her rebranding, Brad and his drugs. Margaret fucked her way onto Bridwell Lane, forced to walk the road there, to feel on the bare soles of her feet the pavement over which she'd driven and run for years. Bits of loose asphalt clung to the delicate bottoms of her pedicured feet, digging in while she walked, making her swear more—fucking county and its paving priorities. She wished she'd taken the longer way around to the other entrance to Bent Creek, where the grassy verge led straight into smooth sidewalk. She straightened her shoulders as she approached Clyde's house, trying to look as though this might be part of a new training plan, walking the side of the road in a pencil skirt, carrying her shoes. She raised her hand as Clyde raised his.

"Right nice day," he called.

"Perfect," Margaret said.

"You taken to jogging without your shoes? Or is it driving without your car?" Clyde steadied himself on the porch rail.

"I ran out of gas."

"Want a ride?"

"I'm nearly home."

"You got a little ways yet."

"It's not far."

"How you getting back?"

Margaret hesitated.

"Come on up and I'll get the truck and ride you the rest of the way. Carry you to the gas station."

"I'm fine, really."

"You're dang stubborn is what you are, turning down a ride so you can walk all the way home, then all the way to the gas station and then all the way back to your car."

Margaret let her shoulders drop. He was right. She didn't want to walk all the way back, getting passed by teenage boys and randy rednecks. She stepped in and up the path, Clyde's eyes on her the whole way.

"You look like you ran out of more than gas, there."

"I'm fine."

"Set a second and gather yourself."

"My car."

"What you think is going to happen to your car? Ain't no gas in it. Cain't nobody drive it away."

Fuck it. Margaret sat.

"That's better. Rest there a second." Clyde did his usual disappearing act, came back with a mug, which he handed to Margaret, empty. He sat, reached beside his rocker, lifted a bottle, poured.

Margaret rose.

"Just set. You need a little nip."

"I need to get my car."

"We'll get her directly. Set. Sip. We'll get you back out to her in half the time it would have taken you to walk."

"How much have you had?"

"Just getting started. Don't you worry."

"I really shouldn't." Margaret started for the steps.

"All right, then. If you're sure."

Margaret sighed. She turned. Clyde poured into his own mug.

The bare grain of the wood under Margaret's feet seemed to scratch an itch she'd hadn't previously noticed. "One won't hurt. And then we'll get my car?"

"Well all right, then." Clyde raised his glass.

Margaret lifted the mug to her lips, paused. Clyde was watching her, hard.

"Something I ought to tell you," he said.

Margaret straightened.

"I saw your girl."

Margaret set down her mug.

"In the woods, on my land, by the creek, asleep. A few weeks ago. Reckon I scared her."

"My daughter? What makes you think you saw my daughter?"

"I followed her home, saw your car. I been wanting to tell you since I saw you with that flat tire."

"You followed my daughter?"

"Not like that. To make sure she was okay. A young girl like that, alone in the woods in the middle of the day when she ought to've been in school." Clyde edged down the porch. "I thought she might be fixing to run away."

"Why would you think that?"

"Them trash bags. Like she'd wanted to pack and then didn't have no suitcase or didn't want no one to know. Just seemed like something wasn't right with her."

"Bags?" Margaret stared into Clyde's face, reading the craggy lines.

"I went back after, thinking I might bring the bags. I looked in them." Clyde hung his head. "I know it wasn't none of my business. I's just worried. Didn't know what to make of it—it was all man clothes in there."

"What did you do with them?"

"Left them, there by the creek. Checked on them. She didn't come back. And then the weather looked like it was going to take a turn for the rainy. Didn't see no sense in letting them waste in the woods. So I brought them here. I kept thinking I ought to bring them to you. But what would you have thought, a strange old man at your door with two big ol' trash bags? And then I saw you out there with that flat tire. I could hear Mildred's voice then, saying, 'Clyde, you get on out there and help that girl.' So I did. I just couldn't find the words to ask about your girl right then. You look right pale." Clyde took her elbow. "Come on and set and sip. Even Mildred liked a little nip now and again."

Margaret eased her elbow out from Clyde's grip. She curled down to sit on his top step. She clutched the mug in both hands, tilted, felt the liquid, honey-colored, burn beautifully down her throat, tracing the inside of her. Clyde lowered himself, slowly, to sit beside her, mug in hand, George Dickel tucked between them. Margaret set down her shoes. One tipped, tumbled down the stairs, landed on its side at the foot of the steps. *Fuck it.* Margaret lifted the bottle.

NINETEEN
Agatha

On a clear summer morning in 1977, Agatha slid out of bed and, instead of padding downstairs to start the kettle, went to Donagh's room, or what used to be his. She slid Donagh's favorite shirt from its hanger and slipped it around her shoulders. The small buttons, white and shiny and smooth, tested Agatha's fingers as she pressed them through the tight slots. How Donagh ever managed it, with his long, broad fingers, she couldn't fathom. The collarless neck, a bit frayed, stroked the skin of her throat. The shirt, white as the day Donagh bought it and flawless except for the loose edges at cuff and neck, turned into a drop-shoulder number on Agatha, the seams landing halfway down her upper arms, at the precise place where Donagh had always wrapped around her. She stood in front of the mirror, rolling the sleeves, one broad turn, maybe five inches. Agatha rolled again and once more. She could have gone out like that, onto the shore, to walk or dig or whatever else might have seemed right. The shirt was long enough. Just that and her Wellington boots would have done. Who would care, anyway? No one was there to see. Only the occasional tourist might pass in a car, and even those didn't see her. She could have pulled on her own skirt or trousers, tried tucking in the long tail of the shirt or just leaving it flapping. The skirt lay rumpled on the floor and her trousers hung in her wardrobe, in the other room, which she'd taken up in the months since Donagh's death.

Agatha stood in the room she'd shared with Donagh every Saturday since that first kiss in the kitchen. She lifted a pair of Donagh's trousers from the hanger, fawn-colored tweed. She was surprised, although she shouldn't have been, at his slim hips, not so much bigger than hers.

Outside, she was surprised again, this time at the weight of the sapling she'd had delivered. Donagh had lifted the willow and the elm easily, slung each one over his shoulder and marched along beside her as though it had been no more than a bunch of bananas or a bag of treacle on his shoulder for Wina and Ellsie. Agatha dragged the sapling for Donagh behind her, gathered the shovel and urn from the shed, stepped in the direction of the stile and beyond it, to the glen, her hair loose, already white.

Seeds could have been sown instead of saplings planted for all three of the trees, but with sheep and goat and deer in the glen, even the saplings were in danger; with osprey and gulls above, a seed or two stood even less chance. And Agatha wanted to be sure the tree would survive, grow tall and strong beside the willow and the elm.

Afterward, wild-haired and dirty-cheeked, she walked to the other side of the glen, climbed to the top of Goat Fell, let fly the rest of Donagh's ashes in the direction of Ireland. She came down the easy way, ignoring the stares of red-faced, potbellied men and their pink-cheeked women with rainbow-striped camera straps wrapped around their necks, the legs that poked out below their shorts like thick lengths of unbaked bread. Agatha strode along in the grass, hair waving behind her, shovel in one hand, empty urn in the other, not breaking her stride until she propped the shovel against the whitewashed wall outside the Sheiling.

Within, she ignored the sudden silence of the room, dimly lit and spattered with the white faces of men given up on the week's work, the whole room like a sky at dusk, darkening with every moment and with a new white star showing nearly as often. Agatha had only once seen this room with its full complement of darkness and white-faced stars: in celebration of Donagh's sixtieth a few years before.

She set the urn on the bar.

"Y'alright there, Agatha?" the bartender asked.

"Quite fine, thank you, Malcolm, or I will be if you'll pour me a dram. Bushmills, if you please." Agatha clasped her hands and rested them on the bar as though preparing for prayer.

"Whisky, Agatha? Bushmills? Donagh's?" He glanced at the urn. "Aye. Right. Fine."

He set the drink in front of her, golden in the glass, a little oil on the top, the residue from the peat through which the waters had flowed. Agatha turned the glass, savoring the idea of drinking in the peat, dark and rick and dead, fuel for the fire that warmed them, flavor for the waters that nourished them, and for the whisky as well. She waited for the whisky to still completely, shunned the water jug Malcolm set on the bar for her; tipped the glass, held it in her mouth a moment, making the burn deepen, linger. *Uisghe beatha*—water of life, water from death, water for Donagh.

She slept that night in Donagh's clothes, lifted the lot of them out at dawn, built them into a mound in the back, put flame to them and watched them smolder, then catch. When the flames made a sure fire, Agatha stripped in front of them, tossed her garments on. Bare, she stayed until the fire smoldered again. She dressed in the cottage, took to the rocks. It was then that she felt the start of the small knot in her belly. She pushed it away. She would keep moving, make herself more useful. She would absorb the grief the way the earth takes on new layers of detritus, fodder for new growth.

It was less than a year before Fiona, daughter of Doreen, daughter of Aileen, arrived at the gate of the cottage, hiding under her hair.

TWENTY
Hope

Hope pulled the layers of blankets up over her body. She was a fossil, there in the dark, leaving an impression on the bed. Her dad was a fossil too, a thing that had left his impression preserved in her bones. Her mother was trying to scrape him away, shedding even his name. Hope closed her eyes.

She dreamed about being with her dad in the snow, wearing his sweatshirt. Both of them wore huge snowshoes. They schlumped along the beach on Arran, side by side, until they got to the curve where Hope had seen Agatha the night she went outside and sat on a rock with bannock. In the dream, when they got to the curve, Dad crossed in front of Hope and his snowshoes somehow disappeared as he walked away into the dark water, as if he belonged there, like one of Agatha's selkies. When he was all the way up to his neck, he turned and mouthed *I love you*.

Hope woke, wrapped her arms around herself, confirming that she was there, wearing Dad's sweatshirt in the room at Agatha's cottage. She told herself everything was okay. She repeated it again and again, rocking herself to sleep with the words. She fell back into the dream again and again.

At a little after three, she couldn't stand it anymore. The dream wasn't okay. She wasn't okay. She pulled back the covers.

Of course, Agatha was there, as if she'd been waiting for Hope to take a seat next to her in front of the fire.

"I keep having this dream," Hope said. She sat down, pulling her knees to her chest.

Agatha peered over her glasses. "Do you wish to tell me?"

Hope shrugged.

"Might help to get it out in the open air, away from you." Agatha poked at the fire.

"My dad," Hope started. She stumbled, then told the dream in a rush, her throat tight and her eyes watery but not spilling over.

When she finished, she rested her chin on her knees.

"*Doithín*," Agatha said.

They sat, silent, for several minutes.

"Shall I tell you what I make of that?"

Another few minutes of just their breath and the crackle of the fire.

"Sure."

"I think you're right on the mark. Your dad does love you. And just at the minute, he's lost at sea. And it isn't at all your fault, pet." Agatha rested her hand on Hope's knee, let the night settle around them for a few minutes. "Can I tell you a dream of mine?"

Hope pulled her legs into her chest, pressed her face into her knees, nodded into them.

"I'd this dream just when your dad left. The same one again a few days before you had the argument with your mother— the one about the pill. I say it was a dream, as that's what your generation would call it. To me it was a visit from *caoineag*."

"A what?"

"A kind of a witch—you can't see her, only hear her when she comes, normally in the night."

Where else would Agatha go but away with the fairies?

"In the old days, every good family had one. These days..." Agatha paused, shook her head softly. "There's not many left who can hear her. Of course nowadays, most people are the sorts of people who are content to buy things like tomatoes in grocery stores, as you call them. They don't pay attention to the whole tomato; they only want something round and red to put on their sandwich to make it look pretty. They don't care about what's inside. You maybe have an idea of what I mean."

"What about your dream?" Hope asked.

"Aye, of course. The *caoineag*. I heard her weeping. That's her job—you hear her cry her warning. I heard her when your granny had her cancer discovered. And then she came to me just before your father left.

"I phoned your mum the next morning," Agatha said. "It was too soon. She was cross with me for asking what was happening. I was never her favorite, but you'll know that as well. I don't think she would ever have phoned me and admitted it on her own. I kept hearing the weeping, though. I knew there was more to it." She turned to Hope. "They say the *caoineag* of the MacDonalds keened before Glencoe, before the Campbells snuck in and massacred them." Agatha came around behind Hope, wrapped her arms around her and rested her chin on her great-niece's head. "You've been caught on a battlefield yourself, I know— one that feels as big and bloody a massacre as ever played out on any desolate moor, and more so when someone disappears altogether. That would bring even the strongest warrior to her knees," she said.

Agatha stayed still, arms tight. Hope wanted to rip away. She wanted Agatha to hold her even tighter. She wanted to cry. She wanted to not cry. Agatha held and held, and Hope's will to hold herself in loosened.

"Mom called me into the den," she started.

Her mother had been tense when her dad was on the couch day after day, not healing, but the arguing didn't really start until he'd begun to heal. Margaret's anger felt like a long, razor-edged rail that Hope had unwittingly leapt onto. She and her father had been riding it. That last night, the raised voices stilled, then Mom called her name. Descending the stairs was like heading toward some unseen end of the rail on her board. There was no way to know whether she'd be able to leap clear and land well or if there would be some hidden obstacle waiting for her.

"They tried to tell me he needed special therapy for something that hadn't healed properly after the accident. I thought that was as bad as it could get."

Leaning into Agatha, Hope let go. She cried freely, shoulders shaking. She let Agatha rock her until the tears stopped, and then she let Agatha pull her up, wrap an arm around her, walk her up the stairs, tuck her into bed.

Agatha hardly had the door closed before the shame crept under the blankets, feeling like a living thing, growing as the hours ticked past. If she'd felt as though she was teetering on the edge of some X-games-sized half-pipe that first day on Arran, she'd surely dropped in, rolled down and down over this new terrain. Instead of gaining the pace that would roll her over the belly and up the other side (had she been so stupid as to think she'd have enough pace to throw in a trick on the way?), she found herself stopped completely, crumpled on the floor of the half-pipe, bleeding her insides out to Agatha. Skaters downed in the belly of the pipe had only two options: be carried off and forfeit the competition, or slither up the slick sides to try again.

Hadn't she been scaling the smooth sides since Dad left? Enough. Her mother could have her stupid name and the bald guy to go with it. Katie could have Josh and homecoming.

Hope pulled herself out of bed, dressed, and left the cottage.

South along the coast road, in the predawn, Hope walked, seeking direct contact with the earth—no help from her board. She would make her own momentum. The wind howled. The sky showed the stars perfectly. Agatha had said that, at the turning points of the year, she could see the Northern Lights. She'd told Hope how, at the top of the world, ionized nitrogen atoms reclaimed electrons. When that happened, and when nitrogen, along with oxygen, returned from its highest state of energy to its lowest, grounded state, the night sky found itself adorned with swirling ribbons of green or red or blue light. The Aurora Borealis typically only showed themselves near the equinoxes, Agatha had said. If you saw them, they'd stay with you for a lifetime.

Agatha had also said that her own mother, Hope's great-grandmother, had known none of the science of the Northern

Lights, and that if she had, she would no more have believed
it than kids Hope's age believed the old fairytale version. Ellsie
believed the same as everyone who lived in the northmost parts
of Scotland: that those shimmering colors in the night were
either fallen angels, jangling indefinitely between Heaven and
Earth, or they were the Fir Chlis, the Merry Dancers. Maybe
in another few generations, Agatha said, teenagers would think
the electron story so much myth.

How could you tell where the truth lay?

Maybe angels weren't unhappy to have fallen. Maybe it
stunk being up in Heaven with all those perfect souls. Maybe
they felt neglected by God. Maybe jumping was the best option
at the time.

Hope steered herself off the road and onto the rocky shore.
The grey of the impending day began to bleed into the charcoal
night sky, as she walked the pebbled beach, turning her face
from the sea spray spatter. The rising tide washed her dream
back to her. Hope turned inland, away from the cottage; cut
through the back of Kenny's garden, crossed the fields, climbed
the stile, and stomped on. She might have heard him call out to
her. She didn't stop or look back.

Just beyond the stile, a goat stared at her and chewed. They
all looked the same. Hope would have sworn they were really
one goat, Agatha's goat, following her everywhere, if it hadn't
been for Kenny. *Hallo? This is Scotland. There are goats.*

By the time she passed the fences in the glen, she didn't
care anymore about the goats. She broke into a run. The sun
reddened the clouds as Hope jumped the Rosa Burn, almost
making it. Her left foot sunk into the mucky edge of the bank.

She passed the sidhe and the thorn tree, starting to sweat.
She unzipped her jacket, and the wind pushed it out behind her
like a bright blue cape. Hope pushed harder and harder against
the wind, feeling as though her feet could move her almost as
fast as her board. She ran for miles across the rock and grass
floor of the valley. She ran with her mother's voice calling
behind her and her father's face in front of her. She ran until

both of them blew away and left wind and breath and heart and then, when she finally stopped on the saddle, only the sound of blood pumping in her ears.

The land fell away on either side. The sun had already passed its peak. In front of her lay the rock-scattered valley, the river wandering down the middle on its way out to the sea. Behind, the valley of Glen Rosa rolled back as far as she could see. Cir Mhor rose to the left. *Alluvalite, peridotite.* Goat Fell climbed to the right. Hadn't Agatha said it took her a full midsummer's day to get to the top and back? Hope picked up a rock and flung it hard. It bounced down the hill, smaller and smaller, bashing itself on other rocks, out of control, finally landing too far out to be seen.

She lifted another rock, then another and another and another, the harsh grey stone leaving tiny indentations in her hand as she gripped and released, gripped and released. She felt she could go on like that forever. The sound of them bouncing down the hill, a rockfall splashing down to meet the water instead of the other way around, was more satisfying than screaming, more satisfying than giving in to tears. She threw and threw, not stopping when the clouds closed in and the drizzle started. Her throws got harder as the rain got faster. All three of them—rain, rocks, Hope—felt like a full-on storm together. Her head and chest and belly pounded and rolled in rhythm with the other two.

At some point she turned and began to climb. She didn't bother to zip up her jacket. Her dad's sweatshirt got wetter and wetter. She clutched a rock in each hand. If Dad had felt at all like this when he drove away from their house, then by now he was totally stuck somewhere too, stuck and ashamed.

And maybe not able to face even me.

Who knew when that might change? Hope climbed, hand over hand in some places where the trail wasn't clear so she made her own way, not stopping until she reached the indicator at the top. Agatha had said she could see Ireland from there on a clear day.

Beyond it lay America and, somewhere, Hope's father. She moved to the edge. The valley stretched out hundreds of feet below her, the stream wiggling through it. If she leapt, how many flips and twists could she complete before she hit the bottom? She tossed one of the rocks, watched it dance, bouncing against the cliff face all the way down. Only something formed from all the elements of the earth and worn by time would be able to survive such a tumble. Hope rubbed the jagged edge of her last rock. She sat.

TWENTY-ONE
Hope and Agatha

Hope still hadn't moved, slowly growing numb in damp clothes and clutching the rock in her haggard palm, when gnarled fingers squeezed her shoulder. Agatha reached over and plucked the rock from her hand the way she would pluck a piece of fruit she was harvesting. She tucked it into her pocket and sat down, there in the rain with a yellow rain slicker that made her look as though she was about to go out hunting whales or salmon or whatever swam in the waters around Arran.

"*Dóithín*," Agatha whispered, wrapping first a blanket and then her arms around Hope. "You're safe here." She sat beside Hope on the top of the mountain, above the valley, the sea, and even her own life. "*Mo caileag, mo luaidh*," Agatha said. Hope understood.

The rain had stopped and the low sun started to sink behind Cir Mhor when they turned in the direction of the cottage. They would have to make the last of the walk home in the dark, feeling their way across the rumpled floor of the glen.

Agatha kept one arm wrapped around Hope for as long as they could manage to be side by side on the descent. In the flat of the glen, the sun cast scant light from behind the hills that hunched over them. In Terra Pines, Hope would have been soaked in sweat had she stayed out the whole of a summer day. Running as she had might have made her dangerously dehydrated. As it was, she began to shiver as the light disappeared. Agatha stopped and pulled the rucksack off her bony shoulders. Cool air dug into Hope's wet skin as she lost the contact. She bounced, hoping to

warm up, her dad's voice a whisper in her head: *If you're cold,
you just gotta work a little harder. You make your own heat out
here.* She'd heard those words so long ago and far away they
might have been said to some other girl.

"There." Agatha strapped on a high-tech-looking headlamp.
"Birthday pressie from another great-niece of mine. We'll need
it later, at the rate I walk these days. Saves me hanging onto my
big torch."

Hope knew Agatha meant flashlight, but she couldn't help
but think of Agatha tromping through the glen with one of
those gigantic flaming torches used to light medieval castles or
lead the way on witch hunts.

"And now for you." One hand produced another headlamp,
the other a pair of pants and a sweater. "There's a tree just there
you can hide behind if need be."

A sapling stretched toward the grey sky.

"You'll end up in hospital if you don't change into something
dry. I should have made you do it before we left the saddle."

Hope squelched off behind the sapling. She peeled her
father's soaking sweatshirt off her body and replaced it with the
dry sweater. When she turned back around, Hope found Agatha
perched on a rock. Next to her, a goat sniffed the backpack.
Agatha poured tea from her flask.

She held out a cup. "Help you get warm before we move on."

Hope took the rucksack when they stepped off, surprised
at the heft of it, surprised at how little progress they had made
by the time the darkening clouds erased the day completely,
muffling all but the slap of their feet through damp grass and the
swish of Agatha's legs against her slicker. The beams from their
headlamps mingled, forming one triangle of light into which
they walked. Unseen ripples of the glen stretched out and away.
How far back was the saddle? How far to the left until the hill
rose, leading to Goat Fell? How many steps toward their little
luminous triangle until they reached home?

In the woods at Issaqueena, trees framed the trail, guarding
sentinels showing the way, affording markers of progress on

even the blackest night—the fallen pine to bunny hop near the start, the water oak with the split trunk whispering that they were halfway, the twisted hickory before the curve saying they were almost home. Dad, warning her not to over-ride her light on the descents, to keep her pace slow enough to reveal hazards—high roots or newly fallen branches or forgotten rocks and ruts—soon enough to make the necessary adjustments.

They were at no risk of overstepping the light there in the glen, sloshing along, side by side. Hope swung her light left, searching for any mark—the little hawthorn, the sidhe, the stream with the humped bridge, the one with no bridge at all, even the stile that said they were not so far from home. She hadn't paid enough attention on the way out to notice anything further. She swung the lamp back, to the right, landed on the Rosa Burn snaking along the valley. Ahead, several tributaries would cross their path, most just narrow twists of water. That much she knew. They would have to make their way over them all before they would pass the sidhe, climb the stile, navigate the last of the glen, enter the cottage, build a fire. How far until they reached any of that? Hope faced forward, slapped on under the sliver of moon rising. A couple of times she thought the goat had given up, but when she swung her headlamp in its direction, it was always there.

"What's with the goat?"

Agatha took her hand. "Funny animals, aren't they? Funny eyes they have, always looking through their lashes as though they know a wee secret. That one following us looks not unlike the one who's been hanging about on my wall, eyeing my snowdrop bulbs, amongst other things. Moira thinks she's a *glaistig*, as she's said to anyone who will listen and a few who won't. I think she's a glutton, waiting to stuff herself when I'm not looking."

For the first time, Hope wanted Auntie Agatha to keep going with a story, even a fairy story, to help them out of the valley, and to distract Hope from feeling like a total jerk—the kind of neophyte who tries a half-pipe far too tall for her and then holds up everyone else while they lie broken or bleeding in the bowl, waiting for someone to cart them off.

When they reached the largest of the tributaries without a bridge, Agatha let Hope go ahead, her light beaming over Hope's shoulder. Hope jumped the stream, walked on. Agatha's light wavered, then disappeared. The goat bleated. Hope swung around, caught sight of Agatha, one foot caught under a rock, hands stretching out in front of her. Hope sloshed into the water, arms and legs swinging as if they could do something to stop Agatha from crumpling down. If she cried out or made any sound at all, Hope didn't hear it. When Hope reached her, she looked like another rumple of rocks in the streambed.

"Never was much of a dancer." Agatha held a hand out, her voice not sounding as jovial as she surely intended.

Hope grabbed her wrist and pulled.

Agatha winced. Hope let go, reached under Agatha's arm the way she'd seen her dad do with a big buddy of his who had tried to show off, bunny-hopping a log at the edge of a steep hill on the Lick Fork Creek trail. She struggled to pull Agatha upright. They nearly fell again just getting her untangled and onto the home side of the water. They stood, headlamp to headlamp, both aiming downward so they wouldn't blind each other, neither wanting to look at the leg Agatha had hurt too badly to put weight on.

"I'll just sit a minute, if you'll help me there by the tree," Agatha said. She hopped away, steadied herself against something that looked as much shrub as tree and crumpled down, gulping in the dark air. The goat ambled over, still chewing, still staring. It bleated aimlessly at the dark. "Maybe Moira's right about you." Agatha patted the goat, her voice thin.

For the next few minutes, none of them made a sound. The breeze whistled through Hope's jacket and sweater and dug into her skin. The goat nuzzled the rucksack.

"You'll need to go for help," Agatha said.

"No."

"I'll be fine. I've the shelter of a tree—a hawthorn, mind—and I've our goat friend here."

Hope took stock. In their favor: two headlamps, the remains of a flask of tea, a goat. Against them: a rucksack full of wet clothes, a soggy, dark glen, and a goat. Help would be nice, but she had no intention of leaving Agatha. And the people to whom she would have looked for help were no longer available. Her gran, for instance.

Granny Mac would have seen to it that it didn't come to this, or if it had, she'd have them up—Agatha under one arm and Hope under the other, roaring across the glen, rolling over the final hill home.

Granny Mac was gone, burned to ashes and tossed to the wild Scottish winds. Tiny granules of Granny could have rested anywhere in the world by then, could be embedded on Mount Everest, irritating the eye of a man in Beijing, dissolved in the Black Sea, churning in some cloud over Siberia.

Hope looked over at Agatha, rigid against the tree. The night was so quiet Hope imagined she might be able to hear the injury setting in.

"Right," she said. Granny and Dad might be gone, but she was there, holding everything they taught her. She slid herself between Agatha and the tree. She grabbed Agatha under her arms.

"You're not strong enough."

"I am." Hope tightened her grip.

"I'm too heavy."

"You're not."

When they reached full height, they faced each other again, headlamps off. Hope propped Agatha, standing on her one good leg, against the tree. She pulled her dad's sweatshirt from the backpack. She turned sideways and wrapped Agatha's arm around her shoulder. Hope bent Agatha's leg so it didn't reach the ground, tied it to her own so she would take all the weight.

As they set off again, wobbly and even slower than before, Hope felt the tension in from Agatha's arm, wrapped around her shoulder. With each movement, Agatha's muscles tightened as they searched for a rhythm, babystepping across the rough ground in the general direction of home. The sidhe appeared in front of them, who knew how much later? At the same time as she noticed it rise there, just ahead, it occurred to her that there was the stile to navigate, and a gate, the kind that only let people come and go, one at a time, but not animals. How would they navigate those? Hope snuck a glance at Agatha; she found her great-aunt so pale as to be nearly luminous. She considered steering them more south than west, in the direction that might get them to the road, above the stile. She'd ridden her board the length of the road, though, and not seen any other entry point. Worse, she'd noticed some sharp drop-offs just at the edge. They would have to follow the path they had set out on and do the best they could. The uneven slosh of their feet seemed to amplify as they trudged along, Hope's shoulder aching. Was Agatha leaning more heavily on her, or did the passage of time just make it seem so?

By the time she saw the stile, Hope's tricep had begun to quiver under Agatha's weight. Her jaw rigid, Hope turned sideways and pulled Agatha to her. With Agatha's weight fully on her, Hope lifted. She felt Agatha slump rather than rise up the first step with her.

"Auntie Agatha," Hope said, her voice high and desperate.

"I'll be all right, pet. I'll just have a wee rest."

Agatha slid farther, leaving Hope no choice but to come with her, off the first step and on, until they both plonked, bums first, onto the grass. Agatha leaned back on the hedge beside the stile. Beads of sweat clung to her hairline and above her lip. She closed her eyes. Hope reached toward her, hesitating before she made contact with the old woman's clammy skin. Hope placed her fingers on Agatha's neck, looking for a pulse the way her father taught her to do to herself during interval training. The beat was too fast and faint. Crouched somewhere between the rough road and the rolling hills, Hope looked around, searching for what, she didn't know. She found heather and gorse and rock and hummocks of grass. *Not even the fucking goat.*

She moved quickly: untying herself from Agatha, she jerked out everything from the rucksack and covered Agatha with the few extra dry garments.

"I'll be back soon," she whispered in Agatha's ear.

Hope rose and planted one foot on the first step of the stile, then leapt over, accelerating as her feet hit the humpy ground on the other side. She began to run in the direction of the town. Clouds blew by overhead, cleared the sky for a moment, revealing a crescent moon as Hope took the crest of the hill and began the descent, gathering speed. She had forgotten the row of cottages at the edge of the trail, just above the campground, whitewashed and bright even in the night. The town was yet more than a mile away, maybe two. And even then, who would be up? And where was the hospital?

Hope watched her fist bang against the first door; she heard herself shouting. "Help me!"

Her fist was red by the time a light came on inside, then another at the door, blinding her. A face at the window. "Calm yersel."

She heard herself say she needed an ambulance, her aunt had fallen.

"Is this your idea of a joke?"

"Please," she said. "She's old. I don't know where the hospital is."

The door opened, and a tall, scrawny man stood in it, glowering down at her.

"Please help me," she said.

"Come in."

"Just call an ambulance." Hope bounced as she said it.

The man's hair stuck out in all directions. Under a worn white shirt, dark hair tentacled across his stomach. He looked her over from head to toe. "And just where shall I tell the ambulance to go?" The man raised his eyebrows, clearly still skeptical. Would it have been faster to run all the way into town? His brows lowered as Hope told him where Agatha was, his expression shifting from doubt to belief.

"We left the saddle too late," Hope said, "and then she fell."

"There's no ambulance can go there," he said. "That's the mountain rescue we'll need to ring."

Hope shifted from foot to foot as the man dialed and explained, looking to her for clarification as he told whoever was on the other end of the line that they were in Glen Rosa, between the campsite and the Glen Rosa Enclosure, near a stile.

"I'm going back to her."

"You're to wait here. They don't need two of you injured in the glen."

But Hope was out the front door and gone. How could she wait while Agatha was slumped in wet grass in the middle of nowhere, and it was all Hope's fault?

The blades of the helicopter stirred even the wiry limbs of the heather. Hope wrapped her arms around her waist, clutched her sides as she watched two men and a woman hunch over Agatha, then lift her onto a stretcher and strap her down. For a second, as she was being lifted, Agatha's eyes opened, connected with Hope's in a look of fear and recognition, the look that takes over in the moment when the skater realizes the landing can't happen. Had Hope's eyes held that expression out in the Cave, the night she'd been polishing and cleaning even after her mother said her father wasn't coming home?

Agatha's eyes closed nearly as quickly as they had opened, her body sliding into the bright insides of the helicopter, her white hair like tufts of wool that the sheep left on barbed-wire fences. She looked so old suddenly, older than Hope had ever seen her in the shadows of the cottage fire. Hope climbed in after her and tried to make herself as unobtrusive as possible.

In the belly of the helicopter, the EMT asked her stupid questions when he should have been focusing on her aunt. What happened? Why were they out so late? And in the glen? His eyes pierced her, accusing. "What where the pair of you doing out here in the dark?"

"She was teaching me astronomy," Hope said, her voice flat and hard. *Fuck you, buddy.* "Can you just help her?"

They peeled back Agatha's layers—hat, jacket, cardigan. They pulled off one Wellington boot and cut off the other with huge shears. Agatha would hate the waste. Perhaps Hope could find another pair.

Agatha had fallen once before, just a little further east on the Rosa Burn. She and Donagh had been racing across the glen, him letting her get a bit ahead. She'd stretched her legs long, feeling the length of them as she hadn't properly done since her days on Skye. She'd arrived at the broadest part of the burn, prepared to leap over, using a flat rock in the middle for leverage. She'd nearly made it, pressed off fully, but then been caught by the giggles in midair as she heard Donagh's voice close behind, promising capture. That little loss of momentum had caused her to falter, landing in cold, clear water nearly up to her knees. Donagh caught her.

"We can't have you walking about in wet trousers, now can we?" He lifted her and carried her round the corner to the shelter of a large oak. The long light of summer afforded them the luxury of staying until her trousers were dry. She felt nearly warm at the memory. Beyond the recollection, in some dim haze of darkness and pain, she felt her body begin to crumple. She heard herself tell the lassie she just needed to rest. She let go. She felt the lassie's breath on her, whispering something. And then strange hands slid under her, clashing with the memory of Donagh's. Lifting. A bright, swirling light. She raised her head. Were there three men? She thought of Da, of Rory, of Donagh. She let go again.

Hope stood beside Agatha's gurney in the emergency room, the pair of them scrunched under the screaming lights that lit up every little hair on Agatha's hand and arm. Agatha's white hair sprawled on the pillow, flowing back to reveal blue veins at her temples. Hope held her hand, lukewarm. She felt for a pulse at the wrist. They were in a hospital. She should feel safe. She didn't trust them to take care of Agatha. The nurses who admitted Agatha to the ER had done a kind of good cop/bad cop routine, alternating between treating Agatha like a piece of meat, speaking too loudly—*Acht yer awright, no sae bad*—and then speaking to her as though she was a baby—*Okay Mrs. Stuart, just you hang on, we'll get you sorted*—the voice too loud and high and getting her marital status wrong while they moved her from gurney to X-ray to the ER bed, where they put on the cast.

"I want to go home," Agatha had said, her voice faint.

Hope had risen then, ready to take her. She'd been here before, her dad seeming like a hero because he'd gone the night with broken bones and acted as though it was nothing. He'd laughed in the ER. Hope had laughed right along with him. She tightened her grip on Agatha's hand.

"Not so fast there, Miss Stuart," the doctor said. Her high cheekbones and too-tight ponytail made her look hollow. At least she got Agatha's marital status correct. "I want my eye on you for twenty-four hours, at least."

"I think I can manage with a hurt ankle in my own home."

"Aye, if it's just that."

Hope clung to Agatha's hand.

"Sometimes bodies take funny turns." The doctor spoke as much to Hope as to Agatha. "Bit of a delayed shock reaction."

"My niece can ring for help."

They all turned to Hope. She felt the color rise in her cheeks.

"That won't be necessary." She scribbled something on Agatha's chart, then patted her leg.

Agatha folded her arms across her chest. "I've not had a day of my life in a hospital and I'm not starting now."

The doctor smiled a thin-lipped smile, sighed, stepped through the curtain.

Agatha's shoulders sank back onto the pillow. She turned toward Hope. "Don't let them keep me here."

Hope nodded.

"Say you promise."

"I promise," Hope said, not fully sure what, exactly, she was agreeing to, but meaning it nonetheless. And then Agatha shut her eyes, leaving Hope at the edge of the gurney, between the IV and the pair of Wellington boots, one flopping and useless, cut right down the side.

Agatha's mind drifted: Aileen, in Canada, in the cold. Never a proper marriage. The children not even realizing they were bastards until they went for their own marriage licenses. A second relationship after the first man died. All this in letters. Never a phone call, until the morning in January. And then not Aileen's voice, of course, but still a Scottish one, speaking Gaelic at that, saying Aileen had gone out skating on the lake, alone, at dawn, they thought. She should have known better. She should have known the unpredictability of January waters. Agatha wouldn't have gone if the body hadn't been found, hair snagged on a submerged limb, face down, as though she'd gone in for a wee swim. At least she'd died outside. The priest said the mass in Gaelic. The congregants murmured along in the white air beside the grave. *In ainm an Athar agus an Mhic agus…*

She'd gone for Anna as well, after the crash. She recalled the click of her shoes against the linoleum, the strange roundness of the voices bouncing off sterile walls, the gleaming silver bedrails and white sheets. Agatha pulled the sheet back. Anna's hair, prematurely white, grey-faced, long fingers wrapped around the rail. Whoever had covered her hadn't been bothered to close her eyes and mouth properly. What last word had she wanted to say?

All of them gone. Scattered to the winds like so many of Scotland's children, walking the world, searching for something better. Dying under cold foreign waters, in strange beds, and on wrong-sided roads.

At least Ellsie had had a familiar hand to hold, an ear for her last words, the dark soil of Arran over which to fly. So many had left and been replaced that Agatha, too, might be taken to death in her own native land by foreign hands. Surely it would happen if the lassie didn't rescue her from the hospital. How many did she know her age—younger, even—who'd taken the smallest of tumbles, been encouraged to the infirmary, never to come back.

Instead they wound up scattered, willy-nilly, by some young relation—or worse, put in the urn, boxed, and left at the back of a cupboard.

Agatha swallowed. "*An Garbh-choire*," she whispered. She wished to be scattered at the feet of the cauldron. She might have said so aloud. Just then, she couldn't be sure.

TWENTY-TWO
Margaret

From within her, the sound of her mother's voice tapped on Margaret's temples the morning after she sat on Clyde's porch drinking George Dickel. *Ocht, it's like a bloody midden.* The phrase had been a syncopation to Ellsie's sweeping and dusting and scrubbing.

Margaret remembered hanging from the bookshelf when she'd been six, one tiny hip wedged against the lip of the shelf for leverage as she pulled the *M* volume of the encyclopedia away from the rest. Mummy had used the word in the usual Scottish sense, meaning a general mess. She learned, too, that the word was of Scandinavian extract, meaning a dump for domestic waste. Archaeologists used the term for any pileup of daily wastes. Lucky ones unearthed middens that held the waste of several generations.

Ellsie had never considered midden a lucky word. They'd had them in the back court of the tenement in Glasgow: bins overflowing with the whole building's waste, everyone's dirty business out in the open, the lids never staying on for long. She had told of them in great detail. She spoke of how lucky Margaret was to live in a place where the trash was so neatly removed. Her mother fought against the slightest hint of decay in the house, always sweeping clean space into their lives, and so Margaret perhaps should not have been so shocked the day she'd come in from school, seven years after learning the full meaning of the word, and been greeted by a mother with hands on hips.

"I cleaned out your little midden there," she said. She took Margaret's thirteen-year-old hand, pulled open one of the bags. "You'll go through that, bit by bit, and see what you'd lose if I was to take all the things you didn't care enough about to put away neatly. Since they're strewn about, I assume they are meant for the bin." Mummy's hands punched into her ample hips. "On you go, then. Get started."

Margaret unearthed a pair of turquoise sandals, a fedora belonging to a boy she'd danced with the week before, her geometry book, a Twix wrapper, her diary (opened), a sock, underpants. She kept going.

"If I find this room being used as a bin again, I will treat everything in it as garbage."

Margaret hated her mother at that moment. Years later, though, she found herself holding up all manner of things when she and Trig roomed together in college, saying, "Keep or toss," demanding cleanliness so their room wouldn't become a midden, attract vermin, or, at least as bad, give away their secrets to anyone who looked.

Margaret hadn't fully understood the importance her mother put on the things she cared enough about to put neatly away— to keep safe from the trash—until after her death, when she'd cleaned out the tenement in Glasgow, abandoned when Ellsie moved in with Agatha to die. The flat had been spotless when Margaret arrived, but as she dug into drawers and cupboards and wardrobes, she found layers and layers of her mother's life—toddler garments, brought from Skye, that fell apart in her hands; a school uniform; desiccated flowers pressed between the warped pages of fairy tales; Ellsie's tag from the World War II evacuation; a treacle wrapper, bits of black still clinging in the creases; a ticket to the festival of flowers—and so on through the emigration and wedding and return.

Margaret took all of it to the midden, except the treacle wrapper. Absently, she stuffed that in her pocket, forgot about it until she reached in weeks later, back home in South Carolina. She pulled it out, unfolded it. Why had her mother considered it important enough to save? What was it about her own room that particular day that had so incensed her mother? She would never know the answer to either question. But her mother's voice still haunted her, returning at strange moments, like in the middle of a hangover on a summer morning.

Margaret opened her eyes. Sunlight jabbed through the gap in her curtains. She scrunched her eyes against it, turned her head away. Her brain felt scrunched too. Her left hand lay numb under the cushion. Margaret opened one eye, met the back of her loveseat, on which she was curled, too old to be comfortable in the fetal position. She sat straight up, both eyes wide, then lay back as fast. She ran her tongue over her teeth, found them too large and textured. How much had she drunk? She closed her eyes, began with sitting on Clyde's top step, tried to move her memory forward. Not much came. She pushed herself up, pulled her skirt into its proper position. Her shoes nestled neatly under the coffee table. Two large trash bags filled the space where the sofa used to be. Margaret braced herself for what standing might bring. Leaning against the arm of the loveseat, she breathed out slowly, waited for the equilibrium to return. Then she made for the kitchen.

If she was Trig, she'd have had enough self-preservation instinct to premedicate. What was it—Advil and B12, or E, or C, or all of them—that Trig used to take before she passed out? If she'd been Brad, she'd have been on a regular roll of self-medication. Hell, even Hope seemed to have begun to get the hang of keeping pain at bay. Through the shriveled mess of her brain, Margaret thought she felt a thread of understanding. She pressed forward.

The kitchen table held her purse, and, beside it, a note on a long, skinny sheet of paper, the kind people used for grocery lists, with little lines and, in this case, blue ducks waddling across the bottom. *877-3650. When you're set to get your car. You wasn't quite up to it last night. These ought to help. CB.* Beside the note lay a blue rectangle: Goody's headache powders. Margaret lifted the note and the powders, edged to the back door. The garage door yawned, wide open, light streaming into the empty space. Margaret dug out her cell phone. She was neither *set to go*, nor did she have Trig's or Brad's pharmaceutical knowledge. She did, however, damn sure know enough to avoid being seen like this. She dialed Clarie, claimed illness, poured a glass of water, knocked back the powder. The gritty aspirin residue clung to her mouth, marking a path, like breadcrumbs being dropped inside her. She steadied herself, eased back to the den.

The trash bag unknotted easily, the musty scent rising, not strong enough to overpower Margaret's memory of stale beer and sweat. Her stomach rolled. She hung her head, waited for her insides to settle, thought of attraction, of bonds, of Brad, of trash bags. She recalled learning in some class long ago about how, when one large molecule begins to feel the attraction of another large molecule, it starts the creation of a polymer. If, after swirling ever closer to each other, the molecules agree to share electrons, a covalent bond may be formed. These bonds, which take hundreds of years to break down, comprised the average trash bag. In the newer, biodegradable bags, the polymers were formed by organic materials—starch, cellulose, soy. Exposed to the right amounts of sun and rain and time, the molecules in a biopolymer released their grip on each other, allowed the electrons to freely move in their own separate directions again. Developers of bags like these—bags like the one Margaret wrapped her arms around in her den—hoped to make lots of money from this notion that larger elements can break apart the strongest of bonds and eradicate the worst of human waste, even things like Brad's sweaters and t-shirts and underpants, which, having been spun and woven from wool and cotton, would have worn away over time on their own if Margaret hadn't bundled them into the smooth, black bags. Margaret settled her head against the bag she'd opened, closed her eyes, drifted.

When she woke, she rubbed her hands across her face, felt the lines from Brad's favorite sweater—a ribbed one with a high collar and zippered neck, charcoal that set off his eyes—

embossed on her cheek. She dug under the sweater, pulled out a t-shirt: 2005 Kiawah Half Marathon. He'd paced a pudgy female client trying to lose baby fat to a 1:50, a time that would have mortified Margaret. She dug to the bottom, landed on the smooth medal Brad had won at the state road race cycling championships that year, the rumpled photo with it. Her Brad. Long and lean. Smiling his crooked-toothed grin.

Oh Brad.

Ohbradohbradohbrad.

She lay her head down, pulled the bag into her hollow chest, closed her eyes.

A knock at the door startled her. She sat up. Another knock.

"I know you're in there, Margaret MacPherson Carver. So get your ass up and answer the door."

The clomp-click of Trig's mules on the garage floor. Margaret put her head back down. The key in the door. Trig knew all her planks. Margaret stuffed the t-shirt and medal and sweater into the bag, stood, straightened her skirt, blew her bangs out of her face.

"Good Lord, I'm coming," Margaret said.

Trig was already in, though, taking in Margaret from head to toe.

"Just clearing out."

"Oh, horseshit, Margaret. I passed your car on the side of the road at eleven o'clock last night. Couldn't find you here, there, or anywhere. Clarie says you called in sick. Says you got a call from Hope yesterday. And now look at you. You look like you belong in that bag you're holding."

"Well, wasn't it you who said I should pull a good old drunk?"

"*Good* being the key word there, not a leave-your-car-on-the-side-of-the-road-get-home-who-knows-how kind of a drunk. You got to do these things with people who love you."

"Really, Trig? People who love me? Why? Because you all have to scrutinize every little movement? Can't miss a minute of the drama?" Margaret swallowed. "Did you come for a reason, or just to get details of the latest fuck-up?"

Trig's shoulders pulled back. Her left hip jutted out. She took a breath.

"I just wanted to make sure you weren't dead, or worse..." Trig turned. "Which I have, so I guess I'm done here."

"Trig." Margaret started after her.

Trig clomp-clicked through the open garage door and out to her car. Margaret followed. Trig pulled down Live Oak Lane without glancing back, just as Brad had. The Shih Tzu yapped on the screened porch next door. Margaret could have sworn her brain felt each of the sound waves individually.

"Trig, I'm sorry." Trig was long gone.

She was likely right about one thing: Margaret must look as though she belonged in the trash bag. She certainly felt as though she did. And if she couldn't even get Brad's clothes successfully to the trash can, what hope did she have of moving beyond him?

The heat of the concrete dug into Margaret's feet. The air, too close and heavy, seemed like a grating wrap with neither beginning nor end. A rumble started overhead. Fat raindrops followed. Margaret shook her hair away from her face, turned back inside.

She stripped at the back door, stuffed her clothes inside the bag, on top of Brad's things, resisted an impulse to run upstairs and dig out everything that had anything to do with Brad or her time with him. Her head pounded as though there was a metal cap over it, held in place by a rod through her temples, being hammered into place. The hamper offered only her soggy running gear. Upstairs, rooting in her dresser, Margaret caught an image of herself in the mirror, turned away. Even the silk of her pajamas chafed as she pulled them on.

A clatter woke her, coming from somewhere distant enough to seem like a dream, she didn't know how much later. She rolled over in her Egyptian cotton sheets. Would cheaper, not-so-crisply pressed ones make less of a ruckus? Another clunk made her sit up. Trig again? But she had already demonstrated that she could get in even when the door was locked. (Margaret owed her an apology. Swearing at a truckload of men was one thing. Swearing at your friend, who had come to make sure you were okay? *Fuck.*)

The next thud felt like a direct blow to her still-delicate head. Definitely in the garage. Surely not Trig. Margaret pulled the sheets to her chin, found the smell of unscented laundry detergent and perfume-free dryer sheets almost too much. Silence, then a scraping she wanted to tell herself she imagined. Had she even locked the back door after Trig took off?

Margaret descended the stairs, heart thumping, head pounding, clutching her phone. At the foot of the stairs, she touched 9-1-1 but not Send. What if it *was* Trig? The last thing she needed was to have the police screaming down the street for all the neighbors to see, only to find some hungover nutcase who had just called the cops on a friend she had treated like shit. Or an old man, kindly bringing her car back. Bits and pieces of the evening with Clyde floated back. Clyde saying he'd seen Hope in the woods. The story spilling out about Brad leaving and Hope getting into trouble and Margaret feeling she could do nothing to help either of them. She'd told him the lot of it. He'd said she should call Hope. And then they'd eaten Vienna sausages out of a can. Margaret clutched her stomach with one hand and the banister the other.

In the door between the den and the kitchen, Margaret hesitated. A shaft of sun poking through storm clouds exacerbated the brightness of the house. Hope's words bounced around her head: *That's what you want. A sunshine girl. All freakin' hap-hap-happy for your Christmas cards.*

The *hap-hap-happy*, battering like a pinball inside her head, came to an abrupt halt at the sound of a door closing—the door to the Cave. Margaret glanced at the back door. Not only was it unlocked, it wasn't even properly latched. Had it been like that since Trig left, or had someone been in the house while she slept?

Stomach roiling, Margaret inched forward, trying to stay below the window in the top half of the door to the garage.

Hand on the knob, she started to press the door closed. From the other side, someone pressed back. Margaret leaned into the door, clutched the knob tighter, touched Send. Dropped the phone to shove the knob with her other hand.

The pressure on the other side released; the door slammed and Margaret's body crumpled into it. Jumping up, she looked through the glass, glimpsed the man turning from the door. Margaret's breath stopped.

From the floor, a voice came through the phone. "What is your emergency?"

Margaret pulled open the door, caught Brad's back retreating across the garage. His shriveled triceps were far too visible; his skin bore the tan of people who spend too much time in the sun and refuse to wear, or can't afford, sunblock: roofers, road pavers, cheerleaders, the homeless. Margaret swallowed back the bile that rose, burning, in her throat. She leapt across the garage, grabbed for his hand, and spun him around.

"Oh," she gasped when he turned, met her with yellowed eyes, one of his front teeth chipped. Face to face with him at the edge of the garage, her chest felt as though the bony cage was shrinking; at the same time, her heart expanded, expanded, expanded.

The operator's voice from the kitchen floor, distant and muffled.

Here he was, at last. How could she ever have imagined this gaunt derelict who stood before her? She wanted to push him away; she wanted to wrap her arms around him and tell him she could save him.

"Margaret?" he said. His voice, coming from the pitted mouth beneath those awful yellow eyes, was still his. Brad. Her hand wrapped around his; her palm tingled, muscles and tendons tightening up her arm and across her shoulders and into her neck and chest. She clutched at him, desperate, disbelieving.

"Brad."

"I didn't think you were here."

"I am. And you are." She tightened her grip. "Come in. We can talk."

"I just came for…" He tugged away, trying to get loose for a minute before his hand relaxed into hers. He took a half step closer to her, his eyes traveling her body.

Margaret's stomach clenched.

"You look beautiful, Margaret," he said. "You look perfect."

Margaret's eyes darted to the windows on the other side of the garage.

"I'm getting myself together, Margaret."

"Come in, we can talk," Margaret said again.

"So I can come back to you." His free hand brushed against her cheek. "Sweet Maggie."

"Just come in."

"I just need a little cash, Margaret."

She pulled him closer. *Who is this man?*

"I just need some of my own money."

Margaret feared she might vomit.

A siren sounded, somewhere outside the neighborhood. Margaret's grip on Brad's hand tightened as he pulled away again.

"Stay. We'll talk."

Brad pulled again, surprisingly strong, freeing himself. "This was a mistake."

"No. Stay. Wait. Wait for Hope."

If she had any real leverage, Hope was it.

The siren again, closer. Were there two? Margaret grabbed for him as he lunged out of the garage. She noticed, then, the car, with its door open. His bikes were already stuffed in the hatch of the 1983 Honda Civic with rusted rims and missing headlight. Didn't Trig have one of those in high school? She stopped at the edge of the garage, stunned.

"Where's your car?" she asked

He slid in. "This is my car." It rattled to life.

"Hope needs you, Brad."

His eyes on her, wide and blank. "You just think you know what everyone needs, don't you, Margaret?" He pulled forward, across the grass, away from her. She took several steps after him, as though she might catch him and grab onto the car, go with him if he wouldn't stay with her. Her hands lifted toward the rusty Civic as Brad rounded the corner of the house; her eyes jerked to the police car turning down her street. Brad bumped across the unfenced back yard and onto the neighbor's drive and away. The house with the larger corner lot had seemed like a good investment when they made the offer; who knew it would also block the sightline of the approaching police car, now pulling up to the edge of the drive?

Margaret forced the hand that had held Brad, now scarlet and sore, down by her side; she felt its heat through the smooth of her silk pajamas, even as her other hand reached out to shake the hand of the police officer, cold, robotic. She could send them after him, say he tried to break in. But legally, this was still his house too, wasn't it? She imagined him making his getaway in his raggedy car while she stood there, clothed in garments meant to be private, right out in the drive.

A mistake, she heard herself saying. Sorry. It was only her estranged husband. Sorry. Could she pay for their inconvenience? One of them asked where her husband was now. "Drove off," she said. "Just before you arrived. Desperate to get away. I'm sorry."

She watched the patrol cars round the corner out of sight, then headed inside, her feet thumping the ground harder with each step as the exchange with Brad settled within her. While she'd been imagining his return, he'd been plotting to take what he could the first moment he was sure she was gone. What if Hope had been there to see what had become of him? Had he no regard for either of them? How had he let himself become such a haggard shell? She had pushed Tim away to save herself for *that*?

In the den, the black bags glistened under the lights. Margaret glanced at her watch. Still time to make the trash pickup. She swallowed the bile in her throat, ignored the contraction of her stomach, the sudden chirping of her mother's voice in her head again, as clearly as if she was alive and well and standing in the den, her hands planted on her hips.

She shoved away her own questions and allowed herself to feel the fresh growl of anger. She lifted one bag in each hand, tried to make for the door, found them impossibly slippery. She might as well have had Brad in one hand and Hope in the other. She dropped the bags, bent, wrapped her arms around them, clenched, stood, stepped forward, the muscles in her arms and back now contracting as well as her stomach, pulling the weight forward. She turned sideways going through the door of the den left shoulder first, readjusted in the kitchen, then right shoulder leading out. Margaret leaned into the breeze as she moved toward the trash can at the end of the driveway. Clyde must have put it out for her. She set the bag down and went back for the other.

Between the blooming crape myrtles, in the soft rain, she opened the trash bags, determined to lift each item and be sure that it belonged in the trash, that it really got there and didn't make its way back to her.

Sweater, t-shirt, medal, socks, boxers, briefs, track shoes, Valentine's cards (1994, '95, '96—her own words in between Brad's torn training shorts and holey washrags). After the last shoebox, Margaret was left holding only the bags. She heard the rumble of the trash truck in the distance. She remained still as the trash man worked around her, rain breaking on the brim of his cap as she watched, bare-armed, covered in goose pimples, hair plastered to her head.

"You want me to take them?" He nodded to the empty bags.

Margaret looked at them, shiny, limp things reaching toward the ground. She shook her head, rain splashing from her like condensation from a cool glass on a hot day. In another season, she'd spun such a glass in some palmetto-shaded bar at Edisto Beach, drops flicking out at her and Brad. He'd spun his glass back, icy droplets tantalizing, waking them to each other in the heat and humidity. Damn him. No, *fuck him.*

She watched the truck's crusher as it tamped down her little midden, mixing the remains of her marriage with number eight plastic, cling wrap, and Styrofoam meat trays, padded and bloody and on their way to be covered over for lifetimes on the fringes of the city, out of sight. Fat raindrops spat at her; the air hung close around her; heat rose within her chest. Watching the truck turn the corner, she felt the urge to run, could almost feel the full extension of her legs in a sprint, the strike of her foot against the ground, the roll forward, pressing the earth away, the tension in her calves and quads, the burn up her legs and into her lungs. Her heart was already racing. She could drop the flaccid bags, turn, run and run in bare feet and creamy silk pajamas. She imagined the perfectly spun fabric, smooth and soaked with rain and sweat, becoming part of her skin. She imagined herself running faster and faster, lifting off, no longer part of the world—this newly molten anger bubbling up through the skin of her arms and neck and face, fueling her until she reached ignition. She began to shake. She feared she might run until the flames reduced her to ashes, a dark and grainy heap, easily kicked aside.

Margaret fought to root herself in, there at the top of the driveway. Something else, a stillness, was what she really needed—a safe container for this rage. She squatted at the edge of the driveway, wrapped her arms around herself. A gust of wind lifted the trash bags, flapped them like dark flags. She shook one open, pulled it over her head, the words THIS IS NOT A TOY facing outward. She pressed her hands flat against the edges. A low, loud sound came from her, somewhere between a moan and a howl. She let it rise, pressed harder and felt the dark material yield, rivulets of strain appearing like stretch marks. Might she, at last, be able to summon and sustain the strength to keep up the pressure until she burst through? Might she then allow herself enough sunlight and rain to break free of the bond? She pressed harder, clawing as though she was suffocating.

TWENTY-THREE
Hope

Hope eyed the doctor as she came back through the curtains and took her place at the foot of the gurney, scribbling on Agatha's chart.

"We're just getting a bed sorted for you," the doctor said.

"I've a bed already sorted for myself," Agatha said. She pressed herself up to sitting, her cheeks coloring in the process.

The doctor continued to write, then handed the chart to the nurse. She looked directly at Agatha, lips pursed. "We can't take any chances, Miss Stuart, at your age. You need care."

"I'll be fine. At my age. And I've plenty care." She nodded at Hope.

The doctor hardly turned in Hope's direction. "Adult care."

Hope's eyes met Agatha's. "I can follow instructions," she said.

The doctor patted the gurney.

"I'll have the bed sorted soon."

The nurse and doctor slipped through the curtain, whispered on the other side. Hope turned in their direction, listening as their footsteps clipped down the hall and away.

"Get me out of here." Agatha's whisper crept up Hope's neck so quietly she might have imagined it. She turned and found Agatha trying to disentangle herself from the sheets. "You don't know what they do to old ladies in places like this."

Agatha leaned forward, freed herself from the sheets as footsteps approached from outside. Hope flipped the sheet back over Agatha.

"You all right in there, then, Miss Stuart?" the nurse's voice called from the other side of the curtains.

"Of course."

"No be long now."

Hope met Agatha's eyes again, saw the familiar fear. Hope could stand there and watch them wheel Agatha into some room—to do who knew what to her and release her who knew when. She would have to go back to the cottage, wait to hear what was supposed to happen next.

They had put a cast on Agatha's leg. They said that was all that was really wrong. They only wanted to keep her because she was old, and Hope was young. Shouldn't Agatha get to choose? Couldn't Hope take care of her? Hope turned. She flipped back the sheets, pressed one Wellington boot onto Agatha's good, pale foot; she wedged the cast as far as it would go into the dissected Wellie. She motioned to Agatha to keep quiet, stepped through the curtain. Hadn't the nurse been gone only a second or two when she got Agatha's wheelchair to take her to X-ray? Heart pounding, Hope tiptoed around the corner. A row of wheelchairs waited, like a miniature taxi stand. Hope wrapped her fingers around the handles of one with a saggy blue seat, swung it back around the corner and through the curtain. Her arm shook as she wrapped it around Agatha's waist and slid her from the bed to the wheelchair.

In the hallway, Hope hurried for the door.

"And where are you two going?" The nurse's voice sent lightning down Hope's arms. Her grip tightened on the wheelchair.

"Just taking her to the bathroom." Hope turned just far enough to show the nurse her sweetest smile, one her mother would have been proud of. She didn't wait for an answer, but pressed on toward the doors, now in sight. Below her, Agatha's bony fingers clung to the arms of the wheelchair.

"I could actually do with a loo," Agatha said.

"You want me to take you?"

"No. Keep going."

At the door, the voice came from behind them again. "Miss Stuart. Just a minute there, Miss Stuart."

Hope hesitated.

"Don't stop now, lassie."

Hope thrust through the front door, out into the shock of a clear dawn.

"Faster."

"Where?"

"Left. On you go."

Hope pressed onto the smooth pavement; she began to trot, taking instructions from Agatha as she went, down the lane and out onto the road. Did the old lady expect Hope to push her the whole way back to the cottage? Wasn't that miles away and on the other side of The String? Wouldn't the wheelchair have a blowout by then? Agatha's hair flew out from the sides of the wheelchair; the sliced Wellington flopped in the wind.

"Where are we going?"

"Ferry."

"What?" How much of an escape did they need?

"There'll be a taxi there, if we're very lucky." Agatha laughed, a small sound, almost a giggle. "Our getaway car."

All the way down the curving road to the ferry, and then loading Agatha in and answering the taxi driver's questions about why the hospital hadn't rung for him, and putting the wheelchair in the trunk (Would they have to take it back? Would Hope be accused of stealing?), Hope's neck hairs stood on end. She knew if she took her own pulse, it would be as fast and hard as if she was entering the final, hard trick in an X-treme contest.

She relaxed, just a little, when they were in the cottage, the taxi driver away—the doors locked, curtains drawn, Agatha stretched on the sofa, her eyes gratefully closed.

Hope crouched, then, on the hearth, still not truly thinking, but moving through the motions of lighting a fire according to Agatha's instructions.

In the fireplace, the paper flamed and smoked. In the time it took Hope to light the next scrunched lump, the one before went out. Agatha had made it look easy so many times, moving her hand from one ball to the next, getting the whole fire started using only one match. Now there were seven sticks with blackened points scattered on the hearth. Others had dropped into the fireplace. Hope's hands shook.

She stood. She needed help. *Mom?* Hope lifted the phone, hesitated. What number had Agatha dialed? Why hadn't she paid more attention? But what would Mom do, from all the way across the Atlantic? She looked at her great-aunt. Agatha needed heat more than Hope needed to hear whatever Mom would say.

Hope bent again, struck another match, and managed to get two balls of paper going before she had to strike another. The kettle whined in the kitchen just as the fire took. Aunt Agatha wouldn't be doing her brisk walk toward it any time soon.

A sliver of morning light snuck through a gap in the heavy curtains. Hope stood in the doorway, waiting for the tea to steep and watching Agatha, laid out on the couch, her long white hair spilling over the side, one hand on top of the other on top of the blanket. If Agatha had looked as old as the mountains around her when Hope arrived, she looked older still slumped there on the couch, like some kind of pale igneous rock that flowed up from the inside of the earth and cooled on top. Hope waited for the rise of the blanket, a snore, a gurgle. She knelt beside Agatha, leaning her face closer so she could feel Agatha's breath, wondering if she'd really done the right thing in bringing Agatha home. Wasn't this the same thing that happened with Dad? Would Agatha be better off in hospital? She didn't realize she was holding her own breath until Agatha snored. Hope snapped upright and let out a small, surprised scream. Agatha opened her eyes and squinted at Hope.

"Are you getting some tea?" she asked.

"Yes," Hope said. She backed toward the kitchen, watching Agatha's eyes close again.

In the kitchen, Hope whispered the instructions for tea to herself like a prayer. *Warm the pot. One spoon of leaves for each of us and one for the pot.* She peeked back through the door between steps.

Agatha had pushed herself to sitting when Hope came back with the tea, steaming and dark.

"Not sure I made it right." Hope handed the cup to Agatha.

Agatha watched as Hope poured. "Looks lovely." She sipped, set the cup down. "I'll just let it cool."

"I'm sorry," Hope said.

"It's lovely tea, pet."

"Not for the tea."

"You needn't apologize for my clumsiness."

"I can apologize for being out there and not being smart enough to come home."

"That you can." Agatha pushed up a little farther. "Apology accepted, so. Enough said. We've just to get on with it. You can make amends by helping me get myself sorted. A bit of breakfast might help as well."

Hope left Agatha with her tea, brought in the paper with its Sudoku puzzle, sliced the bannock, and scrambled the eggs, whispering to herself all the way. She tried to tell herself it was all as normal, except that Agatha didn't cook, that they ate at the coffee table, that it was long past time for breakfast and slightly past lunchtime, and, when she'd finished, Agatha pushed away her plate, dabbed her lips, looked to Hope instead of to the Sudoku.

"We might just be all right," she said, and then leaned back on the sofa and closed her eyes again.

Hope had just finished doing the dishes and settled in front of the fire with a fresh pot of tea when a knock came at the door. Agatha's spine straightened. Hope held her mug in the air, the pair of them frozen.

"See who it is, then," Agatha murmured.

Another knock, louder.

"Just coming," Agatha called. "Wait. Hand me my wee brush there." Agatha dusted a crumb from her lap.

Two shadows loomed outside the door. Hope hesitated in the kitchen, under her jeans, suspended between Agatha's old lady slip and bra.

"Miss Stuart?" the voice, muffled and still sharp, on the other side of the door.

The handle, icy under the heat of Hope's hand. She took a deep breath, turned, and pulled. Backlit by a slant of sun stood the doctor, eye level with Hope, and beside her was a man, slightly shorter, his hair slicked back with an excess of product. The orderly?

"Ah, good, you're here. Is Miss Stuart in?"

"She doesn't want to go to the hospital."

"We're well aware."

"Invite our guests in," Agatha called.

Hope stepped aside, letting the pair pass. "She's in the front room."

"You'll want a wee cup of tea and a biscuit," Agatha said. The pair flanked her on the sofa.

How could she be so calm? Even with the added weight of the cast, the two unwelcome visitors could easily take an arm each, slide their hands under Agatha's legs, lift her up, and drag her away.

"Away and get cups and saucers, Hope."

"This is not a social visit, Miss Stuart."

"And here I thought I'd a pair of new friends."

"Hardly, after the stunt you pulled," the doctor said. She turned to Hope. "You and your accomplice here."

"We just…" Hope began to say—what, she wasn't sure.

Agatha raised her hand. "It's all right, pet." She put her hand on the doctor's leg. "My niece was only doing as I asked."

"Exactly why we want you in the hospital, where we can keep an eye on you."

"I'm not going to hospital. You've sorted my leg. I've my

own healer I can ring for other help."

"And who would that be?"

"Helen Harvey."

"Helen Harvey?" The doctor sighed. "Miss Stuart. You're going to need more than dried herbs to get you going again. You're an old woman."

"And you're an impertinent one," Agatha said. She turned to Hope. "Please away and get those cups."

"If you're not coming to hospital, you need an adult here."

"I am the adult here. I've broken my ankle, not my head. I can direct my niece to do what I can't."

"So you've shown. Which is what worries us." The doctor scooted slightly back from Agatha, paused a moment, crafted a small smile. "Look, Miss Stuart. I'm not trying to be impertinent, but the fact is, you are an elderly woman in need of medical care. I cannot, in good conscience, leave you in the care of a child. And not that it's my provenance, but I can't leave a child in the care of a compromised adult. Where are her parents?"

"She's having a wee holiday. Children do that, you know, with their extended families. It's not as though she's a toddler. She's perfectly competent. And I may be old, but I'm hardly finished yet, young lady."

The four of them were still for a few moments.

"If it will keep you quiet, I'll produce an adult for you," Agatha said.

"Yes, please."

"Hope, away round the back and get Moira."

"Auntie Agatha," Hope said, her voice sounding higher and younger than she intended.

"On you go. They aren't going to whisk me away just yet."

Within minutes, Moira stood, hands folded on top of her rumples of breast and belly, scowling alternately at Agatha and Hope, then smiling at the doctor. "I told her she's too old for this sort of nonsense," she said. She leaned her torso toward the doctor. "She rides a bicycle too, so she does. Or she did."

"And will again," Agatha said. "As you might do well to try."
Agatha hesitated. She lowered her voice. "If only you could get
on one."

"Agatha Stuart!"

"All right, ladies." The doctor stood. "I'm leaving you a couple
of prescriptions here. I recommend getting them filled and not
relying on dried plants to help you with pain and healing. I'll
bring in a walker and a cane, as I suspect you're too stubborn to
use the wheelchair. And I expect to see you in my surgery one
week from today, just for a check. Fair enough?"

"Not really, but I'll come anyway."

The doctor handed the prescriptions to Agatha, who handed
them to Hope as soon as Moira and the others left.

"You'd better get them filled, in case they check. You can away
in and get them and some other messages, including some of
those dried plants. I'll make you a wee list." Agatha patted the
couch. Hope sat. "What do they know?" Agatha said, putting
her hand on Hope's leg. "We'll be all right, the pair of us."

Agatha began to make the list. Her hand shook slightly,
making her script waver on the page. Hope took the pen, leaned
her great-aunt back onto the sofa, lifted her feet, and covered
her. She took down Agatha's instructions, and then watched her
drift to sleep, holding vigil beside the sofa.

TWENTY-FOUR
Margaret

Margaret stood under the storm, tattered bags in her hands. Rain dripped from the ends of her hair. She turned for the house, dropped the bags in the kitchen trash can on her way up the stairs and into the shower. Margaret didn't wait for the water to warm, but stepped into the cold, steady stream of it; she let the heat rise to steaming, her skin reddening under the pulse. She ran her hands across the flat of her stomach, pausing on one of the stretch marks, now faint, from her pregnancy. She wandered her hands up, cupped her own breasts. How long had it been since she'd felt a touch, been held, drawn heat from someone else? She turned the shower back to cold, held herself there, palms braced against the wall of the shower.

In front of the mirror, Margaret took stock: the stretch marks, the scar just at the edge of her right breast from the tumor scare. Would anyone other than her notice that the left breast, engorged more when she fed Hope, was still slightly larger than the right? Was the mole beneath her navel a blemish or a beauty mark? Margaret pressed her hair back from her face, leaned in to examine the crow's feet strutting out from her eyes, the little extra hairs above her lip, blonde at least, thank God. She piled her hair on top of her head, stared into the mirror at herself, showing from the thighs up. Was she wrong to want someone to delight in her body while it still held some of the beauty and litheness of her youth? She held still, her eyes in the mirror reflecting the question, her body reflecting an answer.

She repeated the answer to herself as she pulled on shorts, socks, shoes. She kept on as she made her way out the door and through the neighborhood beyond—as the questions came, which felt good, even though the answers tended to come in the form of questions themselves: Wouldn't Clyde keep? Hadn't Brad just shown her that he was good and gone? These kept her going through the run and getting gas and the car.

She pulled the car back into the garage, climbed the stairs, re-showered. In front of the full-length mirror, Margaret pulled on her favorite jeans, added a draped, pale grey blouse, sandals. She touched the last number she'd dialed before 911 as she made her way back through her cavernous den, held her breath through four rings, almost touched Cancel, and then heard the voice on the other end of the line.

"Tim," she said. "Mags MacPherson."

"Hey there, Mags MacPherson. Did you find me a house?"

Was his voice less friendly than yesterday? Did it matter? What did she have to lose?

"Afraid not," she said. "Actually, I was wondering if I could find you a cup of coffee. I'd like to explain yesterday."

"No need to explain," Tim said. "I thought you didn't drink coffee."

"I'd like to explain. And you like coffee."

"How about something we both like? Something a little stronger."

"Isn't it a little early?"

"I could pick you up a little later."

"Why don't I come to you?" she asked. "And Tim?"

"Yes?"

"I prefer to be called Margaret."

Tim opened his door dressed in crisp linen trousers, a starched white shirt. "Where's it to be, then?"

"We could stay here," Margaret said. She held up a bottle of Tempranillo.

"You sure about that?"

"Not at all, but let's do it anyway."

Tim took Margaret's hand and tugged her across the threshold.

"Home sweet home, then," he said. "Until I can find a realtor who will find me a permanent one." He took the bottle of wine. "Make yourself comfortable. I'll get us some glasses."

Margaret perched on the edge of the leather sofa, held her hands in her lap until Tim returned.

"We'll let that breathe a little while you explain, yes?" Tim sat in a lean leather chair across the coffee table from her.

"Sure."

"So?"

"You must think I'm awful."

"For?"

"Kissing you when I'm a married woman."

"Is that what you want to explain?"

Margaret nodded. She glanced down at her hands, was surprised not to find them visibly shaking. She slapped them against her knees and took a deep breath.

"I am, indeed, married. To an addict." Was that the first time she'd said it out loud? "Who left me and my daughter months ago, to go to rehab." Margaret held her eyes closed for a few moments. When she opened them, she looked down. She might as well have been speaking to her own hands instead of Tim. "He called and told me he'd figure things out his own way. I guess I've been hanging onto the notion that he would come back, all better." A crisp laugh escaped her lips. "He came back yesterday. He thought I wasn't home. I guess it took seeing him again for me to know he isn't coming home." She swallowed. "So legally, I'm married." She looked up, heart thumping.

Tim poured the wine, lifted the glasses, brought hers over. He sat close and wrapped his arm around her. She turned into him, and he cupped her chin in his hand, warm and smooth.

"I'm sorry you've been through all that."

"Thanks."

He held her for a few minutes in silence.

"Must have been rough," he said.

Margaret nodded. She sipped.

"Sure you're ready?"

I'm sure I'm ready for something different than waiting for an addict who isn't coming back. Margaret took another sip. *And blaming myself when he doesn't show, or when he does show and doesn't stay.*

"Yes," she said.

"In that case, may I kiss you?"

Margaret took a small breath. She nodded.

He pulled her to him slowly, as though he was still asking. Margaret held herself still, shut out the questions—the image of Brad, ragged and awful in the driveway, of Hope, haughtily marching away from her. She closed her eyes, breathed in the soft fullness of his lips.

Tim sat back a little, gave Margaret a quizzical look. "Where's your daughter tonight?"

"Still at my aunt's," Margaret said, lifting a glass. "My aunt who lives in Scotland."

"Ah," Tim said. "Well, then. A toast." He raised his glass. "To aunties."

Later, after the wine was gone, she let the buzz of fear wash over her and away as he brushed his lips against her neck and kept going.

In the morning, he nuzzled her awake, took her hand, pulled her to standing. He wrapped a dark robe around her, then his arm, and led her down the hall and out onto the balcony to a steaming mug of tea. They sat side by side, watching the sun rise over Piney Mountain.

TWENTY-FIVE
Hope

Hope listened as Great-aunt Agatha's breath slowed and watched as her face relaxed, the loose skin on her cheeks flowing toward her hairline. Hope risked touching Agatha's leg with a careful hand. Under the cover and her clothes, and under the flat of Hope's palm, Agatha's leg felt sharp; it was harder even than Dad's had been when Hope had scrunched beside him in the back seat of Bert's truck on the way back from the hospital.

The list lay on the table with Agatha's wavery scrawl at the top. Hope would have to leave her to go and get the items Agatha and the doctor wanted. What if Agatha woke and needed something? What if she didn't wake?

If I was in Terra Pines...

What?

She would have called Katie. She had called Katie how many times since Dad left? And what good had it done? The only other person she had trusted, once upon a time—her mother—was too far away to help. Agatha wanted them to do this on their own. Wasn't that what Dad said he was doing, too?

She went for Kenny, hoping to find him outside, as he seemed to be so often. He wasn't. She peered in the windows, trying to see which one was his. She found herself standing at the side of the house in front of his gran, the list flaccid in her hand, stammering about why she had left Agatha even long enough to come across the back, saying she just wanted some company. Damned if she would give Agatha over to Moira.

"We've phones, you know," Moira said.

"Yes, ma'am," she said, surprised at her Southern politeness kicking in. "I didn't think."

"Time you started, is it not?"

Hope felt the heat climb her neck. She held herself in.

"Yes, ma'am," she said.

Hope felt Moira's eyes on her back as she crossed the back garden again and entered the cottage. She paused at the sofa, noted that Agatha's breath was steady and smooth. Some pink had returned to her face and throat. Could Agatha be right, that they could do this by themselves? She'd been right about so much so far. Hope would try to trust that as she ran the errands. She held onto the notion as she stepped out the front door, noticed the shed, thought of the bike. That would get her there faster than her board or her feet—probably even faster than the bus.

She went first to the natural foods shop, where a floral-skirted woman got her the herbs from Agatha's list. After, she made for the pharmacy—on Arran they call it the chemist. The woman behind the counter, a freckly rectangle of middle age, peered through reading glasses attached to a chain of brightly colored glass beads. When she lifted her head to look from the prescription to Hope, her too-black, over-permed curls bounced.

"You are surely not Agatha," the chemist said.

"No, ma'am," Hope said.

"Do you know what this is?" She waved one of the prescriptions at Hope.

"No, ma'am."

The woman paused a minute, assessing.

"I'll have them ready in a few minutes."

Hope hovered nearby, in front of rows of make-up bottles—creams and cakes and powders meant to make women's skin flawless. Hope didn't think it worked; it just made them look sealed in. And anyway, what good did it do? Take, for instance, Hope's flawless mother. Was she any better than Dad, really? At least he had been fully himself before he swaddled himself in Lortab.

"Stuart," the chemist called.

Hope watched the woman slide each of the medicine bottles into the bag. Even through the colored plastic, Hope could see what they were.

"See it's only Agatha who has any of these," the woman said.

Outside again, Hope's hand felt shaky. Her palms began to sweat. Her heartbeat was a blur in her head. She should hurry back to the cottage. She looked out at the Firth of Clyde, herbs in one hand, pills in the other. Tourists drifted past carrying postcards and ice cream cones. Children shouted at each other. Hope felt the press of them, too close. She needed air and space. She needed it now. Across the street and down past the ferry, the crowds thinned to nothing.

Hope found a sheltered section of the rock wall, away from the harshest cut of the wind, the press of tourists, and the searching eyes of locals who knew Auntie Agatha. She plonked herself down on the wall and let her legs dangle in the air. A rare sun gleamed on the water. Warmth gathered under Hope's arms and at her waist and in the palm of her hand, where she clasped one of the little bottles—so similar to the one she'd clung to that first day in the tightly made bed in Auntie Agatha's cottage. It might be called something different here, but she knew the size and shape of the little pills well enough.

Hope lay flat on the rock wall; a quiet corner of the beach or a smooth, flat rock by the shore might have been more comfortable. She preferred the bumpy top of the wall, a reminder. She gripped the bottle tighter, thumbed open the cap without looking, felt one pill in her hand. She held it between her thumb and forefinger, lifted it, and squinted up at it.

Hope's gut tightened. She began to shake, feeling as though it was all starting again, her life in a spiral.

She recalled watching her father take the first pill, there on the sofa. They had laughed together, talked about the rides they would take when he healed. She recalled taking the first pill herself, and then the second one. She remembered the feel of the pill in her mouth, the way it slid down her throat. She'd waited for the slow dissolve, the feeling of her limbs getting a little heavy, as though the muscle was smoothing itself out. Pieces of her—calves and quads, normally tensed and ready for what came next—seemed to flatten; the toughened tissue she'd built up became fluid like the smooth belly of a bowl, easy to flow across. She had rested there in her smooth self.

She closed her eyes. One tear trickled down the side of her cheek. These little pills had taken it all away before, hadn't they? But not in the way she wanted. They had taken her father and she'd done nothing to stop it. Instead she'd followed his lead, let these little pills give her mother an excuse to banish her too. She'd done nothing about that, either. In the car on the way to the airport, she might as well have been watching herself on TV, her insides calling out the way people call out in movie theatres at bad horror films. *He's behind you*, or *run*. She hadn't even heard herself. And now here she was again, at the beginning of the spiral with Agatha.

Hope sat up, swung her feet to the pebbles below. She tucked the pill back into the bottle, pressed the cap on, and tucked the bottle in her pocket. Hope marched back to the village. She would wait five minutes for the bus, then she would ride. Beside her the maw of a trash can gawped. She could dump the pills in there, tell Agatha they didn't have them. Lie. Like her mother and father.

Fuck that.

As she waited, she imagined herself climbing on, rolling over The String to the cottage, pressing the bottle into Agatha's hand. She might not fully trust herself, but she could trust Agatha. She would prepare the fireplace and light a small fire. She would cook their meal. Hope would do it herself; Moira wasn't needed. Hope would not sit still and wish for the right thing to happen. She would try, at least, to make it right, here, with Auntie Agatha.

She clutched the little bottle, still, when she heard Kenny's voice behind her.

"Finally," he said. "I've been shouting your name all the way down the road. My friends already don't believe I know an American, and you're helping them to prove it." Kenny began to tug her across the street, in the direction of a small cluster of teens, pointing at her with his free hand and shouting, "This is Hope, who I've been telling you about."

What had he told them?

"Hiya." One of the girls stepped forward. She introduced herself, Karen, and the other four; she invited Hope to walk along with them.

Here, at last, were people her age. She wanted to drop her bags and follow them. She wanted to scurry back to Agatha.

"I have to get back to my aunt," Hope said. "She hurt her leg."

"We heard she'd to come and save you in the glen," a girl called Audrey said, hip jutting.

Hope turned to Kenny.

"I never said that."

"He never did," Karen said.

"What else would the old bird be doing out there? Planting things? Are you as nutty as she is?"

"She's not nutty." Hope shifted, began to turn.

Kenny grabbed her arm.

"I could see you home."

"I thought you were walking *me* home," Audrey said.

"I never said that, either."

"Another day, maybe you can come out with us, Hope," Karen said.

"Sure, but I have to get back to Aunt Agatha as soon as possible." Hope turned back to the bus stop. Kenny walked along beside her.

"Bus is a long way off yet," he said. "We'd be as well to walk."

"I don't want Auntie Agatha to be alone any longer," Hope said. "I should ride."

"We could ask my gran to check on her."

"No, we couldn't," Hope said.

Kenny blushed.

"Auntie Agatha wants us to do this on our own."

"You could phone."

"I don't have a phone."

Kenny held his out. Hope hesitated, then took the phone. She held her breath as it rang and rang; she imagined Agatha propelling herself agonizingly the few feet between the couch and the phone. She thought about hanging up—she shouldn't be making Agatha move. Wouldn't it be worse, though, to have made her start to move and then not finish the call? A smile overtook Hope's face when she heard her aunt's voice, clear and strong, saying hello and then that she was okay, thank you very much, and that she could do with a few more minutes of peace.

Hope let Kenny roll the bike as they walked beside the sea wall with the waves whispering at their side. After they passed the edge of town, there might have been just the two of them on the whole island, maybe in the whole world.

In the time it took them to reach the last curve before the cottage, Kenny didn't say one word. Did he wish he'd gone with his friends?

"You okay?" she asked.

"I'm great." There was his normal, enthusiastic voice. "Why d'you ask?"

"You usually talk a little more."

"A little?" He laughed. He set down his bike and took her hand, a first for her. "I'm not saying much because I'm trying to sort out how to say something properly."

"What?"

"If I'd got it sorted, I'd have said it."

"You're worried about saying something properly to the queen of blurting it out all wrong?"

"Mmhmm." He took her other hand and they stood facing each other. A slant of sunlight hit him, revealing how serious he looked, how seriously good.

"I know you'll not be here forever and you've friends and a life and everything that you want to go back to, but I've never met a girl like you and I was hoping you'd stay a while longer, and maybe put up with me a bit more, and now Miss Stuart is hurt and you'll maybe have to leave when maybe you were just starting to not hate me."

"I never hated you."

"No? Not even when I laughed at you falling off your skateboard?"

"Maybe a little right then. What I really hated was being sent here."

They didn't move; they stood, hand in hand, Hope feeling the clear air and Kenny's smile, which seemed to be caused by looking at her.

"I don't hate being here now."

"There's something else." Kenny said.

"What?"

"Well, this." He leaned in slowly, holding her hands in his hands, her eyes with his eyes.

In the thin light, at the edge of the land, Kenny's lips touched Hope's, warm against the cool air. They stood like that for a few beautiful moments, the feeling perfect, reminding her of the first moment after being in the air, separate from the board and the world and everything, when her feet reconnected with the griptape and she became one with the board and they cruised along effortlessly together.

Kenny pulled away slowly and straightened. "Thank you."

He leaned in again, offering a quick peck on the cheek.

"Better not push my luck," he said, then let go of Hope's hand and turned toward his house.

TWENTY-SIX
Agatha and Hope

Agatha's ankle throbbed harder at the mere thought of phoning Margaret to tell her she'd fallen. She'd have to, though—wouldn't she? Margaret would be no different than the doctor in her thinking about old ladies who fell. She remembered well what Margaret had had to say when Ellsie had fallen, and Ellsie had been a mere sixty-seven, the injury nothing more than a pulled muscle, years before the cancer. She'd heard the talk in the village when anyone over the age of seventy had the slightest odd turn. All the years would fall away—the feel of cold turves of peat in her hand, the snag of a fish's jaw coming off the hook, the warmth of a coal fire in a tenement. How to build a ship, tend a family, please a man, sew a coat, survive a war, bury a mother a sister a lover, savor a piece of treacle—all these would fall away when the words fell from her mouth that she'd fallen at the Rosa Burn. Her life, in Margaret's mind, reduced to one final mistake. At least it wasn't her hip. At least she had this lovely afternoon. If she could manage to her room, she could collect her favorite photo albums, remind herself of all the years, then stay the night in her own bed before she had to face it.

Agatha pressed one hand down on the arm of the chair and one on the coffee table. She lifted her backside off the couch, just a little at first, testing. It had been one thing to drop onto her knees and crawl the few feet to the phone when Hope had called; it was entirely another to navigate the walk to the door, and beyond, up the stairs. Agatha took one step. She ignored the heat in her leg. She did not break her concentration when Hope came in sooner than she expected, or when Hope grabbed the walker from the corner and put it in front of her.

"I do not need that." She looked neither at it nor at Hope.

"You need it or you need me," Hope said.

"I…" She raised her rump another inch. Her face reddened as she tried her weight on her left foot. She made it one more step, then looked for a new handhold. "I will not be a little old lady with a walker." She took another step.

Hope put out her hand. "You're going to guarantee that you'll be an old lady with a walker if you hurt your ankle any worse."

Hope wrapped her arm around Agatha. Agatha released a small breath.

"Where do you want to go?" Hope pulled Agatha's arm over her shoulder.

"I don't know, really." She looked at Hope, their faces close together. "Yes, I do. I'd like to go to the bookshelves in my room."

They stood there, leaning on each other.

"You should rest. You don't want the doctor coming back." Hope paused and stared into Agatha's whiskery face. "And taking you to the infirmary."

"It's not nice to threaten old ladies." Agatha's spine straightened. "I'm going for my albums. However, I'll let you help, if you must."

As Hope stood beside Agatha on the stairs, she thought about how fast skate tricks go—how the fear turns to excitement in midair, and how it's all over one way or another in seconds. Agatha's palm pressed against the wall, the stair rail unfortunately the wrong height. Her other hand gripped Hope's waist. Hope held onto the area that would have been Agatha's waist if her body curved enough to have one. This was no *leap off and see what comes* moment, the way it was when she dropped in off a steep new ledge. What was the same was the feeling that, once they started, they had to see this trick through, no matter what pain it might bring. Agatha had entered them in an uphill, three-legged race to the bedroom. There was no quitting now.

Hope didn't dare look at Agatha until they were fully on the landing at the top of the stairs. Beads of sweat clung to Agatha's temples. Her cheeks were flushed pink like the first time Hope saw her by the fire. She mustered a smile and leaned away onto the wall, inhaling deeply.

"What is it you lot do over there?" Agatha held up her palm. "The five bit."

Hope slapped her palm and held on, the way she shook hands with someone who had matched her hardest trick, when they both knew that one more ante up would land someone in the ER, when they didn't need to prove it to each other and everyone else was irrelevant.

On one side of Agatha's walk-in wardrobe, four pairs of shoes were lined up neatly as though for inspection: a sturdy pair of lace-ups with a small heel in brown, the same pair beside them in black, a pair of brown suede Birkenstock sandals, and a pair of flat brown lace-ups, which she wore most days when she wasn't using the gardening shoes or Wellington boots that huddled behind the kitchen door downstairs.

Above the shoes, pleated skirts hung at attention; buttoned-up cardigans bandaged hangers, knife-creased trousers pointed blades out as though they were standing guard against an imminent onslaught from the other side of the closet, where the built-in bookshelves were filled with books and papers, huddled together like families in a refugee camp. They pressed against one another, their rippling edges and soft, worn corners clamoring to be pulled out. Though the books were clearly running out of room, and though there was plenty of open space on the floor beside the shoes, nothing from the jam-packed, library side of the closet crossed the center line. It reminded Hope of the time Katie's mom had put a piece of masking tape down the middle seat of the minivan and told Katie to stay on one side and her brother on the other. The papers and rolled-up maps and oversized books reached out from their shelves the way Katie's brother had pointed at her in the car, but never crossed the line. Hope imagined the books and papers singsonging "I'm in my spa-ace," the way Katie's brother had, and sticking out their tongues.

Hope ran her fingers over the spines, most of them wrapped in plain brown paper, Agatha's neat print lining the sides of the tomes in order alphabetically, so that *Gaelic Dictionary* lined up next to *Geometry*, just a few spaces away from *Indigenous Plant and Shrub Propagation* and *Isles: Topo Maps of the Western Isles*.

"There we are." Agatha pointed to a naked green book.

It fell open almost as soon as Hope pulled it from the shelf. On each page, neatly spaced, rested photos from long before she was born. Her attention landed on one on the second page, a woman lounging in a white wicker chair, a young child on her lap. The date at the top of the page was clear. Hope did the math (maths, Agatha called it). Her mother would have been one, so about the size of the baby on the woman's hip—the woman whose body was the same shape as Auntie Agatha's. The woman had the same unruly hair as Agatha, but under the hair, her face looked rounder. She wasn't fat. She just looked strong and comfortable and happy.

"Bring it over, then." Agatha turned toward the bed.

The woman in the picture was definitely Agatha. There were others of her, marking just about every year from 1960 to just before Granny Mac died. At the start, each year held clusters of photos—Agatha with smiling babies, Agatha with gloomy-faced teenage girls, Agatha at weddings and christenings and twenty-first birthday parties. As the years went by, the numbers of photos for each year got thinner. So did Agatha.

"Is that my mother and you?" Hope sat beside her, flipping back to the photo again.

"Aye. She was a lovely bairn, so she was. They were all lovely. Not that you asked this either, but I've been at the christenings of thirty-seven babies. All nieces and nephews and great-nieces and great-nephews. I'm onto great-greats now. I'm godmother to seventeen, you know." She shook her head. "I can only imagine what this cottage would be like if I'd to have the lot of them here at once."

Hope imagined all of them clustered around the fire with seventeen cups of tea and seventeen slices of bannock. Did the seventeen know each other? Did Hope even have a godmother?

Hope turned to a page labeled *Fiona*, featuring a girl whose wild hair flew around her the same way Hope's did. On the next pages, labeled *June* and *Agnes* and *Allison*, Hope felt as though she'd known the girls forever as she recognized a raised eyebrow in one photo, the sure stance in another. "Are these girls related?"

"Aye. All related to each other, and to you. Fiona is a great-niece, like you, and goddaughter. Agnes and June are nieces. Allison is a great-niece as well."

"Why were they here?"

"Same as you, sort of."

"Where are they now?"

"All grown up and mostly happy," Agatha said.

"Did anyone else get you hurt?" Hope looked down at her hands; she picked at an edge of cuticle.

"Hope, every one of them strained or sprained me in one way or another, as people who love each other do, though usually mentally and emotionally rather than physically. Even the ones who just came for their holidays." Agatha patted Hope's leg, then smiled. "You and Allison are tied for making me do the most walking. I did, however, manage to keep myself upright while walking with Allison."

Agatha stroked one of the pages.

"Can you be bothered with another one?"

"Yes," Hope said. She met Agatha's eyes, rested there a minute, resisted the impulse to touch her own cheekbone, the same shape as her aunt's.

TWENTY-SEVEN
Margaret

It was nearly noon by the time Margaret made it to her office.

"Well, you hardly look like someone who was at death's door yesterday," Clarie said.

"Just a twenty-four-hour thing, I guess."

"Mmhm. Want your messages?"

"Sure."

"Mr. Sims wants you to call him about the listing in The Enclave. And Sonja Rupert wants four bathrooms now, and if one could have a bidet," Clarie said. She grinned at the look on Margaret's face. "I'm just the messenger. Oh, and your new client—Tim, is it? Called too."

"Yes." Margaret fiddled with papers on her desk, feeling the color creep up her neck. "Tim."

"He said thanks for the showing yesterday. And he'd like to have another look. He thinks it might be perfect for him."

"I started to feel better in the afternoon," Margaret tried feebly. "Thanks, Clarie."

She closed the door to her office and sat down, unable to stop a smile from consuming her face. She fingered Tim's card. She lifted the phone, then set it down. She breathed deeply, as if that alone could bring her back from acting like a giddy teen to the adult she was supposed to be. Email suited her better—she'd be happy to give Tim another showing. He should call again or email to arrange a time.

"Right," Margaret said. She had work to do, still. She lifted her file on Sonja Rupert. *A bidet, really?* Margaret was laughing quietly to herself when Clarie put a call through.

"Moira something," she said. "She sounds extremely Scottish."

"Margaret, this is Moira, round the back from your Aunt Agatha."

"Yes, of course. Hello, Moira," Margaret said. Her gut wrapped around itself as Moira said she was sorry to bother her, but she felt she had to. Agatha had fallen, been taken to the hospital; Hope had brought her home against the doctor's orders.

"You're very kind to call, Moira," Margaret said. "I'll take it from here."

Margaret clutched the edge of her desk. She stood; she sat back down. Inhale, exhale. Her brain darted around too fast to choose an action. Dear God, what were the two of them up to? She should have asked more questions of Moira. Where had Agatha fallen? How? When? She needed to calm herself before she phoned.

Margaret breathed her way through making a cup of tea. She sat back down. She sipped. Her throat remained constricted, the way she held it for Ujjayi breathing during yoga, only in this case, no relaxation was forthcoming. The best Margaret could do was to keep her breathing steady as she dialed Agatha's number.

TWENTY-EIGHT
Hope and Agatha

Before Hope made it to the closet to get the next album, the ring of the phone stopped her. She turned to Agatha.

"Someone checking up on us, no doubt," Agatha said.

Hope hesitated, her hand on the wall. Couldn't they just ignore it?

"Away and answer it."

Hope pressed through the tightly sealed door into the front room, then hesitated, hand on the phone, in the silence between rings. What if it was the doctor? With very specific questions? What would Agatha want her to say? The next ring made Hope jump. She lifted the receiver.

"Hello? Stuart residence."

"Hope?" Her mother's voice, as loud and clear as if she were in the same room.

"Mom!"

"You sound surprised. Or out of breath. Were you in the middle of something?"

"No. You sound surprised yourself."

"I didn't expect you to answer."

"Then why did you call?"

"I mean, I expected Agatha."

"Oh."

"Where is she?"

"Nowhere. Just here. Nothing to do. Friday night on Arran."
Hope looked at her watch. Middle of the workday in Terra

Pines. Mom hated personal calls in the middle of work.

Agatha pressed herself up, leaned on the bed with one hand until she could reach the wall. From downstairs, Hope's voice, loud and too high. She'd obviously forgotten to close the door to the front room. *Margaret.* At least she'd had some time with her photos, if not the peaceful night in her own bed, before this conversation.

Cool and rough under her hand, the plaster held her weight. In the doorway, she put forward her good leg, as far as she could, lifted her weight onto it, leaned for the banister. On the stairs, she said a quiet thanks for her long wingspan, able to keep one hand on the banister and the other on the wall. She resisted the temptation to slide down onto her bottom and navigate the stairs like a toddler. Wasn't that where they said everyone went in their old age—back to babyhood?

In the front room, face flushed, Agatha squeezed Hope's shoulder, lifted the phone out of her hand.

"Hallo, Margaret, I'll pass you back to Hope in a minute if you like, just want a quick word." Agatha stood with one leg crooked, stork-like, her hand on Hope's shoulder.

"I just thought I should call and make sure everything's okay." Margaret's voice was tense, and Agatha forced herself to relax in counterpoint, keeping her tone especially light.

"We were going to ring you in the morning with a wee bit of news. I've just taken a little fall—some slight damage to my ankle, just to add a wee bit of challenge to things." Agatha smiled at Hope.

"A bit of damage?"

"Aye."

"How much, exactly?"

"Just a wee bit of a break."

"A broken ankle. Auntie Agatha. You should be in the hospital. Who is taking care of you?"

"Calm yourself, dear. I am taking care of me. Hope is helping." She squeezed Hope's shoulder.

"Hope? You need supervision. Medical attention."

"I've had all the medical attention I need. I'll recover in due course. Old ladies get better, you know."

"Why didn't you call me?"

"It just happened yesterday, pet. We meant to ring earlier."

"What happened, exactly?"

Agatha told of tripping on a rock and of how Hope had made sure they got to the hospital safely, and then got them back to the cottage, started the fire, made the breakfast. She'd filled Agatha's prescriptions. All was well.

"Let me speak to Hope. No, never mind. She tried to feed me some story about just another Friday night on Arran."

"She's correct."

"Meaning you break your ankle every Friday?"

"Meaning we were having a chat, as we do. And looking at lovely photos. Including some of you."

Silence.

"I think I've learned enough," Margaret said. "I'll call again tomorrow."

"Fair enough. Mind, if we're outside we'll no hear the phone, and there's no machine. You'll try us again, I'm sure."

"How are you going to manage outside?"

"I told you it's just wee."

"Moira didn't make it sound *wee*."

"Moira? Aye, now the truth comes out. I might have known. You'll remember what Moira's like," Agatha said. "We're fine. We'll keep you posted. Away you go now, and don't worry yourself about me."

"Will you *keep me posted* in a more timely manner than you let me know in the first place?"

"Aye, Margaret, if that's what you'd like."

"It is."

"You can ring as often as you like. I've never said otherwise. Speak soon, pet."

Agatha let go of Hope, set down the receiver.

"Is she going to send you away?" Hope asked.

"Not today."

TWENTY-NINE
Margaret

Margaret set down the phone. She closed her eyes. *Shit.* While she'd been sipping wine on Tim's sofa, Aunt Agatha had hurt herself gallivanting through the glen. How had they even gotten out afterward? Margaret had dragged along behind Agatha in her youth, and again to scatter her mother's ashes. You didn't just call a cab, or an ambulance for that matter. Margaret put her head in her hands. She should have known Aunt Agatha was too old to handle Hope. How could she make it right?

She turned to her computer. She could book Hope a ticket back. Should Agatha come too? Could she even travel? Margaret pictured another invalid convalescing in her house. She thought of her still-cavernous den. Hope would skulk through the door, still angry over the new business brand, looking for something else to demonstrate that Margaret wasn't the mother she wanted or needed, and find the gaping hole where the couch used to be. And that was without Margaret telling her that Brad had been back.

"Shit," Margaret said. She stepped out of her office, face pale, searching for steady ground. She found Clarie first. "My aunt broke her leg."

"Shit," Clarie said.

"That's what I said."

"Are you going over?"

"I don't know." Margaret shook her head. "Aunt Agatha doesn't seem to want me there." She went back to her desk, hung her head, and then lifted the phone and dialed Trig's number, hoping she hadn't totally trashed their friendship.

Trig picked up on the first ring. "Well, look who it is!"

"Trig, I'm sorry."

"You damn sure are."

"And I thought you might like to know that Agatha broke her leg," Margaret blurted out. "Well, not that I thought you'd like that Agatha is hurt, but that you would want to know, and her neighbor called and told me it's bad and Agatha says it isn't anything really and I don't know what to do and Brad came back after you left and I might have alienated my one true friend."

"Shit, honey. Of course you know what to do. Get your ass on a plane."

"Agatha doesn't want me there. Hope hasn't wanted me anywhere near her for months."

"Screw that. You have to go."

"What if Brad comes back again?"

"Did you really just say that? Screw Brad."

"He tried to break in."

"Is that why you're really afraid of going?" Trig let the question hang on the line for a few moments.

Margaret closed her eyes. She scrunched away the tears at the corners of her eyes.

"I'll take care of your house. You can make it up to me when you get back."

Margaret nodded, hung up, went back to the computer, found the least ridiculously expensive flight late that afternoon, booked it before a new round of questions paralyzed her. It would only save her a hundred dollars to wait a day or two anyway.

Bag packed with an hour to spare, Margaret pulled back out of her neighborhood. Clyde. He deserved an update, didn't he? She parked in his driveway, hurried through the garden gate, down the path and up onto the porch, calling his name, pressing her hands against one window and then the other. Light through the other side of the kitchen shone on the empty coffee mug on the counter, the only evidence that anyone had been there at all. She peered around the edges of the porch, half-expecting him to come out of nowhere as he always seemed to. She sat on the top step, folded her arms across her nervously bouncing knees, had almost decided to go on to the airport when she heard the rumble of the tractor. She walked around the side of the house to the driveway and found Clyde rolling across the fields, riding high in the seat.

He pulled up in front of her. "Hop on."

Margaret shielded her eyes, the sun bright again after the storm. "I'm in a bit of a hurry."

"Won't take but a few minutes," He reached down.

In the short time she'd known Clyde, Margaret had learned that it was always faster just to go along with him.

Callused fingers wrapped around Margaret's smooth wrist, mahogany swallowing honey. No one would guess from the grip of his fingers or the pull of his arm that he needed a cane. Margaret felt he could lift her into the air one-handed, perhaps even hold her there and twirl her as her father had when she was very small, spinning her around and around, giving her the lovely feeling of herself turning one way as fast as the world turned the other, beautiful synchronicity. How long since she'd felt any sort of synchronicity?

"Shotgun." Clyde patted the space beside the seat. "That's what we called it when my daughter, Ruth, rode along. Bonnie, I nicknamed her. Get it?"

He turned the tractor back to the field. They rode in silence, away from Bent Creek and Clyde's bungalow, in the direction of the creek that marked the boundary.

"My Bonnie used to ride this land with me from when she was teen-tiny, check the corn and the little bit of cotton we still grew when she was a youngster. Loved to get down and stand in the middle of a row of corn, touch each stalk. Loved to come out under a harvest moon and ride. Being out last night reminded me of her. This ain't about Ruth, though. You call your girl?"

"My aunt broke her ankle."

"Mmhm." The tractor rumbled on. Clyde lifted a weathered hand. "My granddad planted that line of water oaks there. See how it looks like they come from the earth on their own, not in a neat row, but the way the trees would plant themselves? Granddaddy put them in as saplings—dug them up from places they'd of gone wrong and set them down here, where they could grow up good."

They drove, slower now, for a few more minutes.

"She get it seen to, your aunt—her ankle?"

"She says so."

"Don't seem like nothing to worry about. How's your girl?"

"I'm not sure I believe it's nothing to worry about. It could be a big deal at her..." She paused, glanced at Clyde. "Well, she's old."

"Mmhm. Right there, in that corner, I grew my first little crops. Later, I planted a peach tree, only one we ever had. I tended it just the same—lay my hands on it every day until I was sure it was strong. Still come out to her in weather that might not be right for her, just to be sure. Even now she blossoms for me."

Limbs bristled out from the short tree. Clawed branches reached toward the sky. Such a harsh-looking plant to bear the soft, sweet fruit nestled in its bright green leaves.

"I really have to be going," Margaret said. "The airport. My flight's in an hour."

Clyde turned the tractor toward his house. "Auntie can't be too bad or you wouldn't of sent your daughter in the first place."

They rode in silence until they reached the driveway. As Margaret prepared to jump down from the tractor, Clyde put his hand on her shoulder.

"You know my crops and my little peach tree?"

Margaret met his eye.

"I tended them right all the years; thought I was leaving something for my girls. Turns out I was just leaving, dawn to dusk every day. And then they left me. What I got now is too many peaches and recipes for things folks don't want to make anymore." He nodded. "You hear me?"

"I do."

—

The airport smelled of stale sweat, popcorn, and lilac air freshener. Margaret tucked herself into a corner seat with her phone, checking email, setting her clients up with colleagues in her absence, letting people know where she was going. She saw an email from Tim, thumbed over it.

Just as they called for boarding, her phone rang. Tim, on the other end. "You didn't mention visiting your daughter last night."

"I didn't plan on it. My aunt broke her ankle."

"I'm sorry. You should have called. I could have driven you to the airport."

"Thanks."

"How long will you be gone?"

"Just a few days, if I'm lucky. Depends what I find on the other side."

"Look…I know I hardly know you, but I liked last night," Tim said. "I'm here if you need something. And I'd like to see you again when you get back."

"Thanks," Margaret said. Were her cheeks pink? "Me, too."

Margaret paused. Could she say more? Tim had unlocked something in her—reminded her what it was to let herself unfold into joy instead of being the one who held it all together, grim-faced, while everyone else had fun. She wanted to hurry back to that, to Tim. She wanted to believe that she could build a new life with that as a foundation. But not without Hope.

"I have to go. We're boarding."

The belly of the 747 rumbled. Margaret had three seats to herself, the extra space she had so often hoped for when she'd sat next to her mother. Ellsie always seemed to take up more than she ought to, fleshy arms smothering the armrest. During her teen years, Margaret had looked away, nonetheless seeking the soft round of her mother's shoulder when it came time to sleep. Only twice had she boarded a plane since her mother returned to Scotland: once for Hope's gestation and again for her mother's funeral. Then, Agatha had wanted Margaret to help her carry a whole tree into the glen.

"Just a sapling," Agatha said. "To put her with Mammy and Wina."

Margaret had told her she could remember her mother fine without breaking her back planting a tree. Agatha's shoulders had arched back, her chin raised, lips thin, but she hadn't argued. Margaret had felt a small turn of the stomach, low, and almost reconsidered.

Her mother wouldn't have wanted a tree. The ashes were all she needed, scattered partly in her beloved Scotland and partly with her beloved James. She wouldn't have wanted to be rooted to Scotland. Would she? Of all the sisters, only Agatha had chosen that, pulling the family back in again and again from other countries and other continents. Margaret had resented it as a girl—the pilgrimage to Auntie Agatha. Then, pregnant with Hope, she'd resented that she could think of nowhere better to go. She resented Agatha's deep knowledge of the biggest flaws in her life. Margaret clenched her jaw. Her mother had reminded her time and again that they should all be grateful for Agatha and her unfailing generosity. Where would they be without Agatha?

Margaret tried to settle over the Atlantic, the tiny white pillow harder than her mother's shoulder had been. She closed her eyes, drifted into a dream with a black and white tile floor, red spattered walls. She opened her eyes to the flight attendant coming at her, plastic dinner trays steaming. She shook her head lightly, tried to focus on where she was going and why.

She'd thought about abortion, all those years ago; she'd stood in their bedroom, hers and Brad's, after confronting him about the cocaine, the first time, fifteen years ago. She'd wondered if it had damaged his sperm, if she could manage a baby at all, especially on her own. She'd tried to clutch her still flat, tight abdomen. No matter how closely a person looked, they wouldn't be able to see the question she asked herself, over and over: keep or toss?

Even at Agatha's cottage, the question hovered for months, an alternative toss offered in the form of adoption. Even within the family (Agatha's suggestion), such a thing would have felt to

Margaret as though she was throwing her child onto the family's midden. So the answer had been keep, even before Brad arrived at Agatha's gate and asked her the same question about himself.

Now, on the plane, with her marriage in the dump, she tried to muster up a *keep*, but she wasn't sure to what.

THIRTY
Hope and Agatha

Hope brought Agatha's photo albums downstairs. Bunched together on the couch, they sifted through images and years and stories in front of the fire, trying not to be jangled by Margaret's phone call. In the morning, Hope washed the breakfast dishes and cleared away the remnants of Agatha's herbal tea, wiping her wet hands down the legs of her patchwork pants. The bag from the chemist sat scrunched on the far corner of the counter, unopened. As she worked, Hope watched Agatha, balancing on one leg while she laid out flour, baking soda, salt, sultanas, and the sieve on the counter.

Agatha scooped the flour into the sieve and then tap-tapped the edge with her hand, barely touching the sieve each time but coming back again and again so the flour fell to the bowl below like the finest snowflakes, reminding Hope of the snow angels she and Mom made years and years ago. They'd lain in the back yard, side by side, swooshing their arms up and down, sweeping their legs in and out, giggling at the feel of the wet snow underneath their bodies and the fine flakes tickling their faces.

Hope was five. Mom didn't work. She stayed home and cooked desserts on Sundays—apple pies and chocolate volcano cakes and lemony muffins. Back then, Mom even ate those desserts, and Hope had still been amazed that tiny, weightless snowflakes could pile up into something solid enough to make snowmen, to stop traffic, to make her mom lie down and giggle the morning away.

Agatha handed Hope the sieve, a clump of flour in the middle. It seemed right. Hope had learned, since those days of snow angels and volcano cakes, that things could go in the opposite direction—backward from fine, weightless snow transforming into whole wintry scenes. Her life had gone from those solid days to fragments too scattered to catch neatly in a bowl.

Hope tapped the sieve, sending floating specks of flour down in the bowl, flour she and Agatha would mould into sweet scones, buttery circles to nourish them. Could life be like that, going from solid to fragments and back to solid again?

They slid the scones into the oven. Agatha struck what looked like a yoga pose, balancing on one foot and taking down her clothes. Hope had nearly finished cleaning the counters when the knock came. It was Kenny.

"How's the ankle today, Miss Stuart?"

"Getting better, thank you, Kenny. You've come to check on me, have you?"

"I've come to see if Hope wants to come a walk." He turned to Hope.

Hope shook the crumbs she'd gathered into the compost can. She turned to Agatha, tea towel open, ready to wipe or hang it on its hook beside the sink.

"I think I can manage the eating of a scone all by myself," Agatha said.

Kenny's idea of a walk was to hike cross-country to the bus stop, ride into Brodick, buy a bag of fries, which he called chips, and sit on a rock wall watching the ferry dock and making up stories about the people stepping off. Hope's hand rested on the rock wall between them, and Kenny took it in his; Hope rested there, letting Kenny's voice roll over her, his skin making hers tingle.

When they finished the last fry, they made the return journey, only instead of going directly to the cottage, Kenny led Hope out onto the rocks, not far from the place Hope had seen Agatha that first night outside, coming toward her like something from another world—the same place she'd seen Dad in her dream. The cottage was out of view. Behind her, the land rose, rough and craggy. To the left and right, pebbles spread out forever as though nothing else had ever belonged in the world. In front of her, the Atlantic stretched and stretched, swinging its salty self back and forth from the shores of one continent to another.

Hope bent, curled her hand around a fistful of pebbles. She threw stone after stone after stone, trying to make them skip like Agatha could. Most of them plopped and sank. What did it matter? She'd had so much contact with rock in one way or another since she'd been on Arran that it had started to seem like a friend: always there and always honest, even if the pebbles wouldn't always do precisely what she wanted. She turned to Kenny.

"Looks as though I'm going to be here a while," she said. "I wouldn't want to leave Aunt Agatha, while she's hurt and all."

Kenny took her hand. "Is that the only reason you'd want to be here?"

"There might be another one." She looked up at Kenny and dropped the last rock to the shore as he bent to kiss her.

"Good," he said.

Agatha made for the front room as soon as the scones were out of the oven. There, she lowered herself from the couch to the floor. She pushed along the carpet, scone in hand, until she reached the fire. Standing, baking scones, had been more than enough for her ankle. She propped it on the hearth. Surely even a few inches of elevation were better than nothing. She let her torso round to the heat. Agatha took a deep breath, held her lungs full, let go, closed her eyes, bit into the scone. Butter and flour and her own raspberry jam clung to her tongue. She held onto the sweet for a few extra seconds before she swallowed.

The girl had done well at the chemist and the health food shop, up the stairs and down, sifting the flour to just the right texture. She might even be making a friend or two. Agatha bit again, held the morsel, rounded slightly more, the pain in her ankle subsiding. She might lie back, there in front of the fire. Why had she never thought of it before?

All her life, around the fire, they'd sat. On stools or on the floor on Skye, crowded around, curling into little balls of themselves to fit near the fire in Glasgow and again when the lot of them visited the cottage. Even when it had been down to her and Donagh, he'd sat behind her, his legs outstretched, and she between them, back to his chest, upright. For the first time, lying down seemed the right thing to do, as though she was a girl on a picnic blanket, out in the air, lying back to look at the clouds, crumbs from the last sweet bite clinging to the hidden places in her mouth.

Agatha reached her arms behind her, began to lower, landing supine by the fire just as the phone rang. She lifted her head, thought to ignore it. Unless it was Hope, needing something. Surely Kenny would see her okay. But how could she be sure? She pushed up again, pulled her leg from the hearth. Perhaps it was that blasted doctor, checking on her. It could be Moira, threatening food, as if she wouldn't just march right in, or Margaret—or Mags or whatever she was called now— reminding her of her age. Agatha was on all fours by then; she put one arm on the coffee table, thinking to stand, then thought better of it. She'd get there faster crawling. She strained forward, one arm on the chair by the phone. Still on her knees, she lifted the receiver, said hello and heard Margaret's voice, high like a spring songbird, wrong for the season, on the other end, saying she was here.

"Here where?" Agatha asked.

"Here. In Scotland. Glasgow. I just landed. I'm renting a car. Do I need to pick up anything on the way?"

"You're here?"

"Auntie Agatha, are you okay?"

"I might ask you the same."

An audible sigh. "Do you need me to bring anything?"

"Just yourself will be more than enough."

"You're sure."

"Quite sure."

"See you soon, then."

Agatha replaced the receiver, sat back on her bottom, pulled her legs out in front of her. She lay back, reached her arms over her head, added up time in customs, immigration, car hire, the drive to Ardrossan, the ferry, over The String. Three hours, and then Margaret would be there. Agatha stretched her body to its full length, rigid, her gut tightening as it had decades ago at the sight of old Mr. McKechnie striding out of his office at the shipyard in the middle of the workday, no warning at all, his red nose leading the way as he marched past each girl's station, pronouncing their work—and by extension themselves—worthy or otherwise.

THIRTY-ONE
Margaret and Hope and Agatha

An Garbh-choire. For all the times she'd been there, Margaret couldn't for the life of her remember what the words meant. She could recall the feel of Agatha's hand around hers thirty-five years before, lean and foreign. The cadence of Agatha's voice as they stepped down the garden path, Agatha tugging her away from her mother, who was paying the taxi driver and getting the bags. She remembered the wind, cold in the middle of summer. They'd left ninety-nine degrees and landed in fifty-five in Glasgow, grey skies and gathering wind as they crossed the Firth of Clyde. Margaret had huddled inside the ferry, stubborn against her mother's cajoling that she go above and watch the crossing properly.

"This is where we're from," her mother had said.

Not me. Margaret had said a silent thanks that her mother had met her father at the Festival of Flowers, that he'd brought her to America—a series of framed photos in the den told the story of their meeting and marrying and of her mother's emigration. The return trips lived only in memory. Margaret hadn't intended to make any more of those memories, yet here she was again.

Inside her little red hired car, windows steaming, Margaret looked from the sign to the cottage to the sea. Funny how people named their homes. Her first childhood home had a name. Her mother must have carried the tradition across the sea, then dropped it when they moved to a larger house in a new subdivision when Margaret was seven, a brick ranch amongst so many others that curled around cul-de-sacs, each with its mailbox at the end of the driveway. In South Carolina, names were for vacation houses, fanciful places.

Margaret checked herself in the mirror, freshened her lipstick, shook her head lightly, fluffing her hair and trying to shake away a sudden surge of doubt about why she was there at all. Shouldn't she just have trusted Agatha? Or, if not, just made the decision to bring Hope home? Would her mind ever leave off with the fucking questions?

"Jesus, Margaret, what is wrong with you?" She straightened the mirror, opened the car door, lifted one small floral bag, a weekender, from the passenger seat. Between the car and the gate, Margaret stood, one hand on the sign, hair whipping over her head. She thought of naming, of the story behind names, of her mother on the sofa with her in second grade, saying her own name spanned hundreds of years. Margaret, from the Greek for pearl.

Her father had said, "Oh, Ellsie, you know it's really a flower. Margaret is my lovely flower." Margaret looked it up in the school library and found that both her parents were correct, and that there was a third, bastardized version in the Germanic languages, meaning pebble. Had her mother known? Tried to slip a piece of the Scottish coast into her name as well as her DNA?

Margaret looked toward the sea, settled her other hand on her stomach. She turned toward the rocks, dropped the bag, leaned seaward as if she might go. She glanced at the cottage; the kitchen curtain fluttered closed.

At the back door, Margaret hesitated. Knock or walk in? Pull the door open, poke her head round, call out "Yoohoo," as her mother used to do, expecting a full welcome every time? Probably what Trig had expected when she used the spare key. Margaret raised a hand to knock. The door opened.

"Margaret." Agatha's arms extended almost to their full span.

Margaret's eyes landed on Agatha's cast. "Oh, Auntie Agatha! Shouldn't you have a crutch?"

"Lovely to see you, too."

"Sorry." Instantly small again—some awful combination of the little girl being pulled down the garden path and the shamefaced young woman scurrying away from failure— Margaret took a deep breath, leaned toward Agatha for a second chance at a hug. Agatha flapped her away, aimed for the front room, kitchen counter serving as her crutch.

Margaret brushed her hair out of her face, smoothed her trousers, straightened her shoulders. She remembered her mother again, packing for another journey across the sea, body hunching over the open case on the bed. "Sometimes. That sister of mine." Mummy had punched her hands against her ample hips. "'No need for your cardie,' she says. 'Or your Wellies,' she says. 'We've it all here.' As though she has the whole bloody world of foul weather gear there. As though we can't take care of ourselves. We should just turn up naked and see what she does then." Ellsie flopped a coarse wool cardigan into the case. "Who could fit their pinky, even, into one of her tiny wee cardies anyway?"

Margaret had been ten, hadn't been sure her mother even knew she was there, standing in the corner, listening; hadn't needed to ask which sister. Agatha, of course—the one they all flocked to, muttering a litany of complaints like a rosary the whole way and then opening their arms and clucking—the Stuart sisters on their annual migration, until Margaret's mother migrated back permanently after her father died.

And now here was Margaret, following her mother's path, the suitcase in her hand full, she was certain suddenly, of all the wrong things.

Margaret set down her bag, slipped off her shoes, lined them up next to Agatha's Wellies and gardening shoes. Nothing of Hope's. Margaret's stomach knotted. She pressed into the front room, found Agatha standing before her, waiting. Alone.

"Where is Hope?

"She's away out. I expect she'll be back shortly."

"Oh." Margaret felt suddenly deflated.

Agatha placed a hand on each of Margaret's shoulders. "Let's have a good look at you, then." Margaret's muscles, calves to neck, coiled tighter under Agatha's scrutiny. "Flawless. As ever you were. On the outside, at any rate." Agatha pressed her hands inward, then stroked Margaret's left arm. "Are you all right, pet?"

"Of course." Margaret might as well have been naked. Agatha's stare had stripped her already, and she was hardly through the door. If Margaret gave her half a chance, she feared Agatha would have her down to the bone, picked clean, emotional carrion.

Agatha nodded, patted her, turned.

"Will you want forty winks, or tea first?"

Margaret sighed. *I want Hope.* Even in her head, the demand sounded like a petulant child, wanting back a toy she'd given away to the Goodwill. When Margaret put Hope on the plane, she'd been pleased at the thought of Hope with no cable, no computer, no cell phone—just clean, fresh air and space. Now she wanted her reeled in, accounted for.

"We'll take our tea then…"

"I don't want tea." Margaret's hand flew to her mouth, the sudden exasperation risen and then swallowed almost in one breath. "Sorry." Again.

"No bother, dear."

Agatha lowered herself into her chair. She nodded in the direction of the sofa. Margaret did as she was told and sat, too. Agatha raised her eyebrows, waiting for Margaret to speak.

"It's just, well. I came all this way, expecting…"

What had she expected? Hope sitting neatly beside Agatha, sipping tea, reciting the poetry of Robert Burns in pink American Eagle pants? Agatha pale and weak and needing her? A great big sign that said she wasn't a total failure as a mother and a niece? Her life back?

Agatha leaned closer, obviously willing to wait until Margaret found the right words. So calm. So patient. So fucking irritating. Margaret pulled her eyes away, landed on the walker, pushed into the corner, and the wheelchair beside it. "Aunt Agatha! You have a wheelchair and walker and you're not even using a crutch?"

"Calm yourself, Margaret. I haven't needed either, except the wheelchair on the way out of the hospital." Agatha stifled a chuckle and reached behind the sofa. "I've a lovely cane." She pulled it out. "Which I can use." Agatha planted it in front of Margaret. "But you surely haven't come three thousand miles with no notice to make sure I'm using the correct support apparatus."

Margaret shifted in her seat. She clasped her hands in her lap, unclasped them, rested one across the doily on the armrest, rolled an edge of lace between her fingers. "I've just come to make sure you're okay." Margaret stood and turned to the window, one hand scrunching the doily on the back of the chair. "Both of you."

"As you can see, I'm fine. You'll soon see Hope is fine as well. Tell me, so, how *you* are. What have you been doing with yourself these weeks Hope has been with me?"

What would Agatha say if Margaret said she'd kissed a client in the foyer of someone else's house? That she'd been drunk with a man nearly twice her age—a man she hardly knew? That he'd brought her home so drunk she didn't even remember it. That her husband had turned up, ragged and awful, and that, in response, she'd taken herself over to Tim's? That each of these decisions had seemed right at the time—that some of them still seemed right even now, as she lost herself in the deep red upholstery of Agatha's ancient couch? That there were some she wanted to repeat.

"I'd rather talk about what Hope has been doing here."

"Hope can tell you that herself when she gets back."

The Hope who had boarded the plane in Terra Pines wouldn't have told Margaret anything. And now here was Agatha, not telling anything either but expecting her to reveal herself. Margaret looked back at Agatha—the years engraved on her face, the lean body that had survived all her younger sisters, the thick cast on her leg. Still, somehow, stronger than she was. Margaret clenched her hands on her knees, wishing she could muster up just a bit of the joy, the comfort she'd felt with Tim.

"You should consider a wee sleep, Margaret."

"I don't need a wee sleep or a wee cup of tea or a wee dram or a *wee* anything. I need…"

Agatha's eyes were too sharp. "What, exactly?" she asked.

Margaret hung her head. *Answers?*

When Hope got back to the cottage, the goat had given up leaning over the wall in favor of peeing on the driver's-side front wheel of the tiny red car that sat in front of the cottage. Could it be the doctor's car? She turned to Kenny. He shrugged.

"Want me to come in with you?" he asked.

Hope paused, considering. "No, thanks."

Kenny squeezed her hand. "You know where I am." He turned toward his house as Hope started through the gate. What if Agatha had fallen again? What if it *was* the doctor? Hope stepped quietly into the house, listening for Agatha's voice but hearing a different one, far more familiar. She didn't need to make out the words to know that it was her mother, out of the blue, pulling up in a shiny red car, waltzing in. She pressed the side of her body against the kitchen door, listening.

A pause, and then Agatha's voice, more gently: "Might you have come here to get yourself sorted?"

"I don't need to be sorted."

"Ah, Margaret," Agatha said. "You were always a lassie who had to have everything lined up neatly."

"What's wrong with that?"

"Not a thing," Agatha said. Another pause. "I just want to see you all right."

"I already told you I'm all right." The chirp factor in her mom's voice increased. "It's you who's injured."

"I just have a broken bone. But you," Agatha said, "how can you possibly be all right?"

"Of course I'm all right. I have a nice home. I have a thriving business. I have…"

"A missing husband. A daughter thousands of miles away. A life not lining up neatly just at the minute." Another moment of silence. "And not all your fault."

Hope stiffened. She imagined Agatha leaning toward Mom, trying to touch her. Margaret would shift away.

"Did you think you could be the first person in the world to get from birth to death always knowing what would come next?" Agatha asked.

The silence that followed seemed to press the door back against Hope.

"Brad." Margaret's voice sounded small.

"What about Brad, pet?"

In the long silence that followed, Hope almost pressed through the door into the front room, the echo of Agatha's question bouncing in her head.

"I saw him."

"You saw Brad? When?"

Hope pressed her palms against the door. Her gut clenched. Her spine, even, seemed to tighten.

"I was." Margaret hesitated. "He came to the house."

"And?"

And? Hope tilted her head back, breathed deeply to resist the impulse to barge into the front room and confront her mother herself. She listened, feeling warmer and warmer, her breath increasingly shallow and her throat tightening as her mother described her father as a scarecrow, a ragged addict, lost to his pills, car gone. He'd asked for money and she'd refused. Of course she had. When the conversation paused, Hope breathed into the silence, molten anger rising from her core and breaking against her rocky shore. She couldn't resist her own impulse anymore, threw the door open.

Mom's back was to Hope. Her perfectly manicured hands pressed against the white of the windowsill, pearl-passion-pink-tipped fingers trying to hold everything together, even the cottage. In the moment before she spoke, Hope took in the two women: her great-aunt's ridged, pale face, her mother's brown and pink spectrum of perfection. Aunt Agatha was the rough wood Hope loved on her skateboard. Mom was smooth, polished, like the sideboard where she kept the good silver. Impossibly, the wood that made these two women had been cut from the same family tree. Hope remembered Aunt

Agatha's box and comb, the chant that was really a sacred blessing. She took a deep breath. She would not let her mother control this, too.

"Mom," she said.

Margaret turned, eyes wide, lashes battering her cheekbones. "Hope."

"Dad came home?"

Margaret's face slackened, only for a second. Did her chin quiver? "Yes, Hope, he did."

Hope took a step closer. "Dad came home and I missed him because you sent me here, and you didn't even bother to call?"

"What would I have said? He was gone."

"He might have stayed if you'd given him what he wanted."

"Hope, you don't understand."

"I think I understand perfectly," Hope said. "You got rid of both of us. Congratulations, Mom."

"Hope. Honey. It's not like that at all." Margaret started toward her.

Hope swung away from her, toward Agatha, her fists trembling at her sides. "It is like that. It *is* her fault. I don't even know why she's here. We're fine without her."

She gets rid of everyone who doesn't fit in her perfect little life. What will she do to us now?

"Acht, the pair of you, that's quite enough." Agatha's voice, louder than Hope had ever heard it, sliced across the room.

Agatha kneaded the arms of the chair with her lean fingertips. How many times had she seen this? What was it about mothers and daughters, the hate that narrowed their eyes and their lips and their hearts to each other? She'd had none of that with her own mother; she'd only been able to stand on the outside, watching Ellsie quietly fold in and in, never able to get so much as a whisper until that morning her mother asked to go to the sea. If her mother had spoken her loss, even in a venomous murmur, Agatha might have had the thread she needed to pull her mother out of herself and back to them.

Agatha reached for Hope and wrapped her in her arms. "Calm yourself, *doithín*."

She held Hope there a moment and then pulled back.

"What a pair." She shook her head. "Hope. Your father's addiction is not your mother's fault. And your mother, she loves you." Hope rolled her eyes. Agatha held up her hand. "You may not be able to feel it just this minute, but I assure you she does."

Agatha pulled Hope close to her again, feeling the girl's hot, angry breath on her neck.

"Margaret," she said over Hope's head. "Can you turn away from the window and look at your daughter? And as you do it, can you try to see her? Truly see her?" Agatha paused, watching the flickers of unintelligible emotion across Margaret's face and wondering if her niece could see what she saw: the eyes that were brighter, more open than when Hope had first arrived, no longer defiant; the patchwork pants, sewn by her own hand; the cheek bearing just a little flush, as if some lad's young lips had rested there; the long red hair swept back over her shoulders, out of her face. Only after Hope and Margaret had regarded each other for a minute in silence did she speak again. "Hope," she whispered. "You've a lot to tell your mother."

Within Agatha's arms, Hope shook her head.

"Aye, you have. You've to tell her the lot of it. Even what you haven't told me."

Hope pressed her forehead to Agatha's collarbone.

"It's the only way. It will be all right." She spoke louder then, for Margaret's benefit. "It can only be all right if the pair of you tell each other the truth. Where else would you expect to find the right answer?"

THIRTY-TWO
Hope and Margaret

Scrunched in Agatha's arms, Hope lifted her head. Her face was raw; her heart was drumming on her breastbone. Agatha let go and stepped back, leaving Hope exposed with no place to twist or turn. Aunt Agatha flicked her eyes from Hope to her mother, and then reached for her cane, hobbled across the front room and into the kitchen. A moment later, the light slap of the front door against its frame said she'd gone out.

Hope turned to her mother, found dark lines trailing down her mother's cheeks—her mascara out of place for once.

"I do love you, Hope." Her hand reached for Hope's cheek.

Hadn't it been Mom's habit to come into her room when she was five, in the early morning, and stroke her cheek, to wake her for kindergarten with that softest of touches? Hope held herself steady, clenched her teeth so she wouldn't pull away.

Mom sat on the couch. She patted the seat next to her, as though Hope was her favorite house cat.

"What's everything?" she asked.

Hope folded her arms across her chest.

"I'd like to know."

Hope tightened her grip on herself.

"It can't make things any worse between us."

Hope traced the seam of the patches on her pants.

Several minutes passed before Mom whispered, "Please."

Hope sank into the empty chair, rigid and silent. How could Agatha have done this to her?

"Would it help if I went first?"

Hope shrugged. "Couldn't make things any worse," she echoed, although she wasn't sure that was true.

Margaret shifted to face her. She put her hands on Hope's knees.

"About fifteen years ago, I came to stay with Aunt Agatha for a while," she said.

"With Dad?"

"No." Margaret swallowed. "This might be the hardest thing I've ever done, telling you this. Think you could just listen? I promise to do the same for you."

Mom took Hope's hand. Hope started to pull back, then stopped, hypnotized by the black smudges under her eyes, the migration of tiny mascara particles down her perfect cheeks. What could have happened the year before her birth that would be hard for Mom to tell? Hope left her hand where it was and nodded, because her throat was too tight to get words out.

Fifteen years ago, Margaret had hesitated in front of the little gate, a hand on her stomach, still flat, holding the embryo. Agatha had rushed out with her apron on, wrapped arms around Margaret and pressed damp hands against her back, come to life at the sight of the latest Stuart in need of shelter.

Margaret had discovered Brad's cocaine stash when she went to hide her pregnancy test: positive, unplanned. She hadn't even been sure what was in the bag and had taken it to Trig, who, it turned out, already knew. Just about everyone except Margaret knew. "Great for endurance," one of his racing buddies said. Some used with him. Some sold to him. Margaret felt betrayed by everyone she'd trusted, except Agatha and her own mother.

How could she tell her mother that she had an unplanned pregnancy and that her baby's father was a cocaine addict in the same breath? She hid out at *An Garbh-choire* with Agatha, settling for putting the world away for a while.

They quickly fell into a daily rhythm, finding ways to live together while spending most of their time apart. Agatha brokered the conversation with Margaret's mother, who was still working then, in Glasgow. She came to them on weekends. None of it was part of the plan Margaret had made for herself—the plan that said work for five years, buy a house, work for three more, have a baby. Margaret had held the plan in her mind's eye as lovingly as she'd held Brad on the day of their wedding. On Arran, with the plan in shreds, she occupied herself with the immediate tasks of not thinking about Brad, not thinking about any of their so-called friends who had helped him along the path to addiction, concentrating on remaining physically fit and planning for the needs of a baby. Months passed in this way. Without any of them, Margaret or Agatha or Ellsie, saying it explicitly, it became understood that Margaret would stay on Arran with the baby a few months after the birth and then go into Glasgow and look for work and settle, for as long as it took to develop a new plan. Accounting couldn't be that different on the other side of the Atlantic.

The daily routine began with Margaret taking a brisk walk as soon as she got up while Agatha did the day's baking. So it was that Margaret stepped out as usual one Tuesday in June, sat down on the steps, and wrapped her arms around the outsides of her belly in order to get at her shoelaces and see some of what she was doing. Laces tied, she stood and straightened herself. She glanced in the direction of the road along which she intended to walk and the sea beyond. Instead of the sun or the clouds or a threatening squall, her eyes landed on Brad Carver.

She thought of turning and going back inside. She could ask Agatha to come out and shoo him away, as she might a crow pecking at her lettuce or a sheep gnawing on the gate. The baby kicked, mightily. A small part of Margaret wanted to think it was recognition. If that were the case, however, the baby seemed to recognize nearly every man on Arran as its father, along with several sheep and at least one chicken. Margaret felt herself starting to pull in her tummy. She nearly laughed at the reflex. Instead, she squared her shoulders, straightened her lips, and stepped down the path, through the gate, past Brad, and onto the road. She expected him to follow, or, if not, to call after her. She set the briskest pace she could manage, elongating her stride.

"Don't look," she whispered to herself, in time with her footfalls. "Don't. Look. Don't. Look."

When, at last, she did look, just before the curve in the road, Brad was gone. Margaret wondered if she might have imagined him. Her dreams, at that point in the pregnancy, had been so vivid they made her lie in bed in the mornings sorting out what was memory and what was imagination. She walked on, taking her usual route, enjoying the challenge of the headwind on the way back.

The pair of them—Agatha and Brad—were taking their tea in the front room when Margaret got back.

"Margaret." Brad rose, stepped toward her.

"Did I not tell you to let her gather herself?" Agatha asked.

Margaret sucked in her cheeks. Her eyebrows pulled together. She'd walked for an hour. What had Brad Carver told Agatha in sixty minutes? And what had Agatha said to him, other than that he ought to let Margaret gather herself? Given the size of her, that might take some time.

"Away and have your shower, and I'll put on a fresh pot of tea," Agatha said to her.

Margaret sat down. "Isn't there any left in this pot?" She lifted it and gave it a quick swirl, testing the weight. She poured.

"I'll leave you to it, then." Agatha went, of course, in the direction of the kitchen and garden, leaving Margaret in the living room with Brad and the rare feeling that she would prefer to have Agatha there with her. Hadn't Agatha been forced to choose between a man and her family, too?

"I'm clean, Margaret," Brad said.

Margaret lifted the teacup, even though she'd poured out the bottom of the pot, meaning she had nearly as much in the way of leaves as she had in the way of liquid. She sipped a tiny sip and silently called for Agatha. She glanced into Brad's eyes. Pale green. Clear. Healthy. Not the bloodshot, red-rimmed horrors she'd left. She dared another sip.

"I checked into rehab the day you kicked me out."

A third sip, and then she held the cup just below her lips, feeling her body press into itself—ankles, knees, thighs together. Elbows digging in at her sides. Shoulder blades trying to meet. The baby kicking and punching so vigorously it could probably be seen. All this she did while Brad told her he'd stayed in rehab for forty-five days and then, instead of coming for her straightaway, had tested himself out in the world to be sure both of them, all three of them, could trust him.

When he seemed to be finished, Margaret said, "Bannock."

"What?" He leaned in her direction.

"Bannock. I'd like a piece of bannock—warm, with butter. A lot of butter for once. I'm pregnant, you know. And I had a brisk walk. And now I'm hungry."

Brad started to rise.

Margaret pressed her hand on his shoulder, leveraging herself up while pressing him back down. The tears were rising, she feared, faster than she. Her face was turning red, felt as though it was swelling as well. Heat and color crept up her neck and into her ears. Her whole body, in fact, felt as though it was inflating, as though it wasn't already absurdly puffy. She lunged for the kitchen door, for Agatha, for stability. On the other side, she grabbed blindly, hoping Agatha hadn't gone to the garden.

"I thought you wanted bannock." Agatha let her hold on for a minute, and then pushed Margaret gently away and held her at arm's length. She handed Margaret the round of bannock, still warm from the morning's baking, and wrapped in a tea towel. Agatha stepped around her into the front room. Margaret set the bannock on the cutting board and began to slice, listening.

"Away you go, son."

Brad's forehead would be wrinkling, full lips tightening, a protest forming.

"You've said your piece. Now let the lassie digest it."

The clink of teacup and saucer on the tray. Margaret straightened her shoulders and blinked rapidly, hoping to clear her lashes of any tears hanging on. The knife stilled in the air over the bread. And then she heard the door on the other side of the front room. Surely Agatha wasn't taking him upstairs.

The back door, with its peculiar sucking sound, opened. Of course. Agatha would show him out the back.

He stood at the gate again the next morning, just himself, no flowers or chocolates or any other frivolous bribery another man might have brought. Margaret partly wished he'd turn up with a dozen roses, or, worse, something completely out of place and season so she could call him irresponsible or inappropriate or insulting in some way. Instead he just stood there, offering himself, offering apologies for causing her pain, thanking her for helping him find himself again.

Margaret clamped her hands on her belly and looked seaward, mostly because she disliked the nearly irresistible urge she had to look toward the kitchen window and see if Agatha was there, and, if she was, to see if she would meet Margaret's eyes and let Margaret see what she had to say.

"How can I trust that it won't happen again?" She said it as much to herself as to him.

"You can't."

She faced him squarely, looking for the punch line.

"I'm an addict, Margaret. It's like being an alcoholic. You don't get cured. You just stop using."

"I need to think." She turned down the path, toward the cottage door.

"Margaret," Brad called out after her. "I've never loved or wanted anything, any drug or chance or anything at all, more than I love and want you. And our baby."

Margaret didn't dare look back. She didn't dare let her eyes dart to the window, suddenly taken by the need to hold herself in. If Agatha saw her, she might understand before Margaret did.

Inside, Agatha stood at the counter, back to the door, pressing out scones. "Is he coming in?"

"No."

The pair of them stood in the kitchen, Agatha brushing the scones with milk and putting them in the oven, Margaret holding her belly as though it might fall off if she let go. Agatha closed the oven door. "Is he still there?"

Margaret glanced. "No."

"Come a walk with me."

"I just got back from a walk."

"A short one, out to the rocks. We'll take a scone each, in just a few minutes."

Margaret held her scone in one hand, butter sliding out and down her palm toward her wrist. She held her belly with the other, feeling the baby kick and wishing she'd had an ultrasound to determine the sex. She hadn't yet settled on a name and wouldn't have minded making only one list. *This must be how people wind up with those awful androgynous names.* Settling on a rounded boulder on the shore, Margaret felt like another hump, part of the landscape, too large and tired to think seriously about moving herself anywhere significant. And yet, she had thought of going since Brad had appeared.

"Am I an idiot?" she asked Agatha.

"Ah, no, pet."

"I feel as though I've turned into one of those needy little cheerleaders who can't live without her man."

"No one would ever accuse you of that."

"Do you think I should go with him?"

"You're seeking love advice from the spinster of the family?"

"Isn't that why we're on the rocks?"

Agatha bit into her scone. "We're on the rocks so as to have the solid ground under us. We're outside so as to have the air fresh about us. We're both here so's you'll know you're not alone." She licked the butter from her hand. "You'll recall that I'm the Stuart spinster because I sent my lover packing? My sister Aileen, were she able to get the last word in anymore, would tell you I did it for no good reason."

"What do you think about it now?"

"I try not to." Agatha put the remainder of the scone in her mouth.

"I'd like your advice anyway, about Brad."

Agatha told her to send Brad away or tell him to stay, it didn't matter. Brad or not, Margaret should take her own time. She should have the baby on Arran as they'd planned. Gather herself. And then decide.

There on the rocks with Agatha, Margaret had agreed, not just spoken words of agreement, but felt them. As the days went on and she came face to face and hand in hand with Brad, she shifted. At the last minute, against even the midwife's advice, she wedged herself into a rented car beside him and boarded the ferry and then the plane and, three weeks later, had her baby at Terra Pines General Hospital as she'd always planned. Margaret started her family, as she'd planned, with a handsome husband at her side instead of a pair of wrinkly old crones.

Hope had seemed the right name. They gave her McNairn, which they'd chosen in case of a boy, as a middle name. It broke with the family tradition of giving the mother's maiden name as the middle name. Margaret thought it would free the baby to be wholly herself.

Could even Agatha have predicted that Margaret would be back in the cottage, fifteen years later, telling the whole of it to Hope?

"At the time, I thought I made the right decision. And last year, when I found out he was using cocaine again, I thought it would be the same."

"Cocaine? No, it was Lortab."

"Lortab too, but mostly the cocaine. That's how he came back so fast after the last surgery. I thought you were better off not knowing."

"Mom." Hope tucked her head toward her chest, curling into herself, as if she wished to be smaller, or just gone.

"I'm sorry," Margaret said. "I'm sorry I made you feel like I wanted to be rid of him. And you. I just wanted him to be rid of the drugs. Somehow I thought if I did everything perfectly he'd come back. And when it became clear that he wasn't going to be able to do that, I wanted you to be free of searching for him. That's why I put his stuff in trash bags. I thought it would help you—us—learn how to live without him." Margaret lifted Hope's chin. "We have to do that, Hope."

She felt Hope tense.

"Mom?"

"Yes."

"What else do you think I'm better off knowing?"

Margaret shook her head.

"He didn't tell you anything about where he's been? You don't know anything about where he is now?"

Margaret put a hand on each of Hope's hips; she pulled her closer, their knees banging together at the edge of the couch. "He didn't say anything about that. He just wanted his bikes—to sell, I think—and money."

"Did he ask about me?"

Margaret closed her eyes. She tried to force back the tears. "He's not himself."

"Did he ask about me?"

Margaret opened her eyes. "No."

Hope pulled herself up off the sofa.

"Hope, any dad in his right mind would have asked about you. Your dad…"

Hope turned toward the door.

And then they left me. Clyde's voice, out of nowhere, like the man himself.

Margaret pulled herself up. "I hear you," she whispered, and then followed Hope out of the cottage without another word.

Hope settled on the farthest-out rock she could get to, slightly taller than the rest and requiring that she use the full reach of her arms and legs to get there. The sea splashed around her, like it was angry she'd gotten out so far.

Margaret stretched one leg as far as she could, her foot landing halfway in the water, on the slick, seaweedy part of Hope's rock. She wished for Agatha's cane; she needed something to help her balance. Margaret pulled her foot back. Hope turned slightly, her hair wild, her face flushed and beautiful. Margaret's chest clenched. She held out her hand. "I could use some help here."

Margaret's arm began to feel heavy, like when they held Warrior II too long in yoga. She thought she might let it drop, and then Hope reached out.

The pungent scent of seaweed rose to meet them, as it always did; the rocks beneath them felt as solid as if they were rooted to the center of the earth.

Hope took in a deep breath. "You know when Dad left?"

Mom nodded again.

For a few minutes, Hope couldn't get anything else out. "I. I did some things."

"I know, honey."

"No, Mom, you don't know. Can you *please* just listen?"

"Okay," she said. "Okay."

"I liked the Lortab."

Margaret took a deep breath.

"I liked it because I thought it helped me feel what Dad felt," Hope said. "But that's not what you should have worried about."

She told Margaret about the thrill of taking on increasingly difficult tricks at the skate park, how she loved the buzz of risk and then the rush of success when she did something more dangerous than anyone else at the park.

"Sometimes I imagined Dad there, cheering me on. I imagined how proud he'd be."

"Hope, Dad couldn't have been prouder..."

"Mom. Listen. I liked it when I failed, too. When I wiped out right there in the bowl. Remember the time I came home with my chin split and my knee all bloody?"

Margaret winced, recalling the gash.

"The blood tasted good. I wanted more. I thought I could feel him there too. I just want to feel him again. He came back and I wasn't there and now he's gone again."

Margaret felt the press of her daughter's body against her, already taller than she would ever be; she wrapped her arms around Hope, held on tightly.

"It doesn't mean you don't love him if you move forward with your own life."

The wind tangled their hair, ballooned under their shirts. They pulled in, together. Margaret swept Hope's hair out of her face to see her eyes. Somehow this wild girl came from her. So much braver than she was—willing to take risks Margaret would never have dreamed of. Able to take falls that might have broken her.

"I know you think I want you to be perfect. I don't. I just want you to be able to be your whole, best self."

"I know, Mom," Hope said. "But I want to be able to decide what's best for myself. Without someone questioning my every move."

Margaret nodded. Wasn't that what Margaret wanted as well? "Of course," she said. "As long as I'm right there beside you as you figure it out."

For a long time the waves were the only sound between them, the hiss of soft white foam slithering up between the pebbles. Margaret held her breath so she could feel Hope breathing against her. When Hope finally spoke, she felt the words through her daughter's shoulder, vibrating against her cheek.

"I...I want to stay here on Arran. With Agatha. At least for a while." Hope crunched in, and Margaret's arms automatically tightened around her. "Could I?" She didn't say *we*.

Margaret's lips parted, then pinched closed again. When she'd sent Hope to Agatha, she hadn't for a moment considered that Hope might choose to stay. In trying to save them both, could Margaret have lost her daughter altogether? Was it possible that they could find each other again if Margaret stayed, too, trading it all—her house, her business—for a life of walking a rocky shore in a country all relatives but one had given up long ago? She thought about everything she'd left in South Carolina: Trig, Clyde, Brad, the dirty jogging clothes in her hamper, the empty bike hooks in the tool room. Tim. It didn't add up to anything nearly as real or as important as the ache of Hope in her arms, pressed close like maybe she hadn't been since she was a baby kicking in Margaret's stomach, at war already with a world she hadn't even seen. She had never been as still as she was now. Margaret glanced at Hope, who looked out at the sea through clear eyes, no longer hooded and clouded by anger or blame or uglier things that came in little brown bottles. Hope turned and met Margaret's gaze.

"Could I?" Hope repeated.

"Yes," Margaret cleared her throat. "Yes, we could."

She wondered if it was what she should have said, so very long ago.

THIRTY-THREE
Agatha

Agatha set her cane outside the shed, the cool air clutching her. She imagined the temperature rising between the two out on the rocks, hoped they would move close to each other and feel the press of their bodies against each other the way she had once felt the press of the bodies of her sisters against her, and of her own mother, and of Rory and Donagh. All of them gone.

She thought of all the lassies who had come to her over the years, each one a kind of affirmation of her choice on the shore years ago. Each one proof that her family needed her, that she'd been right to send Rory away, to watch him float off to another continent, taking with him her chance at the weight of a body made of her own, of the growth of a life from within her.

Agatha entered the shed quietly. She took a quick inventory of the few spare pots on the work surface, the trowel hanging neatly next to the hand fork, the same one Donagh had used when he lived there, purchased new, after the war, when the rations were lifted and metal didn't all go for arms. How it gleamed, even in the grey of an afternoon, those years ago. There it still hung, dull now but as useful as ever, not unlike herself.

Agatha touched the handle of the pointed spade and the flathead and the fork and the rake, propped in the corner between the bench and the wall, in the way she might have touched the heads of small children, had she had any. She closed the door, leaned her body against it as she lifted slightly to make it fit the space, now out of square. She should repair it, make it true again. It probably wasn't possible. It was more likely that a repairman would declare the whole shed scrap, encourage her to build a new one. And what would be the point of that, when it still worked well? A wee lift and a firm press and everything slid into place. So many things fit together with just the right nudge.

She lifted the spade, ran her hand over the familiar wood of the handle. Its work was done for this season, the soil nourished and prepared. Soon it would be autumn, and then the dead season. That's what people called it, but it was then, when things seemed barren, that the new growth began.

All her life, Agatha had trusted her part in preparing for the new growth. Even in the face of a father and a lover claimed by the waters, in the face of her sisters turning away, one by one, leaving her bare and barren, Agatha had trusted that it was her place to simply do the work—turn the soil, pull the weeds, keep the garden always at the ready—so that, even in the bleak spaces of winter, the new growth would have space to unfurl, silently, underground. She listened to the whistle of the wind through the slats of the walls, hoping for some sound from the figures out on the shore but only deciphering the voice of the waters.

She'd long thought of herself as similar to the hardy *Crataegus monogyna*, the hawthorn, filled with lore and longevity, the enduring native. Certainly *C. monogyna* may live hundreds of years, but eventually there comes an autumn during which she will shed her leaves and never bud again. And then what? Carved into boxes and combs, tokens cast to the world instead of the dropping of a seed for a sapling to come up in her place. Agatha ran her hand along the shelf, breathed in the metal and dirt and wood. Might she be the treasured box and comb that would be passed from generation to generation? Only the years would tell.

At present, there were still Hope and Margaret to consider. Agatha would take her time (what choice had she, in her condition?), make her way to the rocks, and hear whatever they cared to say.

Acknowledgments

I'm deeply grateful to the MFA program at Queens University of Charlotte, in particular to Fred Leebron, Michael Kobre, and Melissa Bashor. I'm grateful to readers there, including Jane Alison, Lauren Groff, and Pinckney Benedict. And I'm grateful to Ashley Warlick, whose reading, instruction, and encouragement helped me get there in the first place.

For their early and ongoing support, I thank Emrys, the Metropolitan Arts Council, and Sue Lile Inman and the Tuesday evening writing group. I'm grateful to Shelly Drancik and Carla Damron for being wonderful readers. Thanks also to the Skye Reading Room, and to Nilly Barr for helping me see the path forward.

Many thanks to Michelle Dotter for her keen eye and thoughtful editing, and, of course, to everyone at MP.

Much love and gratitude to close friends and family for encouraging me on and off the page: Ann Hawkins, the late Charlie MacGregor, Anne Macaulay, Kelly Pfeiffer, Kenneth Naismith, Suzanne Regentin; and Alan Marshall, Stewart Marshall, and Andrea Baker for their steadfast love and support.

And lastly, and most importantly, I'm deeply grateful to my children, Davis, Dylan, and Corey, for more love and encouragement than I could ever have wished.

About the Author

Originally from Kilmarnock, Scotland, Heather Marshall is a writer currently based in the foothills of South Carolina, where she lives with her children, dogs, a set of bagpipes and a Royal Enfield motorcycle. Her fiction and creative nonfiction have been published in a variety of periodicals—mostly recently in *Northwords Now*, *Prime Number* and *Six Minute Magazine*. She holds an MFA in Creative Writing from Queens University of Charlotte.